# SLAYER'S REVENGE

Andy Blinston

*Book 4 of the Rakkan Conquest series*

Falbury

*Slayer's Revenge*

First published in Great Britain in 2022 by Falbury



Part 4 in the book series Rakkan Conquest

First Edition, 2022, Andy Blinston

A CIP catalogue record for this book is available from the British Library

ISBN: 978-1-9993139-9-9



Falbury Publishing

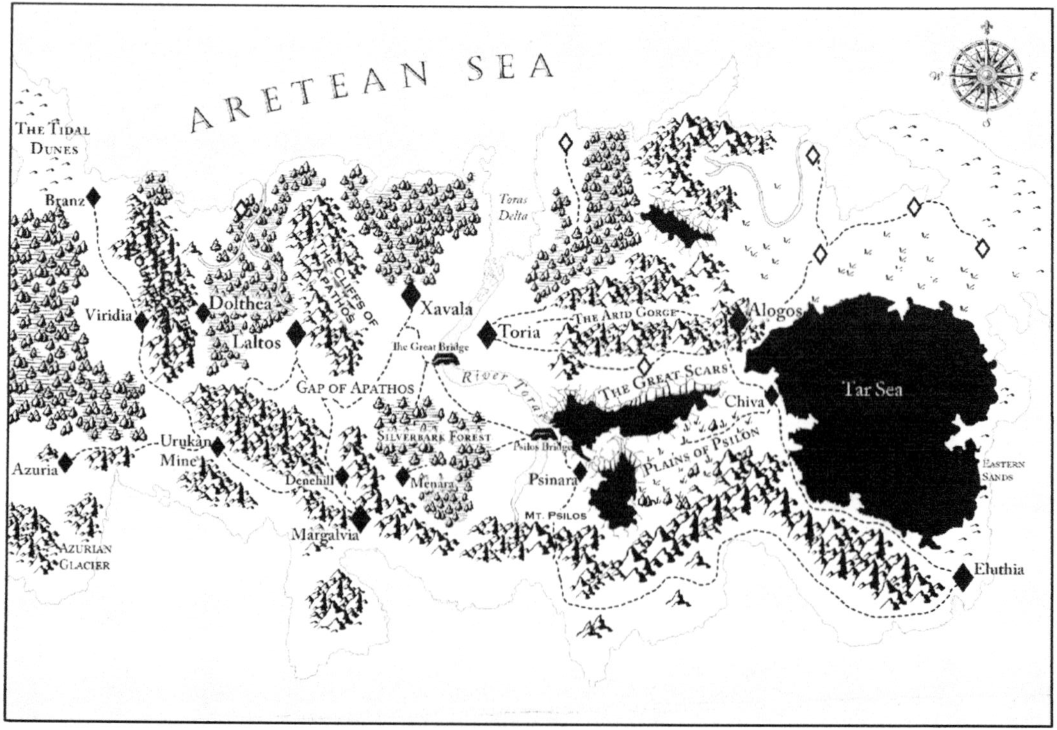
ARETEAN SEA
The Tidal Dunes
Branz
Viridia
Dolthea
Laltos
The Cliffs of Apathos
Xavala
Toras Delta
Toria
The Great Bridge
River Toras
Gap of Apathos
Silverbark Forest
Psilos Bridge
Urukan Mine
Azuria
Azurian Glacier
Denehill
Menara
Margalvia
Psinara
Mt. Psilos
The Arid Gorge
The Great Scars
Plains of Psilon
Alogos
Chiva
Tar Sea
Eastern Sands
Eluthia

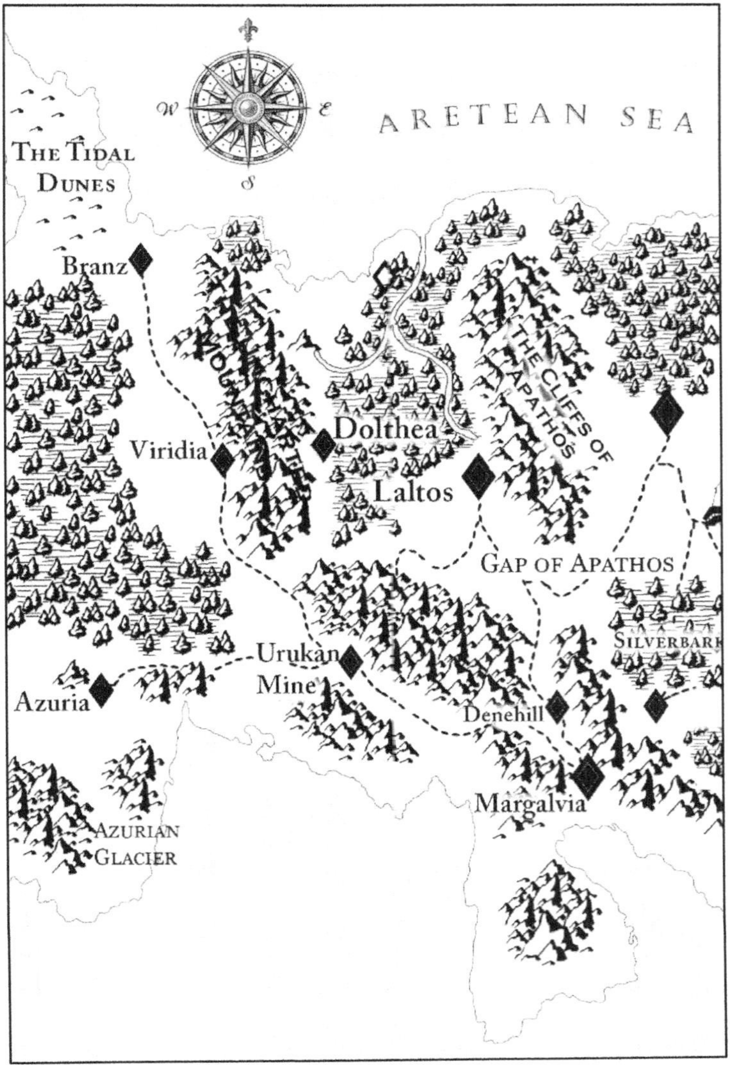
W
E
S
ARETEAN SEA
THE TIDAL DUNES
Branz
Viridia
Dolthea
Laltos
THE CLIFFS OF THE APATHOS
GAP OF APATHOS
SILVERBARK
Urukan Mine
Azuria
Denehill
Margalvia
AZURIAN GLACIER

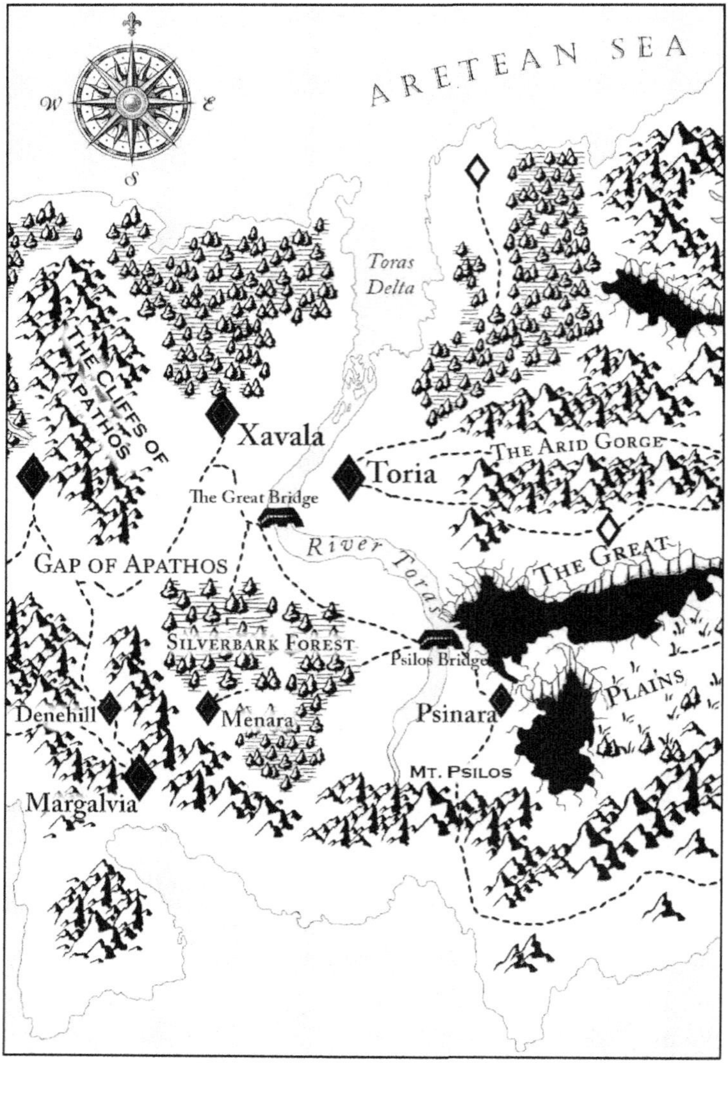
W
E
S
ARETEAN SEA
Toras
Delta
THE CLIFFS OF
APATHOS
Xavala
Toria
THE ARID GORGE
The Great Bridge
River Toras
GAP OF APATHOS
THE GREAT
SILVERBARK FOREST
Psilos Bridge
PLAINS
Denehill
Menara
Psinara
MT. PSILOS
Margalvia

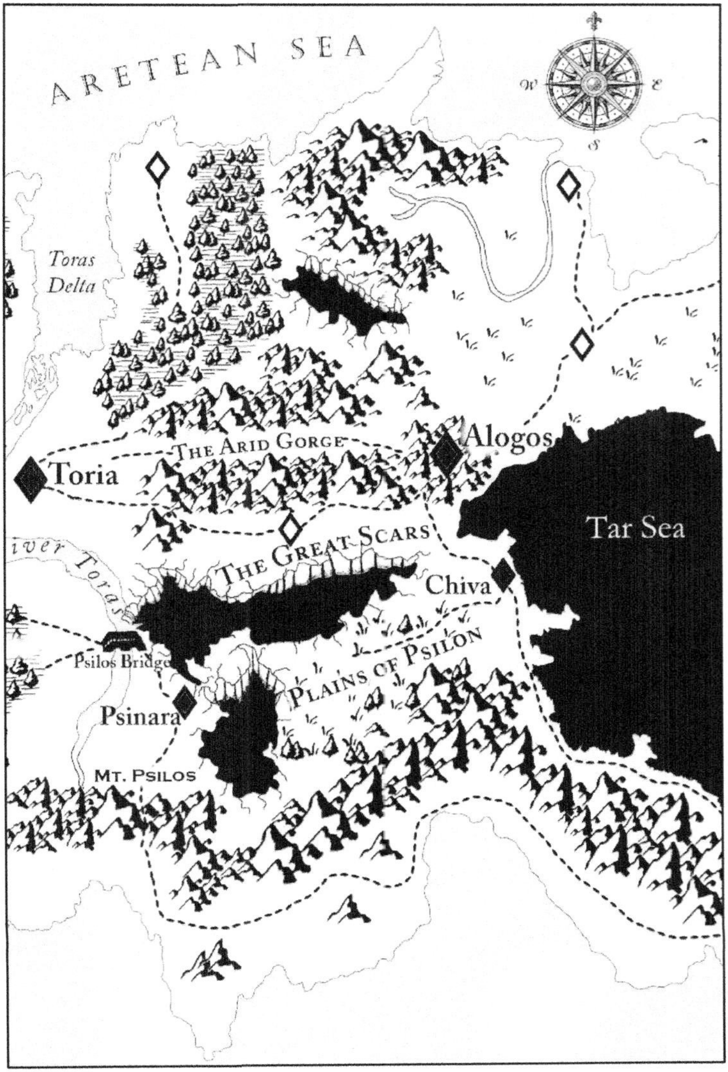

ARETEAN SEA
W
E
S
Toras Delta
Toria
The Arid Gorge
Alogos
Tar Sea
The Great Scars
River Toras
Chiva
Psilos Bridge
Plains of Psilon
Psinara
Mt. Psilos

## Character List

### Margalvia

Darius – Overlord of Rakka

Varro – Warlord of the Black Legion

Sulla – Red Militia Chief

### Former Laltos

Hera – Regent

Lex / Alexandra – Algus – House of Theodoros

Gorgias – Algus – House of Hera

### Viridia

Rufus – Warlord of the Viridian Legion

Pollio – Viridian Commander, brother of Rufus

Piso – Viridian Commander, brother of Rufus

### Toria

King Medus II – King of Toria and the Torian Empire

Ophelia – King's Orator

Jason – Algus – King's Sword

**Other**

Aran – Chief Priest of the Diagathic Order

Aristippus – Regent of Xavala

Selene – deceased Algus, sister of Alexandra

Waif Magician / Shirin – deceased – Half-algus, half-goman

Brutus – deceased Black Centurion

Archimedes – deceased goman commander of the Torian army

Hadrian – deceased Warlord of the Viridian Legion, father of Rufus

Nikolaos – deceased Algus of Laltos

**Escorts**

Lyra – Darius's panther

Tiro – Lex's peregrine falcon

# Prologue

## Lex – Silverbark Forest

They said pain was the body's way—or perhaps the mind's way—of telling you to slow down, but Lex knew the truth; pain was a trial, the stiffest challenge that you had to overcome if you hoped to accomplish anything meaningful in this life. When the time came to fight, a warrior couldn't wait until they were pain-free unless they were prepared to submit, and although Lex's pain now stemmed from a real injury rather than the phantom trauma of the last decade, she'd battle through it nonetheless.

But now it seemed her body wasn't as strong as her mind.

Darius grabbed Lex's waist as she stumbled on the uneven cobbles the Menarans had the nerve to call a "road."

"Enough," he said. He grabbed her arm for support and brought her body unnervingly close to the unsheathed Blades hanging from his waist. "You're going back on a wagon."

She wouldn't argue, despite her ears still ringing from days of listening to the incessant roar of wooden wheels. The pain in her abdomen had intensified within minutes of beginning her first attempt at walking in the last few days.

"Be careful with those swords." She arched her battered body away from them as they headed back to the wagon, keen not to add another cut to her injured leg.

What kind of weapons refused to be carried within a scabbard and burned through leather with an unnatural force of their own? Only a metal chain attached to Darius's waist had been capable of holding them. Whatever power resided within them left a darkness emanating that seemed to be ever-battling with the red spark glowing from deep within the runes etched onto them. And Lex couldn't resist her gaze lingering on the man they called master while he helped her walk back towards the wagon.

Behind Darius, the dense red leaves of Silverbark Forest fluttered in a manner the wind rarely caused, like a thousand bloodstained spirits of the recently slain followed them and their army through the branches, possibly guarding them, possibly haunting them, spitting their shame at them marching with enemies. Darius had spared the Viridians, but did the rakkans have to march back from Mount Psilos at the same time as them? Even though they were a mile behind, their stinking breath sometimes carried in the forest wind and made her retch.

This place had once been tranquil, but now the thumping of the surrounding army broke the peace, and the forest floor grumbled at the disturbance on the road cutting through it.

She continued walking and lost herself in the sight of swaying leaves until a wave of gut pain stole her attention away, made her double over, and go headfirst towards the cobbles.

But Darius caught her in time. "That's it," he said, voice stiff and bristling. "I'm carrying you."

Before she could protest, he lifted her into his strong arms and nestled her head between his shoulder and neck.

"I wish Hera hadn't insisted we up our pace," Darius said.

That damned dagger to the stomach hadn't hurt half as much at the time as it did now after the quick march.

"You shouldn't be seen carrying me," Lex whispered, but without the effort to convince. The relief of not having to grit her teeth with every footstep was welcome. "You're a leader now. Have one of the others do it."

"You think I want another man to have his hands on you?"

She could hardly complain about his protectiveness. It was the only reason she still breathed. "You should save your strength."

"You're light," he said. "I'll still have enough strength when the Torians reach us." Although his words were clearly meant to instil confidence, his tone was morose, reminding her of the loss they'd both suffered at Mount Psilos.

Or was it fear? The Torian army had been spotted a week ago, but the escorts had lost sight of it when the soldiers had left the road and submerged themselves in the forest. Apart from where the road dissected the trees, the woodlands were so dense that all you saw were silver trunks in every direction, crowded with ferns and undergrowth. Thankfully, Darius's panther, Lyra, would detect any ambushes, and at least the King's Sword was decaying in the underbelly of the mountain. With him dead, Darius was finally unrivalled in the Empire.

"It won't be too long until we're in Menara," Darius whispered as if she were too delicate to speak normally to. This time the fear was unmistakable.

"Don't fret," she said. "If the Torians attack, the Viridians will be the first they run into. With any luck, both sides will kill each other off."

"It isn't the Torians I'm worried about." He glanced down, those dark eyes as unstable as she'd ever seen them, as if trembling in the sockets as he focused on her bloody bandages.

They reached the closest wagon, and Darius laid Lex down amongst the sacks of grain she'd spent far too much time resting upon.

"I wish I could fight it for you." His grip was still tight before he finally released her.

"I'll be fine," Lex said. She had to think that. "The Menarans have the best medicine in the Empire."

"They'd better. Your wound reeks."

That was true. It had become so bad Lex hadn't adjusted to it.

"Don't leave me too," he said.

Any anger she'd borne for the man after watching him run through her sister dissolved at the words. He'd had no choice, and as painful as it had been to watch, it had been more painful for him. She'd have done the same for him. She'd killed far more people to protect him in the years they'd known each other, and apart from her daughter, there was no one else's life she'd choose over his.

This wound wouldn't defeat her. "Hell will have to do without me for a while yet."

"Don't jest about the afterlife."

Who was jesting? Lex had no delusions about where she'd end up, but she wouldn't make Darius suffer by speaking further on the topic.

"Sorry," she said, resting her head against one of the sacks.

"When we get back," he began, "we'll—"

A horn sounded, a distant yet frantic howl that froze Darius in place, his body rigid and hard as iron when she grabbed his arm and pulled herself up.

Sulla came barrelling up shortly after from amongst the marching humans. "That's the Viridians in the rearguard. Must be trouble."

Lex pulled herself off the wagon and stood on shaky legs while Darius's eyes glazed over. Only after a few moments did he seem to notice her standing.

"Shouldn't you stay on the wagon?" he asked.

"Not if there's trouble," Lex said. "Sulla, do our escorts see what's wrong?"

The rakkan scoffed. "Don't even get me started on that... Your Regent and algus have been keeping an eye on the Viridians rather than the Torians."

"Damn them," Darius said. "I told Hera to focus on scouting, but at least she might know why Rufus's men are sounding their horn."

The three of them set off to find Regent Hera, Lex requiring some support walking from Sulla while they passed through the ranks of soldiers on the road, and she dwelled on how the Viridians and humans had been at odds since Mount Psilos. Hera wasn't one to let emotions sway her judgement, but who could blame her in this case? The Viridian Legion couldn't be trusted, and perhaps Lex was foolishly optimistic for believing they could be anything but a plague to this world.

When Darius had ordered them to march back to Viridia, Lex had shuddered at the thought and quickly warned him afterwards. A long march through human territory without oversight wasn't something she was prepared to risk; Viridians weren't men that passed up the opportunity to pillage. Plus, she'd rather they stayed to the east of Laltos, near the Silk City. When the time came to destroy it, the Xavalans deserved to suffer the same Viridian brutality that Laltos had, a fervour no other rakkan or human army on their side had the stomach for inflicting.

"I'll speak with Hera about the Viridians," Lex concluded as they walked.

"Can your falcon see what's wrong?" Darius asked.

He could have, had Lex not sent her escort with a request to Eluthia—a city she shouldn't have been conferring with. But that was a matter for another time, planning for a future that might not even transpire. Darius had enough to deal with in the present.

"The forest is too thick," she said. "Tiro wouldn't be able to see."

Darius cursed. "Then it's up to you and me, girl."

At the comment, Lex smacked him in the arm and stifled a grunt at the granite-like muscle that cracked her knuckle. "Don't call me 'girl.'"

Darius grinned while Lyra let out a low growl, reminding Lex she was there.

"I wasn't talking to you," Darius said.

Well... That was fairly embarrassing for her. "You're not a scout. Send others to do that now."

"Yeah, Dar," Sulla added. "The grunts do that kind of work."

The Viridian horn blared again, wiping the amusement from the rakkan's face. The whole army had ground to a halt now, peering back, clinks of metal sounding from within the forest as either men fidgeted or swords clashed far away—she couldn't tell which.

Finally, they spotted Hera just off the road, deep in conversation with many of her highest-ranking algus, her sons and daughters amongst them. The Regent's hair fluttered loosely in the wind, as dark a shade of black as Lex's, and the subtle lines she always drew to highlight her eyes were a little smeared in places but took nothing from the calculated intensity of her stare.

By the time they reached her, Lex was doubled over with gut pain, the world fading in and out of focus.

"I wouldn't even send a rat to help those rakkans." Hera watched their rear out of the corner of her eye, the Viridians now visible in the distance like a dark, acrid mass sweeping through the silver trunks. Whatever had driven them off the roads and into the forest must have been close behind them.

"You'll do as I say." Darius pushed his way into the tight circle of algus.

"What do your escorts see?" Lex asked.

Hera's mouth pressed closed at the question.

"Tell her, Mother." Gorgias slinked from behind the Regent, having been almost invisible until then, to reveal his still bruised and misshapen face. Thankfully, his intercession looked to take the stubbornness from his mother's eyes.

"Fine," she said. "Our escorts spotted the Torian army again a few minutes ago, spread throughout the forest to the east. Their vanguard is already upon the Viridians."

Lex shook her head at the Regent. How could Hera not inform Darius of this until now?

"How many?" Darius asked.

"Not enough to be a worry for us," Hera said. "The Viridians will probably be able to handle them, and we'll survive any that make it through."

"*Probably?*" Darius growled.

"And that's not all. The Xavalan cavalry has been sighted near the Gap of Aphatos."

Lex was glad the woman had at least spared some algus to scout that far away, but she also saw why Hera hadn't mentioned this news. The Black Legion, along with the humans, were soon due to split from the army and head south while the Viridians marched to the Gap alone. The Viridians would meet the Xavalan cavalry without support if not forewarned.

Darius paused, listening to the wretched legion moving through the trees behind them, still far enough away that anyone attacking them wouldn't be much of an immediate threat. Lex guessed he was considering letting them fend for themselves—hell, even Lex was. But was that wise? The Viridians had bent the knee. Why waste them when they could be useful?

She grabbed Darius and pulled him away from the others. "Don't let them die. We need to hold the Gap of Aphatos, and it's a dangerous job. Maybe they're the ones to do it." It would also mean they wouldn't march further west through the human lands.

"They can build your fortress?" Darius asked.

"*Your* fortress. And I don't know..." Rakkan building methods were seldom used on open ground. "You might need human engineers as well, but the Viridians will do the fighting."

"All right. Stay at a distance. I'll go and protect the Viridians." He lowered his head, letting out a nervous laugh. "There's something I never thought I'd say."

He stalked away with Lyra while Lex bent over to combat another wave of light-headedness. *Damn this wound.* When would it just heal?

She scanned around for Nasrin or any other carers or surgeons, but finding none, she spotted a nearby wagon to rest upon once again. Plumes of black smoke now rose from the canopy in the distance, and a grey fog carrying the smell of charred wood eased its way through the trees. Algus ran between groups of soldiers giving orders, and one particularly frantic-looking man headed straight for Hera and said something that stole the colour from the Regent's face.

On second thought, the wagon could wait. Lex hobbled closer to try to overhear what was being said, but someone caught her from behind before she got within range.

"Mistress?" Nasrin's voice had never been so welcome.

Lex turned and the world spun uncontrollably, collapsing her onto the carer.

"Oh, mistress!" Nasrin wrapped her arms around Lex's body, avoiding the belly wound and gripping her under the armpits. "You need medicine. We should find a swift."

If only the Chief Priest had been there; he could have summoned one of his secret escorts.

Lex shook her head, feeling the beads of sweat fly off. If she went under…

"Nasrin"—Lex leant in—"I need a favour if I don't make it."

"Stop fretting about that and focus on—"

"It's important." Lex tightened her grip on the carer's sleeve. "I sent Tiro to Eluthia to strike a deal with Regent Panorea. If she accepts, she'll begin a delivery. You must make sure she's paid." Being in debt to Eluthia was not a position one went into without desperation. That's why Lex had chosen to bear the risk alone and signed requests in only her name.

"What? Stop—"

"My gold in Laltos. It should cover the cost of the first load."

"Load of what?"

Lex scanned those around, ensuring no one could overhear, especially those friendly with the Chief Priest.

"Weapons," she said. "Talk to your friends in the Silk City. I intend to smuggle them there."

Nasrin's face morphed from fearful confusion to abject terror. "Weapons to slaves…?"

Lex had spoken with the Xavalan slaves many times in the past and knew the resentment they bore. News of the Menaran slave uprising would have spread throughout the Empire by now. The seeds were ready for sowing.

"Don't tell the Chief Priest," Lex said. He hadn't the stomach for blood. "And only tell Darius once his attention turns to the Silk City. He has enough to handle before that."

"Stop speaking as if you're going to die!" Nasrin's cry drew the attention of a few soldiers around, but luckily they were soon drawn back to the thickening smoke around them. By now, the clamour of metal on metal, sword on shield, and spear on armour was filling the forest.

"Lex!" Gorgias came hobbling up to her, in almost as bad a shape as she was. "Mother says some Torian algus are making their way around the Viridians. Take cover."

Then there was only one thing Lex could do. "Nasrin, get me a sword."

The carer's face told of her objection, but she scurried away obediently, nevertheless.

Gorgias pulled his own weapon free; then they positioned themselves behind a line of Hera's hoplites and peltasts that had made a defensive formation on the road. The shield wall was similar to the rakkan legionnaires and slingers, but behind this one, Lex felt no safety, no strength of the muscle in front. They wore only steel helmets, shimmering scale armour, and had wooden shields—not black kuraminium like rakkans. Only when Nasrin returned with a sword did she breathe again.

Thickening smoke oozed from within the forest to the east, carrying barbs of ash that scraped her throat. And amidst the smog, sparks of blue began flashing between the trees. Soldiers in front tensed. Nasrin slinked behind her.

At the first sign of movement, Lex's vision wobbled and the sword almost slipped from her grasp. *Not now.* Although Hera had been confident of victory, not everyone survived a battle.

A ring of clashing steel to her right drew her gaze, and she saw over a dozen algus had emerged on the road and were screaming towards their flank. Hera's algus rushed to block their enemies' path and battered them back as best they could, but a few broke through before the regular soldiers could reposition themselves, and one with green mud smeared across his face locked onto Lex and headed straight for her, the eagle on his breast the only part of him easy to track by eye.

Algor flared on his hand, then swept down his blade in a flash of light dimmed only by the smog. His right hand swung upwards as he neared, his teeth bared.

Lex raised her sword to parry, but the weight was almost too much for her wrist, which could only leave the blade hanging timidly in the air. But before the enemy's weapon struck, Gorgias leapt in front of her, his sword held up and close to his body. It took the force from the blow, drove the algus's weapon back against his chest, and the two men collided in the air, butting heads with a sickening crunch.

Gorgias fell back, nose bloody and bent at a cruel angle, but his enemy quickly regained his feet and looked between the now downed man and Lex, then focused his glare on her.

Shouts filled the forest, and soon the silver trunks ahead of them were suffused with the silver armour of Torian soldiers, the scales on their chests rippling as they charged towards the Laltosian front line. The peltasts tossed their javelins, scoring many a hit, but it wasn't enough to weaken the inevitable crash as the two masses collided.

Amidst the chaos that ensued, the algus that had struck Gorgias got back to his feet and stepped forward.

But Lex moved first. Still able to summon a smidgen of her algus flair, she feinted left at the hopefully dazed man, then adjusted her true swing towards the right.

The man read her intent well and dodged the blade, perhaps through skill, perhaps through Lex's paltry speed. Either way, she was in trouble because his next stroke batted the sword out of her grip, then he brought his weapon up, ready for the killing blow.

She adjusted her hips and dug in her heels, ready to spring out of the way when she spied where the blade was heading.

It came left, and she burst right, flying off the road but not quick enough to avoid the point as it sliced through her bandage and added another wound to the side of her existing one. She fell to the soil next to a nearby tree, pain blinding, vision blurred as her body stopped rolling, and she lay face-up, the smoky red canopy above soon just a backdrop to the twisted face of her enemy.

He raised his sword, then brought it down with malice.

But no sooner had he begun the strike than a fiery blade burst through his chest, followed by the hiss of boiling blood. Hot splatters rained onto her face as the runes on the Twin Blade roared, soon joined by the hate-filled roar of its master.

Darius lifted the algus up as he flailed and howled, dripping gore below that Lex rolled away from. Darius's eyes burned red-hot inside his helmet, focused on her, and fired more with every heartbeat until the blaze engulfed the kuraminium guarding his face.

With his free hand, he took hold of the algus's neck and wrenched the sword upwards, the serrated edge tearing through flesh until it burst free at the shoulder and allowed the mangled fighter to meet the soil.

Still, Darius focused on Lex and her fresh wound while, behind him, two blurs closed in.

She opened her mouth to scream a warning, but he'd already turned his head a fraction, then whirled around. Tongues of fire swirled down his blade as he struck the first figure's sword, algor resisting ferven and throwing off a cloud of sparks.

Despite the algus's sword blocking the sharp edge of the Twin Blade, Darius was too strong and continued his swing as if blocked by nothing, forcing the algus's own sword through their belly.

The second figure was a female algus who dodged both of them and went for a strike to Darius's back, but a black shadow flew from behind them, amber eyes like narrowed slits as white teeth emerged from jaws that widened and caught hold of the algus's ankle.

The algus faltered, only for a breath, but that was enough time for Darius to grab her sword arm, snap it with a mere flex of his hand, and finish her off with a savage punch to the temple that rolled her eyes back.

Just by the crack of the skull, Lex knew the algus was dead, and Darius pounced on the closest enemy and tore through them with equal ease while Lyra prowled towards Lex, teeth bloody, and stood guard above her.

Lex tried to wipe the sweat dripping from her brow but only added blood, which soon seeped into her eyes and blinded her all the more. She cursed and tried to stand but knocked into Lyra's hulking mass as the panther straddled her.

It took more than a few wipes of her sleeve to get the blood out, and when she could make out the crimson-tinted scene before her again, she watched Darius's fiery figure slice through the soldiers currently battling alongside Laltos's own on the road. At the flank, Hera's algus fared less well, and if Darius didn't rush to their aid, they'd soon be outnumbered two to one. The Viridians hadn't put up as good a defence as Hera had presumed. Perhaps they'd even let the Torians straight past.

One Torian soldier broke through the melee and headed straight for Lex. She reached for her fallen weapon, but Lyra pounced first. The panther sprang and slammed the man back onto the ground before sinking her canines into his neck.

Lex took the chance to grab her sword and get to one knee, but her vision spun again. The smoke had her dragging ever-deeper breaths into her lungs yet crying out for more air. It was as hot as an open fire despite the absence of flames, and sweat now drenched her tunic.

For the first time, she realised this couldn't be due to the smoke. Fever was seizing her.

"Lyra!" she called. If this was the end, she needed to help Darius and her daughter. If his reign was ever to succeed and see Cynthia grow up safely, the Viridians and the humans had to find a way to settle their differences—by force, in all likelihood.

The panther ran back over and rubbed her bloody face against Lex as if it would cure her wounds.

"Darius…" Lex croaked. Even distracted in battle, he'd comprehend the words. "Make Laltos and"—a wave of pain stole her voice for a moment, the old wound feeling as if that dagger were still embedded—"the Viridians build the fortress together. And Cynthia…" The last words came out as a shriek of pain. "Don't leave…" *Her.* Not only was her vision spinning, but now it darkened from smoke and fatigue.

"Lex!" Darius's cry stretched out in her mind for what felt like forever as the darkness took her and nightmares began.

# 1

## Darius – Silverbark Forest

"Don't bury the dead." Darius wiped the last stain of burnt blood from his new sword now that the battle was over. After surveying the fallen both on the road and within the trees, he knew there weren't enough bodies for burials to delay their march for long, but any delay was still a delay.

Toria's attack had been sudden, and although the numbers hadn't been great enough to defeat them this time, this wouldn't be the last attack, and as soon as they were out of the forest, he expected horses and swifts to join the harrying of his army.

But if only that were his greatest worry.

Despite blood staining his boots a shade of red as dark as the leaves above, despite the surrounding gruesome sights that had even the most-decorated rakkan warriors hurling, Darius was numb to it all, as if in a dream, as if the forest was cloaked in darkness except for a patch of red light shining upon one woman. Lex.

A wagon stood waiting to his side, blood dripping from the gaps in the planks at its bottom and spoiling the road. Oxen grunted, attached and ready to pull, their cargo of grain offloaded to make way for the injured, amongst which Lex lay silently in fever. At her head, Nasrin sat with her bag of supplies to aid, but there was a look about her like she was heading to a funeral.

Whatever the carer expected, Darius couldn't bring himself to imagine the worst, not so soon after losing Selene. Lex *had* to survive.

"Will she make it to Menara?" he asked.

Nasrin put a hand on Lex's sweaty forehead and paled. "I don't know. Their medicine is renowned but can only do so much."

Along with the rot and sickness, Darius also had the Torians to worry about. If he left Lex in Menara and the town was attacked…

"Is it possible to get her back to Margalvia?" he asked.

"If she makes it to Menara, we'll see."

He guessed that was the best reassurance he could hope for right now.

After the road had been cleared of the dead and the living, Lex's wagon along with several others set off with a familiar drone of wheels on uneven cobbles. Darius was left to silently watch its rear with Lyra at his side, soon joined by Hera and Gorgias. The human soldiers and algus followed shortly after the wagons, and finally their army was on the move again.

Darius dropped his head to face Lyra. "Follow her."

Without hesitation, his panther went to walk by Lex's wagon, whether for her own peace of mind or his own, he wasn't sure. Perhaps both.

"My algus are tracking the Torians that retreated," Hera said without a trace of emotion. Perhaps such indifference to battle was how a leader was supposed to react, or perhaps they wilfully projected stoicism, but Darius wasn't sure how they did it.

As they too set off, the mother and son muttered things to one another, but Darius remained lost in his own thoughts until Gorgias nudged him.

"Master?"

Darius ran a hand down his face in a futile attempt to straighten his mind. "Sorry… What?"

"The Torians, shall we stay on them?"

"Yes," Darius said. "Warn me if they rally."

"When…" Hera corrected. "They have more numbers than they committed here. It's only a matter of time."

And Darius wasn't sure where they'd head next. Harassing his army was one possibility, but there were also the farmlands to the northeast as well as the sprawling lands around Laltos that Lex had urged him to defend.

The last thing she'd uttered to him via Lyra came back to mind, about the fortress, and begging him not to leave her… All he could do to help her now was follow the plans she'd sketched out for him.

"Did Lex mention her plans for the Gap of Aphatos to you?" he asked.

Hera nodded. "But if we're to build this fortress, I see no reasons for Viridia to assist. Why not the Margalvians?"

Her question was a good one that Darius had long considered, and while he pondered his most troubling rakkan subjects more, a thumping of boots behind him announced their impending arrival. For the first time after the battle, they'd caught up.

Before the Viridians reached them, Darius decided it best to stick with Lex's plans for now. He'd seen what Viridians on the march did, and these were hungry, angry, and fresh from battle.

Who knew what they'd do to the human towns and villages on their march home.

"The Viridians will build the fortress," he said to Hera, "if only to keep them out of Laltos's lands."

The Regent's grimace was like that of a woman suddenly stricken by a foul odour. "Fine. But I won't provide many of my algus or builders to help them. Just enough to ensure the Viridians aren't up to no good."

"We'll discuss numbers and details later." When Lex had recovered. *If* she recovered.

Shaking off the dark thoughts threatening to overtake his mind, he turned and caught sight of the newly instated Warlord Rufus at the front of his legion with many tattooed commanders beside him, so similar in looks to both him and Hadrian that they must have been his brothers. Although they all had rusty hair of varying lengths, only the Viridian Warlord's was without dirt or blood, and that might have been why his was the only face that didn't strike Darius as rough and unsightly.

Along with marred cheeks and noses, the Viridian Commanders marched like men suffering old injuries, and some had knobbled wrists and elbows, bashed or broken a few too many times.

By contrast, Rufus was a man fresh yet fierce, his slender figure showing no evidence of battle but ready for one at any moment with a flat, measured expression. His arms swung bare as he marched, open to the elements and displaying his intricate pattern of Viridian tattoos that turned Darius's stomach; he knew the blood that Viridians had spilt to earn such accolades from the former Warlord.

Behind them on the road through the forest, Viridian warriors marched, with many on bandaged legs or propped up by scavenged branches used as walking sticks. Those still fit carried casualties much like the humans.

Slowing their pace, Darius, Hera and Gorgias allowed Rufus to catch up as he clearly wished to, and Darius spoke first as the rakkan arrived.

"Slow your march," he said. "The humans ahead can travel no faster, and you're to remain at the rear."

The Viridian Commanders glanced at Rufus, but he merely nodded at the command. "Very well. May I also request your algus withdraw their escorts from tracking my legion? It's been impossible to discern them from Torian spies, and my Subdued will slay any foreign creatures from now on."

That reminded Darius to pick up the subject of Rufus's tortured and broken algus at some point and what their future would be, but he decided now wasn't the time. After believing Selene had been a Subdued for so long, he doubted he could approach that subject yet without anger.

"Very well," Darius said. "Hera, do as he wishes."

The Viridian Commanders all flashed derisive grins at the woman that Darius was tempted to smack from their faces. But Hera denied them the satisfaction of a riposte, and although she gave no confirmation she would do as he'd instructed, he trusted she would. Lex had never doubted the woman for a moment, and that was enough for Darius.

Just the reminder of Lex sent a chill through him, as if to remind him to be afraid of her suffering the same fate as Selene, but he couldn't let himself dwell on it. Lex wouldn't want him to be so distracted.

"While we're on the subject of Torians," Darius added, "I'm tired of their raids, and of the Silk City's too."

"Aren't we all," one of the Viridian Commanders spat. "So, why are we marching home, away from them?"

Rufus looked to Darius as if eager for an answer too.

"Perhaps you shouldn't," Darius said, then watched everyone there carefully for their reaction. Most of the commanders looked to be stricken dumb by his words, but Rufus betrayed a hint of a smile. Although he'd ordered them to march back to Viridia at Mount Psilos, Lex hadn't been keen on that, to put it mildly.

"The Gap of Aphatos," Darius continued, "is the only undefended route for an army to march into the west. The tunnel we created from the Cliffs into Laltos will be caved in, so the Xavalan cavalry will have to use the Gap to get their raiders into Laltos's former lands, as will their Torian allies."

Rufus nodded. "You want to control the Gap, and I can ensure it. But I'll need supplies to maintain enough warriors there." The rakkan spoke in that same self-assured manner he'd had when negotiating with Darius in Dolthea months ago.

"You'll need a fortress," Darius said. "And you shan't build it alone."

"Viridia's architects are the best in the land," one of the commanders said, his walk becoming more of a strut. "We need no assistance in building a fortress."

Tired from the march and the worries weighing him down, Darius hadn't the will to rebut the assertion. "Whether or not you can do it alone, the humans will aid you."

"To a certain extent," Hera added. "And I won't trust anyone other than myself to oversee the construction."

The vocal Viridian Commander baulked. "You mean we'll answer to a human? Is this what we're reduced to?" He and his brothers turned their ugly faces on Rufus.

Rather than pull rank on the rakkan, Darius instead waited and studied his Viridian Warlord; just how capable was the man in keeping his commanders in line? After all, Darius may have sworn to defend the rakkan in any challenge his subordinates might issue, but he couldn't protect the man at every moment, especially when he had friends in far more need of his attention. Rufus would need to fight his own battles.

"I hate to say it," Rufus said, each word slow as if carefully chosen, "but this is one of the rare occasions on which my commander has a point."

The Viridian Commander opened his mouth, ready to respond to the insult, but before it left his lips, Rufus's gaze snapped to him, cold and dangerous yet without so much as a fork of the eyebrow.

"Viridians are willing to obey the Law of the Blades," Rufus continued, "but answering to a human..."

Darius could already see the other commanders watching him, and he realised that undermining Rufus's authority so soon after he'd become warlord would only make them all the more likely to defy him. Plus, Darius couldn't help but be impressed at how Rufus had silenced his brother. Perhaps there was hope for him as a leader after all.

"Rufus and Hera, come with me," he said. "The rest of you carry on."

The two leaders looked a little confused but followed Darius off the road and into the forest, still within sight of the marching army. Darius kept the wagon carrying Lex in view until the red canopy above shook in the wind and drew his attention back to the two others with him.

"I thought it best the others didn't overhear this," Darius said. "Rufus is right. I won't undermine him in front of his new legion."

"Then he will build your fortress without my help," Hera said. "Unless..." She held herself back from the next word, and it wasn't usual for the woman to not speak her mind.

"You'll do as I say," Darius said. "Would you rather leave the Viridians to do as they please while so close to your former home?"

The Regent shook her head with a sigh. "Not really. But if I cannot be there, will you be?"

Rufus gave no reaction to the suggestion, but something changed in his demeanour, standing almost too still.

But rather than think of how he could be of use overseeing the fortress himself, all Darius could focus on was that it meant leaving Lex. She'd begged him to stay with her.

"I'd prefer to command alone," Rufus said. "Your presence will only make my men think of me as your surrogate, a mere puppet that relays your commands and does not think for himself. If I'm ever to lead my legion and change their ways, they must respect me as a man and a warlord."

Conscious of his own bias on the matter, Darius didn't respond and instead looked to Hera.

Her sigh before speaking was one of resignation. "He has a point, but if I can't be there myself, I'll need more assurances."

"I'm happy to build the fortress alone," Rufus said.

But even Hera looked to be unsettled at the thought now. Perhaps she had been bluffing before and was as unwilling as Darius to leave the Viridians to their own devices so soon after the battle at Mount Psilos.

"The humans know the land better," Darius concluded. "Hera, give him workers and algus. As for me, I'll stay with this army, but Lyra will go with you. If *any* of your men get out of line, Warlord, then I'll know and exercise these Twin Blades again. Clear?"

Both Hera and Rufus digested the orders for a moment before nodding in unison. "Yes, Overlord."

# 2

## Rufus – Gap of Aphatos

A rakkan's strength was only underestimated by the most foolish of humans, and when a rakkan clenched a fist, it was as brazen a display of intent to harm as drawing a sword.

And Rufus knew his brother Piso's intent as the rakkan's knuckles turned white and a soft orange glow enveloped his hand, the threat of the ferven eager to flare. Piso's short hair was a darker shade of red than Rufus's mane and showed many a scar on his scalp from all the times those fists had been let loose.

The human soldier before him stood unmoved, naively within striking distance, without a helmet, and around him stood other rakkans and humans bearing as much tension as Piso's fists.

Humans and rakkans squaring up had become a common sight over the last few weeks, and at least this time it was inside one of the rooms they'd finished rather than out in open view of hundreds of witnesses. Although Darius had ordered them all to work together on this fortress, it was unsurprising that tensions were rife because they'd faced each other on the battlefield not too long ago, and Rufus was prepared to let men vent like his father had—but not before he'd banned the carrying of weapons except for guards and patrols.

Outside the crowded room, the building of the fortress sent a clamour inside—hammering of nails and chiselling of unearthed stone as the new walls arose one grey block at a time, preparing to protect the west from the King. Shovels clanged as they hit rock in trenches, and the thump of wooden palisades driven into holes added bass to the chaotic melody that only inflamed the tensions inside the room. At least the space was bare, without a single piece of furniture that could be used as a weapon. Rufus's rakkans were safe.

The human scoffed at Piso. "And why should we tell you anything?"

"Because my men died in that trap!" Piso yelled. "Your patrol should have warned them when they changed shift."

"We couldn't be sure it was a trap," the human said, although his grin told otherwise.

Piso growled. "Your men saw the Xavalans waiting there. What else could it be?"

The human shrugged.

Then Piso's right fist launched upwards.

Before the human saw it coming, the fist had burst with fire and slammed an uppercut into his jaw, shattering the bone and thrusting his head back with such a violent snap that Rufus knew the man was dead before his body slumped.

Shouts and screams soon erupted as the humans and rakkans hurled insults at one another, and Rufus moved at once, not to restrain his brother or the other dozens in the room, but towards the door. He slammed it shut, then peered out of the window to the right-hand side.

He spied the one he feared, the panther lurking in the dirt outside. Lyra turned her head at the sudden noise, ears pointed towards the building.

Killing humans was nothing new to rakkans, but the world had changed from the one the Viridians had known for centuries. Now, slaying humans would undoubtedly invite Darius's wrath, and if Rufus didn't handle this, it wouldn't only be his men facing punishment.

The chaos in the room persisted, but Rufus continued to watch the panther until she turned her head back towards the thankfully deafening noise from the rest of the fort around them.

Only when Lyra had disappeared around a corner did Rufus speak.

"Silence!" he yelled, his focus fixed on his subordinates. But only half the Viridian Legionnaires obeyed him. The rest shoved the humans back as they pressed forward, Piso at the front with his fists raised and ready to spill more blood, more like his adolescent self than the commander he now was.

Meanwhile, his twin, Pollio, leant against the wall at the back and smirked at Rufus with a full set of white teeth, epitomising a warrior who was careful with both his health and which fights he entered into.

Unwilling to risk disobedience to his commands a second time, Rufus reacted with action rather than words. He pushed forward and wedged himself between the line of human soldiers and Viridians, hovering over the brains and gore of the dead man on the dirt floor.

"Enough!" Rufus stared at Piso until his brother finally relented and gave his men a signal to step back.

They obeyed, but it took the humans a bit longer to settle. When they had, Rufus beckoned over the highest-ranking soldier, the one responsible for these humans' treachery.

But by the angry look on the human's face, it was clear he thought only the rakkans were in the wrong here.

"I don't look kindly on men that cause me such aggravation," Rufus said to the soldier. "Give me one reason I shouldn't execute the lot of you."

The man scowled. "Darius. He won't look kindly on you harming humans, and your legion is already on the edge of a precipice."

Rufus stepped up to the man, not usually one to physically intimidate, but he knew his strength outmatched any human's by orders of magnitude. "The Overlord isn't here."

"But his escort is. She knows the scent of human blood."

Rufus leaned his head a fraction closer. "Human blood already wets my boots. What more trouble would your blood be to me?"

The soldier nervously peered down at his dead comrade, a look of submission that Rufus had been seeking. Now he could soften his demeanour.

"We've all been tasked with building this fortress," Rufus said, "because combining both human and rakkan expertise is how we'll achieve the most robust defences. We rakkans are expert builders from centuries of forging the mountains around us into impenetrable walls. But now, we find ourselves in the open plains, relying on wood-and-stone constructions that you humans are most experienced in breaching. Working together is the only way this place will prevail, and allowing my men to be slain helps neither you nor us."

"Old feuds die hard," Piso spat.

Rufus ignored the interruption and continued, "The success of this fortress isn't about protecting rakkans. It will protect all of us." He was glad to oversee every detail of the construction of this place precisely because it was of such strategic significance.

"Not only have I designed a stone fort to house an entire legion if required, but layers of defence—trenches, palisades, spikes—have been plotted out and will render it impossible for the cavalry to get through."

"Why do you waste time convincing them?" Pollio's voice was soft and slippery yet brought a silence to the room so deep Rufus heard the thump of logs outside again.

Pushing himself off the wall, Pollio came forward while his men shifted to make space for him.

"I can handle this," Rufus said.

Piso scoffed, and a lot of his men grunted in amusement.

*Delinquents.* Rufus would remember which ones.

"Piso killed a human," Pollio said, turning to Rufus, "so you know what needs to be done."

"What?" Rufus said. "Arrest him and take him to the Overlord?"

The Viridian Legionnaires there grunted in disgust at the thought, but not Pollio. He smiled, knowing Rufus well enough to know he'd never seriously contemplate that. For all his faults, he was at least loyal.

"I'm hungry," Pollio said. "Can we get this over with?"

Rufus glanced out of the window again, swearing he saw a black tail flick around the corner of a pile of building stones.

"If you wish to leave," he said, "then feel free to do so, Commander."

"Oh… I'm not leaving until I know my brother is safe."

It was times like these when Rufus was tempted to report Pollio and most of his brothers to Darius. But it would be an act so cowardly it made Rufus retch. He refused to be such a man.

But still… Construction was already behind schedule, and relations between the humans and rakkans were getting no better. Lyra's presence had helped abate these confrontations in part, but only Darius himself could enforce absolute peace. As loath as Rufus was to invite the Overlord, if the Silk City's traps began leading to a more perilous situation, he wouldn't have a choice.

"Are you able to resolve this, Pollio?" Rufus asked.

The commander nodded calmly. "Of course, Warlord."

"Then do it. I'm going to write to the Overlord and let him know of the Xavalan ambushes."

"Do you think he'll come here?"

"I doubt it," Rufus said, well aware Darius was practically chained to the sickbed of his lover. After a brief stay in Menara, the Overlord had taken his woman back to Margalvia where they could better protect her. "But I'll ask if more warriors can join us from Viridia. I suspect we'll need them."

Rufus strode towards the door and stepped outside, and as soon as the door had closed, he focused his attention on his exposed arms, on the sensitive skin that could feel every movement of the air around him. The breeze was fresh and cooling in this valley, making it difficult to sense whether the panther was still around. Before he could be sure, yells burst from the sealed room behind him, bones cracked, bodies thumped onto the ground, and men screamed in agony. Without an algus to protect them, the humans had no chance.

"Clean the room up well," Rufus shouted through the door before marching towards his tent.

# 3

## Sulla – Margalvia

"You need to convince him." Sulla grabbed the Chief Priest by the arm and tried to drag him away from all the humans prostrated in front of his altar, but the man somehow managed to slip his arm free to leave Sulla holding only his robes.

Aran halted with an unimpressed glare, his silver hair still neat and styled despite the rough handling. "I'm in the middle of a service."

"No, you're not," Sulla said. "I've listened in on these things before, and you were about to say the final prayer."

Many of the humans stared at him like he'd just spat at the altar, then looked to the Chief Priest as if expecting a reprimand.

"Nevertheless," Aran said, "I haven't finished."

Sulla grumbled under his breath and took a step back. They needed to get Darius to listen, not dawdle.

The Margalvian building the priest had chosen as his place of worship had once been a butcher's, and the whiff of raw meat still lingered in the stained stonework. Perhaps such humble surroundings were why it had taken Sulla so long to discover that this man wasn't just a priest but the head of the Diagathic Order himself, or perhaps it was his youthful looks, that smooth skin around the eyes that hid his age so well any woman would have paid thousands of crests for his secrets. Whatever the man's reasons for not speaking freely of his position, Sulla only cared about what he did, and right now, he didn't do it swiftly like a youngster but as slowly as a senile man.

Sulla occupied himself by cracking his knuckles while Aran said his final words and dismissed the humans with some incantations.

"Are you done?" Sulla asked once everyone had left.

"I usually spend time in silent reflection after a service," the Chief Priest said, but his smile faded a little as Sulla folded his arms impatiently.

"Very well." Aran grabbed his cloak and draped it over his robes. "Let's go."

Seconds later, they were tearing through the streets and straight into the central garrison. It was where the Black Warlord and everyone else of importance resided, and the southern wing was being used to house the sick and injured.

"I still don't understand why you need me," the Chief Priest said.

"You have a way with words," Sulla said. To have just seen so many humans so eager to hear his snippets of wisdom had only confirmed the fact.

Once deeper underground, the corridors grew so dark he flared ferven across his hands to shed light onto the fractured walls for his guest, who seemed to be walking with more trepidation than before. Sulla filled him in on Rufus's message and why he'd rather take Darius to the war front than hide away in Margalvia as they had been doing.

"From what my spies tell me," Aran said, "you're right to be concerned. But why would Darius listen to me when he doesn't listen to his friends?" His question echoed from the black stone that made the narrow walkway.

"Don't you have some higher powers you can call upon? Use some magic or divining."

"I'm a priest. Not a witch."

"Ah. The dress fooled me."

"It's a *robe*. Anyway, I still don't see how I can persuade him where you've failed."

Sulla stopped with a grunt of annoyance and squared up to the man. Although the Chief Priest's eyes betrayed age-old wisdom far beyond his otherwise unblemished looks, Sulla still had at least a few decades more experience than him.

"This is serious," Sulla said. "To be honest, I'm asking you out of desperation, not out of confidence in your powers of persuasion."

The Chief Priest shifted uncomfortably at the last remark, backed into the wall as his long hair slipped for the first time across his face. "I know. But I'm being realistic. I'll try my best, but you'll need more than me."

Sulla could have told the man that before, but it wasn't like he was spoilt for choice at the moment, and judging by Rufus's message, conditions at the new fortress hadn't improved. At this rate, Sulla suspected they wouldn't be finished before the Xavalans or the Torians attacked.

"Can't you just say your gods have commanded Darius to go to the new fortress?" Sulla asked.

Aran's face twisted in disgust. "I'll pretend you didn't suggest such a heinous lie."

"You don't know how many lives this might save."

The Chief Priest pushed Sulla back with his gloved hands in what would have been a futile move, but Sulla allowed himself to shift back.

"Two wrongs don't make a right," Aran said.

"Then let's try three…or four."

The Chief Priest gaped as Sulla turned and pressed on towards Lex's room, where Darius had been holed up for an entire week. Despite being deep under Margalvia, the air coursed through shafts and vents meant to help the sick, but even that couldn't take away the stink of rot and decay. Sulla only hoped it wasn't coming from Lex. The wound she'd taken at Mount Psilos had been healing after the visit to Menara, but her fever and mind still hadn't, and Sulla had seen many warriors go through the same delirium. Worryingly, not many had survived.

The pair rounded a bend and came to a wooden door braced with solid bars of kuraminium across the planks and a large key lock that hadn't been there the last time Sulla had visited. Even ten burly rakkans would have struggled to kick the thing down.

"Is this a room for the sick," the Chief Priest asked, "or a prison?"

Sulla frowned, knowing Lex didn't need such security within this city, but before he could think of an explanation, Aran gave three light raps on the door and stepped back.

"Who is it?" Darius's voice rasped from inside, almost as if roused from sleep.

"A wise, old friend is here to speak with you." Sulla gave Aran a grin. "And I brought that priest along too."

After a few moments' pause, muffled voices came from within the room.

*Lex?* Sulla pressed his ear against the door at once. "Is she awake again?"

But as he listened, the door shuddered and boomed from a strike on the other side, rattling on its hinges and sending Sulla backwards into the Chief Priest with ringing in his ear.

"Back away," Darius shouted.

"All right, you lout!" Sulla said. "You could have warned me *before* bursting my hearing."

The Chief Priest frowned with a rare crease on his brow. "How long has he been so…irritable?"

"There's no need to be so polite," Sulla said. "The guy's been an arse ever since Lex fell ill." But now that he thought more on it, the first week back in Margalvia hadn't been too bad. Then suddenly, the man hadn't allowed Sulla or anyone else to see her.

While Aran and Sulla quietly waited outside the room, three metallic snaps came from the other side of the door. Then, slowly, it creaked open just wide enough for Darius to slide himself out and pull it closed behind him.

Sulla winced at the sight of the man. The deep shadows under his sunken eyes were now so dark it almost looked as if he'd emerged from firing the kuraminium furnaces, and the paleness of the rest of his skin was that of someone who hadn't seen the sun for a long time. His cheeks had lost more fullness since the last time they'd spoken, and his clothes were thick and warm but clearly hanging from a small frame.

"Darius…" Sulla said. "Are you still not eating?"

Darius shook his head. "I can't keep much down these days." But his breath bore the reek of firewater.

"Then maybe you shouldn't be suffering here; let someone else look after her. You're the Overlord of Rakka now. You have responsibilities beyond one woman."

The man's eyebrows forked. "What do you want?"

Momentarily lost for words, Sulla just studied his friend while Aran spoke first. "You've had a message from Warlord

Rufus. Your fortress is behind schedule, and the Xavalans are causing problems. Rufus wants his men to march from Viridia, and—"

"I won't risk that," Darius said. "You've seen what they're like on the march without anyone to rein them in, and without me or Rufus…" He shook his head. "Tell him no."

"I won't say you aren't correct to worry," Aran said, "but my spies predict an attack by the King could come at any time. If you won't allow him reinforcements, perhaps you should go and see that they complete this fortress sooner rather than later."

Darius let out a long breath that seemed to deflate him to half his size. "Your spies? What are you, the King's Orator now?"

"I have eyes and ears throughout the Empire, more than you know. Lex trusted my insights, and so should you."

"I'll trust them when she's recovered. But even if I go there, what can I do? Whip the men to work faster? Redesign the fort to be quicker to build?"

Sulla tried to think of answers to his questions but came up short. "It's better that you're there than not."

"I'd go if I could achieve anything," Darius said.

"And what about if Rufus is attacked?" Sulla said. "You can damn well be of use then."

"If Warlord Rufus is attacked," Aran said, "he hasn't the numbers to repel Toria's armies. Your presence might deter a battle entirely."

Darius sighed and seemed to consider what they'd said for a moment. If Lex had been awake, he'd probably have gone to her for advice, but Sulla considered it a good thing he had to make up his own mind for once—or at least, he would if the half-rakkan chose correctly.

"Did Rufus ask me to come?" Darius asked.

The answer was no, and Sulla knew Darius would use it to decide to do nothing. But as tempted as he was to lie, he couldn't betray his friend's trust like that. "Not in so many words."

"Then he has it under control; he's smart enough to know if he needs me, and I'll see how he responds to my refusal of his request. Now, is that all?" Darius put a hand on the door handle, but Sulla grabbed it and made sure he couldn't twist.

"Whatever you choose," Sulla said, "quit hiding away here! I know you're worried about her, but she'd be the first to tell you that this war is more important than her. Let me look after her until she gets better." Sulla turned the handle and moved to push the door open, but Darius thrust him back so swiftly Sulla gasped.

"No," Darius said, his voice a pitch higher than usual. "No one is to see to her except me and her carer. You have to trust me; she wouldn't want any visitors right now."

"Hey. I'll visit who I please." Sulla stepped forward again, growing tired of his old friend's temper of late.

But Darius squared up to him, the glow of ferven beginning to swell in his hostile eyes. "Don't make me speak as your overlord rather than your friend. Just trust me. No one is to enter this room without my permission."

Sulla had never been more tempted to punch the man, but before he could decide whether he was foolish enough, the Chief Priest came between them.

"Now, now." Aran pushed them both apart but couldn't budge them, and the effort had his sleeves slipping down a few inches to reveal patches and scars across his forearms.

The sight gave Sulla a chance to shift the conversation and hopefully calm all their frayed nerves.

"What happened to you?" Sulla asked the priest.

"Oh…" Aran slid his sleeves back down to meet his gloves. "I need to catch many wild animals for bonding escorts. The big ones can be quite a handful, especially the cats."

"Do you two have anything else to discuss with me?" Darius asked. "Or will you leave me in peace now?"

Sulla scoffed. "Peace or pieces?"

Without a reply, Darius opened the door, passed into the darkened room beyond, and slammed it shut before Sulla could take a peek inside.

As the metal locks scratched shut again, Aran gave a shake of the head. "Something's going on in there, and I think you should trust him and stay out of it. If you're concerned for the fortress, perhaps you can ask your warlord for assistance."

*Great.* Warlord Varro was even less willing to aid the Viridians than Darius was, and a second warlord at the fort would only complicate matters. Whatever the half-rakkan was doing in there, it'd better be worth it.

# 4

## King's Orator – Toria

The death of a spy was such a hassle. Good ones were hard to come by, and it sometimes took them years to position themselves in the necessary places. As the King's Orator, Ophelia had to report every failure to the King, and he usually replaced dead spies with a Numbered, undoubtedly loyal but lacking the experience, intellect and charm to be as useful as her older informants.

"Why did you do that?" Ophelia leaned forward from the rich folds of the padded seat before her desk to see the man's blood trickle within the floral patterns of her once pristine rug, an ugly red that clashed with both the green and blue threadwork and the gold leaf that ordained all the framed fine art in her study.

The King's Sword bent over and wiped his sword clean on the dead man's trousers. "Two days, not a week. He lied."

"They all lie. That's why they're so useful."

Jason shook his head. "Can't trust again."

Because the spy had claimed to have written the report a few days before he actually had? *So typical.* As much as Ophelia would like to think categorising people into such wooden dichotomies was a facet of Jason's adjusted mind, the old Jason she'd known when he'd been imprisoned had had a similar intolerance for those who proved themselves untrustworthy.

"Everyone lies sometimes," Ophelia said. "I can discern lie and truth from the mere twitch of a man's nose, so don't kill someone so rashly again." Who knew what the King would have done if he'd been here.

Jason stood again, frowning. "If everyone lies, do you?"

Ophelia smiled. "I wouldn't have the King's ear if I weren't one of the best."

"To me?" His eyes narrowed.

Not that question again… Sometimes, she forgot how dangerous it was to speak to the man without caution. As easy as it was for the King to correct aberrations in Jason's mind, Ophelia preferred to keep him as untampered as possible, one of the few kindnesses she could offer her friend. Although the King had good intentions, one had to be careful. Ophelia had ensured she was so meticulous she'd been allowed to keep her mind, going to such lengths as not only speaking of the King as a "he"—despite the goman actually being a woman—but *thinking* of the King as a "him" too. It was the only way she'd guaranteed no slip-ups.

As she pondered, Jason still watched her, awaiting an answer and looking to continue what was for him a positively chatty mood.

"Of course not," Ophelia said. "I have no reason to lie to you and the King."

"But you lie to the Puppet…"

Hearing Jason refer to the man in such terms had Ophelia picking at the flaky skin on the back of her hands, only worsening the condition that had plagued her since birth. The Puppet King had to make many public appearances, often with Jason protecting him, but Ophelia had always explained to Jason that the man was a decoy. Had she ever used the word "Puppet," or had Jason come across it somewhere else? Even someone with a warped mind had enough wit to know why a man would be called that—even though Jason wasn't aware of the real King's cogi—and that he was being lied to.

"Our decoy for the King needs to be convincing," Ophelia said. "That's why we act the part even in private company. He's borderline delusional, but he serves his purpose."

Jason chewed on her words for a moment before nodding, and as he did, the black staff strapped to his back peeked from behind his neck, almost concealed within his grey hood. It was a treasured prize that the King allowed only his Sword to handle, a fact that filled Ophelia with pride on his behalf, but the sight now revealed the algus was still more hunched than usual.

"Hide the Staff better," Ophelia advised. "And are you sure you're fit enough for these investigations? Those broken ribs alone won't be fully healed yet."

"I'm fine," Jason said.

"I can see you're not. I worry over you."

Jason's lips curled into a barely perceptible smile. Ophelia was the only one to ever bring the King's Sword close to something akin to happiness, and how special she felt because of it. Unfortunately, she had more pressing matters to attend to at the moment than savouring her friend's company.

She reached across the desk and took the note her spy had brought, then shifted an oil lamp closer, taking in the last scrawl detailing the new fortress the rakkans were building.

When at the end, she asked, "They haven't even finished the palisades? Did you see?"

Jason shrugged. "Didn't see, but not a lie."

The man's certainty had Ophelia dropping the note, panic gripping her. "You didn't...touch him to ascertain that, did you?" How else would he be so sure? Was that why he'd been asking about lying?

But Jason shook his head.

Ophelia fell back into her chair, breathing freely again. Although Jason hadn't the cogi powers of his sister or the King, he was at least able to read someone's thoughts via touch. It was a pity it was so dangerous for them if he used that gift; otherwise, it would have come in quite useful. But the King had no tolerance for that particular rule being broken.

She picked up the note again and moved on. "Are the Silk City's algus and cavalry in the Cliffs?"

Jason nodded.

That meant the pieces were all in place.

Ophelia sprang from her seat so swiftly she knocked over the oil lamp. But she couldn't care. As slaves ran to clean up the mess, Ophelia grabbed the hem of her flowing cream dress so that it wouldn't soak up blood, and she sprinted through the doors of her office towards the King's throne room.

The guards lining the corridors didn't so much as move their eyes as she passed, followed closely behind by Jason, and the grand doors to the King's room were already swinging open, heaved by five men each, when she swept through and entered under the enormous domed ceiling. Dominating the front of the room sat the throne with its silver wings spread out to each side as if a steel eagle were ready to take flight, and as always, rolls of parchment littered the floor and had only multiplied as the King continued his scribblings.

"*What news from the west?*" The King's booming voice entered her mind like an intrusive presence before they'd arrived at the foot of the dais he sat upon. The black mask covering his face, along with the monotone voice, made his mood unreadable, so Ophelia had learned to always tread lightly at first.

"Their defences are ill-prepared," she said.

"*So, that's the scenario that played out.*" The King grabbed a roll of parchment from his lap, covered with so much writing it was almost entirely dark with ink. "*Then we must take this opportunity. We'll not get another.*"

Whenever the King made such absolute statements, it made the skin all over Ophelia's body itch. Resisting the urge to scratch was something she was used to, but only by imagining the warm milk bath she'd need to take soon.

She lowered her head in a gesture of understanding. "Do you mean this battle will determine the fate of the war?"

"*The war? No. The west? Yes.*"

"But if we have the west, that means we'll have…"

"*Driven the rakkans back into the mountains.*"

Finally, all these years after Archimedes's death, they'd be on the cusp of victory again.

"Then we should commit all our resources to it," Ophelia said. "The Xavalan cavalry is already well placed, and the swifts of Alogos could travel west and cross the River Toras with enough time to spare. We have the food stores to support their army. And the algus of—"

"*Don't get ahead of yourself.*" The King placed down the parchment, stood, and paced towards the dais's edge to look down upon the pair. "*The One Mind will not make this battle easy. It will even shift the world against us, for whatever reason.*"

When the King paused, Ophelia opened her mouth to ask for clarification on what "shifting the world" meant, but he spoke again before her.

*"But I won't let that deter us. Jason, are you fit for battle?"*

The algus glanced sideways at Ophelia for a moment before shrugging. "Enough. Not fully."

*"Then you'll remain here."*

Ophelia's shoulders relaxed, only then making her realise she'd been so tense at the question. But if Jason wasn't going, did that mean…?

"What about the Staff?" she asked.

The King raised his head to face the dome overhead. She knew he wasn't taking in the fine art that adorned the ceiling but using his cogi powers to foresee the possible futures before them, during which a silence began that stretched out for so long Ophelia's arms itched again.

But finally, the King moved and looked down. *"Jason, are you certain the Twin Blades of Trogus allowed Darius to fight in the Staff's presence?"*

The algus nodded.

*"How well?"*

"Well enough."

The King's eyes narrowed at the man's curt answers, and Ophelia had to suppress a smile at the frustration Jason unwittingly brought to most that dealt with him.

*"Could any of my algus defeat him?"*

Jason shook his head. "But I could."

The King looked back to the ceiling again for a few moments before concluding, *"Then I'm unsure."*

That was the first time Ophelia had ever heard those words from the King. "You mean the odds are even?"

"*No. Keeping our possession of the Staff between only us three will gift us a decisive victory when the time is right, but the greatest battles are to come, and I want to use the Staff to permanently cripple his armies, preferably after we've dealt with the threat of the Twin Blades.*"

Ophelia had scoured Toria's archives for months in search of knowledge about those weapons and how to defeat them, revealing little other than they couldn't be touched, even by algus using algor.

"Do you know yet whether they can be destroyed?"

The King shook his head. "*And until then, perhaps the Staff should remain hidden. When Archimedes revealed it and razed Gerunda, the other cities retreated into their shells and made it that much harder for us. We'd be best not to overplay our hand again, and wait until we can catch most of their warriors in the field. The numbers at this new fortress won't be significant; we might defeat them without the Staff.*"

"Might? That sounds like either way we'll suffer heavy losses."

The King nodded to confirm her inference.

Ophelia wondered which of their forces would be best suited to assaulting a half-built fort. Algus were best at infiltrating defences and would require smaller numbers, easier to ambush by stealth and evade scouts and patrols. But Xavala didn't have enough. Toria's finest would need to be sent at once.

Ophelia stepped forward eagerly. "We have over a thousand alg—"

"*Send the Xavalan cavalry.*" The King spun on his heel and returned to his throne.

"Cavalry? Against a fort?"

"*Not yet built.*"

"But, my king…" What was the best way to point out a foolish decision to one with the power to execute you? "The cavalry is most effective in open—"

*"I'm not sending them because they're the best choice."*

Then Ophelia questioned why. It wasn't because they were the most fearsome or talented. In fact, they were among the most useless and under the reign of a regent that...was expendable.

Suddenly it made sense to her. When the King had said this battle would decide the fate of the west, she hadn't realised what that meant for the Silk City. If they lost this battle, Xavala would fall, and its armies and horses would either be absorbed by their enemies or slaughtered. Plus, the Silk City was one of the most troublesome in the Empire. Its armies were expendable for more than one reason.

"I'll send your orders," Ophelia said. "And what of Xavala's algus?"

The King once again silently took in the ceiling for a few moments before speaking. "*Send half. The rest will retreat here.*"

"As you wish, my king." Ophelia bowed and turned to leave but realized she'd forgotten one thing. "And the Staff?"

The King leant back, rapped his fingers against the steel feathers that made up his armrests, and looked out at the rolls of parchment.

He seemed distracted for so long Ophelia feared he'd forgotten the question, but he finally said, "*I'll decide in the morning. And before you leave, I have another request of you. There's something I've passed down to myself, message to message, from far beyond my cogi's sight. I don't know why, but—*"

The King suddenly fell silent, scanning the room again except now his eyes were wide through his mask, as if in search of a phantom.

Then Ophelia heard a light rustle and patter of tiny feet that should never have been present there.

Jason's head swivelled too, sensing the danger.

"Find it!" she cried.

He took off in a blink and careened through the piled scrolls as if already knowing where the creature was.

"Don't kill it!" Ophelia howled. How long had it been there? If it was an escort, it could have overheard the conversation.

After batting away a few clusters of parchments with little care, Jason dove, and a shrill squeak sounded not long after. He came back to his feet gripping what appeared to be a mouse in his hand as it tried in vain to wriggle free.

Ophelia knew Jason would be able to tell if it were an escort, to access its mind to see whether there was enough intelligence there to give away a bond. Yet even on escorts, he shouldn't be using his power.

But he was already touching it… Would the King object to even that?

"I'm sorry, my king!" Ophelia turned and fell to her knees. "I'll have the guards flogged for allowing that creature in here. I'll triple the patrols with cats, wolves, lizards…" Any escort that could sense prey would scour the place day and night.

"*Relax, Ophelia.*" The King's voice was strong, as always, but he held out a concessionary hand. "*If it were an escort, I would have warned myself of it.*"

That was true and restored enough of Ophelia's faith in herself to look up, albeit still from her knees.

Jason brought the mouse and handed it to the King, whose eyes clouded over for the briefest of moments before he squeezed the creature in his hand, taking more than a few seconds to crush its squeals into silence.

"*It was no escort. It never spoke with humans.*"

But it could have been. The guards still deserved flogging. "I'm sorry, my king. This won't happen again."

"*See that it doesn't.*"

Already, the list of those responsible for protecting this sacred place ran through Ophelia's mind as she rose but kept her head lowered and made towards the door.

"*Aren't you forgetting something?*"

Ophelia froze. Was this it, a failure that meant she couldn't be trusted with a free mind any longer?

But then she recalled what the King had said before the interruption.

"Apologies, my king. You have a request for me?"

"*Yes, and if you don't stop apologising, I'll remove those words from your mind.*"

Ophelia gave a diffident bow.

"*I need you to bring two people to me, unharmed. I've written down a basic description of the first for you.*" He held out a parchment that she took and noted only gave the details "male," "hair colour black," and a rough height of "average." Was this some sort of test?

"Do you at least have a name?" she asked.

"*He goes by 'Sixty-three' now.*"

At least that name was unusual, if not unique, depending on whether Archimedes had recycled it. The man must have been captured a few years after Archimedes had arrived in the Empire, so he was probably still quite young, perhaps in his early twenties.

"*I've listed what else I know on the back, including when and where he was captured.*"

"I'll make enquiries," she said. "Hopefully, he still goes by that name. Is this urgent?"

"*Not yet. But finding him as soon as possible would be best.*"

Then Ophelia would put her best people on it. "And why do you seek him?" If he possessed any particular skills, that might help narrow down his whereabouts.

The King shrugged. "*I must seek him for something I'll enjoy because my future self didn't reveal the reasons. I sometimes like to tease myself like that.*"

Whatever the purpose, Ophelia would wager Sixty-three wouldn't enjoy being brought here, and finding him in the Empire would be no easy feat.

"And who is the second person you'd like me to bring?" she asked.

"*Alexandra of Laltos.*"

# 5

## Darius – Margalvia

The stink of decay lingered in the room despite the air coursing through the chimney and the ventilation tunnels. No fresh air, no relief. It left Darius's lungs heavy and stinging as if the infected air clawed at his insides. As he sat beside Lex's bed resting his head on the covers of the straw mattress, his nose prickled from the mixture of the firewater on his breath and the rot from her wound, never granting him a moment's peace from the fact Lex was being eaten from within.

And he could do nothing. If only he could take up a sword and fight this fight for her, or see her enemy rather than it being hidden and festering within.

When he'd killed Selene, he'd thought those moments were the blackest depths his mind would ever reach, even worse than his torture in Laltos when he'd asked Gorgias to end his miserable life.

But when Lex had deteriorated and lost any ability to communicate coherently, the torment of his mind had proven that assumption wrong. He could barely eat. He could barely sleep. His mind would focus on little else, not even to spare a passing thought to mourn Selene. Lex consumed every waking thought now in a way that Selene never had.

And Lyra… It had been difficult at first to separate his senses from hers after the Chief Priest had restored their bond, but now it was as if the bond had been shattered. None of what she saw, touched, or tasted broke through to his beleaguered mind unless his grief allowed it. He checked in with her every hour and was relieved she hadn't summoned him to join her yet.

There were tens of thousands of people now looking up to him as a leader, but Hera and the rakkan warlords were in better states of mind to oversee things for now. Until the time for battle came, his place was beside Lex, however painful the sight of her was.

He needed her to recover and pull through. If she died, what would he…?

"Are you sure they won't disturb us?" his grandfather whispered from the back of the room.

Darius lifted his head and peered at the old man sitting on a stool in the corner, running a hand through his long grey beard with a quiet solemnity that had made Darius forget he was there.

"No one will dare come," Darius said, his voice as wan as his hope.

From the opposite side of the bed from Darius, Cynthia stared at her fevered mother with wide, tear-filled eyes the same shade of blue as Lex's. Seeing them so aggrieved was almost agony, but she had a right to be here, and Darius would ensure Lex's wish for her daughter to remain a secret was upheld.

Behind Cynthia, Nasrin stood organising some herbs the Menaran carers had recommended if Lex wasn't winning the fight with the rot. Nasrin's usual smile had abandoned her for a long time now, and her brown curls sagged over her face and cast dark shadows from the oil lamps in the room.

"Are you sure Cynthia hasn't had enough?" Nasrin asked. "It can't be good for a little girl to see her mother like this."

Darius murmured to himself, picked up his latest half-empty bottle of firewater, and began swigging again. He'd had the same thought when debating whether to bring her or not, especially every time Cynthia descended into one of her fits of crying, or when Lex was awake and rambling like a madwoman. Nothing made a man feel as powerless as a child's sobs he could do nothing to relieve.

"I don't know," Darius said. "All I know is I would have wanted to be with my father at the end if I could, and I'm glad I was with Brutus when he…"

Nasrin gave a solemn nod and went back to rummaging through her bag.

But then it began again.

"Mama…" Cynthia's eyes welled, tears fell down her cheeks in an all-too-familiar way. "Mama! Wake up!" She dove forwards and wrapped her arms around her mother's sweaty body.

Darius dropped his bottle and rushed over before his grandfather or Nasrin had moved, using his algus speed, and took Cynthia into his arms.

"Why won't she talk to me?" The girl's sobs became muffled as he pulled her head into his chest, buried her in the folds of his tunic, and ran a hand through her soft, blonde hair that was so like that of her father, Varro.

"It's all right," Darius said as convincingly as he could. "It'll be all right." It had taken him many attempts to learn the right words to calm her down. Who knew whether it was wrong to lie to a child, but those were the only words that worked, and he just wished they worked on himself, wished they'd quell the fear of losing Lex. Still, he repeated them over and over, and the girl's sobs eased. She was so light in his arms, so small, so vulnerable, a delicate thing that could be alive one moment and dead the next—as with all life.

Throughout all his experience of loss in his life, Lex had been there with so much strength and resilience it had rubbed off on him. Without her, he wasn't sure the struggle was worth it.

"It'll be all right." If only he could take away Cynthia's pain, it might ease his own.

"I'll take her." His grandfather came over and took hold of the girl under the arms, but Darius was almost loath to let her go, to let go of the last part of Lex that was still healthy and strong. Eventually, he released his grip, but Cynthia kept clinging to him.

"Come on, my child," Eugenius said softly. "Let's sit over here and rest for a while."

Cynthia sniffled, then relented and let him take her to the back of the dark room.

Meanwhile, Darius dared to look where he'd been avoiding as much as possible—Lex's face. The shine of sweat was so thick her skin looked varnished, and loose hairs clung to her head like dark-black veins. She could have been a corpse if not for her pallid lips occasionally flinching as she muttered about whatever was going on inside her scrambled mind. It was a sight he'd seen too often amongst dying warriors after a battle.

Why had he never told her how strongly he felt about her? All those months and years felt like wasted opportunities now, denying himself something he'd wanted for most of his known life. And now she might die without knowing the truth.

"I think I've got the mix of herbs and fungi right." Nasrin held out a little heap of powder in her palm. "But the dosage is still hard to know. The Menarans weren't very specific."

"Because they're slaves." Darius dabbed Lex's face tenderly with a damp rag. "Their dead masters were the Empire's experts on medicine, and those secrets were hidden from the slaves, so all they can do is guess based on what they saw." That was another reason he hadn't seen the need to leave Lex with them.

"But still…" Nasrin frowned before emptying the powder into a cup of water and stirring it vigorously.

"I'll try it first if you're unsure," Darius said.

"I hardly think that's wise," his grandfather interjected. "Those remedies need to be almost lethal to fight the rot. I still think we'd be best letting Lex fight it herself."

Darius finished cleaning her face, glad of the fact her skin was at least hot and not ice-cold in death. Yet. "She doesn't seem to be winning the fight."

"Well, someone needs to decide," Nasrin said.

Both of them looked to Darius. "Me? What do I know about medicine? You're the carer here."

"I've never used this before," Nasrin said. "And you're our Overlord."

"She has a point," Eugenius said, still stroking Cynthia's head.

Frustratingly, his grandfather was right, but Darius needed some inspiration to make the right call. His thoughts went to the other leaders and how they weighed possible options, then onto the Chief Priest, who always seemed so sure of himself and what he and others should do. Was that because he turned to forces beyond themselves and begged for divine intervention? Did that even work?

Darius supposed it was worth a try.

He dropped to his knees by Lex's bed, clasped his hands together, and closed his eyes to the confused looks on the others' faces.

*Dianoia… Agathos… If you can hear me, one of your followers needs you. Alexandra may not have been perfect, but she fought for you with more courage and vigour than anyone I've seen. To you, she was your warrior. And to me, she was…*

What exactly was she? His friend? His confidante?

*She was everything. She* is *everything. Some people have suggested I'm part of your plans for this world, and if I am, I'll need her. So, gift me enough wisdom to make this choice.*

He opened one eye and was a little disheartened that rather than having miraculously awoken all well, Lex bore a sheen of sweat again.

"What's your decision?" Eugenius asked.

Darius stood and began pacing the room. Many had told him how rare it was for people to wake up once the rot had taken hold of them, but if he gave Lex this concoction and she died, that would be two sisters he'd have killed. Could he live with himself after that?

"Well?" Nasrin raised her eyebrows.

Then again, these remedies were passed down through generations for a reason.

He bent and grabbed his bottle from the floor, grateful for the little firewater left inside that hadn't spilt onto the stone floor. "Give her the medicine."

# 6

## Rufus – Gap of Aphatos

"Another one?" Rufus boomed in a rare betrayal of his frayed temper. He surveyed the command room, so recently built that it only had chiselled stone stools placed in a ring surrounding an empty space where a table would eventually be. On each seat were the most senior rakkans and humans at the fort, and every pair of eyes Rufus met lacked the one thing he needed, the one thing he demanded of them all—respect. And one pair scared him—feline amber balls with slits for pupils, a wordless black presence that represented the true authority all those miles away.

"We've only lost two," Piso said in a voice as rough as his armour. "It's hardly a cause for concern." Rufus's brother always had a knack for saying the wrong thing at the wrong time.

"Three," one of Hera's algus corrected. "We lost another patrol the day before last."

"Four if you include the party that mysteriously disappeared after reporting back here," another algus said with a suspicious look at Rufus. As usual, this woman had the tense face of a person sucking a lemon, which was one of the many reasons he'd immediately disliked her when Hera introduced them. He hadn't bothered to hide his disdain at the time, much to his regret now because she returned the favour.

A stiff breeze swept through the unfinished windows with a chill that must have swept down from the Cliffs, and the humans shivered while the rakkans grinned at their discomfort. Even in the small things, Rufus's task of bringing together the two enemies was difficult. Some shouts from outside came with the wind, likely from more arguments between humans and rakkans that Rufus had no time for.

He heightened his posture on the stool to remind everyone in the room that he sat upon the tallest. The cold, flat stone under his backside was uncomfortable, but he hid his unease as well as always.

"Show me where it happened," Rufus said.

A legionnaire brought a large roll of parchment into the centre of the ring of seats and unrolled it on the floor. It showed the position of the fortress on the main road west, which cut through the flatlands between the mountains to the south and the Cliffs to the north. The latter may have been a fractured mess of land and rock, one rumoured to have been split during massive quakes caused by the stamping heels of gods aeons ago, but in contrast, the fort's lands were unusually damp and flat as if they'd once formed the bed of an ancient lake. Conditions were perfect for preparing the lines of defences Rufus had planned, but they were yet to be finished.

The legionnaire pointed to a spot at the bottom edge of the Cliffs, where the land usually would have been a hellish quagmire protecting the fort's north face. But the rains over the last few months had been feeble, and the ground was no longer saturated enough to bog down men or horses.

"Something isn't right," Rufus said. "Three patrols lost, all ordered to cover the same territory, in only a couple of days? The Xavalans lay traps, but they've always moved them in the past, never striking in the same place twice."

Piso scoffed. "No rakkan patrol has failed to come back. Perhaps the humans deserted or were too stupid to—"

"Or perhaps the rakkan patrols aren't doing a thorough job," the head algus said, face lighting up a shade of pink. "Perhaps my scouts uncovered something that demanded they be silenced."

Although Rufus would never admit it, that's what he feared. Whether it was palatable to his men or not, algus with escorts made far better scouts than rakkans.

Piso waved a hand dismissively. "Nonsense. Rakkans have eyesight better than even bats!"

"Bats are practically blind, you cretin!" the head algus huffed more with frustration than with ridicule.

"Blind? Then how do they navigate so well in the dark?" Piso exchanged a smug grin with a couple of his centurions. "Can you believe her? Blind?"

"Rufus is right." Pollio's sudden voice silenced the room. Although seated directly at Rufus's left, the commander hadn't spoken until now, and his words sent chills down Rufus's back—he knew how afraid Pollio would have to be to support him so openly.

"Patrols don't disappear at random," Pollio added. "We should scout the area thoroughly."

Rufus turned to the head algus. "How many of your algus have flying escorts?"

"None that I can afford to spare," she said, still regarding Piso with the disgust and wariness one gave a rabid dog.

Rufus was done with others not giving him the attention he deserved. He clicked his fingers, but when she turned her head, he knew she'd taken offence at the act. Well, that was too bad. Delay could mean their end. The first layer of trenches outside the planned fortress wouldn't be complete for a couple of days, and if an ambush came, they needed to know sooner rather than later.

"Do any of our Subdued have flying escorts?" Rufus asked Piso.

The commander turned up his nose. "Get the real algus to do it. Aren't you supposed to be in charge here?"

A few of the Viridians smirked and suppressed laughs, but Rufus couldn't care about his reputation right now. Results mattered more than that, and as reluctant as he was to admit he needed aid, a good leader planned for the worst and hoped for the best. It was time to prepare a defence, which called for all rakkans and humans to fall in line. If the Overlord denied him more of his warriors, then their greatest fighter himself had to join the war front.

He turned to Lyra. "The time has come. I suspect an attack, and you'll be needed."

Lyra stared at him with what Rufus could only hope was confirmation that she'd relayed his message to the Overlord. Usually, her reaction would be a growl or some other manner to convey whatever Darius's instructions were, but this time, she did nothing other than watch, shifting her eyes as if awkward with the lack of response she was giving.

Darius might not have been paying attention at the moment, but Rufus would do no more and instead deal with those under his charge.

"Piso!" he called with such gravity a couple of people flinched. "Do you have the escorts or not?"

Piso shrugged. "Perhaps."

"Send them out with an entire century. I want every inch of that area of the Cliffs scoured, from hilltops to rabbit holes."

His brother's only reply was to stuff some flavoured leaves into his mouth and chew.

"Is there something wrong with your ears?" Rufus asked.

Piso shook his head.

"Then leave within the hour."

"Or what?"

Rufus rose from his stool and towered over the man. "Or you'll find yourself nailed to a cross."

Piso moved to stand, but before he did, a sonorous feline growl rippled through the room and froze the commander in place.

Pollio stood and came between the two rakkans. "My Subdued have more flying escorts than my brother's. Allow me to lead the scouting part—"

"No." Rufus shoved his brother aside to reveal the ugly twin behind him once again. "You're not expendable, Pollio."

Piso's expression became as vile as his heart, but the panther had done enough. He stood slowly and gave the most pathetic rakkan salute he could. "As you wish, Warlord."

When the man turned to his centurions to issue orders, the door to the room flung open, and an algus rushed inside in a blur before stopping in front of the head algus.

"We're under attack!" the arrival shouted.

After a moment where the words sank into everyone there, most of the algus and rakkans in the room flew up from their seats and made for the door, but Rufus bellowed over the clamour, "Wait! How many? Where?"

"Mostly cavalry," the algus replied. "Must be thousands coming from the north."

Rufus cursed. He hadn't reckoned on an attack this soon. Most of the defensive plans to keep cavalry at a distance from the fort weren't finished, and the fort itself had enough gaps in its walls and palisades that horses could gallop through.

"Sound the horns," Rufus said to a centurion before turning to his commanders. "What were our numbers at last count?"

"Including the builders?" Piso asked.

"All." They'd fight with picks if they had to.

"Two centuries of warriors, a century of slingers, and another four centuries of labourers."

Not nearly enough to guarantee victory over such a large cavalry, Rufus concluded. He turned back to the algus that had barged in. "Heavy cavalry or archers?"

"More than enough of both."

That limited their options further. Only preparation would save them, and at least the flatlands they'd built this fort upon meant they'd see the enemy from a distance.

"How long before they reach us?" Rufus asked.

"Not long. Maybe an hour before they clash with the first line of defence."

A line of trenches not yet deep enough to stop a horse.

"Where do we have the most building materials stacked?" Rufus asked.

Pollio frowned in thought for a moment. "Logs on the east side, stone on the south."

"Then we'll defend in the east." Rufus set off at a pace and was out of the door in moments, stomping down what was planned to become the central street, followed by his brothers and the algus. "Assemble the men near the piles of wood to give us some cover from cavalry charges and protect our slingers at all costs. Legionnaires should ready their pikes, and all workers take up whatever spears or long weapons they can find."

"That's too defensive," Piso said. "Viridians charge; we don't sit and wait."

"Feel free to charge and die," Rufus said, "but your men will follow my orders."

"I'll round up the workers," Pollio said.

"No. I want you commanding the slingers."

"Hey!" Piso shouted. "They're *my* men."

But slingers were too integral to the battle to trust under the command of a halfwit. Without them, the Silk City's archers would whittle their centuries to dust. Rufus needed his best commander to keep them alive.

At this point, the head algus cut across his path and stopped him. "My men have only spears and swords," she said. "They'll stay in the north and hide in the trenches."

Rufus murmured under his breath. He'd told them countless times they needed archers, not pathetic soldiers. Why were humans always so stubborn?

"What about javelins?" Rufus asked.

"Yes, we have some."

"Then station any man that can throw with our slingers. The rest of your soldiers can stand with the legionnaires."

Piso scoffed. "We can't afford such weakness in our shield wall."

"He's right," Pollio said in the calmest voice there. "Breaking our line will spell disaster."

"I don't mean to mix them," Rufus said. "Stand them in front."

"And be your human shield?" The head algus spat at his feet.

"This is nothing about race," Rufus said. "Your men are too weak to fill holes and rotate into a rakkan shield wall. They'll go at the front." He set off again, barging the algus out of the way, and made towards the log piles east of the half-built fort.

As they walked and gave more specific orders to centurions and other algus, a high-pitched rakkan horn sent out three sharp blares. First contact.

"What do our escorts see?" Rufus asked.

A Subdued came forward with skin as pale as a rakkan's. "They've gone around the first humans digging in the north, caught them in a pincer."

"Soldiers or workers?"

"Both."

So much for the algus's soldiers. Today couldn't be Rufus's last day. He had so much left to achieve—to put his father's and his great-grandfather's legacies to shame, and to help Viridia ascend to its rightful place in the world.

"We need to get a damn move on," Rufus said.

# 7

## Darius – Margalvia

Lex should have woken up by now, even in the worst-case scenario, if the medicine had worked. Yet now she hadn't been conscious since the morning.

Her pulse was weak, her breaths sharp gasps that pricked Darius's nerves. Lyra practically roared into his mind to deafen him to anything else, to force his attention onto the battle that would soon be raging. He heard Rufus's shouts, the panic, the arguments that could be the end of them all.

But what could Darius do now? The summons had come too late. Even if he pushed a swift beyond its limits, it would take him a couple of days to go from Margalvia to the fort.

If only Lex could wake up and put his mind at ease, he'd set off at once and try. He just needed that glimmer of hope to keep him going.

A bang shook the door to the room and woke Cynthia up from snoozing beside her mother.

"Damn it, Darius!" Sulla's voice resonated with the kuraminium bars over the door. "Get out here now, or I'm going to smash my way in there!"

"Call me if anything happens," Darius said, making his way to the door while Eugenius took Cynthia into his arms.

When they were all quiet and safe, Darius slid open the locks, placed his heel down a fraction in front of the door, and slowly opened it.

The door slammed into his foot with a huge force from behind, but he reacted in time, shoved his weight forward, and braced.

"Let me in!" Sulla yelled.

Darius knew the rakkan well enough to know there was no reasoning with him in this state.

"Either let me out," Darius yelled, "or leave now!"

"We don't have time. Your priest says the Silk City is attacking the fort. You need to take a swift there now."

How did Aran know? Was his pteron escort watching the area? *Strange place for it to be.*

"Is that true?" Darius's grandfather whispered from beside the bed in a condemning tone.

Darius gave him a dismissive look to silence him, then heaved the door closed and snapped the locks back in place. The bang, bang, bang continued and joined the throbbing in Darius's head from too many nights without sleep, too little food, too little water. Just closing the door had taken so much out of him he slid down and took a few deep breaths, rocked by every bash of Sulla's fist.

The rakkan was right. Darius had to leave.

"Can you…shut him up?"

Darius scoffed. "Easier said than—" That woman's voice hadn't been Nasrin's.

He bolted up and saw Lex's eyes open, two spots of blue in an otherwise dark and dreary room.

"Mama!" Cynthia dove from Eugenius's arms onto her mother, thankfully landing on the mattress next to her rather than onto her fragile stomach.

Nasrin and Eugenius moved at once towards her, but Darius stood there numb, without words, overwhelmed. She'd woken up. A little colour had returned to her lips. But her voice was as feeble as one choked through a noose, and she barely managed a smile when she noticed her daughter next to her.

Nasrin hurried to get Lex some badly needed water, and after the others began saying things that didn't register in Darius's mind, the fragile woman looked at him and scanned his body up and down with a slight wince.

"Darius?" she rasped. "Are you…all right?"

"I…love you." The stuttering words had come out before a coherent thought had passed through his mind.

Nasrin coughed as if choking, and the shock on Lex's face was one even he shared. He'd thought those words many times while holding her hot hands and praying for her fever to break. He'd never said them before, and only when she'd been close to death did he regret the fact more than anything.

Sulla hammered on the door again in a frenzy that had dust falling from even the ceiling.

"Sulla, stop," Darius yelled. "Lex is awake. I'm coming."

The words seemed to work, and the bangs ceased.

Nasrin and Eugenius fussed over Cynthia in a way Darius knew was to spare themselves embarrassment over what he'd just blurted out.

But soon, even that didn't distract them enough, and Eugenius said, "Darius, you should really eat and drink before you leave. Nasrin and I will go and get something for you. Don't worry about Sulla. I'll take care of him."

Darius nodded, too many things on his mind to do anything else but agree. The pair left without Sulla barging in as promised, and Cynthia returned to cuddle beside her mother, gently this time.

"Am I so close to death," Lex said, "that you needed to say that?"

"I don't know." He stepped towards her, his knees unstable, either through physical weakness or fear. Or both. "But I didn't want to waste another moment without telling you."

She fidgeted nervously, pulled Cynthia into a tighter embrace. "Aren't some things better left unsaid?"

"No. I'm tired of leaving things vague or unsaid." Especially when he couldn't be sure she wouldn't fall under again. This could be his last coherent conversation with her, a gift from the Goddess.

And if Lex did fully recover, why would he waste that second chance without being open and honest and at least fighting for her?

"But I won't say more until you're better," he added.

"There's more?" she asked.

"You really wish to talk about this now?" Darius knelt by the mattress and took her hand, feeling for the first time that her fever had died down.

She shrugged. "Do you have something more important to discuss with me?"

Only the centuries of warriors and algus about to be trampled by the Xavalan cavalry. But he decided against burdening her with that when she was so weak.

"I guess not," he said. "I should leave and let you rest. I need to be somewhere, but I'll be back to talk soon."

"I'm not sure there's anything more to say. Whatever you feel, I'm not sure I can…"

"I don't care," Darius said. "This time, if you recover, I won't pretend I feel nothing, and I won't give up so easily." She was the most stubborn woman he'd ever met, but if he didn't at least try to bridge whatever gap there was between them, he knew he'd go to his grave regretting it.

"Darius…" Her whisper was so gentle and soft, it was almost loving. But he saw the pity in her eyes that betrayed whatever was to follow was going to hurt. "I don't think you understand."

"Then explain it. What exactly is your problem with men?"

"Even if I wanted to risk my heart again, I have a daughter." Lex kissed Cynthia on the forehead as the young girl snuggled in and smiled.

"It takes all my energy just to keep her safe," Lex continued, "to fight so that she can have some semblance of the safety she deserves."

"I can keep her safe too," Darius said. "She's been in this city all this time, and no one is the wiser."

Lex shook her head. "It's not just that. I've never spoken to you about my mother, have I?"

"No." Mothers were something he never discussed, and he'd assumed Lex's had died before her father.

Lex hung her head, looking all the more ill now. "She married my father shortly before I was born and wasn't much older than I was when I had my son. I don't have many memories of her, just a few of her brushing my hair when I was small, neither of us speaking or laughing or… I'm not sure what was going through my mind, to be honest. I just remember being relaxed."

That sounded much nicer than the only memory Darius had of his mother.

"She died a while ago," Lex continued. "She and my father had many children, and either she hadn't the time for me or didn't like me enough to spare it. I was raised by the slaves, even though I never called them 'mother.' And my other siblings were treated the same. Today, over half of them are dead from either battle or disease, and the rest are as miserable as I am."

Painful memories of parents were something Darius easily related to, but he wasn't sure what this had to do with Cynthia.

"I'm sorry" was all he could utter.

"And now I'm as distant to my daughter as my mother was." Lex's voice finally found some strength, but it was angry. "I don't deny I'm a bad mother, just like mine was, but I won't make the same mistake again. I won't bring any more children into this world just to suffer as my family has, whether through war or famine or disease. Two are enough."

He frowned, finally understanding why she refused to entertain the idea of a relationship, apart from…

"But what about the Silk Regent?" Darius asked. "You were to marry him."

"He can't have children. He's spread his seed enough without success to know."

That brought images that made Darius want to vomit. "All right. I understand your reasons, but there are ways to avoid getting…" He couldn't think of an alternative word to "pregnant" that Cynthia wouldn't understand.

"Not with certainty," Lex said. "I found that out the hard way with Varro."

"Well… There is one."

Lex grimaced and turned away. "Don't even contemplate it. Those methods are dangerous, and many have died even while under skilled—"

"Hey." Darius shook her arm and brought her attention back to him. "What are you talking about? I meant…abstinence."

She gaped with such shock anyone would have thought he'd suddenly sprouted horns. "Abstinence? *You?*"

He hadn't really given the idea much thought, was just thinking aloud. But her reaction…

"And what's that supposed to mean?" he said. "I'm hardly promiscuous."

"I…" She frowned and let out a breath. "If you say so. I just assumed. That's how you were before."

He let go of her hand and leant back against the chilly stone wall. Nothing annoyed him more than people assuming he'd done things or was a certain way solely based on his past actions. At times, that man was like a stranger that Darius now took the blame for.

"I've hardly been popular these last few years," he said. "Truth is, I don't trust anyone these days, especially women. All I think of is them pulling out a dagger and trying to end me."

"That's sensible." Lex shifted herself lower on the bed with a trace of a relieved smile playing about her lips.

"So…" he said. "You haven't said what you think about the idea."

She dipped her head, avoided his gaze. "Of abstinence…? I'm not sure I have the willpower."

Although she'd rejected the idea, how she spoke now made her feelings for him clear for the first time. She hadn't the will, so she wanted it too. Perhaps he should just wait until she was old enough not to have children anymore, but who knew how long that would be? The chances of one of them dying in that period were too high for his liking.

"What were you talking of before?" he asked. "These 'dangerous methods'?"

She let out a groan and closed her eyes. "I'm tired. Will you let me rest?"

And just when they'd finally been getting somewhere.

"Of course," Darius said as Lyra once again relayed Rufus's bellows to his men. They were getting into battle formations. Blood was about to water the plains.

"I need to go," Darius said. "I'll be back in a few weeks."

Cynthia's eyes snapped open at the words. "No!" She reached and grabbed hold of his tunic. "Stay."

The girl's plea seemed to stun Lex, but it was a reaction Darius was all too used to.

He lowered himself to her level with a smile that he didn't need to force this time. "The time will pass sooner than you think."

"Where are you going?" Lex asked with a confused frown as she watched her daughter clutch him.

"To see Rufus. There may be…a mess to clean up."

"Then don't go alone. And eat and sleep first. You look like you need it."

Unfortunately, he didn't have that luxury. *Lyra. Go south where it's safe and watch over the battle. I'm coming.*

# 8

## Rufus – Gap of Aphatos

The battlefield shook with a menacing tremor that rattled Rufus's legs.

What was this force that made the soil shiver? Even a hundred thousand horses stamping their hooves in unison couldn't have made a rumble so deep. Some of the men whispered that the dark gods of the underworld had stirred, ready to break loose from their prison.

But Rufus didn't believe such drivel. Those were merely the same ramblings he recalled when the phenomena had occurred in his childhood.

As quickly as it had come, the shudder dissipated into the thunder of hooves as the Xavalan cavalry charged in for another attempt to break their lines. Their hoisted colours of tan and gold matched their cloaks and tunics, giving them the look of a sandy wave rushing forwards.

Having charged down from the Cliffs behind, all the horses and warriors were now on the flatlands, just outside the half-erected buildings of the fort but inside every defensive fortification Rufus had planned. The shallow trenches and palisades hadn't delayed the cavalry for long, as he'd suspected, and now the battle was a simple field one in which all Rufus had to rely on were his tactics and the strength of his men. Their formation was tight and protected at the front by the mighty Viridian shield wall, and his flanks had a mix of algus and rakkans that could manoeuvre swiftly, along with wooden logs stacked high enough to prevent a cavalry charge.

His enemy, on the other hand, showed far less preparation and discipline, but what they lacked in leadership they made up for in numbers.

"Dig those pikes in deeper!" Pollio yelled to his twin's century. Rakkans braced in the second row behind the front shield wall, one end of their pikes dug into the ground, the other ready to taste horse blood.

Rufus rapped the man on the arm. "Worry about your slingers!" Behind the legionnaires, the slingers and human peltasts readied themselves and waited for the horses to come into range again, to gallop into the stretch of land between the armies that was already littered with their skewered brethren.

Not that Rufus's centuries needed much instruction. Without the need of a command, the rakkans sent another volley of molten stones into the front ranks of the cavalry that pierced the attackers and collapsed men and horses alike. Those riders behind eased their charge, but Rufus knew what was coming.

"Shields!" he yelled to the legionnaires. The third row of the legionnaires raised their scuta into a corrugated ceiling of kuraminium above the pikemen as the enemy's javelins loosed, some tipped with algor and streaking blue across the battlefield before spearing into shields and soldiers.

Men screamed and fell; blood squelched into the mud. At this rate, the fact Rufus's army inflicted five casualties for every one taken was irrelevant. The Silk City had the numbers. Attrition would see his demise.

With all his warriors clumped together in such a defensive formation, it made them easier pickings for the horse archers and the javelins, but to separate his forces would leave them far too vulnerable to cavalry charges, able to be hacked apart one group at a time. He was damned either way.

Always, he scanned around them to see where the Xavalans might launch a surprise attack, but so far, none had tried.

For a few minutes, the cavalry regrouped out of range of his slingers, a few algus riding between different groups of men issuing some orders. The enemy algus were all mounted on swifts rather than regular horses, so they could close the distance between the two armies faster than any slinger could react.

Rufus turned to his head algus. "Do any of your escorts overhear what they're saying?"

"Too far," she said. "But if it were me, I'd circle around and take you from the front and rear."

That was the obvious and logical choice, a move Rufus had a contingency plan for. But so far, the Xavalans hadn't tried it.

"Legionnaires, rise!" Piso hollered at the shield wall in front. "Let's take the fight to them!"

"Ignore that order!" Rufus yelled. As tempted as he was to let his halfwit of a brother charge to his death, he wouldn't condemn his men for the foolishness of their commander.

Piso turned to him with a snarl, molten drool falling from his jowls; he pulled out his gladius and looked to his men, but they all stayed rooted to the spot. They may not have respected

Rufus as a man, but they were smart enough to trust his battle tactics.

Rufus opened his mouth to spit another reprimand, but the wind took his voice when he saw the horses turn. The front riders dug their heels into their swifts and became a rapid blue streak coursing across the field. There were only a few dozen at most, and before any orders left the lips of his commanders, the swifts had closed half the distance with their slower cousins galloping behind in a diamond formation.

Rufus barely had time to think. What were they planning?

The swift riders leapt over the first corpses to meet them in the field before a single slinger had loosed in defence, and as they neared, their speed only seemed to increase.

So few? Not enough to punch a hole in a rakkan shield wall, even if it was only half a dozen rakkans deep.

They were planning something else.

And as the regular horses reached the bloody mark of the slingers' range and leapt over the bodies, Rufus realised their intent. No wonder he hadn't thought of it before; this tactic was only worthy of an audacious adolescent.

"Slingers, fall back!" Rufus yelled as he took off to his side. "Legionnaires, raise your pikes to the sky!"

"Raise?" Piso yelled. "Don't you dare. Skewer the bastards!"

"Javelins, be ready," Rufus roared. "Aim above our shield wall, on my mark."

Thankfully the humans had the sense to obey his instructions while the front ranks of rakkans descended into turmoil with a cacophony of mixed commands from Rufus's brothers and the centurions. Only a handful of pikes had been raised above head height when the swifts reached the line, and it was too late.

"Now!" Rufus called.

Javelins flew as the swift riders whipped their reins and sent their steeds into a leap that put any rakkan or algus to shame. They soared over the shield wall and the lowered pikes with ease, only meeting resistance when the sharp wooden projectiles now filling the air tore through the beasts.

The swifts' squeals were agonising as most caught at least a dozen in the underbelly, legs and neck. But they weren't the targets. The targets had been too high, hidden above their equine blockers. And now, they leapt free of their saddles.

The algus landed in the space the slingers had occupied with flashes like blue lightning and set off at sprints. Rufus tracked more instinctually with his sensitive rakkan skin than his eyes and sensed them heading straight for the front lines of rakkans.

The horses splattered into the bloody mud while the Laltosian head algus and her kin unsheathed their swords and rushed to face their counterparts.

Rufus grabbed the unique horn hanging from his belt. He let out a stream of stuttering blares to signal his contingency. This wasn't the event he'd planned for, but his reserves had to act.

At the sound, the top logs from the piles flew up into the air and rakkans emerged from beneath with war cries so hot they threatened to burn the wood around them to cinders. Algus followed them from within the piles, quickly saw the streaks of blue light coming from the front lines, and charged straight in. Piso and a few of his men were battling with one algus, managing to stay alive but losing the tightness of their formation.

Soon, Xavala's algus had peppered the front shield wall with holes, and the rakkans' pikes were tossed and discarded as they drew their gladii instead.

The rest of the cavalry neared, their most heavily armoured steeds at the front.

"Loose at will." Rufus sprinted towards his slingers, who had reformed in a patch of clear space on the other side of the log piles under Pollio's guidance.

But while the fiery projectiles lit up the overcast sky once again, it was too late.

With a crash of metal thunder, the Xavalan wedge struck a hole in the rakkan shield wall without a hint of slowing. Algus dove out of the way as the widening diamond of horses galloped on and on, slicing Rufus's front line in two and spelling the end of their resistance.

Rufus halted in front of his slingers, put his regular horn to his lips, and let out long blares that signalled every centurion now had to direct their men as they saw fit.

He'd spent many gruelling years training his army to fight fragmented, but despite that, the unfolding carnage before him wasn't something he could shift the tide of. They were too outnumbered.

Rufus glanced to the south. The plains leading to the mountains there were clear, bloodless and inviting. But to flee was futile. The cavalry's greatest strength was in hunting down routed enemies.

"We must fight to the last." Pollio's eyes glowed inside his helmet, and Rufus knew the unyielding look that would be upon his face.

"To the last," Rufus agreed, drawing his gladius and feeling the uncomfortable weight tug at his arm. He'd always known he'd die by the sword, but he'd assumed it would be at the hand of one of his brothers. If they'd been smarter, they'd have killed him decades ago.

By now, half of Rufus's rakkans and algus on the front line were dead, but his brother Piso fought on, drenched in blood while hacking at an enemy algus he'd managed to catch in a one-handed death grip. With only two cleaves, the ruptured woman fell under the screaming body of his brother, tattooed arms flexed and rippling.

At least the bastard would take many before he died; good for that, at least.

The slingers around Rufus continued launching rocks into the attackers, now with little regard for their intermingled brothers, given they were soon to be sliced to pieces anyway.

Laltos's algus thinned, their soldiers already hacked and crushed in the melee. Rufus gave them half an hour at the most.

Then the ground stirred again.

This time, it wasn't like the awakening of a god, but a legion of titans breaking free of their chains, sending a violent wave that convulsed the earth until it ruptured, cracks spreading outwards as far as he could see.

Thousands of horses squealed and reared, spooked by the boom of the ground that eclipsed any terror the thunder of the sky had caused in the past. The landscape cleaved further as the ground continued to rage, separating into a couple of vast fissures that changed the land into one more like the marred, fractured cliffs to the north. The new splits ran north to south for miles in only an instant, and the bottom of the cracks revealed the pitch-black depths of the world.

"What's happening?" Pollio's voice broke in a way not even a battle had caused before, in a way that the Viridians and their allies couldn't afford. Pollio needed to keep his head.

Rufus grabbed his brother by the back of the neck and pulled him in until their helmets clashed, letting the fire in his eyes swell.

"Opportunity," Rufus said. "Follow my lead."

His brother found his grit again and nodded. Meanwhile, the ground continued shaking and almost knocked them both from their feet. Every slinger and legionnaire that hadn't been cut down by the Xavalans now gaped at Rufus with an unspoken question: What should they do?

Tilting back his head, Rufus let out a guttural roar that barely carried above the clamour of the earth, but as he set off at a sprint towards the closest fissure, his men all took the hint and bolted after him.

Whatever lurked at the bottom of these hellish chasms, Rufus didn't know. But he knew only death awaited them on the surface. Surely, tales of the underworld were only superstitious nonsense…

As he reached the fissure's edge, the tremors eased a little, and the rakkans that had survived on the front lines, including a wounded Piso, joined him at the precipice. They might have only minutes.

Rufus tossed his sword, flexed his fingers, and conjured ferven across them until they raged hot enough to dig into even the hardest stone.

"You can't be serious!" Pollio said.

A waft of hot air burst from the chasm and would have ripped Rufus's clothes and armour off if it weren't made of kuraminium. The Laltosians wouldn't be able to follow. A pity, but what else could he do for them?

Pulling back the sleeves of his tunic, Rufus brandished his tattooed arms to his men. "Do you see these marks? I gained these through the holiest sacrifice to the warlords of old. They protect me, and by association, they will protect you. Whatever lurks within these depths, I do not fear it." At least the last part was true.

Rufus stepped to the edge of the crevice, feeling the hot, howling winds on his skin. The rock at his feet split again and crumbled away to be swallowed by the mess of splintered stone.

The jagged sides would give him plenty of holds for his hands and feet—as well as being sharp enough to slice his skin open. That's if he wasn't crushed.

Clambering through it would likely be hell, but he and his men would live to fight another day, to retake this fort. Reinforcements would come. The Overlord had more than enough legions to hold this place, and next time, Rufus would ensure their defences were ready.

With one last look at his brothers, Rufus gave a nod, then leapt into hell.

# 9

## Darius – Gap of Aphatos

"Are you satisfied?" Hera's acidic voice cut through Darius like a blade. "All the soldiers and algus I sent here are dead."

"Of course I'm not satisfied," he said. "I've failed you."

Hera's mouth fell open. Unsurprisingly, because this was the first time he'd admitted fault. But given the lifeless, sundered plains before him, how could he not?

"Would you rather I'd let the Viridians march home across your lands?" he asked, genuinely curious about her response.

But she just looked away.

He swung his leg over his steed and dismounted onto what had been the battlefield, the Twin Blades of Trogus at his waist shimmering in the night. Two days of riding hard on a swift had left his legs cramped and creaking, and despite stuffing himself with as much meat as he could keep down along the way, he still felt weaker than he'd been a few weeks ago.

But at least he could stomach something now. Lex was alive, and although he'd tried to hide his pleasure at the fact from those travelling with him, now he no longer had to feign his solemnity.

The lands before him were no longer a flat, green land with grazing cattle. They were ruptured and shifted, showing no life except the birds hovering in the night sky. Two great fissures running north to south had split the land, a sight much like one he recalled in the Cliffs of Aphatos, only there were no rocky outcrops or tarnflowers here, and the fissures weren't large enough that their enemies couldn't bridge them with time. To the west, away from the split land and now somewhat protected by it, the half-built fortress looked like a deserted ruin under the dark rainclouds; its walls were plagued with gaps and toppled stones, and mere husks for buildings stood between them without a roof to protect from the falling drizzle.

Along with Hera and her son Gorgias, the Chief Priest, Sulla, and Warlord Varro had come along to survey the aftermath and decide on what their next move should be.

Gone was his group's light-hearted banter, most notably absent from Sulla. They'd felt the mountains quiver while travelling, and Lyra had witnessed the world open, but it hadn't quite prepared Darius for the sight of so much blood and gore, the limbs of horses, men and women. The night's overcast darkness cloaked the worst of the slaughter, but Darius's rakkan eyesight was a curse for once. If only he'd been here.

"We were lucky." Aran slid from his swift. "If the God and Goddess hadn't intervened, all the Viridians would have been killed too, and your fortress would be nothing but dust."

That wasn't the first time the Chief Priest had asserted this was the work of higher powers. Although Darius considered it somewhat arrogant to assume any being of such might would back him, he struggled to think of any other explanation.

"Are you convinced this was their doing?" Darius asked. "Or are you speculating?"

"I can't be certain," the Chief Priest answered, "but I wouldn't say it if I didn't believe it. You're far from perfect, Overlord, but for whatever reason, the God and Goddess wished for your enemies to fail, just as they wish for me to assist you. Without my help, you won't stand a chance against the King."

Those words would have sounded arrogant from the mouth of most men, but Darius saw the truth in them. He wouldn't be standing here with the Twin Blades if not for this man.

"But why do you have so much faith in the God and Goddess?" Darius asked.

"Why? Because I've spoken with them, of course!"

At the assertion, Darius gaped for so long that Aran waved a hand in front of him.

"How?" Darius eventually asked.

"Through no skill on my part, I can assure you. When I was but a boy, Dianoia came to me in a vision—a giant, winged woman twenty feet tall and bathed in a cloak of light so brilliant it forced me back a few steps. If I were to describe her magnificence in full, you'd think it a terrifying sight, yet it was as if the light washed away any fear or pain or sorrow. It was pure and entrancing." As he spoke, the Chief Priest's face lit up with the same bewitchment he described.

But just the thought was enough to make Darius nervous, and he couldn't understand how a man would remain calm when faced with such power. Now he knew why some people called Aran a prophet.

"And what did her husband look like?" Darius asked. The God of Justice must have been horrifying.

"I didn't see him, but she told me many things about him. He is at a distance from this world to allow us our freedom. For now."

Given the injustice in the world, that absence was apparent to Darius, even if the reasoning wasn't. "And what does she tell you now? To help me?"

The Chief Priest's expression fell a little. "She doesn't speak to me like that anymore, despite my eagerness. Now, I must discern her wishes through prayer and contemplation."

Which Darius took to mean the man couldn't be sure whether or not she'd intervened here. He needed a vision himself to answer some of the many questions he had about life and everything else. Why had she only appeared to Aran and not to him? Wasn't he worthy of a conversation, or wasn't he ready? Given the death before him that he bore some responsibility for, he suspected both were true.

"You'll have to teach me more about your religion sometime," Darius said. If there was a chance the God and Goddess wanted to help him, he wanted to know more about them. Perhaps they could assist him in defending his people and managing his armies rather than having to rely on people he didn't entirely trust. Speaking of which… "For now," he continued, "we have more pressing matters." He turned to Hera and her algus companions. "Do your escorts see where Rufus is?"

"He and what's left of his men emerged a few miles away," one of the algus said. "My escort is guiding them back here while it's safe."

Safe? That was only because the horse masters had run away. On what was now a split landscape, their cavalry was disadvantaged and couldn't cross the crevice without risk, but Darius suspected there was another reason. Perhaps the Xavalans were stricken by the same superstitious fear of higher powers that had him fidgeting nervously.

"Find me some armour," Darius called to one of his men. His swift had only been able to bear the weight of the Blades. "We'll wait for Rufus inside whatever buildings are still standing."

As the man followed his instructions and the few algus set up sentries, Darius made his way towards what had been built of the fort. The quake hadn't damaged the ground near it too much, but some Xavalans had torn down what they could. At least it could be rebuilt, and this time, Darius would ensure it lasted.

No one spoke much during the walk, but Darius could see the rage in Hera's steps, knowing it was directed at him.

So he slowed down until alongside Gorgias, then dropped his voice so that no one would overhear. "How angry is your mother?"

Gorgias's grim look said more than his words. "I don't know who's in for it worse, you or Warlord Rufus."

That was just as Darius had feared. Now that he was able to open himself more to Lyra's senses, she relayed some of the frictions she'd witnessed of late, an issue that was expected but needed addressing.

Bringing the humans and rakkans closer together was a problem he'd puzzled over on the journey here and discovered only one solution to, but that required help from someone he could trust, and the dark-haired algus beside him was the only man that had come to mind.

"What are your feelings towards the Viridian Warlord?" Darius asked.

"I've been in Margalvia," Gorgias said, "so I haven't spoken with him, but my time as a Subdued with him wasn't awful like with some of the other commanders. Why, master?"

"I may have a favour to ask of you, but not if you can't stomach to be around them." After torture, Darius wouldn't blame him if he wanted to avoid them.

But the man didn't shrink away at the suggestion, instead straightening his back with a puff of pride. "I will do what is required of me, as any man should, master."

"Don't promise anything too fast." Darius only continued his thoughts after checking no one around could overhear. "There's too much friction within the Viridian ranks for my liking. I need someone to stay close to Rufus and keep an eye on what he and those around him are doing. All day, every day."

"You mean…live with them?"

"I told you not to promise anything. I don't need an answer now. Just mull it over."

The man seemed to do just that…for all of two breaths before shaking his head. "No. If I dwell on it too much, I'll just think of excuses. I will do as I must."

Unsure whether to accept the hasty agreement, Darius gave him a few moments to reconsider, but the algus stared with more determination than he'd seen before.

"Fair enough," Darius said. "If all goes to plan, I'll give you more details on who to watch later."

Gorgias gave a resolute nod as they all made their way down what looked to have been the beginnings of the main street and into one of the few complete buildings still left standing. After a few corridors, they emerged into a large room with a circle of toppled stone seats around the centre. Furnishings were lacking here, but they all began to make themselves comfortable, the rakkans heading for a darkened corner while the few humans separated and either straightened out seats or found a quiet spot.

"Speaking of keeping an eye on people…" Gorgias glanced discreetly at the Chief Priest, who had sat at the side of the room, despite the dirty floor, and began scribbling on parchment with a reed pen. "He seems to be writing an awful lot these days."

That was true, but Darius had just assumed that was related to the duties of his religion.

"You're suspicious of him?" Darius asked. Gorgias was more familiar with human and religious habits than he was, so he trusted the algus's judgement.

"I wouldn't say that, but there's something odd about him." With that, Gorgias went to rejoin his mother and left Darius to watch the Chief Priest a little longer.

He'd stolen a glance at a few of the messages the man had penned over the last few months, but they were always so innocuous he rarely bothered anymore. Yet now, the man's face was as serious as a surgeon's while battling to stem a mortal wound; perhaps it was time to inquire again while they waited for Rufus.

"What are you doing?" Darius asked, walking over.

"This and that," Aran said without taking his eyes from the parchment. "Just sending word to the King, indirectly, of course."

Darius could never tell whether the man was jesting or not.

"Should I be worried?" he asked.

"You just lost a battle. Probably."

"… About you and your messages."

"The King's spies are everywhere. If you don't confuse them with false reports, the King will know your movements with far too much certainty."

Darius guessed that made sense. "And how do you know people who can whisper in the King's ear?"

The Chief Priest grinned a little but quickly hid it. "My religion is becoming increasingly popular amongst the slaves now that I've torn down the façade that the algus are somehow gods.

And plenty of algus have loose tongues when amongst those they consider inferior. You'd be surprised how useful slaves can be in underhand endeavours."

Darius had certainly witnessed that first-hand in Menara.

"But I have algus contacts too," Aran added. "Giving them escorts has won me many friends over the years, and I'm not proud to say there are times when I've held my nose and assisted people I would rather not have just to gain their favour."

"… Such as?"

The Chief Priest finally looked up from the parchment. "Most of the algus in the Empire, to be honest. And one young man that had a ghastly reputation as some kind of Slayer of Gods."

Darius murmured in acknowledgement. "I guess you chose your allies well, although I've met many unsavoury algus who I wouldn't trust with a pet cockroach, let alone an escort. I'm guessing I'm not the worst you've had dealings with."

"Far from it."

Darius cast his mind back to all the escorts and their masters that he'd met, and there weren't many among the Xavalans that deserved their animal companions.

But one person amongst the hundreds of others stood out as the most heinous. Ever since remembering her recently, he'd been meaning to ask Aran about her escort.

"You know, when Archimedes took my memories," he said, "I went in search of the Waif Magician. I was told I could find her by leaving a dead mouse out to attract an owl that would lead me to her."

The Chief Priest froze, the veins on his forehead swelling.

"That owl seemed an awful lot like an escort to me," Darius added.

Aran began folding away his parchment. "I don't know what you saw, but I can assure you, I never—and would have never—bonded an escort to that woman. She was a foul, bitter wretch, and while the death of anyone isn't something I relish, I'm glad the Empire's rid of her." There was no tell of a lie in the man's expression, and he wasn't one to show such disdain often. But it was thoroughly warranted when it came to the Magician.

"Fair enough," Darius said, but that raised the question of just what her owl had been. Although he wouldn't allow himself to trust the man—or any man—as such, he was at least convinced the priest wasn't lying about either the Magician or his communications.

Turning back to the room, Darius refocused on the problems of today. After such a defeat, it was time to regroup and decide on his retaliation.

# 10

## Darius – Gap of Aphatos

Rufus still hadn't arrived, and Darius went to sit at the largest stool within the ring of seats, cursing that it had no backrest for him to relax. To add to his discomfort, his stomach gurgled to remind him of its neglect over the last few weeks.

He hoped Rufus had some cooks with him as well as a rakkan that could taste the food first. He couldn't take any chances now. It hadn't been long after he'd become Overlord that assassins had come after him in Margalvia. Although he couldn't be certain who had been behind it, he doubted any of the Margalvians would be foolish enough to use such underhand methods. It had been such a shambles of an attempt—lacing food with a fluid that had dyed the meat an odd colour—that his first guess was the Silk Regent.

Sulla and Varro sat at one side of the ring in quiet discussion, Varro running a hand through his oiled blond hair and seeming to enjoy being free of the horned helmet that he usually had to wear.

And for the whole time Darius watched them talking, Gorgias and Hera had sat in the seats to his right, the Regent watching keenly with a perfect posture, pristine tunic and shawl that gave her a commanding look few other humans he'd met possessed. Her dark eyes were similar to Gorgias's at first glance, but there was a ferocity in them, almost feline like Lyra's, that her son's didn't bear.

During the next lull in the whispers of the room, Hera shifted and raised her voice. "We should discuss the situation here before Warlord Rufus arrives."

"I know what you wish to say," Darius said. "The defences here were inadequate. But I won't make that mistake again."

"With respect, that's not what I was going to say." Although she spoke in a calm tone, he knew the words rang disparagingly in her mind.

"Then what?" Darius asked.

"Even before this attack, the tensions between the Viridians and us were reaching breaking point. I won't subject my people to working with them anymore."

But a mixture of the races was paramount for creating this fortress. As soon as Darius had heard Rufus's plans, he'd known choosing the man to oversee this had been a good call, as well as having the benefit of keeping the Viridians occupied with something other than bloodlust. And the humans had too much expertise in building and sourcing materials in these lands to do without them.

"We'll think of a solution," he said.

"We will not." Hera's tone became acidic once again. "We are not among your subjects, and you do not command us."

"Mother…" Gorgias gave her a worried look, but she ignored it and showed none of his trepidation.

"We'll discuss it when Rufus arrives," Darius said.

"There's nothing left to discuss," Hera said. "I've made my position clear."

"Don't push me, Regent." While this did indeed need resolving, other things were playing on Darius's mind too.

He turned to Sulla and Varro. "How quickly could the Black Legion come here?"

Sulla huffed. "We'd have been here weeks ago if—"

"Perhaps," Varro interjected, "it would be best if the Azure Legion bolstered this position. Azuria is far removed from this conflict, and a lack of defences there won't pose much concern. But Margalvia is vulnerable to the King's armies, should he wish to focus there."

The Black Warlord had a point, but "holding this position" wasn't Darius's reason for asking the question, and it was time he floated his real intentions.

"Do you think the Azure Legion could handle a siege?" he asked.

The room stilled at the question, suddenly so silent and motionless he could hear and feel the changed breathing of every person there. Varro was calmest, and Sulla was practically erratic, the first to move and break out a grin.

"I like where this is leading," he said. "End the threat of the Xavalan cavalry once and for all."

"It could take months," Varro said, "and we'd need to defend the farmlands north of Menara to sustain such a siege. We can't afford to keep losing produce to the King's raids."

"Why waste time?" Sulla stood, practically jumping up and down with anticipation. "Let's assault the walls, raze the city."

At the proposition, Hera's and Gorgias's skin paled, and Darius knew why. He'd been in Laltos with them; he knew how bloody and savage a rakkan assault was. But Darius considered that no more palatable than letting people starve and desiccate in a siege.

"The Silk City has no river." Rufus's voice entered through the doorway before his lean, battered frame did, rasping and tired, almost as weary as his eyes. "They rely on wells that can easily be tainted. A siege won't take that long. Disease and thirst will do the brunt of the work for us."

Rufus hobbled towards a stool with his twin brothers close behind.

No one in the room stood to greet them, and Darius didn't blame them.

"How many of your men survived?" Darius asked him.

"Less than a century." Rufus collapsed onto a seat, then pulled back the leather strips of his skirt and rubbed his scratched and bruised legs. "I'll send word back to Viridia for the rest of my men to come."

Hera gave Darius a firm look that reminded him of their argument minutes ago, and he was in no mood to anger her again.

"Before you do," Darius said, "we need to decide on what to do next. The Xavalan attack has set us back weeks and lost us at least a third of our materials."

"We can start rebuilding immediately," Rufus said confidently, although his brothers reacted with more sceptical raises of their eyebrows at the proclamation.

Hera cleared her throat.

But Darius continued. "If we double the manpower, will it halve the build time?"

"Roughly," Rufus said. "Gathering resources was never an issue with enough men and local knowledge."

Darius still saw no way to get around having the humans work here along with rakkans. Hera wasn't one to back down under threats, so it looked like he'd have to find a way to appease her concerns.

"Hera does not wish to work with you again," he said, seeing no reason not to let all the tensions out in the open.

Rufus's face lacked any surprise. "Her soldiers and algus were most difficult to work with. If you're happy for the construction to take longer, we'll proceed without them."

"I'm *not* happy." Darius took the hilt of one of the Blades and slowly lifted it, letting the glowing runes break the dimness of the space; then he held it out and pressed the point gently into the ground in front of him so that everyone could see its ferocity.

"Whatever we do," he said, "whether it be working on this fortress or battling, I will need the humans and Viridians working to the same ends, even together at times. So, I will remain with the Laltosians from now on, and I will ensure there are no more tensions."

"One man cannot oversee everything," Hera said.

"I don't need to. The threat of my presence will be enough."

"And if it's not? If my people are murdered again?"

"Murdered?" Piso grunted from over Rufus's shoulder. "Who was murdered besides our sentries when your soldiers failed—"

"Enough!" Darius's bark echoed about the walls and killed the argument. There had to be a way for these two factions to at least tolerate each other, but he realised a wise leader wouldn't force this for the sake of a fort. After all, someone else could just follow Rufus's plans.

"Why rebuild?" Sulla said. "Why not just head straight for the Silk City and raze it to the ground?"

While that would protect the west from the Xavalan raiders, it would do nothing to stop the Torian armies. So far, they hadn't attempted a march west, but Darius wouldn't be complacent.

As for the siege, that wasn't as simple as Sulla seemed to assume. Lex had told Darius exactly what the Waif Magician had said before she'd been killed: they served a "goman king." All the humans he'd spoken to, including Lex, had baulked at the idea; they'd seen the King for themselves, and he definitely had a mouth, which confirmed he wasn't goman. But something about a "goman king" made sense. Archimedes serving a human had never sat right with him.

Regardless, the King at least had a goman, however secret their identity was, and that meant any attack Darius launched would be known ahead of time. He had to commit overwhelming forces to whatever he did, or he might fail in the face of a meticulously prepared defence.

But first…sorting out the humans and Viridians was paramount. Thankfully, Gorgias had agreed to be of help.

"Rufus, Hera." Darius stood and stalked around the outside of the ring of seats. "It's time for you both to begin building trust with one another."

"Somehow," Rufus said, "I don't see that happening." Although his words were dismissive, there was some dissatisfaction in his pitch, almost like regret. It was enough to give Darius a glimmer of hope.

"Lex once told me a story of two warring tribes," Darius said, "who had such distrust they wouldn't even sleep in the same town."

Hera became more wooden than she'd been even when they had spoken of razing cities.

"One of their leaders suggested a way for them to work together without conflict," Darius said.

"No," Hera said forcefully. She knew.

So Darius figured it would be best to begin with Rufus, then.

"Is your mother alive, Rufus?" he asked. She was the only person he'd ever heard the rakkan speak of with any sort of warmth.

The twin brothers beside the Viridian Warlord shifted with frowns, wondering where he was going with this, no doubt, but Rufus merely stared at Darius as if his intent would reveal itself on his forehead.

Eventually, the Viridian Warlord answered, "I wouldn't know. I haven't spoken to her for a long time."

There was no trace of a lie in the rakkan's demeanour, posture, or facial expression—anything. Yet, Darius suspected it was. The delayed answer and the fact this rakkan's intelligence had struck him as soon as they'd met… Rufus would know that whatever Darius had planned for his mother wouldn't be particularly agreeable.

"Piso." Darius turned his attention to Rufus's insolent brother—or rather, *half*-brother. "Do you know whether his mother lives or where she is?"

The rakkan smiled. "I do." Then he cast his gaze on Rufus as if expecting a reaction.

The stone-faced Viridian Warlord gave none, though, and it was time for Darius to make his intentions clear.

"You will bring her to me, and she will be handed over to the Laltosians in Margalvia," Darius said.

Rufus dipped his head for the briefest of moments before nodding in understanding. "An exchange of hostages. If my people cross the humans, I guess my mother will die."

"The idea is it doesn't come to that," Darius said. "And they wouldn't be hostages. They should live freely in each place."

As the conversation turned, the Chief Priest moved in from roaming the outskirts of the room to join them. "Is this the best way to build a relationship?" he asked.

"Not really," Darius said. "It's to stop them from killing each other. If they prove they can be civil, I'll consider ending the arrangement." When he next looked at Hera, he could see a refusal about to fly from her lips. Although her people were at the mercy of the Margalvians, and by extension their overlord, Darius was loath to use threats to resolve this, so he decided on a different angle.

"Gorgias," he said.

The algus flinched in surprise. "Yes, maste—?"

"No!" Hera leapt from her seat and squared up to Darius, a head shorter but with twice the ferocity. "My son is not a bargaining tool."

"Your son will be fine if your soldiers and algus behave," Darius said.

"You can't ask this of him. My son was tortured by them!"

"And I was tortured by *you*!" Darius's voice became a harsh roar, sparks of ferven flying between his bared teeth. "By your son! Yet I let the past lie."

"I won't have—"

"Mother." Gorgias stood, placed a hand gently on his mother's arm, and pulled her away to face him. "It's fine. If this is what I need to do for the war, so be it. It might be good for me to face my fears."

"Your son can stay with me," Rufus said. "I won't send him back to Viridia."

Hera didn't seem to know which man to be most shocked by, her head repeatedly turning from one to the other. Even Darius hadn't expected Rufus to be so receptive to keeping a foreigner close, and he suspected the rakkan had other intentions.

It took a lot of quiet whispers with her son, but eventually, Hera gave a reluctant nod of agreement.

"I'll remain here," Rufus continued, "and Gorgias will be around some of his own people."

Gorgias looked relieved to be told he'd stay here, but Darius wasn't. While this fort needed building, Darius needed Rufus to set his sights on a new goal because he was the only rakkan who had proven himself capable of the feat of defeating a major city.

"I'm glad that's settled," Darius said, "and rest assured both Gorgias and Rufus's mother shall come to no harm as long as you both work together, and I'm not speaking of just this fort." It was time to discuss retaliation against the Silk City. "Tell me, Rufus, was it your brain behind the assault on Laltos, undermining the walls?"

The Viridian Warlord hesitated before answering. "It was. Father wanted to go through the gates, but I knew they'd be more heavily defended."

Rufus had picked his spot well. The streets in the area he'd breached had run almost directly up to the palace, wide enough for many rakkans to charge through in great numbers. It was clear what Darius needed to do.

"I've taken Hera's concerns on board," Darius said, "and I won't force you to work so closely together for now. You're not staying here, Rufus."

The Viridian Warlord narrowed his eyes. "But I've already planned—"

"I need you elsewhere. Varro, contact the Azure Warlord and tell him to send his legion here to finish the fort and defend the area."

"His entire legion?" the Black Warlord asked.

"Yes. Like you said, Azuria is the safest of all the rakkan cities. Which brings me to Branz. Send word to the Branz Warlord too. All other legions will muster for battle."

As Darius paused to let the words sink in, everyone opened their mouths to respond.

But he cut them off. "Rufus, you'll pass on your designs for this fort to the Azure Warlord and set your mind to a new task. Can you get the rest of your legion here without them disturbing the humans along the roads?"

The Viridian Warlord nodded. "If I travel with them. I can take a swift back to Viridia at once."

"Very well," Darius continued. "And while you collect them, make new plans. The Silk City has been a thorn in all our backsides for too long. Plot its downfall."

Rufus's eyes grew hungry. "I'll have the men here begin construction of siege towers, catapults, ladders…everything we'll need to besiege."

Darius was reassured at the rakkan's confidence, but then the Chief Priest stepped into the centre of the room with alarm written on his face.

"A siege will kill countless thousands," he said, "and not algus and soldiers but civilians, women, children…even slaves that might side with you if only given a chance."

That was the part Darius did his best to avoid dwelling on. "The Xavalans can easily avoid death by surrendering."

"And if they don't?"

Darius sighed. "Where else did you think my cause was heading other than to death and battle? Do you have a better idea to bring down Xavala?"

"I do. Didn't I say the slaves can be of great use? They're as bitter in Xavala as the Menarans were with their masters. They will turn against them if given the courage."

"But would that be any less bloody?"

"It doesn't need to be violent," the Chief Priest urged, but Darius was sceptical.

"The Silk City has far more algus than Menara had," Hera said, finally with a little less tension in her jaw. "I don't think a rebellion is possible."

"It's worth trying." The Chief Priest turned to Darius expectantly, pleadingly. "It was Lex's idea."

Darius paused, conscious that Aran always seemed to pick the words most likely to sway him. "How outnumbered are the slaves?"

"Outnumbered?" Aran baulked. "There are almost seven times the number of slaves as civilians."

Darius was momentarily lost for words. So many? No wonder the city was so affluent. The Chief Priest's idea might just bear fruit, but it was far from guaranteed and would likely turn violent quickly.

Darius's first instinct was to continue with the plan he'd sketched out, but then he recalled how prescient the Chief Priest was, how often the man's advice would have been wise to follow. Perhaps it was worth at least investigating.

"Rufus," Darius said, "plan as if a siege will be necessary while we look into the Chief Priest's rebellion. If I must, I'll go into the Silk City myself and see whether there's the appetite for it."

"I can go with you," the Chief Priest said. "Lex and I already have contacts there."

"Very well. The rest of you, ready the legions and make the exchange I set out." He turned to Hera. "If you want revenge for Laltos, you'll need to work with Rufus."

Only when Gorgias gave her a nudge in the side did she relent with a reluctant bow, and finally, all their plans were settled for now.

The various warlords and leaders then left while Darius lingered and waited for Hera to leave. Gorgias was a little slower in retiring, so Darius pulled him aside one last time.

"Something wrong, master?" Gorgias asked.

"How is she?"

Gorgias had left his escort near Lex so Darius could always know how she fared. It's the only way he'd been comfortable being away from her.

"The same as when you asked a couple of hours ago," Gorgias said. "Eating, resting. Would you like my escort to relay a message?"

It wasn't like a badger could say everything Darius still wanted to say to her. "No… Or, perhaps… Let her know I'm thinking of her."

The algus nodded. "All right, master, but I think she already knows."

Darius hoped so.

For his final instruction, he dropped his voice to a whisper. "One more thing; about the reason I've asked you to stay with the Viridians…"

Gorgias became eager, slicking back his hair with an air of pride. "Anything, master."

"I don't trust any of them, but watch Rufus's twin brothers closely. If you catch wind of mutiny, inform me at once. Don't be afraid to run should you need to. I'll protect you from any fallout."

"Of course, master." The slight smile he'd had faded. "Does that mean I'm to stay with Rufus even in the siege of the Silk City?"

Darius nodded. "One way or another, you'll see Xavala's fall."

# 11

## Lex – Margalvia

Saying goodbye never got easier because there was always a shrill voice in the back of Lex's mind that questioned whether this would be the last time, whether she or her daughter would be dead before they could meet again.

"But I want to stay with you." Cynthia buried her head in Lex's chest and moaned as young girls did when they couldn't get their way. The small room filled with lamentation, a dreary place Lex had been caged within for too long. She had enough strength to leave now. It was time.

Lex leaned away from her daughter and spoke next with a motherly softness. "You'll be safer back home."

Since Darius had left a couple of weeks ago, she'd been agitated, wondering who would accidentally walk into their room and discover her secret. Of course, Darius's grandfather was still there, a former warlord with an angry streak violent enough to scare away even the spirits of the dead, but he was no substitute for Darius. Only the half-human eased her fears.

"Are you sure you don't want us to stay?" Eugenius asked. "Darius is Overlord. No one will dare lay a hand on her now, and he protected her as ardently as his own child."

"It's true, mistress," Nasrin added. "He looked after her so well. I've never seen him be so gentle."

*Darius?* The old Darius had never been one to suffer the presence of children, yet now he not only put up with Cynthia but also cared for her.

"It's not the Margalvians I fear," Lex said. "If we fail, the King can never find out about her."

Eugenius's beard twitched in a way it always did when he had something to say but was reluctant to let it out.

"Say it," she said.

The man grunted. "If you're not afraid of Margalvians, why haven't you told Varro of his daughter?"

Darius had asked the same thing. Was she just punishing the Black Warlord for hurting her? Or was this secrecy in Cynthia's best interests? She'd been so tempted to tell Varro after his legion had saved them when fleeing from Laltos; he'd even asked her who the little girl with her was. But her rage had got the better of her, and besides, he was sharp enough to have seen the truth but had never said anything. So, she'd lied, waiting for him to call her out, and still couldn't bring herself to regret the decision. As the Black Warlord, Varro had enemies, ones who wouldn't think twice of slaying a young girl to wound him in a way they couldn't with a sword. That was probably why he'd never confronted her for the truth, knowing this secret was best kept.

"You should leave," Lex said to Eugenius, "before the guards we sent away return."

Eugenius nodded, and Tiro swooped from the edge of the room to perch on the rakkan's shoulder. Her peregrine would ensure they made it back home safely.

After saying a last goodbye, the pair left, and Nasrin came to help Lex stand from the bed she'd lain in for so long her withered figure was virtually fused to the straw.

"Have more tea." Nasrin handed her a steaming cup.

Lex took it and drank the whole thing, still eternally grateful to the Chief Priest for the formula that had subdued her hip pain. But it was too bad it did nothing for her throbbing stab wound.

"I wish you'd rest more," Nasrin said.

After putting aside the empty cup, Lex pushed Nasrin's supporting arms away and tried to stand, but she had to grab the carer again when she almost toppled over.

"You see!" Nasrin said.

"I'm fine," Lex lied. "Do you know whether the Chief Priest has asked Darius yet?"

"I don't know. His escort hasn't been here for days."

*Damn.* Not only had Lex's infirmity interrupted her vital plans, but also she'd had to rely on Aran to raise the subject of a slave rebellion with Darius, and she hadn't divulged the full extent of her plans to the priest. He'd proven himself to be reluctant to entertain bloody uprisings. If he'd known Lex had been smuggling weapons by the wagonload into the Silk City, he'd have objected. So she somehow needed to inform Darius via other means.

"Has the message from Eluthia arrived yet?" Lex took a wobbly step only with her carer's assistance.

Nasrin shook her head.

Whatever was in it couldn't be good. Their first payment of gold to the city in the far east was now late, and people didn't usually transport weapons hundreds and hundreds of miles, right under the nose of a watching king, for nothing but promises and air. The Regent of Eluthia was not one known for her understanding nature.

"Are we sure the weapons are arriving in Xavala?" Lex asked.

"As recently as yesterday. Some of your algus are in regular contact from there."

*Even stranger.* "They've seen nothing odd? Nothing to suggest the King knows?"

Nasrin gave her a look as if to ask why Lex thought she knew the answer to that.

"Never mind," Lex said. "Surely Eluthia wouldn't speak with the King."

"Not with the amount you're paying them," Nasrin said. "And their regent is hardly friendly with King Medus."

"Which regents *are*?"

"Alogos's, perhaps. The rumour amongst the slaves was that Regent Berenice and King Medus had an affair at one time."

"That could either be a good or a bad thing for us. Still… Have you heard any such rumours about the Regent of Eluthia?"

"No. But their slaves tend not to travel west often, so neither do rumours. Perhaps they don't enjoy our weather."

"Or perhaps they have everything they need close to home—adequate farmlands, literal seas of oil to fire their furnaces, and access to mines with everything from coal and iron to sulphur." That was one of the reasons they were one of the most withdrawn cities in the Empire.

"They must trade and sell things," Nasrin said.

"Would *you* sell weapons to those who might use them against you?" As well as promising to pay an extortionate amount of gold to buy arms from them, Lex had promised on behalf of Darius that Eluthia would be left out of the war, and as long as they stayed in their city, far on the southeast coast, Darius had no reason to bother them. He would have agreed if she'd asked him, so why waste his time and add more worries to his already burdened mind?

As Lex paced across the room, the pain from her abdomen stung, but she didn't let her lips so much as twitch and give away her discomfort. At least her hip was fine, and she was content with that.

"How about we wait another week?" Nasrin asked. "The wound will have settl—"

A knock at the door cut off the carer's words.

"Who is it?" Lex asked.

"The messenger, Algus," muttered someone outside. "I have your note, sealed with the mark of the Regent of Eluthia."

Lex set off towards the door so quickly she gasped at the pain it brought and failed to suppress the sound. Nasrin raised a hand to stop her but was too slow, and Lex had the door open a heartbeat later.

A short, scruffy boy stood there with the parchment in his raised hand.

"Thank you," Lex said as she snatched it, ripped open the seal, and unrolled the message.

*Algus Alexandra,*

*It is not often I must write to those in my debt, for most people, algus or not, aren't so foolish as to deny me what has been promised. To date, I have not received an ounce of the gold due, and I have been patient, awaiting any sign or message explaining the fact it has been delayed.*

*The payment has now increased, with an extra bar due for every ten previously promised. You have until the end of the month before I take your blood as payment.*

*There will be no more warnings.*

*Panorea, Regent of Eluthia*

Not only had the cantankerous shrew put Lex's name at the head of this treasonous message, but she'd also signed the damn thing and put her official seal on it. Clearly, she had no fear of the King and probably not Darius either. Eluthia's assassins were a force to be reckoned with; they'd once slain everything from queens to dogs without leaving so much as a sight of their shadow.

"Bad news, mistress?" Nasrin asked as Lex slowly closed the door and leaned against it.

How could she transport her gold from Laltos to the collection point in the east in under a month? The wagons would have to travel day and night.

She reconsidered whether to tell Darius what she'd done and the danger she was now in but quickly rejected the idea. On top of the issues being Overlord piled on him, the man was one to act rashly and violently. The last thing she needed was him sending a threat or starting another war.

But that left her alone with the problem of transporting so much gold. She needed *someone* to help, even if not Darius.

"Mistress?" Nasrin repeated.

"I need Sulla," Lex said. Only rakkans had the strength to load and drag the tons of gold that far so fast.

"I think he's with Darius," Nasrin replied.

Lex cursed. *Tiro, come back. I need a message delivered at once.* "Then I need whoever he's left in charge of the Red Militia."

# 12

## Darius – Xavala, the Silk City

Nobody enjoyed rain—at least, that's what Darius had always thought. But as he wandered through the wide Xavalan street, he saw people poking their heads out of doors and windows, their weathered faces looking up at the rainclouds above and closing their eyes with a smile as the droplets splashed on their faces.

This corner of the Silk City had a certain whiff about it that Darius couldn't place, but it was a dirty one. Perhaps the slaves here enjoyed the rain because it lessened that smell, but the looks on their faces told of more behind the sight that he should ask the Chief Priest about when they were alone.

Aran walked beside him, both of them wearing unremarkable tunics and sandals to blend into the crowds. Despite being half-rakkan, Darius had no trouble fitting in amongst humans, especially after leaving his armour and the Twin Blades behind. That had been more difficult than he'd imagined, those weapons now almost as attached to him as Lyra.

It was as if they called out to him, waiting for his return, but he'd be a while longer yet, and if he got into a fight, he had a trusty kuraminium dagger safely stowed under his belt to rely on.

The pair soon arrived at the place they sought, a terraced house made of mottled clay that, at first glance, almost lost itself amongst its neighbours, but an axe symbol on the wall outside—one that would have seemed nothing more than a crack to anyone not searching for it—marked this as the shelter they'd hunted down.

A closed door was the only way in, and when Aran gave two bashes on the rusty old knocker, echoes resonated behind. No footsteps preceded the turn of the knob, and the door gently eased open to reveal a blond, fair-skinned man that immediately stood out as a privileged algus. There was something about the look he gave them too that set him apart from everyone else in the street, a smugness, a calmness that a slave would never bear, and delicate features that had never suffered hard labour. If Aran hadn't filled Darius in on who the man was beforehand, he'd have sworn he was one of the lazy boys of this city that sat around being pampered all day. But no, apparently, Thestor was a hardened warrior.

"Greetings, old friend." Thestor opened the door wider and waved them inside, giving Aran a pat on the back.

Eager to escape the rain, Darius passed inside too but soon discovered that the building was barely a few yards deep before opening into a vast space covered only by what looked to be thin fabric stretched across the decrepit remnants of what had once been a roof. Under the dripping shroud, men and women lay on piles of straw, some unconscious or snoozing, others grimacing while carers rubbed ointments onto their wounded bodies.

"The city guard doesn't often check here," Thestor said as if seeing Darius's horror at the state of the place. "It's safest for all those here until they're fit enough to leave."

The Chief Priest had said this was mainly a haven for injured or runaway slaves, but "safe" was far from the word Darius would use to describe it.

As he passed into the open area, raindrops once again pattered on his hair, but he hardly noticed as a woman to his left stole his attention. She was sat in a corner, looking at him with eyes that told a gruesome story, one swollen and sealed shut, the other a narrow purple slit almost matching its twin. Scratches marred nearly every inch of her skin, whether from flails or fingernails, Darius couldn't say, but as a man tended to her wounds, she didn't so much as flinch.

"The other priests are in the back," Thestor said. "Would you like to speak with them?"

"Of course." Aran gestured for Darius to go first.

But Darius shook his head, knowing the religious matters priests spoke about weren't of much interest. "I'll stay here. Call me if you need me."

"Very well. I shan't be long." The Chief Priest left while Darius began walking between the mattresses, sniffing the vinegar in the air.

"Believe it or not," Thestor said, "these slaves are in good shape. Those worse off don't make it here."

"There are so few of them." Darius counted a dozen at most, and he'd been told this was one of their most fruitful recruiting sites. "Are there more safe houses throughout the city?"

Thestor lowered his head. "A few, but not enough. Only the most desperate dare to abandon their masters."

A man at Darius's feet scoffed at the remark. "Masters... The mistresses are the worst. That's what I've seen." He peered up through the long, shaggy dark hair spilling over his face and shoulders, and the sun-worn patches on his skin and tan clothes made Darius suspect he'd been an outdoor labourer.

"How long have you been here?" Darius asked.

"In this bed? A few days."

"And in Xavala?"

The man pulled back his hair until the rain splashed onto his forehead and rocked from side to side, almost like a nervous tic. "All my life."

Knowing Aran would be a while, Darius sat beside the man, soon joining him in peering up at the rain. Now he understood the appeal; the tiny thumps of drops kept one focused on the present rather than dwelling on your troubles.

The man opened his mouth to collect the drops with the same smile the others had had.

"Do you like the rain?" Darius asked.

The man nodded. "The sun always blazes without much of a breeze in this city. I like the cold."

Darius guessed he was too used to the rakkan mountains to share the man's pleasure in that.

"What will you do next?" Darius asked. "If you travel south, it's cooler all year round."

A thoughtful murmur came from the man's throat next, one that seemed to drain all the enjoyment he'd been showing. "I can't leave. I'll return to my mistress before she notices my absence."

But Darius had assumed everyone here would form part of the rebellion. He looked at Thestor, and the algus's eyebrows lifted as if to ask, "What do you expect?"

"I don't understand," Darius said. "Why come here at all if you don't intend to flee?"

The man pulled up his tunic to reveal a nasty wound on his thigh currently sealed with sap but red and angry enough to be a worry.

"I'd have lost my leg," the man said. "My mistress wouldn't give me the medicine I needed."

Judging by the straightness and thinness of the wound, it had come from a blade, and it had struck only an inch from a major vein.

"Was it her that cut you?" Darius asked.

Mouth closing, the man readjusted his tunic and returned to enjoying the raindrops spilling down his forehead, leaving Darius to conclude his suspicion had been correct.

"Why go back to her?" He tried to keep his voice as soft as possible, genuinely confused rather than passing judgement.

"Don't you know what they do to runaway slaves?" The voice was a woman's and came from near the entrance, and when Darius turned to see, he recognised her swollen eyes as the first he'd locked onto upon entering. "Most of us can make it back in a day or two without our masters being the wiser, but to run away… They…"

"I've heard stories," Darius replied, "but I can't say I know for sure what would happen."

"When the cavalry raids in the west," she said, "they bring them back—the bodies, at least. Always thin and starved, having needed only a few blows to send them to the afterlife."

Although the Xavalans probably chose the worst casualties to parade in their city, Darius couldn't deny that the west hadn't been the most inviting place in the last few years. If the rakkans didn't starve or desiccate you, then the Torians or Xavalans might, and the weather did its best to kill you on top.

"So," Darius said, "will you return to your masters too?"

The woman shook her head. "I've had enough. Now I envy even the starved corpses."

"Why don't we leave these poor people to recover." Thestor gave Darius a light kick. "They suffer enough from their past. Come. I have something else to show you, your supplies."

Resisting the temptation to give the man a kick back, Darius instead stood and followed Thestor back into the main building and down a dark narrow passage he hadn't noticed before when passing by. Even here, the air smelt damp, and that only worsened as they came to a narrow staircase that spiralled underground. Thestor flared algor to light the way, but they both still watched their feet because every step was barely wide enough to support their heels.

"I still haven't told Aran or the priests about this," Thestor said. "I'm leaving it to Lex to tell them."

Her keeping secrets hardly came as a surprise to Darius. "Will you at least tell *me* what you're speaking of or where we're going?"

Thestor jerked to a stop. "You mean she hasn't?"

"No."

"But I thought she would have… You're our Overlord."

Darius nudged the man to continue descending. "I'm sure she had her reasons, but let's see what she's been plotting."

Without hesitating, Thestor continued and they soon emerged into a dark room too short for Darius to stand upright. After only a few seconds, a crick began in his neck, but he barely paid attention as his rakkan eyes adjusted and took in the wooden racks lining every spare inch of the cellar. Each had two shelves, bent and reeling under the weight of stacks of short swords, and next to them, wooden hoplons were piled into columns, wedged from floor to ceiling.

"So much for Aran's peaceful plans," Darius said. It didn't take much imagination to see what Lex was planning, and he was past being annoyed or frustrated with her hiding things like this. "Are you going to put these to use?"

Thestor shrugged. "Not without your instruction. We'll wait and see how things go with the Chief Priest and the Order. But don't worry. I'll have a pair of hands for all of these should it come to it."

"I hope they're in better shape than the ones upstairs."

But when Thestor gave no reassurances, Darius's confidence faltered. A slave revolt was hard enough at the best of times, with fit men and women. If left with nothing but feeble, sick or injured slaves, it was no wonder the Chief Priest wanted this to remain peaceful. Darius was even in two minds whether a slave revolt would go any better for them than an assault by his legions. At least during the latter, the civilians might be able to hide away in cellars like this one.

"How quickly do you plan on having these dispersed?" Darius asked.

"It'll take time," Thestor said. "This needs to be planned and well orchestrated. There's too much risk in handing these out for slaves to hide."

"I agree." Once a few weapons were found, their whole plan would be in jeopardy. "Let's do nothing for now and help the Chief Priest as much as we can. Tell me whenever Lex contacts you and what she's planning."

Thestor gave him a knowing look. "You're not enthused about this idea, are you?"

"Can you honestly tell me you are?"

"I've seen people fight and win with less skill or heart. And now that I've met you… As long as you're here, I'm optimistic."

But for the first time in many months, Darius hoped this plan *wouldn't* end in a fight. As much as he wanted to cut the throats of Xavalan algus and crush their skulls, he prayed he wasn't forced to do that in battle.

They both carried on surveying the weapons for a while, checking the strength and sharpness, until four bangs on a door above disturbed them.

"Are you expecting anyone?" Darius asked.

By the fear in Thestor's expression, Darius knew that was a no. The two hurried back upstairs just as more bangs shook the door, and as they did, slaves within the building grabbed blankets and clothes before scurrying inside and down the stairs from which they'd emerged.

Letting them past, Darius pressed his body into the wall beside the door while Thestor approached and slid open the locks. Only once the last slave was nothing but soft footsteps padding downstairs did Thestor crack open the door.

"Yes?" the algus said.

"Where is she?" a man bellowed.

Darius put a hand on his dagger.

"She's still not fit," Thestor said. "She can barely see through the swelling."

"'Barely' is enough to walk." The door burst open, knocking Thestor backwards, and a man wearing the tan tunic of a Xavalan algus stepped inside, his brown leather boots thudding and showing barely a scuff on them. That told Darius one of two things—either the man had been shopping that day, or he was the type of algus that didn't fight.

When the algus turned and saw Darius, he turned up his nose with a slight scoff. "And who's this? Another carer?"

Darius didn't cease leaning against the wall and left silence as his answer.

"No one you need to be concerned with." Thestor closed the door and quickly positioned himself between the two of them as if afraid Darius would rush and break the algus's jaw. Given his past, Darius couldn't blame the man.

"Let me guess," Darius said. "You own one of the slaves here?"

Thestor nodded. "The one with the two black eyes."

"She's my father's," the algus replied, "and if he finds out she came here, she'll get more than a battering. Where is she?"

Darius shrugged.

"Downstairs," Thestor admitted, much to Darius's shock. "But can you really not give her another couple of days?"

Surprisingly, the algus frowned as if considering the idea, but he soon shook his head. "My father will expect her this evening. I gave her the morning."

"How generous," Darius said.

Thestor gave him a sly kick to the shin. "Ignore him. I'll go and fetch her, then, if there's no other option, but please keep her out of your father's way until she's healed."

"You know I try." The algus turned away and grabbed his neck as if nursing an injury, but Darius guessed it was from lying down for too long on a goose-down mattress rather than fretting over that poor woman.

Thestor headed towards the stairs, but Darius grabbed his arm before he could leave. "Are you sure we should…?" He stopped the question at the deathly stare Thestor gave him, a sight that told him something far worse than he could imagine would happen if they resisted this algus's wishes now.

So he let Thestor go and stayed alone with the algus, glad only to have to see the back of his head now. Judging by the thinning of hair at the crown, he guessed he was in his late thirties and far beyond the age a man should be beholden to his parents.

Despite Thestor's look of warning, Darius couldn't resist a question.

"Who did it to her?" he asked.

At that, the man spun. "You dare address an algus so informally? I forgave one disrespectful remark, but I'm not generous enough to forgive two."

Darius had never been more tempted to flare ferven and reduce the man to a cowering wreck, but he resorted to squeezing his fists and bowing a little. "I meant no disrespect. It would just be useful to know what caused her injuries so we can better treat her." Or perhaps better "treat" the one that had inflicted them.

"What difference does it make?" the algus replied with a nervous shake of his head. "You cannot treat her. If she's not back before he finds out…"

Dwelling on that would only rile Darius up further, so he instead turned to another question that had struck him. "How do you know of this place?"

"I was one of the first donors," he said. "Believe it or not, we algus aren't all heartless."

But the man didn't display much heart as far as Darius could see. Any algus with a heart would have taken that slave far away by now if they were so worried for her safety.

"Then why haven't you sold her?" he asked. "Get her out of your father's way."

The algus paled. "She'd more likely be treated *worse* by someone else."

In response, Darius had nothing but silence to offer again. He'd heard tales of how Xavalans treated slaves, but still, that answer surprised him.

Thestor returned a few moments later with the battered woman beside him, hanging her head with barely the energy to walk—or perhaps she didn't have the will. She'd spoken of wanting death before, and Darius saw no evidence that had been a lie, was even tempted to aid her either by killing her or the man that had come to take her. But that would only put this whole safe house in danger.

So, he instead did nothing, kept his lips and weapon still while the algus visitor grabbed her arm without a word and then rushed towards the door. The two were outside and gone before Thestor had a chance to open his mouth and whisper goodbye, and Darius still leaned against the wall staring at the closed door. How long would it be until this city was under his control and he didn't have to stand idly by?

"Who's his father?" Darius asked.

Thestor shook his head. "Don't get personal. This is only the start of what you'll see here. Remember our goal, and remember, it cannot be rushed."

"It already is personal," Darius said. Seeing this only reminded him of Laltos and Brutus. However Darius came to defeat this city, whether through peace, revolts or conquest, it couldn't come soon enough.

# 13

## King's Orator – Toria

Slaves had a nasty habit of becoming a nuisance. Ophelia knew that better than anyone because her mother had been one, and she'd been the model that Ophelia had imitated, the one from whom she'd acquired all the guile that had lifted her to one of the most powerful positions in the Empire. When someone owned nothing but their own cunning, it was dangerous to underestimate them. Uprisings were nothing new. She'd quashed them before and could do so again.

The banquet table before her overflowed with slices of fatty meat so juicy it appeared as if sweating, and such a lavish variety of eastern vegetables had been cut and steamed that she only knew the names of half of them.

Although not the largest table and hall the King had at his disposal, this one seemed to be his favourite. Perhaps that was because of the room; the prismatic glass ceiling caught the sun's golden rays at this time of evening and locked in the heat until toasty, which had the added benefit of easing the itchiness of Ophelia's scabs.

At the other side of the table, the masked King had cleared a space around himself where he'd stacked more rolls of parchment, paying the food little heed as if he enjoyed only the smell. In all the years she'd served him, she'd never seen him eat and couldn't help but wonder what orifice, if not the mouth, he used. Only in private did he enjoy food, almost as if the practice was so intimate it couldn't be shared with others. That's why she'd never asked.

Ophelia hadn't taken a bite either, so the only plates there disturbed were those in front of the King's Sword, who carefully chewed with such regularity that his jaw seemed mechanical.

"*Have you made any progress capturing the two people I asked for?*" the King asked.

Ophelia hung her head. "No, my king. My spies are still searching for the man, and others report Alexandra is in Margalvia, where we can't get to her yet. But they have confirmed she's involved in this slave rebellion you've foreseen."

The King nodded without looking up from his scrolls and thankfully didn't seem too displeased at the lack of progress.

"When will this revolt occur, my king?" Ophelia asked.

"*We have at least a few weeks,*" the King replied. "*At most until the end of next month. There are a few ways they could spark it.*"

A waft of air laced with a salty pork aroma hit Ophelia's nostrils, reminding her to eat. Her mouth salivated, but it wasn't just because of the food. This could be the chance she'd waited years for. That swine Aristippus had been nothing but a nuisance since his inauguration.

"If the Silk Regent cannot contain it," Ophelia said, in a voice as silky as her tunic, "then is he not failing in his position as your surrogate?"

*"Has he ever been anything but a failure? I haven't kept him there for his intellect."*

That went without saying. "Then why?"

*"The Silk City's wealth has always been too great a threat to entrust to anyone with brainpower. Plus, it's useful to have a buffer with the west, and who better to be that than a man more loathsome and despised than the King?"*

"He's certainly that." Just the thought of the man's smirking face sent a shudder through Ophelia. "But surely you don't intend to allow the slaves to overthrow him?"

*"It would likely be disadvantageous."*

"But you trust the Silk Regent to quash an uprising?"

*"No. That's why I'll send you. Why else do you think I've laid out this feast for you?"*

The King's Sword suddenly ceased chewing and gave Ophelia a rare look of worry from under his hood. He wasn't the only one concerned. Ophelia recalled the King had implied the Silk City was as good as doomed now that they'd failed to take the Gap of Aphatos, and although she was the King's loyal servant, her fealty didn't extend to dying.

"I'm honoured you would trust me with such a task, my king." Ophelia bowed her head slightly and left a respectful pause before continuing. "But I'm unfamiliar with the city these days. Am I best placed to—"

*"Did you not quell three slave uprisings in the past?"* The King's dark gaze broke from his scrolls for the first time and pierced her.

Ophelia cursed her reputation and past accomplishments. It was never plausible to feign a lack of skill for a given task.

"That's true, my king. But we've been making progress in raiding Menara's farmlands. I was planning to—"

*"I'll handle that and use the Silk City as a distraction. But don't worry, Ophelia. I shan't leave you there before the horrors that are to befall that city come to pass."*

The words were more comforting than any others, but Jason cleared his throat with a subtle flick of his eyebrows. She knew what he wanted.

"Is Jason to come with me?" Ophelia asked. "The Silk Regent rarely listens to me. If I am to go, I'd prefer he was removed."

The King's eyes faded in colour and misted over for a while before he answered, *"Aristippus cannot be assassinated. The other regents will know my hand was behind any dagger that ends him, and it's imperative I have the trust of the Regent of Alogos. I sense I'll need to request a great sacrifice from her city when the time comes, and she is much beloved by her people. The only way to be rid of the Silk Regent would be to let the slaves take Xavala. I can't say I'm not tempted."*

Ophelia bit down on her tongue to stifle a curse. "But that would deprive us of many algus, horses, and soldiers."

*"Perhaps..."*

"And if we lose Xavala to slaves, what's to stop the other cities from following their example? We might end up with only Toria's army and the rest of the Empire's cities against us. Then our cause is lost."

The King shook his head. *"Even if the whole empire falls, we'll have reinforcements."*

Ophelia wracked her brain but couldn't think of who the King spoke of. She cleared her throat. "Who—?"

*"I digress. You're right; we can't allow slaves to take the Silk City. You'll quash this uprising, then evacuate anyone loyal to us."*

Alone, that would be a challenge. "I'd still prefer Jason came with me. My spies in Xavala won't be able to unearth all the conspirators. If Jason could be allowed to read the thoughts of suspects and—"

*"No. Jason won't be needed. The Silk Regent will handle the revolt with your guidance."*

"But why not use Jason's abilities for once?"

The King's eyes lit up in anger. *"You know why."*

But Ophelia still considered it a waste. She knew that it was somewhat dangerous for Jason to see into the minds of others and perhaps learn of his real origins, but that was hardly likely from strangers in the Empire, and from her experience with Jason, she knew that he had no power to manipulate other minds like gomans.

The King's sonorous voice filled her mind again. *"Leave at first light. And be sure to guard the city's springs and wells. At some point, the rakkans will attempt to poison them."*

"As you wish, my king." Ophelia stood and bowed, then made to leave the room, brushing past the King's Sword with an outstretched hand to reassure him as she went.

The man stood at the touch. "I'll see her off." Then the pair left and headed straight for Ophelia's quarters.

"You don't need to help me, you know?" she said as they walked through the palace hallways.

The man grunted and ignored her polite remark. Truthfully, she was glad to be with him.

"Don't worry too much over me," she said. "I'll stay in the shadows."

"But I do."

How touching. She reached out and stroked his arm. "Part of me wishes you wouldn't, but another part is glad you care for me as well as a brother."

The man suddenly stopped and frowned at her. "Aren't I your brother?"

Ophelia let out a nervous laugh. Where had he got that idea?

"Did the King tell you that?" she asked, not wanting to contradict anything implanted.

Jason shook his head. "I just…thought I had a sister."

If only she had time to spare, she'd find out exactly where that intuition had come from. But with time short, she decided it best to ignore the man's confusion. If she informed the King, she knew what would happen and was damned if she'd allow it. For a period after the editing, the man's personality was blander than plain rice.

So, she'd let it slide as one of the common anomalies among the Numbered.

"I think of you like a brother," she said. "I can see why you'd think we're related." In hindsight, she should have just lied and said she was his sister in the first place; she made a far better sibling than the Waif Magician, after all.

The man nodded, but his expression still bore some confusion, and he turned to leave as if Ophelia had just become invisible.

"Will you see me off later?" she asked.

Jason nodded but without turning and headed back towards the King.

*How strange.* It wasn't uncommon for him to become confused, but she could usually afford more time to ease his fears.

Right now, though, she had to focus on the revolt. She headed back towards her room, already dividing Toria's armies in her mind. She'd take some with her to the Silk City, enough algus that she could handle the Silk Regent if he resisted her instructions.

And she'd better not take any nice clothes with her. Quashing revolts was a bloody affair.

# 14

## Darius – Xavala, the Silk City

"Watch it, you oaf!" A rotund yet handsome man staggered as he leaned over his table while trying to point a bleeding finger at the older man opposite. "If you injure my hands, I'll be no use to my mistress!"

"Apologies," the old man croaked, bowing his head with hair so stringy and thin everyone could see the lash marks on his scalp. He'd struck Darius as odd since he'd first spotted the man, the only unsightly person in a vast room of well-groomed, appealing faces.

"Give it a rest," one of the women farther down the table called. "He didn't mean to break the cup."

The elderly man ran his trembling bony hand across the wooden top to scrape up the pottery shards, wet with ale so poor Darius could barely drink it without retching. But what else could be expected of a slave house? These people were probably grateful for any perks the Silk Regent gave them because most didn't even have proper beds and simply slept on folded sheets at the sides of the large open hall they now drank in.

Hot wind eased through the gaps in the wooden walls but did nothing to dilute the stench of perfume prickling Darius's nose, an offensive floral musk that the many hemmed-in people seemed to have been drenched in. The stink flowed over the three long tables and stools, ruffling the hair of all the slaves enjoying the little peace they had after a harsh day's work—although you'd be pressed to notice their fatigue through the heavy layers of makeup painted on both the men and women. But their burdened eyes said it all.

Above them, settling within the joists and struts holding up the ceiling, many giant moths that had escaped the silk farms fluttered about in the night.

At the far corner, on an empty stretch of the table, the Chief Priest and Darius sat with Thestor, the disguised three studying everyone in the room as furtively as possible, waiting for opportunities again.

Aran nudged Darius and gave a look to the now arguing pair of men. Surely he didn't intend to recruit them for the rebellion.

For the last couple of weeks, they'd managed to keep a low profile, sneaking into the rest houses during the night and drumming up support from anyone who appeared bitter about their lot in life. Those people weren't hard to find, and some were even fit and strong.

Aran was more heavily concealed than Darius had ever seen him, losing all of the usual glow of his skin but still fitting in well with the beautiful crowd, and Thestor had similarly required heavy cloaking; his fair skin marked him out as a privileged algus to anyone with half a brain, and even the blackened hair struggled to fade the algus aura from him.

By contrast, Darius had needed no aid to fit in, and his only struggle in blending in had been not to get too distracted by Lyra's senses, which continued to confuse his mind. But he did his best to block them out and focus on where he was. Everything at the fort was fine, for now.

A crash from farther down the table stole his attention, and he saw the rotund man leaning so far across that his distended belly mopped the pottery shards as he grabbed the old man by the collar.

"Bastard!" The rotund one punched the old man across the jaw, knocking him to the floorboards as others rushed over to help him.

"Saman, that's enough!" a woman shouted as she stood and squared up to the man, a full head shorter than him, but judging by the size of her shoulders, she had the strength to handle Saman without much trouble. "You're just bitter your mistress doesn't want you any longer. Do you really think him injuring your hand is going to change anything? Because it won't. She doesn't want you anymore. Maybe if you weren't such a lazy slob, you wouldn't have gained so much flab, and your mistress wouldn't have sold you to a Torian fisherman."

"Shut it, whore." Saman let out a huff in her face that made her hair flicker.

"I'd rather be a whore than a shipmate. Enjoy the boats after they cart you off tomorrow."

"Aren't you going to do something?" Aran whispered to Darius.

He shrugged. "If I did, it might get them into trouble. The guards will be back patrolling in a little while."

The Chief Priest shook his head. "It's the conditions they're made to live in that creates men like that, driven to be short-tempered and aggressive by what they have to put up with. This place may be clean and the people preened, but it's stifling and crowded. Two days here is enough for me, never mind years."

"I know." Darius took another swig of the thin beer. "I can't imagine living like this. I'd be surly too if given only this piss to drink."

Aran rolled his eyes. "Must you jest? Don't you see their suffering?"

"I have to jest." Darius set his cup down and ran his hand across the smooth pottery. "If I think too deeply about it, I may not be able to contain my rage." Although he'd lost all memories of his childhood except for one, he knew his family had lived as slaves, hiding within the Empire until forced to flee. His mother was hardly one to evoke any pity within him, but even that horrid woman didn't deserve the torment he'd witnessed others endure these last couple of weeks. The first house of the sick he'd visited had only been the beginning. This place may have been cleaner and cushier than the rest, but still, no one here was happy.

He'd had to stand by and watch the whippings and the beatings…and that was just the men. Always with one hand on his dagger, the only thing between him and a bloodbath had been the gentle words of Aran. These were the people they were fighting for. If Darius made a mess of this and gave himself away, the only way for this city to fall would be an assault by his legions. Then, the slaves would be in for a different kind of hell than the one they currently knew.

The Chief Priest laid a gloved hand on his, almost as if to hold it down in case he became violent.

"I understand," Aran said. "Your anger may be righteous, but it needn't turn into violence."

"What do you think we're doing here, Aran?" Thestor asked. "Isn't what we're planning violent by definition?"

"If you follow my advice, it doesn't need to be. Only a few need to die."

"And what if more than a few *deserve* to die?" Darius watched Saman as he staggered around the table towards the old man, who was only standing thanks to the aid of two other slaves.

The Chief Priest retracted his hand. "Don't let your position go to your head. Who are you to judge that?"

"Didn't you say the God of Justice vindicated me? Broke the earth to justify my cause?"

The Chief Priest swallowed. "Those are not the words I used. And don't think I'm so ignorant that I don't know what you're doing." His eyebrows forked as he turned to Thestor. "I know what Lex has been smuggling into Xavala."

Thestor smiled. "I'd heard of your remarkable talent for knowing things which you ought not to, but still…I'm impressed. I'm glad you're on our side."

"But what other than violence can topple this city?" Darius asked. As much as he'd ruminated over Aran's plan, he still couldn't envisage it.

"Xavala only survives on the backs of slaves," Aran said. "If they don't work, those at the top don't eat."

"Even if we don't make it bloody," Thestor said, "the Xavalan algus will."

"They *might*. And that's why the slaves need you," Aran said. "Do you think even a hundred armed slaves could take on an algus without our protection?"

Darius watched as Saman had now rounded the table, only separated from his elderly rival by the woman trying to budge his hulking frame back.

"Do you think that slave will join us?" Darius asked Thestor.

The algus raised an eyebrow. "I'd prefer a sober one with a smaller belly."

"Not the fat man. The woman."

"Ah." Thestor studied her intently for a few moments. "I think she works in the Regent's palace, and most attractive women that work there serve the Silk Regent himself."

She certainly wasn't offensive to the eye. The rambles of Saman were good for distracting everyone else from their hushed conversation, but now, Darius had tired of the ruckus. If guards passed through, he didn't want more called to sort it out.

He stood and marched over as Saman retracted a fist to swipe at either the woman or the old man, but Darius caught the hand before it flew.

"Enough," Darius said calmly.

Saman tried to wrench his hand free, and Darius allowed him a little wiggle room so that his rakkan strength wasn't too obvious.

"Get off!" Saman turned and swung his other fist at Darius.

But Darius ducked and slapped the man on his large belly, using less than a quarter of his strength but enough to knock the wind from him and crumple him in two.

The woman rushed forward, kicked the man in the temple while he was down, and left him garbling on the ground in the last vestiges of consciousness. And as she pulled back her leg again, Darius nudged her shoulder just enough to send her off balance and divert the kick.

"Bit of a cheap shot, don't you think?" he said with a grin while she regained her balance. A woman not afraid of a fight—especially a dirty one—was exactly who he was looking for.

"If he deserves it, he deserves it." Her eyes narrowed slightly as if judging whether he'd block her if she tried again. Up close, she had a more distinctive look than he'd first noticed, high cheekbones with the elegance of a queen and a straight nose almost a little too perfect, making her seem like a sculpture meticulously crafted from hundreds of hours of an artist's labour.

"Won't you be punished if the masters catch you incapacitating a fellow slave?" he asked.

She gave a slight shrug. "What do you care? And who are you? I haven't seen you here before."

"Me and some others were bought yesterday. They threw us in here and said we'd be collected for whatever duties they need in the morning."

The woman glanced over his shoulder at Thestor and the Chief Priest, who were still deep in conversation with stern faces.

"Lucky you," she muttered sarcastically.

So far, he'd seen enough signs of her rebellious nature to risk testing her with a wayward remark.

"We make our own luck," he said. "I don't plan on being here to be collected by morning."

Her eyes suddenly shifted to meet his, nervous yet curious. "Don't even jest about that."

"I'm not." Darius made his face as serious as he could and was relieved when the corner of her mouth curled a little.

"I wish you luck," she said. "Hopefully, I won't walk past your crucified body tomorrow."

That comment was enough to give him some comfort in taking this conversation a step closer to what he'd really come here to discuss.

"Would you like to sit with us?" Darius asked. "I can't promise anything better to drink, but the company will be an improvement on what you've had recently." He gave the downed man a light kick.

She considered him for a few moments, a grin still on her lips. "I don't drink with people I don't know."

"Please yourself." He abruptly turned and began walking back to his table, having had enough similar conversations in the last week to know the woman's curiosity would eventually get the better of her.

"Wait," she called after him.

He halted, turned his head a fraction.

"That was your cue to give me your name," she said.

He smiled. "Was it?" Then he carried on walking until he joined the other two at the table again. By now, their conversation had stopped, and they sipped their drinks while waiting.

It took her a little while longer than with previous slaves, but eventually, the woman came over with a new cup of pissy ale and set it down beside him. "Fine. I'll drink with you."

Darius extended an inviting palm to the seat in front of him, and she sat, not bothering to pay much heed to either Thestor or the Chief Priest.

"Your name?" she asked.

"I'll give you mine if you give me yours," he said.

She gave a little pause before answering—a woman that was cautious as well as bold. "Farideh, but most people just call me Frida."

"That's a pretty name."

The compliment brought a slight blush to her cheeks, and he thought it best to continue flattery and idle chat before delving into more weighty subjects.

"Do you work in the palace?" he asked.

"Everyone here does," she said. "That must be where they intend to take you."

That explained why everyone here looked so preened and hygienic. "I see. Perhaps I'll be lucky enough to serve Regent Aristippus."

"I doubt it. It's mostly women that serve him and the other algus that live there."

"Do *you* serve the Silk Regent?" Darius asked.

When she nodded, a flutter of excitement ran through him. Finally, they might have found someone that could get him access to this city's ruler. But for now, it was too soon in the conversation to jump to that.

"I take it you're popular with your masters," Darius said.

"Why do you say that?" Frida replied.

He took her hand and lifted it, slid back the sleeves of her tunic to reveal her smooth olive skin as she watched him nervously, gooseflesh beginning to prickle her arm.

"No scars," he said, turning her hand over. "And soft hands. You aren't made to work hard."

She jerked her hand away. "Just because my work isn't backbreaking doesn't mean it isn't hard. And don't think you'll get anything for free because of what I do."

It came as no surprise that he'd said something to unintentionally irritate her. When it came to conversation, he still had the skills of someone that had only lived for a few years. But it was intentional for him to speak first rather than Thestor or the Chief Priest. It gave him a chance to see how much of a spine people had, whether they smiled and nodded along to an awkward man or whether they put him in his place. Thankfully, she'd done the latter.

"Apologies," he said. "I don't always choose my words wisely."

Her expression was still wary and irritated, but it did soften a fraction.

"And don't think your duties are why I wanted a drink with you," he added.

"That's a pity," she said. "I can call over one of the men if they're more to your tastes."

Darius again studied the men in the shack, some of which were young and strong, with skin that looked as soft as Frida's.

"These men do that too?" Darius asked.

"Of course. Every palace slave will at some point. Many of the algus have insatiable appetites for that sort of thing, and I'm not just speaking of the men."

But now that Darius watched the others, something else struck him that he hadn't really paid attention to before.

"There are no children," he said. "Do they live somewhere else?"

Frida shook her head. "No one here has any."

That was odd. "Even with the work you all do? Do you…" He couldn't even bring himself to say the words. He'd heard of parents leaving their young children to succumb to the elements when they couldn't provide for them, and he wouldn't be surprised if these slaves' masters made them do the same.

"Really?" Thestor nudged Darius with an elbow. "You invite this poor woman here to speak about this? She'd have had more fun with that unconscious fat man."

But Darius wasn't finished. Although this had nothing to do with the rebellion, all this talk had reminded him of what he'd spoken with Lex about.

"The men here…" Darius said, "if they do that, don't they leave their mistresses with child?"

Frida's face scrunched with confusion. "Why are you so interested in this? You must know what they do to them."

"The men?" Darius leaned closer. "You mean they stop them having children?"

She digested what he'd said for a moment before breaking out into a smirk. "Why do I feel like these questions are about you and a particular woman, an algus you've perhaps got your eye on?"

He was glad he'd chosen a perceptive woman as a potential recruit. "Maybe I'm just a curious man."

She sat back on her stool. "I don't know about curious, but you're a *strange* man, and you still haven't told me your name. There's nothing worse than a man that breaks his word."

"I promised to tell you, but I didn't say *when* I'd tell you."

"… So, when will you?"

He shrugged. "Perhaps when you help me with the algus woman I've 'got my eye on.'"

Frida's cheeks flushed again, but this time along with a scowl. "Is this why you invited me here? To tease and frustrate me?"

"Forgive him," the Chief Priest interjected, and it was about time he spoke. It was a wonder she hadn't stormed off already.

"As hard as it is to believe," Thestor said, "that's him at his most charming."

She took a sip of her ale, but Darius noted she didn't swallow anything and was keeping her head clear.

"And what is he trying to charm me for?" she asked.

"We're just trying to make friends," the Chief Priest said. "Or rather…allies."

"Ah. Well, people usually befriend whores for only one reason."

"I can think of plenty of uses for whores," Darius said.

"Is that so?" she said. "Like what?"

Darius paused and let her study his face, let her see that his next word hadn't a trace of humour. "Assassinations."

Frida's expression flattened in an instant. She shifted her cup away, swallowed, and stood. "I think you have the wrong person."

"You're leaving?" Darius asked.

"I've heard whispers about foreigners mingling with the slaves," she said, so softly it almost faded into the sound of the wind on the walls. "I suspect I know what you're here to say. I won't—"

"If you suspected, why did you join us?" Darius let the question sink in for only a few moments, seeing her wariness build. She was torn. She needed confidence.

"It was a mistake." She turned to leave.

But Darius stood so suddenly it halted her. "Before you leave, I owe you my name." He leaned across the table, waved her to put her ear to his mouth.

And when she did, he whispered, "It's Darius."

She jolted back as if he'd just pulled a knife on her.

"Yes," he said, "that one, but I'm not here to harm you." Slowly, he eased himself back into his seat and took another gulp of his drink. *Please don't run.* It hadn't happened often, but any slaves that baulked at his revelations couldn't be left to report him. They had to be removed from the city, and that was never easy to do covertly. If the Chief Priest hadn't been there, some of those slaves would probably have found themselves buried instead of hauled out of Xavala.

Thankfully, after standing silently for what felt like an hour, she sat back down and leaned across to him. "Prove it."

That was a welcome response Darius was used to by now. After a quick glance from side to side to check no one was looking, he conjured a trace of algor in one eye and ferven in the other to display his unique blend of powers.

Frida flinched back.

"If I tell you why I'm here," he said, "can you keep it a secret?"

She nodded, a little too quickly for his liking, suggesting it was automatic rather than a reasoned answer.

"We're helping the slaves rise up," the Chief Priest said before he could. "Your masters have oppressed you for far too long."

Shouts and curses began filling the hall as slaves at the other side broke into arguments again, Saman back to his feet. The noise might be useful to smother their talk, but it would also likely draw guards' attention.

"I need your help," Darius said quickly. *In more ways than one.* "I've heard the Silk Regent has escape tunnels into and out of the palace, and I need someone that can give me access when the time comes. Can you do that?"

This time, her answer wasn't immediate. Her inquisitive eyes fixated on him, then on his other two companions. She must have realised what a risk he'd taken in revealing himself to her, that he had no reason to be here other than for the reasons he'd stated. To his surprise, he'd found slaves far more trusting than most other humans or rakkans he'd met.

"You'll kill Regent Aristippus?" Frida's voice had now lost all unease. Instead, it was eager, heated. They'd chosen well.

"That's probably the nicest thing I'll do to him," Darius said. That swine had betrayed Laltos and slaughtered tens of thousands.

"Then I can get you in."

Darius and Thestor exchanged a smile, but the Chief Priest's brow was still furrowed as he watched her.

"Do you know any others that will side with us?" he asked.

She nodded, the smile returning to her lips. "Many."

Meanwhile, a crash from the other side of the place stole Darius's attention. Splintered points of wood jutted out from one of the tabletops that had been split in two, and in the middle of the broken wood, Saman towered over the old man, who shook on the bottom with blood dribbling from his nose.

"I'll give you a name," Thestor said to the woman. "He's a slave master on the other side of town that's coordinating things. He'll be in touch soon."

"You're not staying here?" Frida looked at Darius, but he was still busy watching Saman now mash his fist repeatedly into the old man's head while half a dozen others tried to drag him away.

"I'm not," Darius finally replied. "But I want to speak with you more and pick your brains. Wait here." It was time to end the commotion before it drew too much unwanted attention.

He stood and stormed over to the warring slaves, watching the old man's eyes roll back in his head as he could no longer raise his hands to block the strikes.

By the time Darius neared, a huddle of bodies now surrounded Saman like a fleshy armour, clawing and restraining him. But they weren't doing a good enough job.

One by one, Darius ripped the slaves away until he revealed the man's ale-stained tunic and portly belly. The oaf pulled up a knee to stamp on his foe, but Darius kicked first, using only a smidgen of his algus speed, and hit straight at the supporting leg of the man.

Although not intended, he felt the knee snap before he heard the sound, before Saman let out a shrill howl of agony and collapsed to the ground under the gaping slaves around.

Damn his rakkan strength.

"What are you doing?" one of the women yelled and tried to shove Darius back but didn't manage to budge him. "If he can't work, they'll kill him!"

Ignoring her, Darius knelt, took the old man's head in his hands, and gave his cheeks a little slap to try to bring him to. But there was no response, eyes open and vacant, and Darius's rakkan skin sensed no air leaving the mouth.

"He killed him," Darius said, almost to no one but himself as Saman continued yelling. If Darius let that continue, it would draw in guards.

So he leapt up and stepped towards the man. He grabbed him by the tunic, lifted him up, and swung around to his back with an arm around his throat. A gentle squeeze was all it took to cut off the man's voice. The veins on his forehead bulged as the blood supply stemmed, and Darius waited a few seconds until the man's struggles ceased.

Darius eased the unconscious man to the ground. He'd only be out for a few moments, but that was enough time for him and his companions to scarper.

By the time he looked over his shoulder towards the others, Thestor was already beside him.

"Why must our nights always finish with you killing someone?" Thestor said.

"*I* haven't killed anyone." But if Saman's masters ended him, Darius wouldn't waste an ounce of pity over it.

The Chief Priest came scurrying behind, but there was no sign of Frida.

"Where is she?" Darius asked.

Aran looked back with a frown. "She was right here."

"Damn it. We'll find her later. For now, let's be gone."

# 15

## Lex – Gap of Aphatos

Lex sat in the recently finished throne room and twirled the old roll of parchment in her hand, knowing by now every word written on it by heart but still unsure why it reported what it did and what the implications were. *Did Sulla's men steal some gold?*

But rakkans had little use for it. No, the Torians or Xavalans must have found some of her hidden underground vaults in Laltos, and the rakkans' reports of some being already emptied were true. She knew there had been more inside, but this message said that what remained was enough for only the first payment to Eluthia. At least the wagons were already loaded and on their way to deliver it.

"Alexandra?" Varro called from beside her.

Lex looked up at the man staring from within his dark, horned helmet. "Yes?"

"Warlord Flavius has arrived."

"I know." Even if she'd had the strength to, she wouldn't have stood—a feverish haze still troubled her at times, especially after a long journey here from Margalvia in a rickety cart.

Everyone else in the throne room was standing except for Lex and Sulla. And Lyra, of course. As a proxy for the Overlord, she stood for no one, and Lex would be damned if she'd pay any respects to a rakkan that had fought against her people. Varro should have remained seated in a sign of disgust too, just like his sour-faced Militia Chief.

The fortress around them was now back on the route to completion thanks to Warlord Quintus and the Azure Legion, and this room had been completed first. At the heart of the fortress, surrounded by corridors and layers of rock fused with ferven and angled in such ways that made battering through them arduous, the throne room Rufus had designed was simple yet shared some of Toria's defensive structure. Maybe he'd even based the design on the King's palace.

At the front, next to where Lyra currently sat scanning everyone below, the throne stood before a black-walled façade and was on a dais that lifted it to see even the far reaches of the lengthy room. The seat itself had been chiselled from stone and was plain, not even polished, almost unassuming and leaving all attention for the one who would sit upon it. On the floor in front of each stone armrest was a slit, perfectly straight and thin but currently empty. Each was just deep enough to contain but not hide the flaring runes of the Twin Blades of Trogus when the ruler resided here. Although designed for Darius, Lex suspected Rufus had envisaged himself lording over this place in the not-too-distant future.

Through the centre of the room, a thin path marked by darker-coloured stone led from the door to Darius's seat, and along the walls facing it were smaller thrones and chairs, currently designated for the four rakkan warlords and the Regent of Laltos, but with plenty of space to accommodate the rulers of other allied cities. Only one of them was taken at present by the slave Cyrus from Menara. He'd been their point of contact with the town and a most valuable ally at times.

Hera currently stood in front of Laltos's throne and would hopefully soon sit upon her real one in the city itself. To the Regent's right, Lex sat in defiance as the Branz Warlord strode with heavy steps at the side of the black stone walkway that led to the seat of power.

Only when the Branz Warlord sat did Warlords Quintus, Varro, and Rufus lower themselves, followed soon after by the commanders at their flanks.

"I thought he'd at least be here," Warlord Flavius said. "If his panther can't talk, what's the point?"

"He'll return from Xavala at any moment," Lex said. The journey west would only take him a couple of days' hard ride on swiftback.

"Who was that?" Warlord Flavius leaned out and scanned the room until he spotted Lex. "You? Only leaders should speak freely in this room, girl."

Lyra let out a long, ominous growl until the rakkan had leaned back in his throne and averted his gaze.

Unfazed by the condescending warlord, Lex went back to her ponderings while the others conversed amongst themselves. This was the first time the Branz and Azure Warlords would meet Darius, and Lex prayed he made a good impression—or, in other words, exuded his power. Warlord Quintus was as sharp-witted as her father had been and predictably a little unimpressed at the commands Darius had issued via a messenger before even meeting him face to face.

But Lex had bigger issues to worry about. Darius would take care of himself; the gold she owed would not. It wasn't like any of the other cities had enough gold either. Rakkans traded mainly in kuraminium and other practical materials, Laltos had only what Lex had stashed, and Menara barely had iron, let alone gold. As determined as she was to sort this on her own, she wouldn't risk their cause. If she didn't think of an idea soon, she'd ask Darius and the others for help.

Before she'd had time for an epiphany, the thuds of boots outside grew, and soon the doors flung open. Darius strode in like a man with a purpose and focused solely on the throne rather than regard his guests as he walked past, each of them standing in a show of respect to him—or perhaps respect to the two swords hanging naked from his belt and sending a red glow from their runes.

Behind him, Thestor entered with less bravado and took a seat near Hera while the Chief Priest walked to the side of the room, looking around as if deciding whether to stand in the alcoves or leave.

Lex waved the man over to a seat near her, and thankfully, he obliged in joining her.

Darius gave Lyra a scratch behind the ear as he walked past, then withdrew the Twin Blades and hammered them into their allocated slots with a boom so loud it was almost as if the ground shook again. He turned with a sweep of his cloak and lowered himself onto the throne, rapping his fingers on the armrests in a fashion he must have learned from the Black Warlord.

"Are we missing anyone?" Darius asked.

All the leaders in the room shook their heads, but someone else did enter, a woman who slinked through the doorway and caught Darius's eye. He seemed pleased to see her and watched as she quietly settled herself against a wall at the side of the room.

She was a sturdy-looking woman but had all the signs of one of Aristippus's concubines: the delicate glow of her skin, the bounce in her hair, and the shape and size of her bosom that the Silk Regent always preferred.

"Let's begin." Darius paused, acknowledging each of the warlords in turn with the confidence of a man who had been a ruler for decades, not months. "I thank you all for making the long journey here, and I see from the camps outside that it wasn't alone. Rufus, I hope your legion's journey here was uneventful."

The Viridian Warlord gave a nod, and Lex had already checked out that his men hadn't been their usual nuisance on the march.

"I hope you've enough food for us all," the Branz Warlord said.

Everyone focused on the rakkan except Lex; she instead studied Darius's reaction. Unusually for him, he remained calm, not even clenching his fingers, which still rested on the throne's armrest inches away from the hilts of the sources of his authority.

"You must be Flavius," Darius said.

"That I—"

"You will speak only when spoken to." Darius's eyes lit deep red, a shade Lex had never seen from a rakkan before but that matched what emanated from the Blades. Even the Branz Warlord's mouth hung open at the sight.

"If I may…Overlord," the Azure Warlord said, only continuing when Darius gave him a nod. "You must understand there are no laws or standards for how we must conduct ourselves here. None of us have ever answered to an overlord before. If there are any customs or protocols we must adhere to, you will need to explain them before expecting us to follow them."

Darius's eyes dimmed back to their usual darkness. "Point taken, Quintus. But I wasn't setting out a rule for you all. Only Flavius must ask for permission to speak."

The Branz Warlord scowled, unspoken curses in his hateful yet silent glare.

"And why is that?" Lex asked. She suspected she knew the answer, but the others might not, and a leader whose instructions were ill understood could appear reckless and unhinged.

"Because I fear for his life," Darius said.

Silence fell upon the room, and Lex struggled to grasp his meaning.

Sulla scoffed. "Let Flavius speak freely. Let him anger us enough to wash these newly laid stones with his blood."

Flavius raised a hand lazily and waited for Darius's nod before speaking. "You needn't fear for me. If Varro or Sulla wishes to settle our feud, I'm more than ready."

"It is not them that shall kill you," Darius said. "Rufus has informed me of the deal you struck with Hadrian, and anyone that helped that brute is lucky to still breathe, whether Viridian or Branzian."

Flavius shot the Viridian Warlord a filthy look that Rufus took without a blink.

"But Rufus also convinced me to let you live," Darius said. "He said you have your uses. Don't prove him wrong."

"Very well, Overlord," the Branz Warlord muttered through his clamped teeth.

"As for food," Darius continued, "there are still the old farms of Laltos to our west that will be worked again once this fortress is complete, and the farms northeast of Menara are on rich, fertile land. They've yielded enough for the time being."

"If we aren't raided again." The weak voice came from the far end of the room, and Cyrus gingerly leaned out from his chair.

"This fort will do nothing to protect Menara, and our farms have already been raided a few times from across the river. We can only keep bringing supplies to your army if we're protected."

"We'll have to deal with the raids later," Darius said. "Xavala is a far greater threat. But first, I want to make sure we all understand why we're here and what our future looks like."

"I think we can guess," the Azure Warlord said. "We all know the Law of the Blades. You expect to command us."

Although the rakkan's tone verged on rebellious, he'd marched his whole legion here as instructed and got to work constructing a fort without even having met Darius. Quintus was not one to worry about unless mistreated. Hopefully, Darius saw that.

"You will all form my assembly," Darius said. "I will seek your counsel on many issues, and it is here that we'll decide our best steps forward.

"But I expect you to do more than just talk. I expect you all to fight. I do not wish to live looking over my shoulder, wondering when the King will next upheave my life or kill those I care about and anyone else that gets in his way."

"So, you ask us for blood?" Quintus said.

"We've already paid blood." Varro spoke so quietly that the rest of the room hushed to hear what followed. "While you rested on your glacier, the Black and Viridian Legions have shielded you from the King with the blood of our brothers, our fathers, our sons. The Overlord is not starting a war. We're already in one, and I have every intention of helping him end it."

The Azure Warlord bowed his head a little and seemed to digest the words, but the Branz Warlord rolled his eyes.

Perhaps Rufus was wrong. Perhaps Flavius was better off dead. Lex knew one whisper from her into Darius's ear was all it would take.

"This could be our only chance." The Chief Priest stood abruptly and stretched out his hands as if preaching to his followers. "The King is a far greater threat than you know. Without Darius, you rakkans have no future except extinction."

"And how do you know this?" Rufus's keen eyes fixed on the old man.

"He knows more about the King than any other," Lex said, eager not to let the conversation dwell on *how* he knew things. All his escorts were their greatest, most secret asset. "It was he that knew Darius needed to reach Mount Psilos before you. If we'd only listened to him sooner at that time, Darius would have had the Blades long before Hadrian had set foot on the mountain."

The Viridian Warlord's gaze shifted back to the Chief Priest with more fascination, which wasn't a good thing.

"He's had more success than my spies," Hera added. "My algus can't even get an escort into Toria's palace, let alone themselves. Killing the King or his goman quietly isn't looking likely."

It had been a long shot anyway, but one worth taking.

"Keep trying," Darius said. "But we'll plan as if that isn't feasible." He continued laying out what they did know of the King and his goman—which wasn't much—and then onto how their armies might approach an attack on the city one day. Most seemed unimpressed with the idea, but Lex knew it was a reluctance born of fear. Since Archimedes had driven the rakkans back deep into their lands, most had barely contemplated launching an offensive.

"And what about the Staff of Arria?" Quintus asked.

"It was lost," Lex said flatly, without betraying that it had plummeted to the depths of the underworld along with the gushing body of her sister—or a warped version of her, at least.

"Now I see why you've mustered all the legions," Quintus said with a pensive bite of his lip. "Only unstoppable force will counter their goman knowing our plans."

"There's another thing besides battle to be concerned with." Rufus turned his attention to the humans in the room. "The goman's puppet once fooled you. What's to say there isn't another among us?"

"You're not the first to suspect that," Lex said. "But what use is a spy when the goman sees all possible futures, what we might plan, which actions are most likely to succeed? If you ask me, we should be more worried about assassins."

"I have connections within the King's ring of spies," the Chief Priest added, "or rather, the King's Orator's. I would discover if there were spies here. But, to be honest, the King has no need for them."

"And how do we know you're not a puppet?" Rufus asked.

"I can vouch for the Chief Priest," Lex said.

"And who will vouch for you?"

"I will," Darius said. "And let's have no more baseless accusations."

"Darius is guarded by rakkans day and night," Lex said, "safely watched by those immune to a goman's influence. I suggest you all make the same arrangements."

"There's only one way to end this threat," Darius said. "The King and his goman must die, whether or not they are one and the same. But first, we need to deal with the Silk City. Aran, explain the plan for the rebellion."

The Chief Priest obliged and provided them with details of all his contacts in the city, where the slaves had been able to gain most support, and all the critical locations they'd have to overpower to prevent the Silk Regent's algus stopping them by force. He had the stomach for a little violence, but his plans were mostly an attempt to frustrate the functioning of the city while eliminating those in power.

"I can take care of the Silk Regent," Lex said.

"No." Darius leaned back on his throne. "You're in no state to fight. I'll deal with the Silk Regent myself."

Lex opened her mouth to respond but paused. Although her friend, Darius was now the Overlord. She couldn't question his commands—in front of others, at least.

"Very well, Overlord," she said.

At the remark, Darius raised an eyebrow. No doubt he took pleasure in her submitting to him for once. *He'd better not get used to it.*

"Cyrus," Darius said. "You've been in a slave revolt recently. Give us your insights."

The Menaran stood and relayed how their uprising had played out, the bloodshed, the victims, but also had the awareness to identify where they'd made mistakes and how events could have played out differently. As the man spoke, the Chief Priest looked down with a defeated look. He'd probably forewarned them, but they hadn't listened.

The warlords continued discussions with Thestor and Hera also giving their input on how the uprising would begin and which algus needed to be in the city to end any resistance quickly.

After hours of talks and disagreements, Darius had finally heard enough, silenced them all, and set out how they'd proceed.

"We have the day," he said. "We must lure out the Xavalan army first if the slaves are to have any hope. Rufus, you'll oversee that. Get the cavalry as far away from the city as you can."

The Viridian Warlord nodded while Darius continued laying out the details. And when he'd finished, he waved forward the woman that had up to now been listening in silence.

"This is Frida," he said. "She has a plan to get a few of us inside the palace. If you will…" He extended a hand of invitation, and she came forward to address all the leaders in the room.

While she spoke of her plans, she gave most of her attention to Darius, always seeming most comfortable when their eyes met, a sight that had Lex eager for the woman to hurry and leave.

And when she'd finished, Frida stepped back to the side of the room and lingered rather than departed as an informant usually would have.

"You all know what you need to do," Darius said. "This assembly is finished. Go and prepare your soldiers."

While the others filed out of the room, Lex was mindful that she still needed to solve her gold problem, and Darius seemed in control enough to accept the news without acting rashly.

But as she tried to catch his attention for a quiet word, he was too distracted by Frida to notice. The woman stood leaning against the wall with seductive elegance while fixating on him like a woman with an aim. And worse, he returned the heat of her stare and eventually stood to go and greet her.

When the two met, Darius kissed her on the cheek in a way that brought a little redness to it, and Lex could feel her own face burning.

The woman's mouth curled in a playful grin, something returned by Darius. Clearly, his talk of not being promiscuous had either been a lie, or he'd reverted to old ways. Lex had seen that handsome smoulder of his before, full of charm, seduction, and lust. Those subtle touches of her arms as they spoke told Lex all she needed of what was going on.

After a few private whispers, Darius first gave a sly sideways glance to Lex before saying to Frida, "Why don't you go and wait for me in my bedchamber. They tell me it's just been finished."

The woman gave a little curtsy before slinking away.

Lex's face burned all the more. Why was she surprised? The old Darius had told Lex he loved her too before jumping into bed with a whore. *Men.*

And to think she'd believed the man had changed, had grown into his position as leader when likely all he'd done was got a taste of the fruits of power and let them intoxicate him.

Lex stood, only then realising that Varro had stayed behind too and was watching her for some reason.

But she couldn't be concerned with him right now. Her gold issue still had to take priority, and while Darius hadn't any to help her with at the moment, she still had to inform him.

So, she made her way over and watched him frown at her approach as he must have seen her anger.

"I need gold," she said, glad to be able to speak curtly now they were alone with only Varro.

"… For what?" Darius asked.

"To repay a debt. I know the rakkans don't have much, but may I ask them for what they have?"

His next words were slow and careful like he knew he was only one mistake away from her raking her fingernails across his face. "I don't think they have much. Hera's already asked Rufus about what he looted from Laltos, but he's denied taking any. After Xavala's counter-attack, he didn't deem lugging gold back to Viridia a priority."

Lex had suspected that, but the Viridians must have taken something. Still, if they hadn't admitted it to Darius, they wouldn't admit it to her, and she wasn't going to go to Viridia and try to find out more.

"I don't suppose you have any?" she said.

He shook his head. "Should I be worried?" As he asked, Lyra's attention shifted to her, his posture stiffened, and she knew from past experience how quickly his worry and fear turned into violence. She didn't need that. Yet.

"It's fine," she lied. "When it's time to worry, I'll tell you."

Still frowning, he opened his mouth to no doubt ask her to explain herself, but she hadn't the patience to continue looking at that face when it had just been so flirtatious with another woman.

Before he could speak, she turned and began striding away, unsure how she'd solve her problem but as determined as ever that she would.

# 16

## King's Orator – Xavala, the Silk City

"If you don't act tonight, it will be too late." Ophelia leaned forward in her seat until almost resting her elbows on the Silk Regent's desk.

Opposite her, Aristippus's face melted as the slave woman pleasuring him under the table probably hit the right spot. "Can't you see I'm busy?" His gold teeth glinted in the candlelight as his grin widened.

"Busy?" Ophelia held down the rising vomit. She waited with her fingers clenching the table until, soon after, the slave extracted herself from below the desk and scurried away so quickly she was probably going to empty her stomach by any means necessary. *Don't blame her.*

"Fine…" Aristippus leaned back on his chair and adjusted his tunic, giving Ophelia a sight that would haunt her that night. "Let's get to work."

His office was far cleaner than any Ophelia had ever seen. Not a single scroll sat on either the shelves nailed to the walls or the grand mahogany desk that had thankfully spared Ophelia the sight of the gruesome act. There weren't even any pens. This narcissist hadn't the first clue of how to administer a city. If not for the King's orders, she would have left him to be garrotted in his sleep by a rebel. Her only consolation was that this city could soon fall after she'd extracted every worthwhile algus and soldier she could—not including this man if she could help it.

The walls of his room were sadly not as plain as the furnishings. Erotic images best left in the imagination were common in the Silk Regent's palace but had a disturbing edge to them here. The lewd animals were the least offensive thing to Ophelia's eyes, and the sooner she was out of this place, the better.

"I've given you the names of the ringleaders," she said, keeping her voice so forcibly soft that it came out strained. "And I have parchment already bearing the King's seal with the execution orders." Only she in the Empire was entrusted with blank decrees, one of her greatest sources of pride. "All I request is that you formally permit my men to round them up. I'm happy to organise it myself. Timing will be key; we must strike each place at the same time, using the city's bells to coordinate. Otherwise, they'll be alerted and could run."

"Shouldn't this be handled by Xavala's guards?" Aristippus asked, finally giving her the attention she deserved. "Outsiders will only undermine my city's competence."

*Trust him to only care about optics.*

"We can work together," Ophelia said, "but that shouldn't be our primary concern. My men have the names of those we suspect, but there must be more out there. To quash this for good, we must make an example of those people we know about."

"Say no more. We have plenty of wood for the stakes. Their screams will be heard from outside Xavala's walls."

"Burning will do for some, but not those most guilty."

The Silk Regent's dark eyes narrowed. "What do you suggest?"

Ophelia thought back to the most effective techniques she'd used in the past. "Do you know how the King came to choose an eagle as his symbol?"

"I thought he didn't. He inherited it from his father."

"Of course. I meant how his father came to choose it."

The Silk Regent frowned. "He didn't have an eagle escort. Perhaps he enjoyed falconry."

The naïve fool. "Have you ever heard of the blood eagle?"

"I…" Aristippus's frown morphed into a smile. "Now I recall. You wish to do that to my slaves?"

"We'll flaunt them on pikes in every corner of the city."

"Ha!" The Silk Regent slapped his desk with pride as if he'd been the one to come up with the idea. "That will scare any slave that thinks about rebelling again. I can't imagine a more painful end."

"Truth be told, it's not the most savage of deaths. It kills faster than other methods, but as a sight, there's nothing more horrifying. King Medus I's enemies knelt with fear when we began using the blood eagle."

"But the list of people you gave me won't cover the whole city," Aristippus said.

"Then take their families, their wives, husbands, and children. This is not about punishment. This is about fear. The more we can create, the better. People will not revolt if it means their families will die."

The Silk Regent smiled. "I can see why the King sent you."

# 17

## Darius – Gap of Aphatos

"Darius, you're a fool," Varro muttered as he watched Lex storm out of the throne room.

Darius shot the Black Warlord a glare and felt a red haze descend across his vision. "Have you forgotten who you're speaking to?"

"My apologies." Varro gave a slight bow but didn't meet his glare. "You're a fool, Overlord."

Darius strode up to the man, fist clenched and ready to fly, but Varro stretched out an arm silently and shook his head.

"If you have an issue with my commands," Darius said, "then raise your objections in the assembly like a man so we can discuss them."

"I'm not speaking of your strategy," Varro said. "Don't take it personally."

"How the hell am I supposed to take it?"

"Take it as adv—"

The doors crashed open again, and Lex came back towards him with strides so long it almost split the seams of her trousers. She came to a halt only when nose to nose with him, her blue eyes flaring as much algor and rage as they had before she'd left.

He knew he shouldn't have gone along with Frida's idea, but she'd been so confident rousing Lex's jealousy would work.

"Give my pendant back," Lex said.

"Your pendant?"

"Now."

The silver weight hung safely on his chest and had done for a while. It hadn't been too long since he'd promised to return it to her when she asked for it again, and as much as he wanted to keep it, he didn't want to anger her any further.

He reached under his tunic. "Look, if this is about Frida, then—"

"I don't care." She thrust out her palm and poked him in the chest with her tense fingers. "Pendant."

He gently lowered it until she snatched it and stormed away again, this time kicking the doors open with such force they crashed into the walls behind.

"See what I mean?" Varro grinned. "Fool."

"What do you know?" Darius said. "You lost her too."

Varro sighed. "I know you, Darius. And I know Alexandra. Did you really think she'd get jealous? Does she strike you as someone that would react well to seeing you so suggestive with another woman?"

It wasn't like he'd lain with Frida. All he'd given her was a peck and a suggestive invite, which was actually just a meeting for her to relay more insights she'd gathered in Xavala.

As Darius pondered and cursed himself, Varro's smile became a light snort of a laugh, which only infuriated Darius all the more.

"Is this amusing to you?" Darius asked.

"No. It's just that you tried the same thing before. At least you didn't go to bed with the prostitute this time."

*That* was why he'd betrayed Lex? To make her jealous?

"Damn it." Darius sat on one of the empty seats and buried his head in his hands. "I really am a fool."

"At least it's not irreparable this time."

Maybe, but this was Lex they were talking about.

"Why are you being helpful all of a sudden?" Darius asked.

With another sigh, the Black Warlord sat beside him. "Hate is tiring. You're my overlord now, and if you carry on like this, it will only be a distraction to you. Distractions can get my men killed."

Darius saw the truth in that, and the last thing he needed was the blood of more people on his hands through poor leadership.

"You know Lex better than most," he said. Who better knew her than the father of her child? "What should I do now?"

Varro mulled the question quietly for a few moments before answering. "She needs to know nothing's going to happen tonight between you and that woman, but don't even think of approaching her. Let her cool off. Come up with an excuse for her carer to stay with you for a while, show her you dismiss Frida, and accidentally let it slip that you arranged the whole thing to make Alexandra jealous."

"Won't that make me look like a weak fool to her?"

"Better that than a betrayer, believe me."

It was a good suggestion, and Darius's foolish brain could think of no better remedy. "Thanks for the advice. You're a useful man to have around when you aren't being an arse and exiling me."

Varro let out a breath. "I caused Alexandra a lot of pain that I wish I hadn't. Now she denies herself happiness. I owe it to her to advise you however I can."

To think, if Varro hadn't got her pregnant, Darius might have had a chance with her.

"What happened between you two?" Darius asked. The reason she seemed more bitter than Varro by the failure of the relationship had always intrigued him.

"I tried my best, but…feelings don't always bend to our will, and I just wasn't in love with her like she deserved." His pitch almost sounded regretful, like he'd somehow failed.

That explanation certainly made sense of Lex's animosity; hearing that must have been like having your heart frozen with algor. Was that why she punished the rakkan with ignorance of his daughter?

The Warlord was being so amicable, so helpful. Did Darius owe him the truth he'd concealed for so long? Did Cynthia have a right to know her father?

"Varro…" But Darius's voice trailed off as he realised the gravity of what he'd been about to say. This wasn't his secret to share.

"Yes?"

"Do you…" But there must be some way to repair whatever had gone on between them. "Have you ever thought about clearing the air with Lex? There may be things you two should discuss."

"Like what?" Something changed in Varro's face then, but there wasn't anything Darius could glean about the rakkan's thoughts from it. There was just an alertness about him, as if they'd suddenly drawn swords.

"Nothing particular," Darius said. "But I may need you both to work together."

Varro's obsidian eyes pierced him. "Is that all?"

"Yes," Darius said. "And thank you for your advice."

"Really? You've nothing else to say?"

"No. Why? Do you want a peck on the cheek too?"

The Black Warlord's face reddened and stiffened with strain. Something was on his mind, and Darius suspected he didn't want to know what.

"That's all," he said. "Why don't you retire and—"

"For over a year, I've waited." Varro stood. "Maybe I deserve this after what I did to you, but does the child deserve it?"

Darius's blood ran cold as if algor had filled his veins. "Child?"

"Don't feign ignorance. Do you think me as foolish as you?"

Darius suddenly became aware that the Twin Blades were out of his reach. "Varro, don't forget who I—"

"Did you think I didn't notice how Alexandra treated that little girl she brought back from Laltos? Do you both think I don't know the difference in the look she gives family as opposed to those in her stewardship?"

"I—"

"Well, I do." Varro's breath carried such heat Darius winced.

He stood and backed up a step. "This is between you and Lex. I've kept myself out of it for that reason."

Varro looked away, allowing coldness to return to his features. "I'm disappointed in you both, and I'm tired of waiting for one of you to do the right thing. I really do wish you both well, but I can only hold my tongue for so long."

Darius risked a step forward. "Speak with Lex. It's time you worked through whatever issues remain."

"She won't." The Black Warlord's voice was lifeless and defeated, such a stark contrast to the man he was on the battlefield that Darius was prepared to risk pushing him.

"Isn't your daughter worth it?" Darius asked.

Judging by Varro's face, the reminder brought him physical pain. "Alexandra is not one to push. She must choose of her own accord."

In Darius's experience, that was too true. "I'd offer to help, but I'm not sure she'd listen to me at the moment."

"Is the girl at least safe?" Varro asked.

Safe… Was there such a thing? "For now. She'll be safer once the King and this goman are dead."

"Then I'll do all I can to see it done."

"If you…" Darius's thought trailed off because Varro turned and left the room without another word, leaving Darius to contemplate the multiple new problems he'd acquired besides the war. Sometimes, Lex's policy of avoiding relationships made so much sense; it gave a person the luxury of focusing on one less thing or even several.

He retrieved the Blades, then left the throne room with Lyra and made his way to his bedchamber. Outside, he ordered one of the guards to find Nasrin and bring her to him, then entered to find Frida resting on his most comfortable chair with a cup of his favourite firewater in her hand, a gift Gorgias of all people had given him back in Margalvia. For all the man's faults, he knew his booze well.

"Glad you've made yourself comfortable." Darius tossed the Twin Blades down with such force they hissed in anger.

Frida winced. "My plan made things worse, didn't it?"

"She seemed jealous," Darius said, "and furious."

"I thought you said nothing was happening between the pair of you."

"It isn't. I… I don't see much point in trying to understand why she acts as she does. I need damage control now."

"Then perhaps I'd best leave you alone." She took her cup of firewater and downed it in one.

He grunted. "That was a gift, you know."

She smiled without a regret, and something told him she'd been alone in a room with many powerful men before to be so relaxed. What secrets she must have held in that mind about Xavala… Which reminded him that he had more than Lex to worry about.

He collapsed into a chair beside her. "Before you go, I need to know what you learned about the Torians we saw entering the city."

"Ah." She tipped her cup to lick out the last drops of firewater. "Is that all we should discuss?"

"What else would there be?"

Now her eyes narrowed playfully. "Is she the one who doesn't want children?"

"… I never said anything about anyone not wanting children."

"You didn't need to. You were most curious about how the male slaves avoided getting the algus pregnant. I fit the pieces of the puzzle together."

"Aren't you insightful." It seemed he'd chosen a good person to win over to his cause. Too many had turned out to be lacking in wit, which probably shouldn't have surprised him considering fools attracted fools.

"Would you like to know the answer?" Frida asked.

"That depends. Are you trying to gain favour with me?"

"Of course. Isn't that what any sensible person would do in my situation?"

"No. A sensible person stays as far away from a ruler as possible and says as little as they need to. Most are unstable, violent creatures."

She sat back and gave him a look only an equal would. "Are *you*?"

That was a question he couldn't be sure of, although there were certainly times when he'd been unstable; "violent" went without saying.

"Why aren't you more afraid of me?" he asked.

She smiled and poured herself another generous cup of firewater. "You freed me from that city, and if you were going to harm me, you'd have done it already."

"Fair enough. So, will you tell me what you found out in Xavala?"

"I know you want to know about the male slaves first." She leaned forward, hushing her voice. "Some call it a potion. You can get it in quite a few places in the Empire, but the Menarans have the best reputation for it. They suffer far fewer fatalities."

Darius swallowed, never having considered such a remedy would mean risking one's life. "How few is 'fewer'?"

She shrugged. "I'm no herbalist. Out of the men sent from the Silk City, half didn't return, but they could have been sold on. It's impossible to say. There is an alternative, of course."

"What's that?"

She made a cutting motion with her fingers.

Darius scoffed and crossed his legs with a wince. "What am I, a farm animal?" As far as he was concerned, removing parts of his manhood wasn't an option. But what she'd said piqued his curiosity. "This 'potion'… Can a man still…?"

"Of course. Otherwise, they wouldn't give it to the slaves."

That made sense. "And do any male algus take it?"

Frida shrugged. "Not that I've heard."

That probably meant it was too dangerous to be worth it. Without knowing how lethal this remedy was, it was too great a risk. But part of him couldn't help but be intrigued to look into it further.

"Can you give me a contact in Menara? Maybe I'll inquire one day."

She gave him the details of a reputed medicine man, then they moved on to discuss what she'd heard of the Torians entering the Silk City, during which Nasrin joined them. He pretended to have an injury to his knee to give her an excuse to remain there massaging and flexing it while Frida continued talking business. So far, nothing had changed in Xavala, but that was only more worrying. The King had a goman.

"You're sure it was the Orator?" Darius asked.

Frida nodded.

That couldn't be good. Whatever was happening, they'd best accelerate their plans, and that meant speaking with Lex.

Frida took another sip of her drink, but she hadn't even swallowed before she coughed and sprayed him with it, seeming to have taken it down the wrong pipe.

"Thanks," he said, wiping his face dry. "Had enough? That's strong stuff, not pissy ale."

She placed her cup down with a wince. "Don't know. Caught in my throat, and it's turning over my belly something nasty."

It was probably a good thing Nasrin was here to help settle her stomach, then. But then again, he'd rather Nasrin helped him find Lex tonight and perhaps calm her temper.

"Nasrin." He turned to the carer. "Have you seen Lex recently?"

The carer dug her thumb hard under his kneecap, sending a jolt of pain despite it not being injured. Then she gave him a look which told him not only had she seen the algus but she'd also been filled in on what had happened at the assembly.

Darius cursed. "I only invited Frida here to make Lex jealous. How can I patch things up with her?"

Nasrin eyed him suspiciously but eventually seemed to believe him and sighed. "Damned if I know. She's not the forgiving type. But I suppose if she believes you never intended to do anything, maybe she'll get over it in a few months."

*Months?* Was this mistake that bad? Or was she that bad at holding on to grudges? After dwelling on the questions a little, he knew the grudge thing was definitely a part of it—just look at Varro.

"I suppose I'd better face her sooner rather than later."

"Rather you than me," Frida said, voice still hoarse.

"Not much choice. Sounds like something's going on in Xavala, so I need to pick her brain." He stood, grabbed the Twin Blades, and ushered Nasrin with him. "Come. Let's go and find her. Frida, go find a tent when you're finished drinking my best firewater."

The two made towards the door when Frida began heaving again behind him, and by the sound of it, this time she was expelling far more than a cough. Some people just couldn't hold their liquor.

He turned back with a shake of his head. "You'd better clean up your—" He froze when he saw her on all fours on the ground, her mouth spilling liquid a deep shade of red.

"By the Goddess!" Nasrin squealed and hurried towards the woman.

Darius reacted slower but reached the woman before Nasrin, took hold, and felt her tremble and threaten to break out into a fit.

"What the hell…" He stared at the cup, suspecting immediately what poison this was. The King had tried it before. But his tasters had tested the bottle that morning.

"We need charcoal!" Nasrin pulled the woman down to the floor and onto her side before scraping her mouth clear.

"Guards!" Darius roared so loudly it would wake up the entire fort.

Two rakkan legionnaires came inside and gaped at the dying woman.

"Charcoal!" Darius shouted, and they both set off at once, knowing the drill by now.

The woman's shakes became violent, and Darius had to hold her down as her hands clawed at Nasrin's face.

"How long do we have before she's too far gone?" he asked.

But when Nasrin didn't answer, he knew he was asking the wrong question.

"Is there hope?" he tried.

The carer's face told of the lack thereof. His first taster had been lost the same way.

He pulled up the woman's tunic at the waist and saw what he feared—a deep-purple shadow spreading under the skin on her stomach.

"Oh my…" Nasrin choked back tears.

"Is it hell's gold?" Darius asked.

The carer nodded. That meant Frida's end would be painful; hell's gold was a mineral poison from Mount Psilos that took time to kill.

"How can we help her?" he asked.

But Nasrin's only answer was a wince and shake of her head.

He'd suspected it was too late but needed someone with more expertise to confirm it.

"All we can do is…" Nasrin trailed off and exchanged a glance that let him know they were both thinking the same thing. With grief etched at the wrinkles by her eyes, she gave a nod, then turned away.

At this stage, Frida's stomach had been eaten through, and the toxin would be pulsing through her veins. Charcoal wouldn't do a thing, and although trace amounts of hell's gold relieved pain, the woman was clearly far from relief. Only Darius could offer that to her now.

"I'm sorry, Frida," he whispered as he shifted his hands to her neck. A sharp twist was all it took, but the sound of the crack made Nasrin flinch.

Frida's trembling stopped almost instantly, and she stilled as Darius placed her head down gently, returning it to a natural angle.

The doors flew open and one guard came in with a handful of charcoal and Sulla right behind him.

"What the hell?" The Militia Chief gaped first at the woman, then at the empty cups, and finally at Darius. "Don't tell me you—"

"I'm fine." Darius stood and wiped the bloody vomit from his trousers. "It was the firewater, and I last drank from that bottle yesterday. I'd be long dead if it were poisoned then."

Sulla breathed and closed his eyes with what looked like a prayer. Perhaps he was right to thank a higher power. Darius could easily have drunk that, and if it hadn't been for his distracted mind, he might have been watching her right now in the knowledge that he was only moments from joining her in death.

"This is too damn close," Sulla said. "How the hell did someone poison your bottle? Who gave it to you?"

Nothing good could come of giving Gorgias's name to Sulla.

"It wasn't poisoned when I opened it," Darius said. "This was done later." He fixed his attention on the guard. "Who's been in here recently?"

"No one but the woman, Overlord. I swear," the rakkan replied.

The room did have a window and was on the top floor, so someone or their escort could have entered via the roof and hidden their tracks well. But whoever had done the deed or how they'd done it wasn't Darius's main concern. His anger at his enemies magnified, the Twin Blades heating so much he felt them through his trousers.

But another more disturbing thought occurred to him, one that made him grab the hilts of his swords. If they'd broken into here, they could have got anywhere.

"Nasrin," he said. "We need to find Lex. Now!"

# 18

## Lex – Gap of Aphatos

Lex ripped back the flap of her tent so fiercely the fabric almost tore, and she stormed inside without even bothering to search for a lamp to light the dark place. Her walk around the camp hadn't settled her temper; it only reminded her how loud and crass most of the Viridians were. Today was certainly not a day where she could hold her nose and tolerate them.

Familiar pains began to sting her hip again, reminding her of her need for more tea. *Great.* Now she had to go out again and find a fire or a rakkan she could stomach to speak to.

With a groan of frustration, she just about made out her bed in the dark and collapsed onto it, wondering whether cold tea would be effective enough. But that wasn't the only thing on her mind.

She grabbed the sheets and squeezed them as hard as she wanted to wring Darius's neck. How dare he say he loved her and then do this? Why did he have to utter those words? Why couldn't he have just stayed silent as usual if this was how he planned on carrying on?

"Bastard," she growled.

"I'm not that bad when you get to know me." The sudden male voice had Lex bolting upright, reaching for her dagger, and flaring algor to shed blue light on a strange man that was reclined on her chair in the corner, squinting from the other side of the tent.

The man didn't move as she swept across, using all of her algus speed, and she only halted when her knife pricked the man's neck.

"Who are you?" she said. He certainly wasn't wearing the clothes of a man from Laltos; his were old and torn, dark as a shadow yet a natural mesh of green shades that would have melded him into whatever undergrowth he hid within. Few people dressed like this, and none of them brought welcome greetings.

The man's eyes were the only part of him that moved, young but clearly accustomed to threats as they focused carefully on her weapon without fear.

"There's no need for that," he said. "I'm not an algus, so I couldn't fight you even if I wanted to."

"Like I'm going to trust that," Lex said, though if he'd wanted to harm her, he wouldn't have wasted the element of surprise. "Who are you?"

"I'm Javad. Nice to meet you, Alexandra."

It was a slave's name, but he hadn't the look of one, so she pressed the knife a little harder to his neck. "Don't speak too soon. Why are you here?"

The man's eyes flitted to the side. "I brought you a gift."

Lex couldn't make out anything in her peripheral vision other than darkness, so she risked a glance sideways. On the floor, rolled up to the side of her tent and almost lost amongst the rug on the ground, lay a tied and gagged man, who looked to be unconscious. His clothes were similar in plainness to Javad's but lacked the same intricate lattice of colours.

"And who's that?" she asked.

"A very dangerous man. Perhaps this will explain..." Javad carefully reached into his pocket and withdrew a small slip of parchment.

Keeping the dagger biting his skin, she snatched it off him and opened it to reveal only her name written along with the official seal of the Regent of Eluthia. She'd heard of but never seen such orders before—they were given to the assassins of Eluthia's highest order. If it was a forgery, it was a good one, but she'd met a few that could pull off such a replica of the seal in her life.

"You think I believe your lies?" she said. "An assassin would have destroyed this before leaving Eluthia, yet you expect me to believe he had this with him?"

Javad swallowed as blood trickled from under the point of her knife. "No. This order wasn't his; it was mine."

Of all the lies he could have told, she hadn't expected that. "Then you do seek to kill me. Eluthia's assassins never reveal their marks." She bet the man thought he could outsmart and overpower her after gleaning some information.

"If it had been anyone but me, you'd already be dead," Javad said with an arrogant lift of his chin. "But I'm sparing your life and repaying a long-overdue debt."

"I don't forget faces," Lex said, "and I've never seen yours. You owe me nothing."

"It's not you I owe the debt to." The man spoke with unreasonable stubbornness and almost made Lex believe him.

"Darius?" she asked.

Javad nodded as best he could with a dagger pressed to his throat.

After a few moments' pause, she concluded that if he were going to try something, he would have done so already, so she backed away to a safe distance with her weapon still ready.

Javad sighed and wiped the blood from his neck. "I've heard rumours of your relationship with Darius in the far east, so when I heard your name would soon make our list, I did everything I could to get assigned the job. I knew I wouldn't follow through with my task."

"And risk your life?" she said, knowing well that the city was as ruthless to traitors as all the others. "What debt do you owe Darius?"

"Something much greater than my life." But Javad pressed his mouth shut to any elaboration on that.

"So, if you're here to warn me," Lex said, "what's this man doing here?"

Javad looked at the restrained figure with a raise of his eyebrows, as if he'd forgotten. "Yes, our friend here… Eluthia's assassins are almost impossible to spot or track, mingling themselves amongst your men or even the wild when necessary. But luckily for you, this man is no Eluthian.

"If I had to guess, he's Torian, and an easy hunter to spot for someone trained. I noticed him lurking around your tent, and he couldn't have been up to anything good. I found a pouch of hell's gold on him along with something foreign and nonlethal, so I presume he had a job here. But I think I got to him first. I assume either you or the Slayer is the target, as I struggle to think of anyone else."

That was certainly a fear Lex immediately shared, yet she wasn't sure how to react to this or whether to believe everything this stranger claimed.

As Lex deliberated over how to proceed, the sound of rapid footsteps grew outside, and soon after, Darius charged in with such haste he almost brought the tent down. His eyes bulged with fear as he first locked onto her and then Javad facing her.

The Eluthian's face dropped when Darius bared his teeth and readied his sword with a roar. "Who are you?"

Javad held up his hands as the tent flaps sprang open again, and this time, Nasrin and Lyra charged in with as much furore as Darius had.

"A friend," Javad said quickly. "I haven't harmed her; ask her."

Darius looked to Lex with a madness she'd only ever seen in him after waking up from her fever.

"It's true," she said. "He's been telling me an interesting tale."

"We met before," Javad added hurriedly, "in Menara. You don't…remember?"

Darius shook his head. "Got hit in the head by a goman. Very convenient for you, isn't it?"

Javad frowned and seemed lost for words, so Lex spoke again and relayed what Javad had said—except the part about him being an Eluthian assassin after *her*—while Darius glared at the man and seemed one flinch away from lunging and hacking him to pieces. But he held his temper enough for Lex to finish.

"And you trust him?" Darius asked.

"Of course not," she said with a scoff. "But he could have easily ambushed me or poisoned me. There's at least some truth in what he says."

Darius murmured to himself at the last remarks, taking a few moments to form coherent words. "This certainly isn't a coincidence. My firewater was poisoned today. Someone's dead, and I'm lucky not to be."

Javad's face paled. "Then I was too late. I'm sorry, Slayer."

Darius's eyes narrowed. "Not as sorry as you may soon be. If your slumbering friend turns out to have a different story when he wakes up, you'll have to answer to me."

But Lex lost interest in these strangers after what Darius had just said.

"What do you mean, 'poisoned'?" she asked. "Who? And did you drink any? Did you eat or drink anything else?" If his firewater had been poisoned, there could be more. "Nasrin!" The squeal of her voice took even her by surprise, but she didn't care. "Get him some charcoal. I don't care if he feels well, he needs—"

"Lex…" Darius lifted a hand to her. "Relax. I'm fine. I'm more concerned with what you've been eating and drinking. Did you—"

"When's the last time you drank?" she asked.

"Long enough ago that I'd already be dead if I were poisoned," Darius said. "And you?"

"I'm fine," Lex said. It was too late to do anything now, which probably meant the same was true for Darius, regardless of how much she wanted him to chomp on charcoal even if it only shrank his risk by an infinitesimal amount.

"We'll know for sure who's at risk when he wakes up." Darius gave the unconscious man a kick. "We'll get the truth out of him."

"But…" Javad's voice faltered. "He won't talk. Even if he's not Eluthian, he'll be trained to withstand torture and worse without breaking his silence."

"Then I'd hate to be you right now."

For the first time, Javad's eyes betrayed fear, and they suddenly searched the faces in the tent, only seeming to relax when they reached Lyra. "Her! She will remember me!"

Everyone turned their attention to Lyra, whose amber eyes hadn't blinked at the man.

"You're claiming to be a friend of my escort now?" Darius said.

Javad shook his head. "Not a friend, but it's because of her we met in the first place. Does she remember Menara? … Or here!" He ripped up the sleeve of his tunic. "Perhaps she remembers my scent."

If Javad was lying, he certainly was setting himself up to fail. For the first time, Lex suspected he was being truthful after all.

Darius looked down at his escort and shrugged. "Up to you."

The panther regarded the man for a few moments before stalking forward and arching her neck towards his exposed arm, taking a sniff. Then she quickly turned away while Darius's frown deepened.

"Interesting…" he muttered.

"So?" Lex asked.

Javad's eyebrows rose in anticipation, and Darius answered while pulling back his weapon. "She recognises him, doesn't feel threatened."

That was enough for Lex, and she too lowered her dagger. Although an escort didn't have the cognition and memory of a human, they could at least distinguish friend from foe and remember such.

"I'm glad we cleared that up." Javad dared to stand slowly. "I have to say I'd expected more gratitude for saving your lives."

"And what did I do for you," Darius asked, "to deserve such kindness?"

Javad paused, and when he answered, his voice was noticeably quieter. "Even if a goman hadn't got to you, I doubt you'd have remembered, might not even have believed the person you met that day would go on to become an assassin. It was just another day for the Slayer, but for me, it was…both the best and worst day of my life."

Whatever had happened, Lex struggled to think of anything that warranted such a sacrifice on this assassin's part except for a child. Had Darius saved Javad's son or daughter? Perhaps they were hidden, and that's why the man was being so cagey.

"I should return to Eluthia," Javad said, "and come up with a story for my failure. I could lie and say Alexandra is dead, but it wouldn't take them long to discover the truth. Be assured that I won't be the last assassin sent. Stay vigilant, both of you."

"Wait, it's *Eluthia* that wants Lex dead?" Darius gaped at her.

Gritting her teeth, she nodded while turning her attention to the unconscious man and thinking of a way to move the conversation on. It was true that assassins had never been broken, but she hadn't heard stories of rakkans trying.

Javad spied her watching the man. "Be sure you don't let him go."

"He tried to kill me," Darius said. "Trust me, he hasn't long to live."

"Good. Then I'll be on my way."

"Before you go, wait outside. I have a few more questions for you."

Lex considered whether to thwart an interrogation, but she doubted Javad knew anything of the reasons she'd been chosen as a mark. She'd just be another name to him, not knowing anything more than he should, so she allowed him to leave without objection while Darius turned to her, a thousand questions probably on his mind.

"Want to explain why Eluthia is sending assassins after you?" he asked. "Anything to do with your gold problem?"

Slaughter was in his voice, and she couldn't let him be distracted. There was still nothing he could do for her other than focus on the Silk City, so she'd tell him everything once her debts were sorted and when he wasn't inviting other women into his bed.

"It's all in hand," she said. "I'll get more guards."

He opened his mouth as if about to argue but seemed to think better of it. Instead, he said, "Fine. You're sure you're all right?"

"Well enough to remember you're a bastard, so feel free to run back to your harlot."

The man's face fell. "She's dead. Poisoned."

Lex was lost for words, and was a little guilty that her first thought was wondering why Darius had offered that woman a drink from his personal supply, something he only did with people close to him. But regardless of Lex's anger, she knew no woman deserved that end.

"I'll let Nasrin fill you in on the details," Darius said. "In the meantime, I'll find you a taster for all your food and drink and have my guards watch you at all times."

Lex scoffed. "I'm quite capable of—"

"And don't think you're taking part in the attack on Xavala."

As if she needed any more reason to slap him. Did he think he could command her?

But before she could respond, he left the tent with Lyra at his heel.

Only Nasrin remained with a sheepish look, but her bloodstained clothes made Lex reluctant to ask for any details of what had happened with Darius's woman.

"Sit down," Lex said. "Have..." She'd been about to offer a drink, but that definitely wasn't wise at the moment. "Are you all right?"

Nasrin nodded and sat on the bed. "Just a little glum. You never get used to seeing people die like that."

"I can imagine." Lex sat and wrapped an arm around the carer's shoulders. "Was anyone else hurt?"

"Not that I know of. That poor woman… Darius had only—"

"It's fine," Lex interjected. "You don't need to go over it."

"But… You'll want to know this."

Would she really? Wouldn't it only make her more annoyed? Not many scenarios would make her less angry with the man, even if he had just come within a sip of death.

But Nasrin sat up and seemed eager to spill what she'd seen, and Lex was so exhausted from both injury and these events that she wasn't sure she had the resolve to deny her.

"Fine," Lex said with a groan. "Tell me."

# 19

## Rufus – South of Xavala

The last few weeks had hardly been enough time to properly plan an assault on the Silk City; Laltos's fall had taken months of preparation plus rolls and rolls of parchment with countless details from spies to lay the groundwork. Now Rufus had to make do with what he had, even if it was just a contingency in the event their uprising failed.

But did the Overlord really think Rufus intended to let his men be chased like hares by the howling dogs of the Silk City?

Not on Rufus's watch. Even if not called upon to assault the city, he wouldn't just draw out Xavala's armies during the revolt; he'd reduce them to ash and blood. Then his brothers and all the warlords would see him for the leader he truly was, and whatever happened within the city would be irrelevant. Rufus would have won Darius Xavala.

As he marched with the vanguard of his army, behind him, the thumps of thousands of boots coalesced into a metallic rumble as the Viridian Legion marched across the plains towards the city. Dusk had fallen and painted a red hue across the sky that would soon be mirrored on the battlefield. Clouds had parted with no threat of rain, and the lands that had shaken so recently hadn't a crack this far north, leaving a vast untouched expanse that any horse would love galloping across. Conditions couldn't have been more inviting for the Xavalans, knee-high grass swaying with a mix of tawny and green that brought peace and calm to the soon-to-be-grisly land.

Alongside him, his brothers strode, armoured and ready for war but yet to issue his commands to their centuries.

"Are your men wearing the clothes I ordered?" Rufus asked but already knew the answer.

"The green cloaks?" Piso snorted. "Cloaks only slow my men down and block their senses."

Overhead, one of the falcons screeched as it dove and attacked a lower-flying bird, possibly an escort, possibly wild. But Rufus's Subdued rid the skies of both. The Silk City couldn't be allowed to see what he was planning.

Another bird approached, and one of his Subdued took her bow, aimed, and loosed an arrow that hit and sent a burst of feathers into the air.

"Distribute the cloaks at once," Rufus said. "The ditches ahead are a good place for your men to hide and wait." With cloaks melding them into the greenery, those centuries would ambush when the cavalry gave chase after Rufus's first wave feigned an attack then retreated.

Pollio took off his helmet and spat. "Ditches? Do we hide like mice now?"

"We'll be the laughing stock of the legions," Piso said. "I won't subject my men to that."

The Subdued and other commanders glanced sideways, probably sniffing for any weakness in the face of disobedience.

Rufus's father never had to deal with this; he'd crushed the skulls of any that talked like that to him, whether family or not, and alike the late Viridian Warlord, Rufus couldn't back down now and instead had to channel his father's energy. Both he and his brothers knew where this kind of talk would inevitably lead; perhaps that's why they'd chosen now, on the battlefield, where there were no overlords or saviours to come to Rufus's rescue. This might have been orchestrated, and he had no choice but to rise to the challenge.

"Pollio," Rufus said. "You will take command of Piso's centuries."

"What?" Piso said.

"Piso. You're relieved of command."

The twins halted, but Rufus continued walking with no intention of deviating either physically or mentally from the path he'd chosen.

"You can't be serious." Piso hurried to catch up and tried to shove Rufus from behind.

But the Viridian Warlord felt the air shifting on his neck, spun just in time for his brother's fingers to only graze him.

Rufus glared at the rakkan. "You should be thankful you missed. If you hadn't, I'd have you crucified in this damned field."

Piso growled inside his helmet, a ringing metallic sound that their father had often utilised. Out of the two twins, Piso was physically the stronger, so Pollio was Rufus's best hope in a confrontation; plus, there was the added possibility that Pollio could be talked around.

Rufus turned to face Pollio. "Do you have an issue with leading those centuries?"

The rakkan looked between his brothers but eventually settled his glower on Rufus. "I do."

"Really?" Rufus said. "We must do this now? The Xavalan cavalry could emerge from the city at any moment."

Pollio's lips curled, and Rufus realised his brother cared not one jot about this battle; his mind was not for turning. Unfortunately for the twins, though, Rufus wasn't one to see a threat on the horizon and not have a contingency.

"I'll warn you only once," Rufus said calmly. "Don't force me to do this. I'll need you in this battle."

"Well, we don't need you," Piso said.

"I wasn't talking to you." Rufus didn't cease staring down Pollio.

"I won't ask my men to bury themselves in foxholes," Pollio said. "They'll fight and die on their feet if fate deems it."

"There's something to be admired of foxes." Rufus stepped back and flicked back his cloak behind the hilt of his sword—the signal. "They're cunning. They don't fall for traps and will find a way through whatever obstacles are put before them."

Piso scoffed and ripped his gladius from its scabbard. "But they don't live forever."

The evening air filled with a ring of steel as every Subdued slid free their swords and pointed them at the twin rakkans. At Rufus's right, Gorgias stepped forward, his blade already shimmering with a faint blue tinge of algor.

There was a good reason Rufus had volunteered to oversee much of the Subdued programme; not only were they fiercely loyal to Viridia, but they'd give their lives for Rufus himself. Darius's man was just an added bonus on an already sturdy reinforcement Rufus had built.

Pollio grimaced. "You'd dare let outsiders interfere with a leadership challenge? You know the law. Even our brothers-in-arms cannot interfere. It's unum ad unum."

"You will die before the challenge has left your lips." Gorgias twisted his sword, sending a purple glint down it under the dusk sky.

Algus were fast, but that fast? Rufus couldn't be certain, but it wasn't like he had much choice but to rely on them. Unless his brothers saw sense.

The other commanders' faces were mostly obscured by their helmets, but Rufus knew their thoughts just from the slight shakes of their heads. Hiding behind humans was a somewhat cowardly thing to do, but this wasn't much different to hiding behind Darius, the only reason he was the Viridian Warlord.

The whole rakkan system struck Rufus as foolish anyway. What did a man's skills one-on-one prove? That he was a great fighter, not a great leader. One day, he'd hopefully convince Darius to change rakkan ways.

"Pollio," Rufus said. "You will take command of Piso's centuries and hide them ready for the ambush. Do you have an issue with that?"

His brother's jaw tensed, opened and closed as if chewing his tongue so that his next words were bloody.

"... Warlord?" a voice called from behind.

Rufus didn't dare take his gaze from his brothers, but one by one, the other commanders suddenly turned their attention towards the Silk City with grunts. Had the gates opened? Was the cavalry already galloping across the plains? What dreadful timing.

"Warlord... Something's wrong." This time it was a commander fixated on the city.

Even Piso and Pollio turned to see, and only then did Rufus allow his attention to shift.

But he found no horses or men in the fields. Instead, black smoke rose from the Silk City in so many places it created a cloud of gloom over the place, cursing those below with shadow. Had the revolt started ahead of time? Surely not.

"We should call off the attack." Gorgias gaped at the burning city.

Rufus suspected Darius would agree with the man, but this could be the opportune moment to assault the city. They shouldn't waste it.

"Warlord…" Gorgias gave him a stern look, a warning that this decision was above Rufus's rank. And as bitter that fact was to swallow, Rufus could ill afford to get on Darius's bad side.

"Send word to the Overlord," Rufus concluded, "and make camp. We'll await instructions here."

# 20

## Lex – Gap of Aphatos

Lex dodged as she almost collided headfirst with a rushing algus.

"Apologies," the man called before zipping along the muddy trails between the tents.

So many were getting ready for battle, but Darius had forbidden her from joining them. Did he think he had the authority to command her? It wasn't like she could go into the Silk City anyway, but hopefully he knew that she wasn't going there because of her own problems, not because of his commands. But that would involve divulging the full extent of her problems to him.

The first payment of gold had made it safely to her rendezvous point with the Eluthians, so their assassins would sit at home with their knives sheathed for now. But it wasn't long until the next payment was due. And where was that gold going to come from? At this rate, she might have to bargain with Eluthia to accept kuraminium instead of gold.

Interrogation of the assassin had revealed nothing before he'd somehow swallowed poison, just as Javad had predicted, leaving Lex no choice but to conclude Javad had been telling the truth. Perhaps it was time to admit defeat and explain the whole situation to Darius. After all, he wouldn't get mad at her after his shenanigans of late. She could get away with more than usual, and after Nasrin had explained what happened with the Xavalan woman, her rage at him had cooled.

No sooner had she thought of the man than she rounded a tent and came face to face with him, his tan skin slick with sweat and grime. Although usually wearing armour, today he donned only a tunic and cloak, looking nothing like the overlord he was apart from the domineering swords at his waist.

"There you are," he said. "I've been looking for you for days."

"Really?" Of course, she knew. She'd needed some time to herself, and now that Eluthia had been placated for the time being, she'd slipped the guards he left spying on her, avoided any of her closest allies recently just so he couldn't track her down, and had even travelled within the camps masking her scent so Lyra couldn't trace her.

"Rufus is marching on Xavala," he said. "I'm to leave soon."

"Then I wish you well. Be careful. Don't risk your life for anyone."

Her sincere words seemed to fill his expression with sorrow and shame. "Look, about that woman…I didn't—"

"It's none of my business what you get up to in your own time."

"But I didn't 'get up' to anything. I only invited her there to…" He swallowed, looked at his muddy boots sheepishly.

"To what?" she asked. Nasrin had already told her, but she wouldn't waste an opportunity to make the man admit it to her face. Such discomfort was a suitable punishment for acting foolish.

"To make you jealous," he said.

It had worked, and the fact would be clear to him as well. Perhaps that was why she was still annoyed.

Living a life of temptation was difficult enough as it was without having him pursuing her. Perhaps shifting his focus onto his relationship with her late sister would make him feel awkward enough to leave her be.

"Open your tunic," she said.

His brow furrowed, but he obliged to reveal the necklace he never removed. She grasped it, but instead of the two keepsakes she'd expected, she found only a lump of aeternus.

"Where's Selene's bear claw?" she asked.

Darius murmured, "Gone."

"You lost it?"

"I gave it back to her before…" He pulled the necklace back inside his tunic and re-covered himself, holding his hand over it for a few moments as if seeking comfort.

"Do you regret it?" Now Lex wasn't just trying to focus his attention on something else. She was curious; just what were his feelings on the woman he now never spoke of?

After a few moments of silence, he answered, "No. It was a relic of the past, and the past is where it belongs."

"Then why carry Brutus's aeternus?"

"Because I don't wish to forget Brutus. He didn't betray me." His gaze dropped to Lex's chest, to the Agathos pendant that he'd returned to her. "I miss that," he whispered. "Didn't you say it was given to leaders?"

"It is. I suppose now that you're Agathos's instrument in the Empire, you'll want me to buy you one."

He shook his head. "I don't miss it for religious reasons."

Now that Lex had calmed down, she regretted demanding it back. The fact he'd always worn it had brought some peace and satisfaction that was now lost, but she couldn't return it. That would only encourage him to keep his attention on her when he should be focused on war.

After a few moments of silence, he next spoke with a stony face. "May I have it back?"

The nerve of the man to ask.

"I don't think that's wise," she said.

"What if I were to command you to return it?"

Lex returned his stone-faced stare. "You know I don't answer to you."

He stepped forward, expression stiffening with a coldness that clashed with the red beginning to consume his eyes.

"What are you doing?" She stepped back, shielding the pendant with her off-hand.

But he took another pace, mere inches from her. "I'm not giving up, for a change. Are you holding the figurine to give it back to me?"

She shook her head. The man before her now was more like the old Darius than at any other moment, the stiff features, pitiless, masking his true intentions in a manner that made Lex uneasy.

"That's fine," he said. "I haven't commanded you to return it. Yet."

"Just try it," she said. "See what I give you when you do."

He lowered his head, breathed deep. "What if I go to my death today? Won't you allow me to die with a memento of you?"

She smacked him on the arm. "Don't even tempt fate by saying that. Make sure you return to me."

"To you?" He lifted his gaze. "Am I yours?"

"You know what I mean."

"I'm afraid I don't." As if finally submitting, his eyes regained their alluring darkness and he smiled. "Don't worry. I have no intention of leaving you."

"Overlord!" An algus tore between the tents in a blur and skidded to a halt beside the two of them. "We've had word from our algus in Xavala." The angst on his face told Lex this wasn't good news.

"What's wrong?" Darius asked.

"The slaves… They've been executed."

"All of them?" Lex asked. How could that be?

"A lot. Our contacts were rounded up first, then the other slaves began to rebel. But there were too many algus there. Many have been burned in the squares, but some have been…blood eagled."

"What does that mean?" Darius asked.

The description was so hideous Lex couldn't bear to recall it. "I'll explain later," she said. "Is there anything of the resistance left?"

The man shook his head. "Our algus that survived have fled. There's nothing left in that city of our support other than blood."

Before Lex could string together a sensible response to the news, Darius stormed off towards his quarters with a grunt.

Lex took off after him. "Where are you going?"

"I want to see it for myself."

"You mean go into the city? Do you think you'll get in?" Even Darius couldn't take down a city on his own. That place would be teeming with Xavalan and Torian algus. This had to be part of the goman's planning; perhaps it was a trap to lure Darius in.

Lex rushed in front of him and tried to halt his strides as he entered a building, but he didn't slow a fraction and instead lifted her out of the way.

"Please, Darius," she said. "Be smart about this."

"It seems being smart doesn't come naturally to me." He traversed a long corridor and reached his bedchamber, flew inside, and began putting on his cuirass. "I'll go to join Rufus, and we'll attack the city."

In a few moments, he'd be armoured and rushing towards Xavala, possibly to get himself killed by a heavily prepared defence; then she'd be out of options. There was only one way she could think to stop him.

She yanked the figurine from her neck and slapped it into his chest. "You can have it if you stay."

He froze with his armour half over his head before slowly sliding it off. "You're that afraid for me?"

"Of you rushing in without a plan? Why wouldn't I be?"

His studied her face as if more intimate knowledge of what was going on in her mind would reveal itself. Whatever he saw in her, he didn't react to it and merely shook his head. "I don't want it as a bribe."

She gently closed her hand around the figurine and stepped back, trying to think of other ways to make him listen.

"But maybe you're right," he added. "I shouldn't act rashly when our enemies seem to know so much. I'll send word for Rufus to retreat and summon the assembly. Make sure the Chief Priest is there."

Something about the way Darius said "Chief Priest" betrayed anger and resentment. As relieved as Lex was that he'd listened to reason, a new worry gripped her. Surely Darius couldn't blame Aran for whatever had happened in the Silk City.

# 21

## King's Orator – Xavala, the Silk City

*The Silk City is doomed.* Ophelia repeated the beginning of the King's last message in her head several times while she stalked Xavala's streets. By now, no slave dared set foot outside without their master or mistress, and the fetor of burning flesh still lingered, carrying a terror more intimate and infectious than any other. It was an unmistakable stench that was both instantly recognisable yet difficult to describe, one so pungent you could taste it.

People never forgot that smell, a scar in their minds far deeper than those made by a whip or rod. Slave masters usually resorted to physical punishment, but Ophelia had far more effective methods involving all five senses. Smell and taste were just two of the others Ophelia had utilised for the most effective infliction of fear she'd accomplished within her lifetime.

For sound, the screams had long since faded with the ashes of the dead but would last a lifetime in the ears of the Xavalans. For sight, one never forgot witnessing a blood eagle.

Ahead of her, the royal square outside the Regent's palace beckoned with its surrounding fountains no longer shooting thin lines of water into the sky. Now they were appropriately quiet and still, letting the troughs of water rest around the gruesome sight at their centre. There, a dozen algus—traitors to the throne—hovered above the bloody stone beneath, dripping and decaying within a cloud of flies, brandished between iron poles as a warning to everyone entering. Their backs had been slashed up the spine, each rib carefully broken and pulled until jutting out. The sawing didn't kill them, but when their lungs were torn and stretched out across the bones, creating the bloody wings, they were most certainly wading through the river to hell.

"It's a glorious sight, isn't it?" The Silk Regent's smug grin was apparent just from the back of his head. His flowing orange robes hadn't a stain of blood on them, but there was more than enough on his hands. If this incompetent narcissist's reign had been more effective, they wouldn't have had to cull so many working hands.

*The Silk City is doomed.* Again, the thought brought Ophelia a little relief, but as tempted as she was to let this city's inhabitants meet their demise, she wouldn't deprive Toria of the fighting men and women they needed. Some might have thought it pointless to inflict such terror on a doomed city. After all, what use was fear in a place soon to be dust and ash? But Ophelia would make use of even the slaves here. They'd be sold around the Empire, carrying those scars of terror from the burnings and blood eagles, like a disease infecting every nook and tainting every soul these people touched. That was how one spread real fear. That was how one slew any thoughts of revolt in the other cities.

It was just a shame that evacuating the Silk City might involve saving the gold-toothed reprobate swaggering in front of her.

"I've had word from the King," Ophelia said.

The Silk Regent tilted his head up to absorb the sight of the blood eagles as they approached. "There's no need for him to thank or congratulate me. I did this for the good of my city."

Did what? Roll around with his concubines while the clashes of steel rang in the streets and putrid smoke filled the sky?

"Along with his pleasure at our success," Ophelia said, "he sends a warning. We are to abandon the Silk City."

The Silk Regent spun so quickly that his gold chains swung to his back. "Is he insane?"

"Quashing the slave revolt was only to buy us time. My men have already begun giving instructions to the most affluent algus houses. The slaves are packing. The people and whatever treasures you have will travel east, cross the Great Bridge and go into Toria."

Aristippus gave a snarl, leaving sunlight glinting from his metallic teeth. "They will do no such thing."

"This is not a request." Ophelia's voice became biting and sharp. If only the King's Sword was at her side.

"They will do no such thing! I just scored a victory over those traitors and their leader. I will not surrender my city to them."

"You will surrender it or die within it. Their *leader* is now the Overlord of Rakka. His retribution will be swift and unstoppable."

The Silk Regent rushed towards her, displaying a rare flair of algus tempo. "I'll never abandon my home."

"What did you expect? Over half of your slaves are dead. Did you think you could carry on as usual? Do you think those slaves were not integral to the functioning of this city?"

"Slaves are replaceable."

"Slaves do not grow on the riverbanks within a season. And this is not a debate. The King has issued his commands."

"To hell with the King!" Aristippus spat each word, splattering Ophelia's face as she stepped back casually with a disgusted grimace.

"I'll pretend I didn't hear that," she lied. Hopefully, this would be enough for the King's Sword to finally end him if all else failed.

"I will not abandon my city," the Silk Regent growled. "Do you think I don't know what the King plans? He wants to empty my coffers and bring my hard-earned riches into Toria, but whatever he promises or however much he reassures me now, it will all be undone within months, and I'll be left as the laughing stock of the capital. For over fifteen years, I've been Regent of Xavala. Do you think I'll go from this to living like all the other algus in Toria, with no status, no power, no respect?"

That's what he deserved, and he was right in expecting ridicule in Toria.

"No," Aristippus said. "My algus and my soldiers will stay and defend their home even if the King will not, and our slaves will stay too; they'll feed our defenders with their own flesh if they must. We'll die here if that's our fate, and the whole Empire will know our bravery and will know the coward we have for a king."

"If the rakkans breach your walls," Ophelia said, "you'll last a few hours at the most."

"Then we'll ensure they don't breach the walls. All of our defence will be focused there."

There were many ways Ophelia could convince the Silk Regent to back down and swallow his pride. Any number of her algus could have taken him on—even some of her soldiers—but she hesitated. One sentence of the King's message came back to mind. *Save whoever you can.*

The King had to have known this would happen and that a complete evacuation was not only too bitter a medicine for the Silk Regent to swallow but likewise for many other Xavalans too. So, she'd use her influence on more important people and leave this man to meet his demise.

"Very well," Ophelia said.

The Silk Regent frowned with suspicion. He was right to be distrustful but too dense to figure out why.

She turned to head back to her men but paused. Perhaps she should give the Regent a crumb of advice; it might help delay whatever assault the rakkans planned.

"If you wish to defend the city," Ophelia said, "I have a suggestion."

"What is it?"

"Keep guarding the wells, and ration your food. Under a siege, you could last months. But if they attack quickly, it means what we've done has angered them. I sense they have a soft spot for these workers—after all, Darius still bears a slave's name."

"So?"

"I've read many reports of the assault on Laltos. The rakkans used slingers to whittle down the defences on the walls, and I expect they'll do the same here. Use your slaves as human shields. I suspect Darius will be reluctant to kill his own."

"Why would he care about slaves?"

Without another word, Ophelia left the egotistical fool to it. She wouldn't press the point. Part of her hoped he ignored her, even though it would make her evacuation more rushed and prone to error.

She breathed deep, satisfied with the knowledge she'd never have to meet that lecherous weasel again. The final sentence of the King's message finally made sense and was now more refreshing than a milk bath. *Worry not if Aristippus is proud, for it means he will soon meet the Slayer of Gods.*

# 22

## Darius – Gap of Aphatos

"A siege will save the lives of hundreds, if not thousands, of our men," Rufus said to the hushed throne room. "Patience is all that's required."

Although the conversation over the last few hours had been fiery, the room was as cold as a mountain river. The clear night outside had leeched any warmth that had endured from the day, and now only lamps shed their tangerine light onto the grim faces of the warlords and human leaders.

"A siege will also sap our resources," Darius said from atop his throne. "And the southeastern side will be vulnerable to Torian attacks." Although rakkans had the strength of many humans, their numbers were fewer, and surrounding a city would spread them too thin; it wouldn't take much for an army to cross the River Toras, march north for a couple of days, then punch a hole through Darius's lines. He'd probably have to blockade the

Great Bridge to prevent that and maybe even the Psilos Bridge farther south.

"A siege will also kill the rest of the slaves," Cyrus said. The warlords acted as if he hadn't spoken, but Darius most certainly took the words of the Menaran leader to heart.

He turned his attention to the Chief Priest, who'd been nothing but a mute, pallid phantom of a man for the last few days.

"What's your counsel?" Darius asked.

The Chief Priest just continued staring at the cold stone ground.

"Aran!"

Finally, the man flinched and looked up. "Yes?"

"What do you propose we do to fix the mess we've created?"

The man sank back into his chair, and only then did Darius see how much weight he'd lost, as if he hadn't eaten since long before the Xavalan massacre. Even the lamp beside him couldn't break the shadows in his sunken cheeks or eyes. "Do you still trust my judgement?"

"You couldn't have known the rebellion would end as it did."

"But I did know; this isn't the first rebellion quelled. I risked their lives. I condemned more to suffer the blood eagle…"

Darius winced, having had the infamous torture ritual explained to him. It was best he hadn't witnessed it himself. Then there'd be no delay before his armies marched to raze the city.

"This priest has little to offer." The Branz Warlord stood. "Rufus is right; we shouldn't risk the heavy losses an assault would result in. Starve them out. Even if we haven't managed to poison their springs, they can't grow food within their walls."

Murmurs of agreement rippled through the room, but Darius noted most of the humans—Lex included—didn't show as much enthusiasm.

"We've been speaking for too long," he said. "The assembly will break for refreshments and meet back within the hour."

Everyone took their leave to stand and replenish themselves—all except the Chief Priest, which was perfect because Darius had more questions of the man.

He left the throne and the Blades behind and came beside Aran, and the Chief Priest only looked up when Darius's heavily armoured body thudded on the seat beside him.

"What's eating you?" Darius asked. "You can't blame yourself."

"Was it not I that pushed for a rebellion?"

"I'm the Overlord here. I bear the blame. Focus on the future." Without the man's wise advice over recent months, they'd all be in a much worse position than they were now.

"That's the problem," Aran said. "Whether or not I am to blame for the past, I don't know if I should be a part of your future."

Darius had assumed the man was troubled by doubts, but to abandon their cause entirely…? Things inside the priest's mind were worse than he'd feared.

"If we give up now," Darius said, "more will suffer under the tyrants of this world."

"Do not think yourself any better than they… I assisted you while ignoring the risks, praying that what I knew could come to pass would not. Well, it has. There are many paths that lead from this point, and they're all so dark. If we aren't careful, we'll lose our footing and slip onto a bloody and dangerous quagmire that leads to a place I cannot see. Is that really the route the God of Justice intends for me?"

Whatever Agathos's plan was, Darius bet it hadn't involved the Silk City Massacre.

The Chief Priest twisted in his seat to face Darius head-on. "Why do you wish to continue?"

This had all begun as revenge for Selene, for poisoning the mind of the woman he'd once loved. Not to mention the countless others slain by the King of Toria, whether in Darius's memories or those he'd forgotten.

"Justice," Darius muttered. It was an honest answer he was unsure of the reaction to.

"Don't you think you need better reasons? Isn't it selfish of you to make your warriors and innocent slaves suffer and die for your perceived justice and those you care about?"

Not for the first time, Darius feared the man was seeing deeper into his psyche than ever before. Aran had a point. Darius had every right to fight for those he cared about, but others? Should they fight?

Was this war far bigger than him?

"Answer me truthfully," he said. "Does the God of Justice support this war?"

"I've asked the Goddess that many times, and she has given no clear answer. But I must confess, I no longer believe it to be so."

Darius didn't know what to think, but if the Chief Priest didn't believe it, then he'd be a fool to do so. Still, even if not backed by divine forces, Darius couldn't stop. This war would continue for centuries, slaves would be butchered, and gomans would shape the fate of yet more people. Wise rakkans like Brutus would never have thought of giving in.

"You say there are many paths ahead of us," Darius said, "but you're wrong."

The Chief Priest lifted his brows. "You see a clear way?"

"No. There are no paths; we're already knee-deep in the bloody quagmire." He took the lump of aeternus from around his neck and held it out, conjuring ferven to set it alight in its dim glow that would burn almost forever. "But even the weakest light penetrates an otherwise unbreakable darkness."

The Chief Priest almost gave a pitiful smile. "I guess you're right."

"We can at least see our enemies, the enemies of justice. The Silk Regent not only deserves death for Xavala but also for Laltos. Such a betrayal deserves punishment."

"But the rest of his city may not. More slaves do not deserve to die."

"Whatever I do, more will die. Aren't you with me?"

The Chief Priest sighed under what sounded like a ton of iron atop him. "I don't know if I should, but I will advise you however I can if it avoids more innocents dying. On anything else, I cannot assist you."

That was good enough for now. As the two exchanged more details, the others filed back into the chilly room with stuffed bellies and a slight slur to their words. Time had passed quickly; every sigh and pause the pair of them gave had lasted minutes rather than the mere fleeting moments they'd felt like. While the last warlord entered and sat, Darius returned to the throne and gave Lyra a stroke.

"Rufus," he called.

The Viridian Warlord stood. "Overlord?"

"How confident are you in breaching the Silk City's walls?"

Lex shot him a questioning look, but she didn't seem opposed to the suggestion of an assault, more surprised, like he should have discussed the details with her first.

"I'm confident," Rufus said. "They are of different construction than Laltos's, initially built to keep out humans rather than rakkans, so they don't have the thickness they need to stop us. But still, the casualties—"

"Yes. You said." As far as Darius was concerned, no one deserved high casualties more than the Viridian Legion after what they'd done to Laltos.

"The cavalry may pose a problem," Lex said. "And the Silk City has far more archers and ballistae than Laltos had."

"Archers do not concern us." Rufus's tone was thankfully devoid of any emotion that might spark bitter feelings. "Our slingers have a greater range. The cavalry can be held at bay until we are through the wall."

"*Through?"* Darius asked. Usually, tunnelling through a wall was impossible because its loose earthen centre collapsed when a rakkan dug into it.

"Yes," Rufus said. "We need not undermine it like Laltos; it's solid stone, just heavily protected behind trenches."

What concerned Darius more than Rufus already knowing all these minutiae about a city he'd never visited was that his commanders had begun grinning as soon as Darius had suggested the assault. They'd argued for a siege but were hungry for the hell of raiding a city. Unfortunately for them, this time, there was no way he'd allow a repeat of the chaos that had unfolded within Laltos.

"Then it's decided," Darius said. "A siege will require patience, and I will not be a patient man. The Viridian Legion will assault the Silk City under cover of darkness."

"I suggest you mobilise the Branz and Black Legions," Lex said, "to cut off any Torian attempts to support the city."

"Indeed." Darius gave the Branz and Black Warlords a nod.

Meanwhile, Rufus stood. "It would be my honour to lead my men to destroy the city that has harassed us all for so long."

Darius stretched out his fingers from the throne's armrest, just enough to scratch the Blades' hilts, making them give a fiery shiver in anticipation of being wielded again.

"You will not lead the Viridian Legion," Darius said.

The Viridian Warlord frowned, and a new hunger arose in his commanders that was soon to be disappointed.

"You will direct our forces," Darius continued, "but *I* will lead the attack from the front."

Something overcame Rufus's expression then that Darius couldn't interpret, like a sudden thought had struck him that he concealed his reaction to within a heartbeat.

"As you wish, Overlord," the rakkan said.

"Will you kill the Silk Regent yourself?" Hera hadn't spoken until now, and her voice was devoid of its usual authority.

"Not at first," Darius said. "Death would be too kind. But I promise you this: he'll pray for it when I find him."

# 23

## Rufus – Xavala, the Silk City

Xavala's walls poked above the horizon, miles of shadowed, sandy dunes Rufus would slice through as easily as the silk the city was famous for. *The Silk City*. Such an apt name; the might of the Viridian Legion would trample the place as if its very foundations were fabric-thin.

"My centuries are in position." Pollio's focus locked onto the city that had plagued the Viridians for so long. Finally, the time for revenge had come. And this time, there would be no retreat.

All that stood between them and their enemy was a mile stretch of swaying grass, but Rufus knew of the unseen trench running parallel to Xavala's outer wall, a dozen yards in front of it, as well as the traps lying in wait within the greenery. It had all been revealed by the falcons of his Subdued, who ruled the sky again, the escorts gifted by the Chief Priest before he'd lost his appetite for the blood-soaked conquest to come. Although Rufus hadn't intended for tonight to be the night of the assault, the rains had fallen heavily during the day and left the ground soft and malleable, horrible for riding horses across. Conditions were too perfect to pass up.

Cities didn't fall in one night; usually, it was days or weeks of relentless efforts to break inside, especially against such a large city whose defence outnumbered Rufus's warriors. He hadn't even enough rakkans to block every exit and would need to defend his workers in a tight formation.

But could Rufus do the impossible? He planned to. That would undoubtedly solidify his position as Viridian Warlord.

Behind them, the legion stirred with that unique murmur that marked the genesis of every battle. It was more than a sound; it was an energy that made the night air turgid, more than a hunger—a lust for blood, riches and women. These rakkans had been left inert for too long and were soon to indulge their greed. They had the tools to do it, everything from towers to ladders. Getting through the outer wall was still his best option, as it had been in Laltos. That was plan A. Humans always underestimated the speed at which rakkans dug through stone and filled in ditches.

Rufus turned to Piso. "How many shovellers do we have?"

"A thousand. They'll carry the tools along with their pikes, Warlord."

The rare title of respect from his brother met his ears as a sweet harmony, and one day, Rufus would earn it and others purely by his own accomplishments rather than by the presence of the domineering Overlord.

Darius growled to himself as if aware Rufus's thoughts lingered on him, staring at their enemies unblinking like an alpha wolf ready to set the pack on the hunt. But he wouldn't be the one to give the order.

At least the Overlord knew his weaknesses, knew when he should defer to Rufus. Hadrian had required so much effort to coerce into a sensible course of action that it was a miracle the assault on Laltos had succeeded.

"March with thin ranks," Rufus roared to his commanders. "Make it appear we're setting up for a long siege. Protect the slingers. Every rakkan without a shovel will use his shield to dig the ditches at our flanks."

Although they'd trained in creating well-hidden ditches to take charging cavalry by surprise, the long vegetation on these plains would simplify the task; that's why Rufus was content to let Piso take charge. Plus, there was the added bonus of leaving his brother in the most dangerous position.

"Have you picked your spot?" Darius asked.

Along the miles of high, thin walls, there were three points of most advantage for a breach. Rufus hadn't been sure which, but now was.

"At the southwest corner," he said. "It's farthest from their garrisons. We'll be through the wall before their algus have roused from their slumber."

"Very well." Darius took a few steps forward until in front of the vanguard. "The Black and Branz Legions are in place near the Great Bridge. Lyra will keep me updated on any developments."

"And what of us?" Hera stood in front of her algus, ranks upon ranks of armoured gods that every rakkan glanced at with caution.

"I will make use of you," Rufus said.

The Regent spat a curse.

"Enough!" Darius turned with that fearsome scarlet returning to his eyes. "In battle, there will be no arguments. Hera, you and every other human and rakkan will follow Rufus's instructions. I don't care if you think them foolish. I don't care if you think them malicious. Hierarchy rules. Battles have been lost through confusion. After we are victorious, *then* he will answer to me for his commands. Is that clear?"

Hera gave a measured nod. "Very well, Overlord."

"Are you to take my instructions also, Overlord?" Rufus dared the question because of its importance. As their most fearsome warrior, where the Overlord fought could shift the tide of battle.

Darius paused for thought before answering. "I will follow your instructions until I don't."

Given his mood of late, it wouldn't have surprised Rufus if the man scaled the walls alone and went in to wreak havoc. Too bad his dark-haired beloved wasn't here to keep him rational.

After taking a beat to savour the last few moments of bloodless silence these fields would enjoy for a while, Rufus gave the signal. The Viridian horns blared, a deep, violent sound that brought pain to one's ears and set the centuries into their march. Rufus's moment to prove himself had come at last.

As the army moved in formation, the Subdued reaffirmed every few minutes that the exits to the city were clear. The cavalry hadn't emerged. Yet. But there was other movement.

Atop the beige walls, shadows multiplied until forming a solid black mass across that even rakkan eyes couldn't pierce. The defence was heavy. They knew an assault was coming.

A horn of the vanguard blared twice. Once it blared four times, they'd be in ballistae range.

Rufus slowed his walk, leaving the Overlord to lead from the front, and instead took his favoured position at the rear, where he oversaw best and the formations on the battlefield could shift and rearrange in his mind.

That's all a battle was in effect: shifting pieces like aeternus on a katakto board. It was a pity most rakkans shunned the game. They said, "Who but a traitor plays a game humans made?"

Conquerors did—that's who.

The horns blared four. And the bolts flew.

They pierced dirt, metal, and flesh, blue missiles of death as long as a Viridian warrior's body. Rufus's front line raised their shields, hurried their march, and loosened their formation. Many commanders drilled their men to tighten ranks in these situations, creating a smaller target that was harder to score, but not Rufus. Rakkan reflexes were second to none. Given the space, the legionnaires and slingers could dodge.

Some did just that, rolling to their side. Others were too slow, the weak spots of the army being whittled away and discarded.

Once close enough, Pollio roared the command, and the slingers drew back without pause and let the front ranks charge onwards while they spun their instruments.

Thousands of molten rings lit up the field in the night and soon unleashed into a red wave that splashed onto the top of the Xavalan ramparts. They were too far to hear the screams, but shadows fell, and soon the red stones became an unceasing hail of torment.

The legionnaires increased their pace as they neared the first traps and random holes left in the ground to snare feet and break ankles—human ankles, that was. Rakkan bones took more than a great force to snap.

Five blares of the horns filled the air, and arrows from the city began flying, a thousandfold in number compared to the bolts, but despite most being tinged with algor, the kuraminium shields of the Viridian Legion held strong.

"Warlord," a Subdued called. "The cavalry is coming. Southern gate."

Predictable, but irksome all the same. They could have given Rufus another quarter of an hour… But at least that meant the traps on the next stretch of ground would be fewer. They wouldn't risk their own horses falling prey to them,

"Piso!" he yelled. "Pike centuries mobilise, right flank! Pollio, cover."

His brothers relayed the commands to the centurions, who knew the drill. Each took direct command of their century, shifting to the right flank in clusters that could react to wherever the cavalry decided to strike. And moving along with one of the groups of pikemen was the looming figure of the Overlord.

Perhaps they wouldn't even need ditches. Better careful than careless, though.

The first sight of the cavalry was a moving dark mass to their right. For now, the slingers marched with the pikemen while still peppering the battlements, stymieing the torrent of arrows enough for the legionnaires in the vanguard to carry on, shields raised, shovels and picks ready. From what his Subdued spies had said, Xavala hadn't sulphur to use as the humans had in Laltos. Rufus had plans if that intelligence was false, but he had confidence such contingencies wouldn't be required.

The cavalry wheeled, taking advantage of the wide expanse and seemingly intent on a charge square at the right flank. Whoever the Silk City's commanders were, they were clearly unfamiliar with the realities of a large battle. Katakto skills only extended so far, and there was no substitute for the schooling of the battlefield itself. Skirmishes wouldn't do.

As Rufus watched his men display a flawless shift to face their enemies, he sensed something else.

Air rushed into the eye socket of his horned helmet and washed across his exposed lips.

He lurched to the side just in time, feeling an arrow rip through the air and crash into the dirt behind him. They were all in range. Xavala's final trench and outer wall weren't far away from the front of his army, dark figures now constantly toppling from the battlements under the heavy slinger assault.

An hour, they'd said. An hour to smash a molten hole into Xavala's walls.

Rufus had plotted how to hold the ground at the site for three.

"Rufus!" a woman yelled.

He knew it was Hera but chose to ignore her. The cavalry had hastened into a gallop. Legionnaires raised their pikes, and slingers now hurled their hate onto the horses and brought rows of them splattering into the damp ground.

And out in front of the Viridian defence was a lone figure, two swords unsheathed and roaring with a fire of their own. Then the Dreaded One became a blur.

His red streak cut across the battlefield, then swung upwards in a leap and slash that severed the heads of two riders.

The horns blared six. The legionnaires had reached the trench in front of the wall and would be shovelling in dirt to ease the passing of the rest of the army. But as Rufus turned to look, an angry-faced Hera blocked his sight.

"Rufus! My algus's escorts have surveyed the ramparts. The archers aren't being hit; they're using slaves as shields."

A body was certainly better protection from slinger shots than a wooden shield.

"Does the Overlord know?" Rufus asked.

"No."

That was for the best, given the man had a soft spot for the working classes. But it didn't solve their problem. Kuraminium shields could only last so long against bombardment from above, and even rakkan arms tired from holding up a testudo.

The shovellers soon partially filled in one strip of a trench and warriors began their creep towards the wall while hell rained on their raised shields.

Behind them, Rufus's siege towers had stopped to wait for their time to cross the trench while Hera's archers atop tried to respond to the battlements with a barrage of their own. But under heavy fire themselves, men fell from them every few seconds.

And the cavalry assault on their right flank continued. His katakto pieces were being attacked on two fronts, and of the two threats, Rufus deemed the archers the greater.

"We need to control the ramparts," he said.

"My algus can't climb sheer stone," Hera replied.

Even though the outer wall had been marred by wayward slinger shots to leave chunks missing all over, anyone that lost their footing would die from the fall, a difficult climb even without defenders dropping things on them.

Rufus had the numbers to last, and a great leader would devise a way to lose as few men as possible.

But before he'd decided on their best reaction, a new tactic from his enemies befell him.

People sprinted atop the ramparts, ablaze in blue flame and screaming as they dove over the parapet and onto the testudo below. The sparks as algor and ferven clashed burst out with a clap, and the legionnaires held up the bodies until the algor had died, then let them slump through gaps in the shields and braced for whatever was to follow.

Hera gasped.

"I haven't seen that before." Rufus was almost impressed by the tactic. Slaves didn't require tossing like stones would, and there was only so much oil the Xavalans could store on the parapet and tip over. But slaves were easily mobilised.

Pollio came running over. "We need the slingers to break the cavalry charges. I've shifted some centuries over."

Rufus's brow furrowed. That would weaken their attack on the wall.

As the shovellers filled in wider stretches of the trench, masses of more legionnaires began to reach the wall, and in response, more men and women came running over the battlements with spears at their backs and plunged into the metal sea below. When they landed, the algor engulfing them spread and extinguished any ferven around, opening up the rakkans' armour to the algor-tipped arrows now raining down harder. After only a few moments, dozens of legionnaires had fallen dead with more screaming and clutching limbs frozen with algor.

"We *really* need to control the ramparts," Rufus said.

A crash to his right stole his attention for a moment as the cavalry collided with his pikemen, toppled and trampled the rakkans but was thrust backwards by a sudden cloud of molten projectiles slamming into them. It was true; without the slingers, the horses would punch a hole through eventually.

"How long would it take to build a ramp up to the battlements?" Hera asked.

"Longer than to break through the wall," Rufus replied. Shovels were slower than picks and slower still than climbers. He had rope, from as thin as wire to as thick as a man's leg. Such a useful thing it was; he was never without it. But as he contemplated the scenario of his hookers climbing and securing the things, he foresaw the algor the Xavalans would send down to frustrate the rakkans unable to conjure ferven for fear of burning the ropes. He needed another solution, and Hera's suggestion of a ramp sparked an idea.

These walls were high, but as he surveyed them, he realised they weren't high enough. His warriors were heavily armoured at the head and shoulders, so they stood a chance of defending a route up.

He called over one of his commanders. "Send word to the front. Halt destruction of the wall for now. Bring forward the ladders."

"To the wall?" the commander asked.

"Get the freshest recruits to defend them first." Chances were that most of them would die; ladders were too vulnerable, especially wooden ones, and he avoided them wherever he could.

But he'd never had so many fighters with supernatural speed to call upon before. Now, ladders were his best bet.

The commander nodded and went to relay the orders as Rufus turned to Pollio. "I need all slingers bombarding the battlements or the ladders will be destroyed."

"But the cavalry..."

There was only one thing for it. It meant sacrificing even more men, but men were dying anyway.

"Lake of fire formation," Rufus said. "In front of the pikes."

Pollio hesitated for a few moments before nodding and rushing to give Piso the orders.

Meanwhile, Rufus turned to Hera. "You'll soon have your way up. Ready your algus. Claim the ramparts so my men can get back to breaking through the wall."

Hera nodded and left too.

Using ladders and the lake of fire were desperate moves, ones seldom proven in the field. Time would tell whether his gamble would pay off.

# 24

## Rufus – Xavala, the Silk City

Fifth attempt. The men scrambled while warriors fell dead around them as they tried to steady the bases of the ladders propped up against Xavala's outer wall. The algus were halfway up this time, but atop were the waiting Xavalans, cobalt slaves still hurling themselves to their doom.

The bodies piled. But at least it stabilised the base of the ladders.

"What the hell!" The Overlord's shout bore all the fury he'd displayed on the fields.

Rufus turned to face the origin of the call. "They're sacrificing their slaves."

"I can see that!" Darius came alongside him. "This city's algus are such cowards."

Rufus took a moment to check the right flank to see how it was faring. In the land between Rufus's warriors and the enemy cavalry, warriors lay prone at regular intervals and shielded their necks and organs with whatever armour they had while conjuring ferven and spreading it out as far as they could across the earth, creating an orange lake that even fearless warhorses dared not gallop into.

The bright fire spread farther by the second, extending back and looping around in case the cavalry tried to bypass it.

With most slingers focused on the ramparts, the horsemen hovered around the edges of the lake and picked off warriors with arrows and spears while being harried by a few archers to deter them. With any luck, the legion would be inside the city by the time they killed a path through it. And then they'd still have to get through the pikes.

"If you want the Xavalans to cease sacrificing slaves"—Rufus turned back to Darius—"make them." There was no other warrior he'd have chosen to seize control of the ramparts.

The Overlord growled. "You want me up there?"

"You'd rather stand here and watch?"

"Fair enough. But I might be tempted to head straight for the Silk Regent's palace. Maybe the battle will be over if I cleave the heads of all the algus leading this city."

"You know that's not how things work."

Darius grunted as an algus reached the top of the ladder and took hold of the parapet, the first to reach it. The way up was ready. And the Overlord sprinted forward at once.

The other algus had enough sense to let him pass and watch him use his forearm to bat away the blue slaves still tumbling down. What a fearsome man Rufus would be with both his smarts and the brawn of such a rakkan, but the hand he'd been dealt in life left him only imagining such.

Darius's swords tasted blood as soon as his head crested the battlements, then he disappeared behind the merlons with only flashes of red and blue light betraying the horror he was unleashing.

More algus followed him up, and the blue slaves soon stopped falling, but Rufus could see they hadn't enough ladders left to get all the rakkans they needed into the city, not even accounting for their heavy kuraminium armour being too much for the wooden rungs. So, when the last dozen clambered up the ladders, Rufus gave the signal and the horns blared. Only a few rakkans remained to steady the ladders while the rest returned to their picks and shovels.

It was time to get through this wall.

Picks soon flared with ferven and began clawing and smashing away the outer layers with ease. Shovellers both hauled away the debris and dug more hidden ditches to their flanks should the cavalry try to cut off their route out of the city. All the while the ramparts lit the sky until almost as blue as a summer's day, and not an arrow or slave came from them again. They ruled this part of the city. Soon the Viridian Legion's true might would visit.

The slingers shifted the focus of their fire onto the cavalry again, forcing them back with more ease now they hadn't as many arrows to dodge, and eventually, the riders retreated.

An hour had been the correct estimate. After that had passed, Rufus marched right up to the wall to check the progress, and on the mark, the first miners broke through to the other side to be greeted by Hera's algus and the Dreaded One panting over piles of slain algus and soldiers. There were no opponents left, no resistance struggling to contain them. The place was deserted, and who could blame the Xavalans for retreating behind the next set of inner walls?

Rufus stepped through as diggers widened the hole and the hungry legionnaires on the other side began to growl, lust lighting fires within them.

"These streets are clear," Darius said flatly. "We'll smash straight through all the other walls and head towards the palace."

"Why rush?" Piso stepped through the gap, wiping blood from his gladius and confirming that, unfortunately, he hadn't been killed. "We'll enjoy the local sights first."

"You'll do no such thing." Darius turned to the commander. "There'll be no pillaging or harassing the civilians this time."

"You think we fight for free? We demand our loot and women."

Darius moved so fast that Piso was dangling by the neck in the Overlord's hand before he'd flinched. "This city is not yours to loot. Everything in it belongs to me now. Every man, woman, and child is mine. Will you dare steal from your Overlord?"

A rasp of an answer left Piso's constricted throat.

"What was that?" Darius pressed his ear closer. "I didn't hear you."

"I won't," Piso growled, somehow managing to ooze contempt even while strangled.

Darius dropped the man with a clank, and Rufus soon realised every rakkan and algus had frozen to gape at the reprimand.

"That goes for all of you!" Darius roared.

Rufus allowed the command to sink in a little before speaking. "You heard him. Ready the centuries. Pikemen guard the flanks and our path of retreat. The rest of you head to the palace as planned."

The commanders and centurions began barking orders to organise the men, and soon the army marched through the streets and battered through another set of walls on the path Rufus had chosen.

These fortifications had none of the strength of the outer ones, seeming to be made to withstand humans more than rakkans, and it took only minutes for the Viridians to burst through and overwhelm the defences.

This wasn't a frenzied charge like it had been in Laltos, with warriors spreading like floodwaters through every street. They met some further resistance but not much because most of the city had holed up with the bravest merely peeking out of high-up windows.

Until they reached the palace a couple of hours later.

Under the shadow of many lofted blood eagles in the square outside, lines of algus waited on the grand steps, their loyal soldiers formed in ranks behind. The fools would have been better off attacking them in the streets from the rooftops to slow Rufus's advance. Did they really think they could match a rakkan legion in the open?

The Overlord's gaze lingered on the blood eagles, every passing heartbeat seeing his jaw clench tighter. Rufus had to admit there was something about seeing them in the flesh that tales and stories couldn't describe, a depth of emotion that even the most genius musician or writer could never convey, and those emotions were visibly overcoming Darius.

"Pollio," Rufus called. "Circle around. Seal off the palace exits our spies discovered."

His brother obliged and took the centuries while one of Xavala's algus stepped forward, sword sheathed.

Based on the descriptions Rufus had heard of the Silk Regent, this wasn't him, but he was intrigued to see whether they had anything to say for themselves.

Rufus began walking towards the man while his legionnaires remained ready in their offensive formation. Only Darius followed, a yard behind Rufus and clearly prepared to allow him to do the speaking.

At first, Rufus expected a surrender, a plea for mercy that he wasn't sure he'd listen to, but as soon as he drew closer to the Xavalan algus, the hate on that face told him this wasn't a resigned man.

"How dare you…" The algus spat a brown wad of phlegm at their feet and stopped. "Leave this city at once."

Darius burst into a laugh, an almost maniacal sound to which the algus's disgust deepened.

"Do you have anything less futile to say?" Rufus asked. Why did men always speak when they had nothing to say?

"We have the backing of the King," the algus said. "If this city falls, there will be no mercy for you."

Darius moved forward slowly, each step landing like a memory of the quake that had rocked the lands. He squared up to the man and cracked open his mouth as if to growl a warning.

But his sword arm moved before his tongue, a red blur that slashed through the algus's body from groin to skull and left the spilling halves to fall and splatter.

Every algus flinched back at the savage blow even Rufus hadn't witnessed so cleanly before. Some but not all of the soldiers turned and ran, a move that soon spread through the ranks like a plague. Those were the smart ones.

As Darius dropped the Blades to his sides again, the fires dimmed, and not a stain of blood remained on them. "Who's next?" He stepped forward, brandishing his weapons widely in a challenge. "Anyone?"

Perhaps he thought he could intimidate them into surrender, but after decades of war with the humans, Rufus knew these people's hearts by their faces. They weren't waiting to surrender and bend the knee; they were summoning the courage to die. That's why they weren't putting up a sensible defence. That's why they were unwilling to use tactics that might give them a chance. After enjoying a life hoisted on the backs of others, some people just weren't prepared to live as one of the many insignificant names in the Empire.

Well, if they wanted death, how could Rufus deny them that? He was a considerate man, after all.

"Legion!" he bellowed.

His army answered with a stamp of their feet and the raising of shields.

And between the gaps of the centuries, Laltos's algus stalked forward. Rufus was loath to deny them their dues, but why waste lives by letting them fight in close combat? Although not *his* men, he had to preserve every sword in the Overlord's army.

Behind the rakkan shield wall, Rufus's slingers twirled their weapons as trained to do.

"Loose!" he yelled before the two armies of algus met.

The stony wave flew over the shield wall and had barely time to arc down before blitzing its targets. Most of the Xavalan algus tried to dodge, but every inch of air bore the lethal shards cutting through. Even those algus with shields took many stones to the legs, bones snapping, knees buckling. It was only a single wave, but it did enough.

"Hold!" Rufus yelled as Laltos's algus sprang in to attack, led by the roaring Overlord.

Although technically a battle, the only word for what Rufus beheld next was "slaughter." The Xavalans stood no chance as Darius unleashed his fury on those few lucky ones that had gone unscathed from the slingers' assault.

In only a few minutes, every algus's throat had been slashed, and Rufus's men stomped unhindered up the bloody steps and into the palace.

Darius turned before they reached the barred gates. "Pull down those blood eagles. Burn the bodies."

Rufus waved at a centurion to arrange it. "Do you know where the Silk Regent's quarters are?"

"I've had the path described, but my guess is he'll try to flee in his secret tunnel."

A boom echoed as Rufus's men swung a battering ram at the outer gates.

"Pollio will have that covered," Rufus said. "Assuming the harlot was correct in its location."

"Let's pray she was."

Another bash of the ram split the wood and metal of the gate.

"Can't you just burn through this?" Darius asked.

"Of course we could. But this thunder will shake the whole palace. They'll know we're coming, as if we're knocking on the door."

Darius grinned, but it was an ugly thing, no humour. "Fear. They deserve it."

"Indeed." Whether they did or not, instilling fear won battles, and Rufus was too cautious a man to assume victory even now. In his youth, he'd many a time lost katakto from a dominant position due to losing his home spaces. The cavalry could rally, or there could be unknown traps awaiting them in the palace.

A splintered crash announced the first break of the gate, and it was only a few dozen more bashes until the metal braces behind clanged and thudded as they fell away. The fractured gates swung open to reveal the next layer of defence—a portcullis.

"Batter through that too," Rufus called. Again, it would have been easier to melt it, but he knew those enemies inside felt the same tremors in their boots from the rams.

The metal stood up longer than the wooden gates, but eventually, the rakkans battered a hole through with only a little ferven required and revealed the palace's final set of doors.

They fell much more quickly, and once open, they revealed an empty, clean courtyard in stark contrast to the gore outside. Clearly, the Silk Regent hadn't enough loyalty from his algus and soldiers to make them mount the fierce defence Rufus had planned for.

The Overlord stormed in first, leaving a trail of red footprints, and headed straight for the main staircase at the far side, one almost wide enough for an army to march up that split into two opposing paths at the top. Rufus followed with his guards, but as Darius turned to bypass the staircase and head down the passageways anyone fleeing would have taken, Rufus led his warriors higher. The Overlord may not have wanted to check on the Regent's quarters, but Rufus knew that's where the rarest riches were always hidden, and he could use a little added flamboyance to his attire. Although not a materialistic man, a warlord had to display a certain degree of wealth to command respect, and he was lacking in that regard.

A few Xavalan guards scurried around in the hallway upstairs, but none bothered to challenge Rufus's warriors. It was difficult to navigate the place, but when they passed by a gilded set of doors, Rufus sensed the air shift through the thin gap between them.

He skidded to a halt, noting the rugs in the hallways of this wing were exceptionally plush. The Regent's chambers?

"Inside," he whispered.

Two warriors took up position on either side of the door, shoulders ready to barge, and the rest of the legionnaires held their swords and shields ready.

When Rufus gave the nod, the two warriors launched shoulder-first and almost burst the doors from their hinges to release a flood of candlelight into the hallway.

Inside, paintings flickered on every inch of the walls, and a dozen algus stood ready, guarding a man seated at the back of the room.

Judging by the sparkle of his golden jewellery and the perfumed musk of the room, that had to be the Silk Regent.

"You should have brought more men," the Regent said.

Bolstering the taunt, the algus flicked their blades and sent a wash of algor down the steel.

It was true; Rufus was outnumbered at the moment. But he wouldn't shed a bead of sweat over it.

"I'll strike a deal with you." Rufus dared a step inside the room, now in front of his men.

The Silk Regent wiped his brow. "Your band is no match for my algus."

"But the Slayer of Gods is." Rufus took another step, sword still sheathed.

The algus didn't react and glanced back to their leader.

"And what deal will you offer me?" the Silk Regent asked.

"Point me to any gold and jewels you have stowed here, and I'll kill you."

The Silk Regent shot up from his chair and cursed. "What kind of deal is that?"

"A merciful one. I'll make it quick. But if the Overlord finds you first…"

The Silk Regent cursed again but mulled over the proposition for a few moments until his gaze shifted from Rufus to the doorway.

Rufus didn't need to turn to know what the Regent was looking at. He felt and heard the heavy breaths from behind, like a bear readying itself for a fight. Each exhale seemed to heat the room until it became a furnace, and all the algus backed up a fraction.

A foot stomped, followed by the metallic clank of a greave.

Finally, Rufus looked back to see the man he expected, only the Overlord no longer looked like a man. Now without his helmet, his pupils were white and red with fury, shedding a brilliance that spread and covered almost every inch of his body. Ferven dripped from his snarling mouth, and his hands gripped the Twin Blades so tightly it was as if they screamed in pain as ferven spat out of them.

It was as they said. Not only was this man a demon, but it could have been the prince of the underworld himself.

And then, most wicked of all, Darius smiled.

# 25

## Darius – Xavala, the Silk City

There he was, the man that had betrayed Laltos, the man that had ordered the raids in the west, the man that had massacred the slaves, the man that Lex had almost married. The affluent gold silk he wore was a repulsive sight; it may as well have been red with innocent blood. Darius still recalled the conditions of the hospice and was determined to leave this room just as horrid when he was through.

Rage forced the ferven from Darius's pores against his will, and it took considerable effort to keep the soles of his feet cold and plain so he didn't burn a hole through the floor as he stalked forward.

One of the algus finally plucked up the courage to charge, and Darius felt the Blades flare as he swung both towards the algus's lifted sword. The kuraminium weapons didn't pause when they met steel, cut through armour and flesh and hissed with burnt blood while sending the foul reek into the air. At least it masked the perfume in the room.

The other algus dared not rush forward after that and tried to back up, but Darius charged at each one and cut them down more quickly and mercifully than the slaves of this city had been.

Soon, only the Silk Regent remained, backed into a wall so hard the paintwork smeared across his sweaty tunic, and a wet patch grew at the coward's groin.

"If you're only pissing yourself," Darius said, "then you aren't as afraid as you should be."

But there was something off in the man's eyes. Yes, they were wide with fear, but not filled with nearly as much terror as they should have been. And Darius's body was flaring so brightly all the others had squinted, yet this man's pupils were open and black, a tell that he'd taken precautions.

"You caitiff." Darius went nose to nose with the stinking man. "What poison did you take?"

The Silk Regent trembled violently, yet his lips curled into a grin. "You don't have long."

Darius dropped one of the Blades and punched the man in the gut with such force he felt the bottom rib snap. Aristippus bent and hurled instantly, forcing Darius to grab his hair and angle his face away to avoid the filth that was spilling out. It was likely too late to get rid of the poison in the man's system, but it was worth a try before inflicting some real pain.

Once the Silk Regent's stomach was empty, he began groaning and wincing. Darius pulled his head back up and let go so they were both standing face to face again. He caught another glimpse of those cowardly eyes before he thrust out his hand and grabbed the man's infamous groin. He squeezed until even he winced at the shriek of agony that filled the dead halls. This man deserved to be strung up with the other blood eagles.

"Was it worth it?" Darius asked. "Were the deaths of all those people worth the pain you'll now suffer?"

The Silk Regent's grin returned. "What is a…fleeting moment of pain in a…lifetime of indulgence?"

To see the man so unrepentant, so boastful… Darius couldn't control himself any longer.

"Your smile sickens me." He grabbed the Regent's jaw, ripped the bone from its sockets and almost tore it off completely, leaving it hanging by only inches of skin.

The man howled through a garbled mess of tongue and blood and dropped to his knees, finally embodying the pathetic state he was underneath the luxurious exterior.

Darius wouldn't give him the satisfaction of dying by the poison he'd swallowed. He'd be the one to slay the weasel.

He raised one of the Twin Blades and cut off the ferven from it, letting the Regent feel the sting of metal pressed to his neck.

But he paused. The neck brought too swift a death.

Instead, he kicked the man in the head, knocking him onto his back, then hovered over him, blade swinging invitingly towards the abdomen.

Ferven flared again from the metal edge, then he slashed and opened up the man's bowels, letting the shrieks wash over him for a third and final time. If only all the people the Silk Regent had betrayed could hear him now and see justice. Darius hoped they would from the afterlife.

Even when Aristippus was dying, Darius couldn't bear the sight of him, so he turned back towards Rufus before Aristippus's screams had eased.

"Leave him to die," Darius said. "There isn't much more resistance in the palace. Most seem to have fled."

The Viridian Warlord nodded. "Then we're close to victory. I'll send centuries to barricade the gates and drive away the cavalry with slingers."

"Good. And when the horsemen try to retreat across the Great Bridge, the Black and Branz Legions will be waiting for them. Thankfully, Lyra hasn't seen any Torians coming across to support this cursed place."

Darius and Rufus went on to discuss what to do with their army and how to quell any remaining resistance in the city in more detail as other commanders and algus eventually joined them, most savouring the sight of the whimpering Regent dying with as much dignity as he deserved.

Apart from the slaves killed at the wall, the assault couldn't have gone better. The city was still mostly intact, and whatever citizens and slaves hadn't left were holed up in their homes. Although unsure what lay in Xavala's future, at least the city had one, and Darius had avoided a repeat of Laltos.

Pollio was the first rakkan commander to enter as they talked and approached Rufus. "Warlord, the cavalry has already been routed. The lake-of-fire tactic was enough to hold them back, though we lost many men."

"Regrettable but unavoidable," the Viridian Warlord said.

It had certainly been a novel idea. There was something about Rufus's tactics that weren't just effective but imaginative. It was a pity the same couldn't be said of most of his legion.

A deep part of Darius took some comfort in the heavy losses the Viridian Legion had taken this night because they deserved a far worse punishment than he'd given them. He hadn't forgotten Laltos, and Viridia was lucky it hadn't suffered the same vengeance as this conquered city.

Pollio slipped off his helmet and regarded his brother. "I underestimated you. We could have easily failed tonight. That's two cities taken in a single night now, thanks to you."

Rufus blinked with the same surprise hitting Darius. Pollio's words didn't sound like another one of his passive-aggressive ploys; these were the first kind words to leave the rakkan's mouth when it came to Rufus.

And to top it off, Pollio gave a rakkan salute to the man just as his brother Piso hobbled into the room, bloody and ragged.

"What the hell?" Piso grimaced.

Pollio gave a quick glance to his twin, then dropped the salute. "I see you survived, Piso."

"No thanks to…" Piso's voice faded away as Darius glared at him.

"Give credit where it's due," Pollio said.

But rather than oblige, Piso scowled at his brother, then turned and hobbled away while mumbling curses to himself.

Rufus ignored the rakkan and faced Pollio again. "Does this mean I have your backing, brother?"

A few of the other centurions and commanders in the room silenced at that question, letting the Silk Regent's groans be the only disturbance in the room.

Pollio grinned. "You do. Father would have lost three times the number of warriors we did tonight."

Finally, at least someone in that damned legion gave their warlord support, and the commander's words seemed to mellow the scowls of some of the others there.

As much as his friends and grandfather had pushed Darius to be a leader, it would take a lifetime to gain the wisdom of battle masters like Rufus. But it was apparent Darius didn't need expertise in every field to be effective. If he was surrounded by competent people, he could leave them to it and focus on those areas where he excelled. Slaying.

The room suddenly quieted into deep silence. The coward had departed, swept away by the reaper to hopefully meet justice, and it was only now that Darius took in the lewd, violent scenes painted on the walls of the Silk Regent's bedchamber. He shivered, suddenly feeling as if within the warped sexual fantasies of the former Regent.

Shaking off his discomfort, Darius knelt by the broken body and ripped out one of Aristippus's golden teeth as proof for Lex that he'd slain at least one of her targets.

"… Master?" Gorgias's voice behind him made him flinch. It had been years since the torture chambers of Laltos, but sometimes the smallest of things could give him a vivid flicker of recollection.

"Gorgias…" Darius rose to see the man looking too clean to have partaken much in the battle. "Glad to see Rufus is keeping you safe."

But there was no gladness in the algus's expression as he looked at the dead Regent. "I hope he suffered."

Darius couldn't call it suffering when compared to the horror recently inflicted on this city, so he left the comment unaddressed.

"Gorgias?" a woman called from the doorway; then in rushed Hera and quickly took her son in her arms. "How are you?"

"I'm fine, Mother." Gorgias pulled himself away, and Hera soon began inspecting him, despite her own arms being bloody and one hand definitely having a couple of fingers bent at unnatural angles.

"You need a surgeon," Darius said.

"Alexandra is on her way into the city," Hera said, an obvious deflection.

But it worked. "But she's still not fit to fight," Darius said. Who knew what dangers still lurked in Xavala's streets.

"Take it up with her." Hera ran a hand across her son's cheek.

Darius would. The palace was secure, and there were enough competent people here to handle things. So, without another word, he marched out of the room and went in search of Lex, clasping the golden tooth tight.

# 26

## Lex – Xavala, the Silk City

"Please, we need you!" The cry was one of unison. Many slaves and citizens had flocked into the dangerous streets as soon as they'd spotted the Chief Priest walking past, not seeming to care about the invading rakkans still charging through their city.

Lex moved away from her algus guards and ushered Aran to the side of the street—or rather, the ghost of a man that he currently was. He laid his gloved hands gently on anyone that approached, but he uttered no words of comfort, no promise of hope, not even a breath of prayer.

And who could blame him? Not a few feet away from the living lay the dead, a sight enough to scar the soul of any veteran of war. To see the man's eyes as he'd passed the butchered corpses at the wall, the black piles of ashes and bones that remained of his slave rebellion… Anyone would have thought the man was witnessing the slaughter of his children.

Perhaps that's how he viewed it. After all, this had been his idea, and Lex knew better than most that guilt was the heaviest yoke to bear.

"Go back to your homes." Lex placed herself between the desperate crowd and the holy man. "The battle is not over, and you're not safe."

But the Chief Priest came up next to her and cleared his throat, a gentle sound that nonetheless carried above the noise of burning and collapse of buildings.

"I'm sorry." The man's voice was weak. "What has happened here is not the will of the God or Goddess. I pray earnestly for you and your families, but do not lose hope. Justice will reign whether it be in this life or the next."

Most seemed placated by the promise of eternal justice as if it blinded them to the blood trickling through the gutters, but Lex wasn't and hadn't been for decades. A few grabbed the hem of Aran's cloak before leaving, as though it would bless them with a prayer of protection, but eventually, she was able to lead the Chief Priest away and slink into the palace with only her guards following.

Inside, some Viridians argued over silver and gold rings cut from the fingers of algus. Looting had been happening in many places in the city they'd just traversed but far from the scale seen in Laltos. She'd only had to kill a couple of Viridians who'd ventured into an abode they shouldn't have, a punishment even the Chief Priest hadn't objected to.

But Lex couldn't worry about the aged man now. She took a quick turn down the slaves' corridors and tried to recall the location of what she sought. When betrothed to the Silk Regent, she'd taken care to learn all she could of him, particularly his resources and wealth. And, most importantly, where he stowed the riches since bolstered with Laltos's spoils. Right now, that might be the only reserve that could save her from Eluthia's assassins.

But as she neared the iron-plated door she sought, she found it ajar, and the clanging of heavy metal already revealed looters within. Surely, the Viridians hadn't found it first…

Before she could enter and verify, a strong hand took her shoulder.

"Lex?" Darius's breath brushed her ear and sent a pleasant shiver down her.

Then the coppery stink of blood hit her nose. She whirled and stepped back but bumped into the Chief Priest, who stood frozen as if still digesting everything he'd witnessed.

"Have you allowed the Viridians to loot here?" she asked Darius.

He shrugged, then dismissed her guards with a wave of his hand. "I don't think the Silk Regent needs his possessions any longer."

"But they're *your* riches now. They'll never respect you if you let them take what they wish."

"They'll respect these." He tapped the hilts of the Twin Blades.

That was true, but that didn't help Lex's gold problem.

"I'm going to call another assembly now," Darius said. "I've just learnt of bad news from Menara. We don't have time to waste if we're going to take the fight to the King."

At those words, the Chief Priest's mournful gaze swept up. Lex paused and waited for him to speak his mind, but nothing but silent air left his lips.

"But three of the warlords aren't here," Lex said. Rufus was too wise a man to be left unchallenged on rakkan ways in an assembly.

"I have you, and I'll consult them when I need to. Come." Darius began walking back the way he'd appeared.

"But the treasures…"

"I'll discuss it with Rufus," Darius called over his shoulder.

"And what's the bad news?" she asked.

"Later."

Gritting her teeth, she had no option but to follow him. But as they set off, he suddenly stopped and turned to her with a fresh seriousness on his face, then held out a hand with dry blood still in the cracks of his skin.

"I forgot," he muttered. "I took this for you."

As he opened his palm, a gold tooth lay nestled in the centre that triggered an old hatred in her to surface.

"Is he dead?" she asked.

"By my sword. He'd taken poison, so I didn't have much time to make him suffer."

"Hasn't this city witnessed enough suffering?" the Chief Priest asked but didn't look up from the floor for a reply.

Xavala's rulers certainly hadn't as far as Lex was concerned. She should have known Aristippus would take the easy way out.

She batted Darius's hand away and sent the gold tooth tinkling onto the marble floor.

"I don't want to touch that filthy thing," she said.

"Fair enough." He turned his bloody hand over and studied it. "Probably best you don't touch me again. You don't want to know where this hand's just been."

They set off again, and Lex considered many times whether to just ask Darius for the gold now, but something held her back. Was it pride? Was it the shame of needing to beg for help after a life of being the person others relied on? Or would Darius be angry she'd never discussed smuggling the weapons with him, promising gold she didn't have? Perhaps those weapons had led to the blood eagles.

Whatever the reason, the words wouldn't easily leave her mouth, but the fact that Eluthia's assassins might come again was too great a threat. For her daughter's sake, she couldn't risk it.

"Darius?" she called.

He came to a halt and turned. "Yes?"

"I have something to ask you." She stepped forward, took his arm, and led him a little farther from the Chief Priest so he couldn't overhear.

"I need…help." She couldn't look him in the eye when she said it, staring instead at his sodden boots.

"With what?"

This might take a lot of effort to get, possibly involving an argument. "I still need gold because I…owe a debt to a dangerous person. I haven't the funds, so I need whatever is stowed here."

"All right."

"Don't ask about—" She froze, met his gaze to see no anger or suspicion within it, only kindness in those dark eyes. "All right?"

"Take what you need."

"This… I'm not speaking of a small amount."

"I gave no restrictions." Darius had never been one to be tight-fisted, so she shouldn't have been so surprised. But he'd never given in so easily without asking for something in return, and she knew what he wanted most—her affections.

"Why are you being so generous?" she asked.

A spark of anger now flickered in his pupils. "Is that so unlike me? Don't you think you can rely on me?"

"It's not that, just—"

"You said you need it and already had an assassin come for you. I know you're not a woman to ask this of me unless in grave danger. Are you?"

She considered lying, not wanting him to fret when he had enough to worry about, but one assassin would just be the beginning. So, she lowered her head and nodded.

He grunted in acknowledgement. "And I'm guessing that Javad fellow won't be able to save you again."

Again, she nodded.

"Then take what you need. And hurry before the Viridians have siphoned it all. I'll get them out of Xavala as quickly as I can for you, but who knows how long that will take." With that, he stomped away before she could respond.

She'd got what she wanted, but why did it leave her feeling guilty? Perhaps she should have expressed her gratitude to him and returned the kindness he was showing.

She hurried after him while he rounded up Rufus, Hera, and a few other algus that had proven themselves trustworthy; then they found one of the Silk Regent's old offices, still effusing luxury but soon smeared with blood as the tired warriors sat down for a much-needed rest around a large table so gleaming with varnish it was as if it hadn't been touched before.

Of all of them, Rufus looked the sharpest, eyes not closed a fraction from fatigue. He hadn't fought, but Lex knew that wasn't why he seemed fresh. Directors of battles needed an alertness that didn't easily fade and kept you awake for sleepless nights with warriors manoeuvring and battling in your mind.

Although Lex hadn't witnessed the battle up close, she knew Rufus had achieved something monumental here. Taking a city in a single night? Again after Laltos? It was unheard of.

"Update me," Darius commanded.

"The palace is secured," Rufus said. "My men have reached the main gates and will soon have control. The rest are flushing out any resistance in the districts. The city is ours."

"Mine." Darius's eyes narrowed on the Viridian Warlord. "And I hear your men are pillaging."

Rufus placed his hands together, fingertips fidgeting before he answered. "You said there was to be no pillaging of civilians, Overlord. But the algus are not mere civilians in the Torian Empire, and my men do not fight for free. I pay them no wage. They eat and live from the land."

"This city is not 'the land,'" Darius replied. "It's mine."

Rufus didn't respond, and he was right not to. This was for Darius to decide and clarify his commands.

But perhaps Darius's idea of marching quickly to Toria might avoid arguments with the Viridians. If they were to leave soon, they'd leave those that remained here in peace as well as leave more treasures and options for Lex.

Yet she couldn't let what Rufus had said go without pointing out one gnawing fact. "Let's not forget"—Lex waited for everyone to focus on her—"that much of the gold stuffing this city's coffers was stolen from Laltos. Is it not rightfully ours?"

"Indeed," Hera added.

"All debts will be repaid," Darius said, "as much as they can be, including returning what was stolen and paying warriors their dues. Now, I didn't call this assembly to divvy loot. The west is still not safe. We control every major town and city, yet our enemies amass on the other side of the River Toras. I am minded to march and join the Black and Branz Legions near the Great Bridge, then cross into Toria at once."

Rufus's fingers suddenly stopped moving, and Lex knew he'd been struck with the same immediate aversion as her. One didn't rush a conquest of the Empire's heart.

"We need time to plan an offensive," Lex said. "Toria's walls are not straight like Laltos's and Xavala's, and they're thickset with bastions all around. You'll never undermine them or break through before they tear your army apart."

"Not to mention they have a goman," Rufus added.

Darius murmured and leaned back in thought.

"The defence of this city was paltry," Hera said. "The King emptied whatever he could, so you can be sure he has something planned."

"That's what I'm afraid of." Darius stood and began pacing around them all. Then he grabbed a dagger, leaned beside Lex, and scratched two waving lines on the pristine tabletop. "The River Toras has two bridges." He stabbed two points along the lines. "Without those, no army can cross. If I were the King, I'd destroy them."

"Unless he *wants* us to cross," Lex said. "In which case, it would probably lead to our defeat."

"But if we move quickly enough, and if we take care of the goman…" Darius looked at Lex, Hera, and Gorgias. "You have more experience with gomans than most. Do you think assassins could get to him?"

Eluthia's might have been able to.

"I doubt it," Hera said. "Even my spies haven't had much success getting near the palace. But it's worth a try. If it only distracts this goman, it can't be pointless."

"Do you have anyone that could try?" Darius asked. "Or perhaps I should go myself."

"No!" Lex's shout echoed around the room, so sudden and sharp that everyone held their breath and stared. "I mean…you'd never get close to them undetected. You've tried an attempt on the King in the past, but Jason…"

Darius raised an eyebrow. "I couldn't defeat Jason?"

"No." Everyone turned to the Chief Priest at the sudden sound of his voice, having forgotten he was even present. "And while Jason may be dead, we now know the King has a goman to command his army of algus. If I thought it would end the war, I'd use every connection I have to get you into the King's palace myself. But you'd never get to him."

"You can get people into the palace?" Hera asked Aran.

The Chief Priest swallowed. "Possibly, but not without considerable risk to myself and others. In truth, I'm far more concerned with the bridges. If you don't act quickly, the King will retaliate, and what he did here is only a taste of the hell he intends to inflict." His last words were strained, as if forced out, and Lex noted he'd switched from saying "we" to "you." When she next had a quiet moment with him, she needed to pick his brain and figure out what he wanted now. He was clearly losing the stomach for war, like many men who had only heard tales over campfires and had never seen the bloody reality for themselves.

"Retaliate…" Darius cut a circle in the table near his tracing of the river. "The King has already struck. We've just heard from the Menarans; Toria raided their farmlands while we've been taking Xavala, far worse than before."

This was the first Lex had heard of it. "Did they reach the town? Or their stores?"

Darius shook his head. "Not yet, at least. They're a long way from Toria, so they must be using somewhere else as a base."

"There's a town on the other side of the Psilos Bridge," Hera said. "It's only a few miles away from the river. The raids must be coming from there."

"We cannot afford to let this continue," Rufus added, his voice casual. "I'm happy to lead the Viridian Legion to take the town."

The Chief Priest paled at the suggestion. "Is that wise?"

"It makes sense." Darius scratched a couple of crosses on the map he was sketching. "The Branz and Black Legions are close to the Great Bridge so will deal with that. And our human soldiers might be able to handle this city. We can send the Viridians to drive the raiders from the farmlands, but perhaps it won't be enough. We may need to plan an assault."

The Chief Priest shot up from his seat. "*Assault?* I was speaking of defending the bridge!"

"But would that be possible to maintain if we don't take the town on the other side?"

Even Lex gaped at the half-rakkan's leap from defending lands to contemplating an assault on a town. When had he become the kind of man to condemn a place he'd only just learnt of, whose inhabitants might not have opposed him in significant numbers? These were the thought patterns of a tyrant. He should have known better. He knew what the Viridian Legion did to human settlements when unconstrained, and although he'd promised her to get the Viridians out of Xavala quickly, this wasn't what she'd had in mind.

"My legion can be ready soon," Rufus said. "If the Menarans can supply some food along the route, we can march for the Psilos Bridge without much delay and be there in under a month. But we could be there more quickly if I take a smaller army. How large is this town?"

"Less than a quarter the size of Xavala," Hera answered before Lex could interject.

Rufus nodded pensively before concluding, "It could be taken with only a thousand rakkans and three weeks' travel time."

"Do you even know the name of this town, Overlord," the Chief Priest asked, "that you're so quick to condemn?"

That seemed to give Darius pause, stole some of the fervour from his stare, and his first reaction was to look at Lex.

"Is this town not a threat to us?" he asked.

Of course it was, but that didn't justify sending Viridians. She considered lying if only to buy time, but after he'd looked to her for guidance, she couldn't deny him an honest answer. "It's called Psinara, and it's the only settlement close to the Psilos Bridge. Any raids across the river must come from there, but we shouldn't rush into action."

"To delay will only allow more raids," Rufus said. "And if we lose more food… There's nothing worse than a starving army."

Lex knew the horrors of that, but she hadn't seen an assessment of what their food situation was or whether they needed to be concerned. Darius would have already been told, and perhaps his urgency was because their situation was more dire than he was letting on. Plus, he'd have heard more details about these raids, and if they were as brutal as the Torian and Xavalan ones had been after Laltos fell, Darius would have vengeance on his mind. That may have been why he seemed intent on sending the Viridians to handle this.

"Rufus is right," Darius said before anyone else responded. "But so is the Chief Priest. I won't attack a town unless there's no other option. Rufus marched his men here from Viridia without incident, then took another city within a day, so I trust him to handle this. March your men to the farmlands and slaughter any raiders you find. Once they're driven back across the Psilos Bridge, sit there and defend it."

The Chief Priest let out a slow breath while closing his eyes, probably feeling as relieved as Lex was.

Darius paused for a moment before adding, "And contact whoever is in charge of the town. Demand they cease their raids, return whatever they stole, and surrender." The way he growled the words told Lex he'd made up his mind. It was so like the old

Darius—resolute and vengeful but with one stark difference. The blood still smeared across his clothes would have repulsed the old Darius and had held him back many times from inflicting horror. Yet the new Darius had conquered that fear. This new man was stronger in a way Lex couldn't help but admire as well as fear.

"Must it be the Viridians?" she asked him.

Darius nodded. "The more infamous their reputation, the more likely the town won't dare continue the attacks."

"Then will you go with them?" she said. Who had a more infamous reputation? And at least if he was there, she could have a little faith that the town would yield without bloodshed.

"I don't know," he answered. "I'll be needed at the Great Bridge."

"Then send a human army with them," the Chief Priest said. "The King may not yield the Psilos Bridge as he did this place. The Viridians will need all the help they can get."

Darius turned to Hera. "Do you have soldiers to spare if you're to deal with Xavala too?"

Lex's heart sank as the inevitable shake of the Regent's head followed.

"Then Rufus's men will march without them."

"... With you?" Lex suggested again.

But Darius didn't answer.

# 27

## King's Orator – Toria

A sweet chuckle swept through Ophelia's mind, not a sound from herself but the monotone thrum from a goman. The noise was so foreign that Ophelia gaped at the King and saw the delight lighting up his eyes as they stood buffeted by the winds atop the Torian palace's highest tower.

Whatever the King had seen to spark such a jubilant mood, Ophelia couldn't see it in the sprawling city below or the river beyond, and the gruelling stair climb up here usually left one in a foul mood.

On the ground, the city's citizens bustled in the streets, making them appear to wriggle like the land itself was alive, and in the distance to the west, the Great Bridge leaned over the River Toras, beginning the route she'd led the evacuees across to safety before the rakkans had moved in to cut off the path. The Xavalan cavalry would never make it here now. Did the King even care? His high spirits certainly had nothing to do with the Silk City, so

Ophelia had to conclude such enjoyment was a result of one of the men she'd sent to the King earlier.

"I take it by your mood," she said, "that one of the Numbered I sent to you is the man you're looking for."

But the King shook his head. "*Keep searching, and don't give up on Alexandra. We'll get her eventually.*"

Despite the disappointment, the King's mood didn't dampen.

"Then why are you in good spirits, my king?" Ophelia asked.

"*My pleasure is from what I see.*"

He definitely wasn't speaking of the city below, but whatever it was, Ophelia shared none of his jovial mood. It had taken considerable gold and time to try and fail to get close to Alexandra, and even more to gather just those half a dozen Numbered that might be the man the King sought. No one in the Empire now went by the name "Sixty-three," which made her task next to impossible. Failure was not something she tolerated, yet this might end up being another one to add to the list.

"I won't give up, my king." Ophelia gave a small bow. "Then, if I may ask, what do you see that has pleased you?"

The King bent and leaned on the decorated parapet, closing his eyes for a moment and breathing in the fresh air that lacked the city stink that eddied at ground level.

"*I see the rakkans' confidence growing.*"

Whose wouldn't after taking one of the most affluent cities in the Empire? "Is that a good thing?"

The thrum returned to Ophelia's mind.

"*It is when confidence becomes overconfidence.*"

"So, will you act soon?" Would the swifts of Alogos finally muster? Would Jason finally go to battle wielding the Staff of Arria?

*"I've consulted the One Mind, and the chances are they will go for the bridges soon. We should act."*

"Launch more raids?"

*"No. I see more clearly now. We'll face them in battle."*

A flutter went through Ophelia's stomach, having waited too long for this moment. "Does that mean you have a plan to thwart the Twin Blades?" If they could be removed from consideration, Toria's victory would surely only be a matter of time.

*"I have the beginnings of an idea. From what I've seen, we cannot destroy them, but perhaps lost will do, like within the depths of Mount Psilos as the Staff almost was… I shall need to think longer on it."*

But then what had the goman meant by seeing things clearly? Could it be something Ophelia was yet unaware of?

There was one remark that had stuck in her mind ever since the King had made it in passing, some unknown variable in her plans, and now she needed clarification on it.

"Perhaps…" Ophelia said, "you speak of the reinforcements you mentioned before. Will we utilise them? After all, why wait until the Empire is on its knees to call on them?"

The King's eyes came suddenly back into focus. *"It's not in my power to call upon them. They will come when they come, be it in a day, a year, or ten."*

If Darius's progress up to now was anything to go by, they didn't have a year.

"But I'm confused," Ophelia said. "Who are they? Where are they coming from?"

*"My homeland. The gomans have been waiting for the Aretean Sea to calm for decades. As soon as it does, your liberation will follow."*

Ophelia felt a fool for not realising that sooner. Of course the goman had been speaking of his own kind.

But it had been so many years since he'd spoken of his kin travelling here that Ophelia had assumed the event was no longer possible.

"Do you not see when they will arrive?"

The goman's eyebrows forked, and Ophelia swore a low growl resonated in her mind.

"*No. But they will come.*"

Ophelia hid her sceptical reaction. The King had never been one to cling to foolish hopes, but she wouldn't place as much faith as he did in the gomans. If the King hadn't seen them coming, then they *weren't* coming.

"How can you be sure?" she dared ask.

"*Because they said they would, and gomans do not lie.*"

But they could change their minds. The two gomans had arrived in Toria well over a decade ago, so what good were promises that old?

She hadn't the nerve to voice that question, and rather than sour the King's mood any further, it was time to return the conversation to what had given him cheer only minutes ago—their upcoming battle.

"If we are to fight," she began, "then we must protect Toria first." Spies had reported armies amassing to the west of the capital, and Alogos was too far to send support now, so a battle close by wasn't in their interests. "We should destroy the Great Bridge. Who on the other side is there to trade with now anyway? That whole land has fallen, and there's little use in taking it back. Besides, if left long enough to their own devices, the rakkans always turn on each other; then we could take advantage."

"*Patience. I'm more concerned with the Psilos Bridge.*"

*Strange.* Although it was the only other major crossing on the River Toras, the only route to Toria afterwards was around the Great Scars, then through Alogos and hundreds of miles of plains that were ideal for ravaging an army with cavalry. Of course, it wasn't a good thing to let armies cross it, but it was hardly concerning.

"Will you defend it?" Ophelia asked. "Do you wish to continue the raids?"

The King's eyes misted over. "*That would be best. I'll defend the nearby town… What's the name?*"

"Psinara?"

"*Yes. And send Jason.*"

Ophelia winced as a gust of wind almost tore off her cloak. She wrapped it more tightly around herself. "Is he needed? Are we at that much risk of losing the battle?"

"*Even with Jason, our odds are even at best. This Warlord Rufus will prove quite a thorn in our side. But don't fret. Even if he's victorious, it could work in our favour.*"

Ophelia frowned. Losing a town had no benefit that she could see, but she wouldn't question her wise King. "I assume Jason will survive either way…"

The King paused as if he hadn't listened to the remark. "*You're right about the Great Bridge. I'll destroy it myself from the river.*"

The abrupt declaration stole Ophelia's stream of thought. "*You* will destroy it?"

"*With a little help.*"

Whatever that meant, it had Ophelia imagining giant waves crashing down on the bridge, but even gomans didn't possess the kind of magic to do that. No, she suspected it had something to do with the hundreds of fishing boats commandeered while she'd been away. The King hadn't filled her in on the details of what they'd been up to, but her spies had reported a few things, including the fact the King had sailed with them for a while.

After her mind had wandered for a few moments, she suddenly recalled what she'd been asking before the King had digressed. He'd given no answer to her remark about Jason surviving, no assurance, no relief, and Ophelia wouldn't let the shift in conversation continue. "I'll tell Jason to retreat if things aren't going his way. There's no sense in—"

"*No. Don't confuse his mind with the likelihood of failure. He will know to retreat if he must.*"

Ophelia pulled her cloak tighter around her, suddenly itching all over. "He doesn't like it when I keep things from him." And even he wasn't mindless enough to fail to realise the King saw much of the future.

But the goman didn't react to the words.

"Will he at least take the Staff?" Ophelia asked.

"*Not yet. We could use it to destroy that army, but their tactics would adjust. Our first strike will pierce deep into all the legions. It won't just win a battle but win the war. The One Mind has shown me more of what will come. Their army will unify. Then we strike.*"

"Very well, my king. And when will that be?"

The King's thrum began to build again.

# 28

## Darius – The Great Bridge

There wasn't a single enemy on the Great Bridge, only the rush and hiss of water coursing between the colossal pillars holding the structure clear of the torrents. It was a barren, lifeless thing, stone grey with age, weathered and lying in the noon sun like a corpse pecked to the bone but still strong enough to allow Darius's legions across. This was all a little too easy.

His journey here with the other leaders hadn't taken long on swiftback, and the Black and Branz Legions were already fed and fighting fit, although running low on food and mostly unaware of how hard the raids had hit their future supplies. They needed to cross and get to the Torian farms.

Wherever the Xavalan cavalry had headed, they'd avoided clashing with the might of two legions camped here, so the warriors were fresh.

But still, there was an alien energy blighting the men behind him, a restlessness that had often turned to violence among themselves. Men on edge. Men waiting for a fight that hadn't come for weeks.

Lyra stalked between the warlords and regents alongside Darius, then carried on ahead, her nose confirming the barrenness of the place he witnessed. Why hadn't the King tried to defend it?

"I reckon we scared them away," Sulla said beside him with a grin, as if knowing his thoughts. "If I were a piddly human and saw a hulking specimen like me in the distance, I'd run too."

Darius raised an eyebrow. "When have you ever run from anything?"

"It's happened…once or twice in my younger days. Can't remember why; just remember having to slip on my breeches while clambering out of a window." He chuckled. "These days, I'm too brave to run."

"… Or too foolish to know when you should."

Sulla scoffed. "Well, I know right now only a fool would run from an empty road to our enemies."

And this bridge was just that. This was the first time Darius had seen the place, and now he knew how it had earned the name "Great." The weight of an entire army marching across in full kuraminium armour wouldn't have been a worry for the stone supports and the giant archways bearing the platform, regardless of how old they were. Even the river hadn't defeated the stone pillars sunk into the shrouded riverbed, green with algae but with the same sharp edges they'd likely had when built. They said it was centuries old, yet one wouldn't have thought it.

The hunks of stone laid together were larger and heavier than a dozen men apiece and must have been built by rakkans capable of manoeuvring them into place. The structure was as straight as a sword and long enough that a man who set off in the evening would have to worry about darkness falling before he reached the other side.

"Escorts scout ahead," Darius said to Hera. "The King must be planning something."

She nodded, and soon the birds soared across the water to search the other side. Meanwhile, Darius considered how someone could destroy this thing. Fire wouldn't do it—even rakkan fire would take a while—and it would take men with picks days or even weeks to bring the thing down.

"I wish Aran were here," Darius said to the other warlords. "He said the King would destroy this. Do you see how?"

Both the Black and Branz Warlords shook their heads.

"Perhaps catapults," Varro added. "But they'd need to get into position first. Our slingers would splinter any that tried."

But the King must have had a plan to have left it clear. This was supposed to be close to a major fishing point, yet the wooden jetties on the other side hadn't even a wreck of a boat attached, and the only disturbances of the river's surface were from birds and fish.

"Maybe there's something on the riverbed," Darius mused.

"The river is deeper than it looks," Varro said. "A man could dive and not reach the bottom before he drowned. They'd have to destroy the bridge from above."

So, as long as Darius held it, they'd be safe. Apparently.

Had he just got lucky? Was the Chief Priest wrong for once? The man had remained with Lex in Xavala, probably to mournfully wander the streets more and lament at his failed peaceful revolution. Ever since the Viridian Legion had left, the priest had barely lifted his head.

One of the algus came sprinting up and bowed before saying, "My escort sees something. Algus are waiting on the other side, hidden within the trees."

"How many?" Darius asked.

"Hard to say. He's only spotted a few dozen so far."

Not enough to faze two rakkan legions, but how many more were unseen? This had the stink of a trap, but perhaps Darius's best option was to spring it and see exactly what it was.

He looked over the Branz Warlord, at the rakkan who had suffered no ill consequences yet for siding with Hadrian against Margalvia. A smart leader wouldn't risk his men, even if he disliked them, but Darius was still tempted.

After all, what was his other option? Wait here and do nothing?

"Flavius," Darius called.

The Branz Warlord turned to face him. "Yes?"

"Yes, *Overlord*," Sulla corrected.

"… Overlord," Flavius muttered.

"You'll cross the bridge first," Darius said.

The Branz Warlord took another couple of glances at the place. "Alone?"

"Well, you'll have your men with you."

Flavius scowled. "I mean, you won't come with us?"

"I won't." Darius waited while the Branz Warlord stared, hoping that once the idea had time to sink in he'd be more open to it.

But Flavius's scowl only deepened with every passing moment.

"Don't tell me you're afraid." Sulla smiled.

But Darius shot him a look of warning not to bait the rakkan, which he seemed to ignore, instead leaning towards Darius and whispering, "Don't worry. Leave this to me; I have a way with words."

That he surely did, but that "way" usually earned him a thump to the jaw.

"Look, Flavius"—Sulla wrapped an arm around the Warlord's shoulders, much to Flavius's visible disgust—"someone has to be the first across, and think…the first rakkan ever to cross the Great Bridge could be a Branzian. They'd sing songs about him and the brave warlord that sent him."

Darius had to suppress his shock when the words seemed to wipe the irritation on Flavius's face and instead stir a little pride. Perhaps he'd underestimated Sulla.

"Look at it this way," Sulla continued, "the worst that can happen—the absolute worst—is your men will walk into a trap and be slaughtered like rats. But they won't include *that* in the song, will they?"

… He just never knew when to shut up.

"It isn't a request," Darius said, bringing Flavius's attention back to him and tired of waiting. "It's an order."

"Very well, *Overlord*." Even though the title was laced with sarcasm, Darius wouldn't put him in his place. His gut told him the Warlord would soon suffer.

The Branz Warlord turned to his commanders and cracked open his mouth to give orders but paused before turning back around. "With my whole legion?"

That struck Darius as foolish. "Take enough that you can fight on the other side if you need to," he said.

"I'll need algus to keep me updated on scouting."

"Hera." He turned to the Regent. "Give him who he needs."

She nodded while Darius once again studied the river, just about making out what appeared to be fishing boats on the horizon to the north, nearer where the river met the turbulent Aretean Sea. But they were so distant they could have easily been fins or floating gulls.

It took a few hours for the Branz Warlord to get his commanders and centuries into formation and at the foot of the Great Bridge. Darius watched every moment, prepared to call them back at the first hint of trouble, but their escort scouts saw nothing stirring in response.

The Branz Warlord himself decided not to go with his men, instead entrusting the brave task to one of his commanders. *So, it's not just me that suspects something is awry.*

As the men set off, Darius found a nearby hill that gave him a better view of the entirety of the bridge and the distant banks on the other side. The army marched in loose formation, the vanguard heavily armoured, the slingers following with their weapons hanging by their side.

The heat of the day reached its peak by the time they'd got halfway, and now all the warriors had feet on the bridge, at least a thousand.

"Still no movement on the other side," Hera confirmed.

Darius watched the marching ant-like figures, then caught sight of something strange on the river's surface in the corner of his eye. When he shifted his gaze, he found nothing there, only the usual ripples, but there was something odd about them, something he couldn't put his finger on that made the water eddy unnaturally.

"Do you see that?" Darius pointed the area of water out to Hera and the warlords.

But as he did, the surface shifted again like the shadow of a cloud had passed over it. Perhaps it was a cloud. The afternoon sky wasn't clear.

"Flavius," Darius called. "Get more slingers ready on the riverbank."

"To cross?"

"No, to..." What exactly did he want them for? His gut told him to be prepared, but for what, he couldn't say. "Keep them off the bridge."

He recalled sneaking out of Laltos within its river, using crude reeds to breathe. Surely an army couldn't do that. He'd almost drowned with just himself.

Branz Centurions left to organise the slingers while Darius watched the far side. His men had almost made it.

But the water stirred, quickly, and this time definitely not the reflection of any cloud.

He saw it before the crash resounded, a white behemoth exploding from within the river at the far side. Its giant body leapt fully clear of the water like a whale thrice the size of anything he'd heard songs of.

The beast arced over the bridge, its mass dwarfing the structure underneath, before it came down and smashed atop the stone.

An almighty crack of stones yielding followed heartbeats later as shattered pieces flew out from the impact, spinning into the water and sinking beneath the creature as it disappeared into the deep once again.

"What the..." Darius's voice was the only sound above the echoes of crumbling stone. The beast hadn't hit any of his men, but the cleft it had created in the bridge looked too far to leap over. The legionnaires soon turned back, now sprinting rather than marching towards the other side.

Meanwhile, a new shadow moved within the water towards Darius's end of the bridge.

He took off down the hill and rushed towards the waiting centuries of slingers, who were fixated on the carnage but had enough wits to ready their weapons.

As Darius arrived, the shadow neared, and the slingers began spinning.

"Do you see that?" Darius yelled. "Aim for the air above it. They'll try to destroy the other end." He needn't ask Flavius whether his men could swim. Most rakkans couldn't.

The shadow neared and the slingers loosed, the fiery balls hissing as they hit the surface of the water before the shadow morphed into a white mass once again. It burst from the depths and careened into the bridge side on, slingers hitting its flank over a hundred times but not inflicting so much as a scratch. The beast's skin must have been tougher than kuraminium, and sharp teeth jutted from the upper jaw of its closed mouth, each one as large as a Margalvian building, probably capable of biting through rock.

A shudder swept through the ground as the bridge buckled, stones flung high in front of the roaring mass as it began lowering again into the torrents.

But Darius spied something more shocking, more confusing: on the beast's back was a dark figure the size of a man, who looked to be strapped on and rode it as one would a horse, only lying flat on his front.

Darius looked back at the bridge and the stranded warriors. A couple of thousand men. He'd suspected a trap, but this?

Before he could formulate a response, thuds began echoing. The ground shook, followed by the groan of stone protesting. The bridge shook like a shuddering snake, with the boom, boom, boom of a drum as it went. Piece by piece, the bridge began to collapse, the pillars underwater knocked out two at a time, leaving only air and water to bear its weight.

The Branz Legionnaires still atop the bridge were too far away to hear their cries, only apparent as specks of black falling with the bridge and soon consumed by the dark waters until every shard of stone had sunk, leaving a white fizz on the water and a few floating, splashing rakkans, the few that had had enough sense to shed their armour.

Then the fins appeared. At least half a dozen, black as coal, rising to reveal the black-and-white bodies and jaws of orcas that snapped at the rakkans and dragged them under into a wet death.

Even had the behemoth not been lurking in the depths, these orcas would be able to prevent boats from rescuing the men or crossing here or anywhere with deep enough water.

Darius froze as he took in what he'd just witnessed, what it meant. That beast hadn't needed to leap clear of the water, hadn't needed to boast its size and crash down upon the bridge. From the beginning, it could have taken all the pillars out as it had at the end. This was a show of strength, the King bellowing from his throne that Toria ruled these waters and Darius should give up.

So, the goman *had* known they'd try to cross the Great Bridge, and Darius saw little he could do in answer to such a foe. Was assassination the only way they'd be rid of this threat?

The curses of the other warlords and leaders soon greeted his ears again, Sulla's the most foul.

"Have you ever seen anything like that?" Darius asked the rakkan.

"In my nightmares, perhaps," Sulla said.

"And those orcas… Can they be trained to do that?"

"No." Hera stepped beside him, worry lines cratering her brow. "They must have been escorts. I've heard of some algus opting for swimmers, but that…"

And if they were escorts, there was one man could have forewarned them but hadn't.

Darius whirled until facing west, where the Silk City lay. "Bring me the Chief Priest."

# 29

## Rufus – Psilos Bridge

Rufus had thought Viridian raids were brutal, but the wreckage along the road to the Psilos Bridge brought a hush to even his most hardened warriors. The raiders were no longer in sight, having had enough sense to flee his advancing army, but enemies kept watch in the distance, meaning it was only a matter of time until his warriors saw action.

It wasn't the sense of death that stunned them—his men's stomachs were more accustomed to the dead than the living—but the extent of the waste, the untold tons of food stores that had been either stolen or torched to feed only maggots.

Those farmhouses still standing in the night were charred, wooden skeletons of what they'd once been, and the barns once rammed with produce were now collapsed heaps of black timber too.

Most human remains they found were tiny fragments, a skull amongst the ash or a hand not consumed by the flames. But despite the lack of corpses, the foul air betrayed the mass of death these lands had buried within.

"How could people do this?" Gorgias said from beside him.

Rufus hadn't seen the man so despondent since soon after they'd broken him and turned him into a productive servant.

"In war," Rufus said, "qualms will only hinder you. The King has none, it seems." And it didn't bode well for them that Darius often shared Gorgias's inability to emotionally detach.

The last time Rufus had trodden through these fertile lands had been with his father and a smaller army, and at that time, they'd been alive and plentiful, allowing his warriors to take what they needed without a farmer being any the wiser. But now…his warriors had been reduced to rummaging through the remnants like rats.

"I'm bloody starving," Piso grumbled beside him. "I'm sick of eating charred grain."

"Be grateful we have anything extra," Rufus said. Thankfully, some glum-looking Menarans had brought a few meagre supplies from the town a few days ago to keep them going for a while, but only enough to survive, not feel satiated.

"If the Overlord had a backbone," Piso said, "he'd demand blood for this theft. If they keep running from us, we shouldn't stop at the bridge. After all, aren't we owed a debt? You let the Overlord take our spoils from Xavala, so you should let us reap our dues from the next town." The rakkan dared to speak as if it was his own spoils that had been stolen. Even though he was always irritable, Rufus's brother had been as annoying as a stone in his boot on this entire march. It was almost enough to make Rufus draw a dagger and shut the rakkan up for good.

But luckily for Piso, Rufus never lacked self-control.

And so the moaning continued as they pressed on all the way to the bridge and were across it a day earlier than he'd planned and ready to make camp.

In the distance, only a mile or two from them, the town of Psinara waited with its gates sensibly shut and escort scouts roaming the skies. Its walls were reportedly made of weathered limestone and barely comparable to Laltos's or Xavala's, and the town was built in a perfect square—or as near perfect as human engineers could manage—doubtlessly by men that had either had insufficient funds to build effective defences or that had never defended a city from rakkans before. They'd even built Psinara on flat land rather than the hill not too far away, with only grass sprouting in between it and the bridge it guarded. It was almost inviting Rufus to attack, but sadly, he hadn't been given that command yet.

"How far away should we set up camp?" Pollio asked.

Rufus's Subdued had done as thorough a scouting as they could given the limited time, so he knew what kind of weapons the nearby town had to defend itself and where his army would be safest.

"Set up camp where we can be seen from their walls," he said, "but close enough to block the bridge. Assume their ballistae have a long range. Don't cross into it."

Pollio nodded and went to organise the men while Rufus took a long-overdue rest. A few hours crawled by before the camp began to take shape, their movements not going unnoticed by the Psinarans if his scouts' escorts were correct, and soon a group of a dozen mounted algus were spotted leaving the town gates under a flag of parley.

"That was quick," Rufus said more to himself than anyone else. He hadn't even flexed his army's muscles yet, and the enemy wanted to speak with him.

"Do you think they'll surrender?" Gorgias asked, the worry in his voice plain.

"Based on what we've just seen," Rufus said, "they only engage in a fight when they have an unfair advantage, and I'm too pessimistic to believe ending their raids will be so easy. Our best bet is to expect hostility and use intimidation. No one does that better than Viridians, so I think it would be best if you didn't speak when we meet them."

Gorgias seemed hesitant to agree but eventually nodded. Rufus placed on his horned helmet, then took Gorgias, the twins Pollio and Piso, and a dozen of his Subdued along the road connecting the bridge to Psinara to meet the approaching group, only halting when on the limit of where Rufus estimated the town's ballistae could strike.

The Psinarans all proudly wore white tunics with King Medus's black eagle emblem stitched onto the front—that's if they even were Psinarans; Rufus suspected these were Torians, with their chins held high and that arrogant smirk that soldiers far from a war front bore.

Unfortunately for them, the war front had just reached them.

The riders stopped on the road and dismounted a few yards away, with one woman coming to the front to face him, cautiously scanning everyone in Rufus's party, and it wasn't a stretch to know she feared Darius was among them.

After her survey, the woman's gaze rested on Rufus with a little of her smirk returning, enough to make a rakkan want to smack it from her plump face. The rest of her body almost burst from the seams of her large tunic, and Rufus concluded that she hadn't done much fighting recently and was too young to be a commander.

"Who am I speaking with?" the woman asked in what Rufus recognised as a subtle Torian accent.

"Who do you think?" he asked.

"Don't even try to bluff that you're the Slayer," she said. "We know he isn't with you."

"If you knew, you wouldn't have looked worried when you arrived," Rufus said, glad when his remark wiped away her smirk. "Have you come to surrender?"

The woman looked to either side of her, her fellow algus seemingly amused at the suggestion. "I was going to ask you the same thing."

"Good." Rufus took a step forward and let a forced chuckle rasp in his throat, just like his father used to do. "My men are restless for a fight."

"You're damned right we are!" Piso grinned with malice, and his interruption was one of only a few Rufus was glad of. Some men took pleasure from battle that couldn't be feigned, and Piso's was undeniable.

The woman glanced at him but mostly focused on the Subdued in Rufus's party.

"You traitors fight for him?" the woman spat. "You'd come to join us if you have any spine left in you."

"Save your breath," Rufus said. "The Viridian Legion instils discipline and obedience, and my people are loyal."

"Ah…" The woman's smile returned. "So, you're the Viridian Warlord."

She really hadn't known? *This* was the pathetic creature the King had sent to speak with him—a woman so blind she couldn't see what was staring her in the face?

Rufus was as insulted as he'd ever been in his life.

He held out his arms, flexed his admittedly slender muscles, and brandished the tattoos and the three signature bands that marked him not only as a Viridian but also as a warlord.

"The fact that you didn't know," he said, "tells of your ignorance to even trivial rakkan details. Did the three Viridian bands tied to my arm not tell you all you needed to know? Do you think you can resist us when you don't seem to know the first thing about us? I suggest you surrender because you're far out of your depth. I am the rakkan that conquered Laltos and the Silk City, and this pathetic town will be crushed like an ant under my boot if I so wish. You have until dawn to surrender and return everything looted from Menara's lands, otherwise, Psinara will become nothing more than a scribble added to the list of my conquests."

Either the woman was too stupid to be intimidated, or she knew something Rufus didn't, because her grin didn't vanish at any of the threats he uttered. Did she know that Darius had forbidden him from attacking the town?

"Psinara will never surrender," she said. "The King commands we fight to the last."

"I'd wager the King is not here," Rufus said, "and rational people fear the tyrant on their doorstep rather than the tyrant many leagues away."

"Fear?" the woman snorted, grimacing. "Fear will never conquer loyalty."

Without warning, a rush of movement sent the hairs all over Rufus's neck on end as the figures in front of him became blurs, ripping their swords out with a flash of blue power.

Rufus leapt back instinctively as his Subdued reacted quickly; Gorgias was the first to bolt into the enemy group and hack at the woman that had been speaking.

Although Rufus sensed the movement of the fight as it began, his eyes barely tracked it, and only when Piso grabbed hold of an algus's arm could he make out a face, see the algus scream as Piso pulled her arm almost from the socket before smashing her skull with one almighty right hand.

The leading algus scored a cut on Gorgias's arm, but the dark-haired man's sword bit her chest a heartbeat later, carrying on through until showering him with blood.

As they fought, two algus came straight at Rufus, easily outmatching him even if he'd been the greatest swordsman in the legions. He ducked under one of their slashes and batted another away with his kuraminium armguard before two Subdued rushed to his aid and cleaved the heads from the enemies in moments.

Rufus took another step back, surveyed the scene before him, and saw that his party now had the advantage in numbers, and it wasn't long before the last Torian algus fell and had his throat sawn through by a laughing Piso.

"Cowards," Gorgias spat, clutching his bleeding arm.

Rufus shared the disgust. What kind of dishonourable cheats attacked under a flag of parley? He'd thought even the King above that, but apparently not. The man had no more respect for Darius's army than he had for the blood eagled slaves in Xavala.

And Rufus couldn't bear to think what would have happened to his mother if Gorgias had been killed.

He suspected the Psinaran's attack had been their intent all along, to assassinate him and hope to leave the rakkan army with a halfwit like Piso in charge. That woman likely wasn't the leader in the town and was just someone those higher up deemed worth risking the death of.

Before Rufus could collect more of his thoughts, more movement in the air began, soon followed by thuds and sprays of dirt as bolts spiked into the ground around them.

He cursed. The ballistae had a longer range than even his largest estimates.

Ducking and weaving through the torrent of projectiles, he and the other rakkans quickly made their way outside their enemy's range, but not without losing a couple of Subdued who hadn't their reflexes.

"Don't worry," Gorgias said, catching his breath. "A town that size won't have a large supply of bolts."

"I'm more worried about the algus," Rufus said. Any town that could afford to waste the godlike warriors was one that made him think twice of camping so close to for any length of time. If Darius hadn't forbade it, he'd have planned an assault immediately rather than wait for algus assassins to make attempts on his life.

"We can dodge through the bolts," Piso said. "Let's call the men and rush the bastards."

"When has that ever worked for you?" Pollio said with a shake of his head. "Let's calm ourselves. The camp's outside their range, and if Gorgias is right, we can bait them into wasting their ammunition in the night-time hours."

Rufus almost smiled at the wise idea. Perhaps some of his tactics had rubbed off on his brother; such a pity the same couldn't be said of Piso.

"Pollio's right," Rufus said. "If we spread the men thinly enough, our slingers can dodge the bolts. Once they're low, they might reconsider surrender." It was a long shot, but even if they didn't, they might be baited into an attack and subsequent field battle that Rufus was well within his authority to order his army into.

"So we'll just stand around taking casualties?" Piso spat.

"Less than we would in a direct assault. Trust me."

Piso huffed and began marching back into the camp. "I don't."

"Aren't you forgetting something?" Gorgias shouted while still battling to stem the bleeding from his arm. "The Overlord told us to defend the Psilos Bridge, not attack Psinara."

"Sometimes, the only way to defend is to end the threat of an enemy for good," Pollio said.

Gorgias gaped, then turned to Rufus. "Warlord?"

"Are you surprised?" Rufus said. "We're here to fight, not sit by our fires cooking what's left of the rotting food. I won't assault the town, but unless they feel the weight of our presence, they'll never surrender, and I'll have failed in what I was ordered to do. Piso will ready his men, and before the night is over, this field will be knee-deep in wasted bolts."

# 30

## Lex – The Great Bridge

"You should be begging for my forgiveness after what you did," Warlord Flavius shouted. "Your orders got my men killed! Was their sacrifice worth it?"

Lex moved in front of Darius before he could reach for the Blades. A growl resonated in Darius's throat as the Branz Warlord glared at him, and if Lex didn't do something, they'd have a dead warlord to contend with.

For a few moments, Darius's heavy breaths were all that left his mouth until he said, "Speak again and they'll be your last words." Then, he stormed away towards the River Toras, whose waters stirred and held a darkness that now seemed to strike fear into every rakkan there. Lex had heard what had happened but wouldn't have believed it if not for the hundreds of witnesses.

She followed alongside Darius, tempted to take his hand and cool his temper, but left that task to the night breeze that currently swept through his dark hair. She knew he enjoyed overlooking water while feeling the sea winds, and this breeze had travelled hundreds of miles from the delta downstream and brought the fresh saltiness that always seemed to ease his temper.

But this night's silence also brought an eerie chill, like the air bore the ghostly curses of drowned warriors. This place should have been their gateway to justice, but now…

"What was all that shouting about?" Sulla called as he joined them. "Old Flavius there looks like he's sucking piss."

Trust him not to sense the mood.

"Things became a bit heated," Lex said.

"Well, that's rakkans for you. Fire in our hearts and out of our mouths, and after a good meal with sprugenroot, out of other places too." He grinned at Darius, but it soon faded as the Overlord ignored his jests.

"Don't feel bad for the bastards," Sulla said. "Those rakkans were killing us in the Urukan Mine only a few months ago."

"Still," Darius said. "The scale of the losses is…"

"Losses are inevitable," Lex said. "If we're ever to achieve our aims, we must make sacrifices. There's no way we could have known what would happen, so don't feel guilty."

"I'm not," Darius said. "I'm wondering what the hell we do next. It seems like fate wishes me to fail now."

"We'll figure it out," Sulla said. "It's up to us to decide our future, not fate. You know what they say: every man is the architect of his own destiny."

Lex raised an eyebrow. "And what about women?"

"Ah." Sulla scratched the scars on his chin. "I'll rephrase: every *single* man is the architect of his own destiny."

Lex rolled her eyes, but Darius didn't seem to be paying much attention, instead staring at the far riverbank that had been his aim.

"Something on your mind?" Lex asked him.

But Darius was too wrapped up in his thoughts to hear her. After a long pause while the others behind muttered amongst themselves, Darius asked, "When will Aran be here?"

"Soon." Lex had travelled with the Chief Priest from Xavala, and he was just washing himself before the expected grilling. The journey hadn't taken long but had been a good chance for Lex to quiz him on the news from the Empire. His many escorts had seen much, but he was more caged than usual.

It was only a little wait until Aran joined her, Darius, and Sulla, silently looking across the water as he arrived. There was a hollowness to his eyes, no shock in them, no awe at the ruined bridge before them. Just emptiness. They'd heard of what happened, but even Lex had gaped at the sight at first, as if the Great Bridge had simply vanished, leaving only its shattered ramp on the riverbank. Had one of Aran's escorts witnessed the destruction?

"You don't seem surprised," Darius said to the man as if mirroring Lex's thoughts.

"What do you expect?" the Chief Priest said. "I have no more shock left to give or tears to shed after Xavala. You could rend the world in two and I'd feel no more desolation than now. I don't even know if I'm doing the right thing anymore."

It wasn't surprising the man's spirit was broken, but Lex had faith he'd heal with time. He had to know their cause was a just one, and the King they were trying to defeat was the one responsible for Xavala.

"I take it you heard about the orcas," Darius said. "You could have warned us that algus have such escorts."

The Chief Priest walked towards the riverbank, knelt, and ran a glove through the water. "An orca in this river is a rare sight. I've seen it only a few times, always caught in old fishing nets near the Torian boats. I bonded them to algus before they were freed, and I believe they used them to help the fishermen near the delta. Never heard of them used in war. They can't stay in the river for too long at a time; they prefer the sea."

"If they're given feasts like they had today," Sulla said, "I'm sure they'll come to like it here."

"That may explain the orcas," Darius said, "but not that behemoth. You could have mentioned *that*."

The Chief Priest stood and faced them. "I think I'd remember such a thing. It isn't anything I've seen before."

At the revelation, Darius looked at Lex as if to see if she had any answers, but she only saw one possibility if Aran hadn't bonded that creature.

"You once said there was another person that could bond escorts," Lex said.

Aran's eyes flitted, a nervousness in them. "My sister… But it's impossible. She's dead."

"Perhaps she bonded it before she died."

"No. It's not possible." Although the man's words were certain, his face betrayed doubt.

"You're sure she's dead?" Darius asked. "When? How?"

The Chief Priest swallowed. "I'm certain of it, and I was not alone in witnessing her death. She was killed by…my late brother."

Darius gave Lex a look from the corner of his eye, and she suspected they were thinking of the same list of questions just raised.

"Why would your brother…?" Lex couldn't even finish the question, the mental image of her lost son killing Cynthia sending a shudder through her.

"I don't think he knew what he was doing," the Chief Priest replied. "He was always an honourable boy, couldn't stand hypocrites or those that didn't live out what they expressed. But at some point, he changed."

"How old was he? Had he gone mad?" Darius asked without the delicacy such a question warranted.

The Chief Priest shook his head. "Not mad, just very disturbed, wasn't himself anymore. As for his age…I'm ashamed to say I cannot even remember when he was born or how old he would have been. It's been so long."

Although the man's face told of the pain of such memories, Lex had one more pertinent question given this man's powers. That behemoth had to have come from somewhere.

"How many other family members do you have?" she asked.

"None that are alive. My parents are long dead, and there were only three of us siblings. My sister was the only one ever to replicate my gift. Not only is she dead, but she had no reason to give any algus an escort. She'd have wanted no part in helping anyone from the Empire."

"Well, she must have done," Darius said. "What other explanation is there?"

The Chief Priest's head dipped, either in prayer or defeat. "There is one. As we know, my gifts aren't unique. The Goddess could have bestowed the power to another."

The thought had Lex's mind racing at the implications. Surely, they'd have heard something.

"I think I need the latrine," Sulla said. "If they have anything like that beast on the ground rather than the sea, we're in trouble."

"You're certain it wasn't wild?" Lex asked.

"It was definitely an escort." Darius faced the dark waters as if watching the beast again. "How else would someone be able to ride it?"

"What?" Lex gaped at the man. "You never said someone was riding it." Why would they? Not only would they have to surface far more regularly, but it would be so perilous as to be foolish.

"That's odd," the Chief Priest muttered.

Something about this struck Lex as off. People didn't ride escorts unless for convenience, and how was that convenient? There was no need to mount it, unless…

Lex gasped as she realised the truth, which drew the concerned looks of the others.

"What's wrong?" Darius asked.

"It wasn't an escort," she said. "The only reason to ride it is if there was no other option."

"You mean they tamed it?" Darius asked. "Like a horse?"

"No. It must have been the goman."

The Chief Priest murmured, "Yes… That makes sense. They can control whoever or whatever they're touching."

"Like a Numbered?" Darius asked.

"No," Lex answered. "Animals aren't intelligent enough to have their minds poisoned into obedience. The beast had to be controlled directly."

Darius cursed, but Lex saw the silver lining to this realisation.

"It means the beast can't patrol the waters for long," Lex said. "The goman would either drown or freeze. It may give us windows of opportunity."

"But he can see his future," the Chief Priest added. "We cannot surprise them. He'll be in the right place at the right time."

Darius spat a curse. "Damned cogi. Why would the God and Goddess give gifts to such heinous creatures? It isn't right. It isn't fair."

"Don't be so quick to judge what is fair," the Chief Priest said. "I imagine cogi is not only a gift but also a curse. Would you want to know the multitude of ways you could die, or know that the ones you loved would soon meet their end? Or how about be paralysed by indecision when contemplating the almost infinite possibilities for your destiny?"

Sometimes, Aran was too sympathetic for his own good. Gomans had proven they deserved no sympathy, and while their cogi meant Darius's future battles would be hard-won, the fact this behemoth couldn't constantly patrol here at least reduced the danger. Perhaps a smaller boat with assassins could make it across.

"Maybe we lure the beast out again." Sulla hammered his fists together. "If we can kill that thing with ballistae, the goman will fall soon after."

"Or we'll lose another thousand warriors," Darius said.

Lex agreed he was right to be cautious. For the army, the best option now was to cross the Psilos Bridge and take the long route to Toria.

"Have you heard from Rufus?" Lex asked.

"Yes," Darius said. "But he didn't say much. He's cleared the raiders out of the farmlands, reached the bridge, and has already been forced to defend it against the town's algus."

"The little runt's turning out to be quite useful," Sulla said.

"The small ones are usually the most underhanded," the Chief Priest said.

Whatever he meant, Lex didn't have time to decipher. "The Psilos Bridge is our next best option. It crosses the River Toras at a shallower point, so the behemoth won't be able to protect it, and even orcas will struggle to swim there."

"And what if we get all the legions across?" Darius asked. "Can we get to Toria?"

"Yes, but it's a long journey. The east is fractured with mile-wide, deep fissures blighting the land. We'll need to travel east towards Alogos, around the Great Scars, then march back west to Toria. It will cost us more men, but the Empire *will* fall."

"Cost…" Darius said. "Why must all good things in life come at a price?"

"What, did you expect victory in war to be free?"

"War?" He looked at her confused for a moment before shaking his head with a sigh. "Yes, the war. Of course it will cost us."

Whatever was clouding his mind, Lex didn't know, but what she did see was that the Chief Priest also picked up on his distraction and watched him with suspicion.

Sensing Darius needed a little time to collect himself, she gave Sulla a subtle signal to leave them alone for a moment.

"Come on, Aran." Sulla wrapped an arm around the Chief Priest's shoulders. "The woman wants some alone time with her overlord."

After they left, she waited a while next to Darius, ready for him to voice whatever was on his mind, but all he did was stare into the distance as if she wasn't even there. Eventually, she tired of waiting and broke his concentration by taking his arm and moving closer.

He glanced down at her hand resting on his bicep. "What's that for?"

"You have that look about you." One of a man struggling.

He smiled, then slipped his arm away until her hand fell and met his. "I hope it's a handsome look."

Deflecting from something uncomfortable was so alike the old Darius it warmed her as well as concerned her.

"What's on your mind?" she asked.

"Nothing. Everything. Sometimes, I question what I'm doing here, whether what I want is really worth it."

Without thinking, she slid her fingers between his and gave his hand a squeeze. "It's worth it."

"Perhaps. You may be right about the Psilos Bridge, but it has me wondering… The road there passes near Menara, right?"

"Close enough," she said. "Why?"

"It'll take our army a few weeks to march to the bridge, and there's something I need to look into first."

She held her questions, waiting for him to say more, but he didn't.

"Something as in…" Again, she waited for any elaboration, but he just studied their interlocked hands in a way he must have known made her nervous about what he was imagining.

"Is your gold problem sorted?" he asked.

"Yes." Not only had she found enough to make the next payment but also for the entire debt owed, along with plenty to cover more shipments too should they wish to attempt a revolt somewhere else, like Alogos. The gold wagons had already set off and would make it over the Psilos Bridge as long as Rufus and the Viridians held it. Tiro was travelling with the caravan, and she was still a little nervous over whether the Viridians would be an issue at the bridge, but not enough to concern Darius with right now. Her debts weren't paid until her gold was delivered, but things looked well for once.

"Is that what's bothering you?" she asked. "Are you fretting over my safety?" She scoffed playfully but his face remained stern.

"Perhaps, but not that alone… If I ask you a question, will you give me an honest answer?"

That was too dangerous a condition to agree to. "Perhaps."

"Is it foolish to risk death for something you desire?"

*As if I don't have enough reason to worry.* "Depends on what you desire. Aren't we risking death now to bring justice to the King?"

At her question, he smiled, a sudden warmth lighting up his face as if he snapped out of his musings. "So, if there's something I want more than that, I guess I have my answer."

It was at times like these when she wished she were a goman. How else could she learn of what the man was thinking?

"Tell me what you're speaking of," she said. "What can you want more than the fall of the Empire?"

He looked at her and his smile widened. "I'm just thinking aloud, not talking about anything specific. Sometimes, I have so much on my mind that I question the same things over and over, but once I'm finished in Menara, I should have more focus. While I'm gone, I'll need you to march with the armies to the Psilos Bridge."

"Or I could keep you company." It would be a good chance to fill him in on the details of her dealings with Eluthia now that all was well.

"That's a tempting offer, but I'll take a swift while you all march. I need to speak with someone there."

"Without me?"

He hesitated to respond, his reluctance clear, but she'd find out why.

"I'll go with only a couple of algus I trust for protection," he said finally. "Lyra and your guards will keep you safe."

As tempted as she was to argue, she also realised she'd be wise to head directly to the Psilos Bridge, just in case of any issues with her travelling gold.

"Can you at least tell me what you're going to Menara for?" she asked.

He shook his head. "It's best no one knows. If it somehow got back to the King in the future, he'll know now what I'm doing and might send more assassins."

"But *I* won't—"

"And there are more important matters for you to deal with. I need you with the army for a reason; you will be left in command."

The shock of his pronouncement was almost enough to make her forget her worry over him disappearing. He'd never asked this of her before, always preferring to retain control through Lyra or the warlords.

"Why me?" she asked. Although on his assembly, she hadn't the authority with the rakkans to do anything other than relay Darius's commands.

"Because I trust no one else," he said.

"But what about Sulla, or Varro?"

"Varro's too indecisive, and Sulla… I love the rakkan, but would *you* entrust all your armies to him?"

Lex knew they were both good points, but still.

"And if we don't recover some of the food stolen from the raided farms," he continued, "we might be in trouble. It sounds like the Psinarans aren't afraid, so perhaps they'll be cooperative with humans."

But leaving Lex in command also risked stepping on Hera's toes as leader of Laltos. "I think—"

"It's no use arguing. I've decided, and those are your orders, which I've given throughout my soldiers already. Remember who I learned my stubbornness from."

She shoved him away, breaking from the warmth of his hand, only just realising she'd been holding it all this time. "I hope you're not referring to me. I'm decisive, not stubborn."

He grinned. "Call it what you will. Stay with my army, and I'll meet you again at the Psilos Bridge."

As frustrating as it was, he was Overlord. If he'd decided, she could do nothing without undermining his leadership now that he'd apparently announced his intentions. Perhaps it had been better when he hadn't had enough wits to use such tactics to leave her no option but obedience.

"Take Thestor with you. I trust him," she said. But based on what he'd been saying before… "And can you at least assure me you won't be in danger?"

He paused before answering. "Why? If I will be, do you wish to confess something to me? Give me a farewell kiss?"

So, he wasn't jesting about not giving up on her. "Perhaps, if you were dying in front of me."

"Interesting…" His smile returned. "Then I'll ensure I wait for you before I die. I wouldn't want to miss out on a kiss." With that, he turned and headed back towards their camp.

# 31

## Rufus – Psilos Bridge

Rufus dove to the side as two ballista bolts screeched through the air towards him. The first pierced the dirt until its blue iron tail vanished, but the second grazed his inner thigh as he landed, splattering into the mud.

*Argh.* That stung.

There was only one thing about battle Rufus detested: being unprepared. And when Darius had ordered him not to march his army to take Psinara, that had left it hard for him to make preparations for the most optimal defence of the bridge, especially after getting immediately attacked.

This was his army's sixth night near the town. He'd set up a safe distance from the camp to draw their enemy's barrage away after a few stealth attacks had damaged supplies they couldn't afford to lose. He had to at least look like he was planning an assault on the town, so his slingers had set up and begun harassing the walls, but with no follow-up attack, the Psinarans were becoming bolder.

Within a few heartbeats of Rufus taking the hit, half a dozen warriors planted themselves between him and their enemies, raising their scuta to form a kuraminium wall.

Despite the pain, Rufus sat quickly and wiped away as much blood and dirt as he could to get a look at his thigh. Blood seeped from the wound, but it wasn't gushing, so they'd missed the vein. If gods existed, it appeared they'd looked upon him favourably at that moment, but how long would that last?

"Bloody ballistae." Pollio knelt beside Rufus and inspected the wound. "They've increased the range again."

"I'll live." Rufus pushed the rakkan away, relieved his brother hadn't had a dagger concealed in his hand. "How long has it been?"

"Hours. The damned sun will be rising before they run out of ammunition."

Rufus turned to Gorgias. "You said they'd run low within a day!"

"They should have," the algus replied.

For such a small town, they sure had a lot of ballistae and a seemingly endless supply of bolts. For almost six whole nights, they'd loosed without pause from both inside and outside the town at times, and it was taking its toll on the men, despite Rufus rotating the centuries of slingers spending time within range.

He could feel his frustration growing like a knot in his stomach and knew that if this was how *he* was feeling, the men must be raging inside. He could see the fire in their eyes as they watched one of their brothers take a bolt through the head, if they were lucky, and the stomach if they weren't.

What this town had lacked in cunning design they'd made up for in volume of anti-siege weapons, and hidden them well too, sheltered in outcroppings from slingers—probably a later addition by a person with sense. It was always size or wit with humans. Never both.

Apparently, the King wasn't going to let this place go as easily as the Silk City, which was all the more reason to see it fall.

Rufus waved over one of his Subdued, whose escort flew overhead. "Have you assessed the gate yet?" It was the same question he'd been asking for two nights.

The algus nodded. "Finally got close. It's made from elm wood, not even a foot thick and hardly defended. I think they assume you'll go through the walls again."

That was handy. Clearly, they didn't know a wise man never pulled the same stunt twice. But elm…that was a good choice. Highly resistant to shock.

Yards in front of him, his legionnaires held their line, protecting the slingers behind who continued pelting the walls and ballistae from a distance the town's archers couldn't reach. And they had archers, according to his flying scouts. Many.

His brother Piso lumbered back from the front line, coated in rakkan blood. "They still aren't relenting."

"Do you think I'm blind?" Rufus clambered back to his feet. Only cowards stayed down. "I'm aware of our situation."

"Then do something!" Piso's voice rang in his helmet. "Our slingers aren't deterring the onslaught, and this town isn't going to surrender. We need to attack!"

Usually, the only thing Piso ever got correct was his own name, but as loath as Rufus was to admit it, this time his tactics were becoming the most sensible, and even Rufus yearned for the satisfying crash of a town being breached.

He glanced at Gorgias, seeing the worry in the man's face and wondering whether he'd report to Darius that Rufus now had no choice; defending his camp and the bridge without unacceptable losses was impossible unless Psinara fell. When the Overlord had given his orders, he hadn't known there would be such a fierce defence, and he'd surely understand the change in circumstances.

Retreat or assault were Rufus's only options, and he'd rather die by the Blades than destroy the legacy he'd just built for himself.

"Ready the battering ram," Rufus called. "This calls for a lightning attack." They'd storm the gates and get in as fast as possible. Ballistae and archers were of lesser use inside the town's walls.

Piso scoffed. "About bloody time." He turned and rushed back towards his warriors as more bolts thudded into the dirt.

"You were given orders not to attack," Gorgias said, but there was hesitancy in his words, not the firm voice of a man opposed to what Rufus had ordered.

"I was given orders to defend the bridge," Rufus replied. "And the only way to do that is to storm the gates. The Overlord will understand."

Thankfully, Gorgias gave no further argument.

"Wood or kuraminium ram?" Pollio asked.

They'd brought both types, and the metal would allow ferven. But it was also damn heavy.

"Wood," Rufus said. "I want the men sprinting. And send a couple of the centuries first with ladders towards the walls as a diversion. I don't want the humans to know what we're doing until it's too late."

Pollio nodded and went to ready the men while the legionnaires and slingers prepared, and it wasn't long before every centurion knew what was needed. The men murmured as if their empty stomachs hungered for human blood, and after being pelted for so long without much ability to reply, they'd be like wolves released on young sheep. This town wouldn't last long.

Pollio came jogging back. "Ready."

Sure enough, the centuries were tight in formation—narrow, deep ranks—that would attack like a bolt into the city and present a tiny target to the city's foolishly flat defences.

Once satisfied, Rufus nodded, and the centurion to his right blared the horn with such a force it was as if he'd held his lungs filled for the last six days. The centuries began the quick march along the invitingly flat land while blue bolts lit up the dark clouds filling the night sky, soon followed by thousands of fainter but just as deadly algor-tipped arrows.

"Double," Rufus said, setting off with a limp. The horns blared again, and the men picked up the pace, shields raised. Even the slingers barely broke their run to hurl a defence. A lightning attack was all about speed, overwhelming the enemy.

Men dropped as projectiles crashed into them, but the rest were too battle-hardened to let it faze them, so hungry for close combat that they roared all the louder and ran all the faster.

The diversionary forces reached the wall first and began hoisting their ladders, but the arrow barrage from atop was relentless; the rakkans' shields barely withstood the blows.

By the time the rakkans were near the gate, everyone was sprinting, and the diversion had worked to draw away the archers.

Rufus's rammers broke free of the shield wall protecting them. The first strike against the gates sent a clap of thunder through the battlefield, closely followed by a rakkan howl from the rest of the army that sent gooseflesh over Rufus's skin. The thrill of battle wasn't something that usually moved him, but there were rare times it did, like after a long, frustrating wait.

The second strike wasn't a crash so much as a shattering, splintering sound of triumph. Ferven blazed at the gate soon after, and rakkans tore at the thing and ripped it apart like the wolves Rufus pictured them as.

For a wooden structure, it lasted far longer than it should have under the battering, and the town's archers soon realised what was happening and redirected their arrows.

But eventually, Rufus's men triumphed. Legionnaires smashed through the gates, leaving only shards hanging from the hinges, and flooded through, shields first.

Now within the gateway, defenders poured barrels of everything from algor-tainted oil to sulphur from above. But the Viridian sprint continued. Men ran as they'd been trained, carrying on no matter what the enemy threw at them.

Rufus set a slower pace at the back, helped along by Gorgias and some of his Subdued guards, and as he limped through the entrance, rakkans and algus already fought atop the walls on either side, the algus outmatching his men when facing only one or two at a time but soon overwhelmed by the sheer scale and speed of the attack.

The oil and mud almost stole Rufus's good leg from under him, but he rebalanced, grabbed a spear from a dead legionnaire, and used it for support. He made his way into a large square just inside the gates, then for a long walk to the nearest staircase with roof access. Whatever was happening in the town now would be impossible to follow, but he needed a high vantage point to get a rough idea.

"You need to control your men better," Gorgias said, as if that was possible within a rakkan legion.

Ignoring the remark, Rufus let his Subdued clear a route up to the rooftops first, meeting only a few young algus and defenceless archers in resistance, and by then, the city's ramparts were a bloody mess of dead archers and triumphant legionnaires. Almost every building in the town had a flat rooftop of uniform height, square tiles laid out perhaps to intentionally allow algus or archers to traverse them easily. But there weren't many atop, most having been stationed on the ramparts or perhaps having fled as his army had rushed up and displayed their giant leaps, leaving them nowhere to safely shoot from.

Considering how heavy the ballistae defence had been, it struck him as a little strange there was such feeble short-range resistance here. If they'd had time to haul in thousands of ballista bolts, they should have spared a few hundred algus. What was there…a dozen that he could see?

But as one of his centurions helped him clamber ungracefully onto the roof, he spied something in the distance that made his stomach drop.

Hundreds of algus had been a close enough guess. There, standing on a large rooftop less than a mile away was a cluster of figures, each with armour thin enough to be mail, clothes bright like the white tunics of Torian algus.

"Look at them!" Gorgias said, but peering down at the Viridians rather than the enemies. "They've become crazed."

Rufus was already well aware. He spied the now undefended bloody square with the same frustration. The streets filled with the rabid barks of his men as they careened in a hundred different directions—into buildings, down side streets, onto roofs, tearing apart the town that had shot at and killed them for days. Those long hours had left them hate-filled, and the pathetic resistance all the archers had put up inside made them cocksure, already thinking as marauders rather than as warriors.

But Rufus knew there was a time and a place for pillaging—*after* a battle.

In one street near the gate, Rufus spied his brother. "Pollio!"

The rakkan thankfully heard the shout above the clamour of clanging metal and looked skyward.

"Get your men into line!" Rufus bellowed. "We've got a battle to win."

Pollio nodded, rapped the first legionnaire he saw across the helmet with the flat of his sword and barked an order.

Rufus caught the attention of more commanders and centurions and relayed the same order, but as he watched them scurry around and try to drag men from rushing into homes seeking loot or women, that sinking feeling became a stone dropping all the way to his bowels.

"Warlord!" a Subdued called.

When Rufus lifted his gaze, he spotted why the man had yelled; the figures in the distance were now blurs flitting from rooftop to rooftop towards them.

Rufus could only think of one way to get the men's attention and avoid a massacre, and no matter how reluctant he was to use it, victory was most important.

"Sound a retreat," he yelled at a centurion.

"Retreat?" The centurion stood frozen.

"Now!"

The horn blared, an extraordinary, feverish pitch that any self-respecting Viridian never used in battle. The legionnaires knew it from drills, not combat, but they'd damn well better answer to it. It might just be the only thing that could shock them enough to let go of whatever human peasant they'd latched onto and seek out their centurions again.

By the time the hornblower's lungs emptied, the first algus of the group had leapt from a rooftop into the large square below, his grey hood flickering with his lightning pace but remaining up to keep his head concealed.

Black eagles were emblazoned on the front of their tunics; these were the King's own.

Rufus cursed. "Pollio!"

His brother looked up.

"Slingers to the rooftops!" Where they should have damn well been already.

By the time Pollio had begun ordering the men, more algus had descended from the rooftops and tore apart any legionnaire that came close.

One algus in particular was surrounded by rakkans but sliced everyone around him with such ease even Gorgias gasped. There was something about the algus's movement that looked eerily familiar, almost like a dance. That grey tunic. That long blade.

Rufus grabbed Gorgias. "Do you recognise that one?"

The algus's face paled. "I thought he died… It's the King's Sword."

So, Jason had been in hiding since Mount Psilos while Rufus had terrorised the Empire. He was almost insulted the King hadn't sent his fabled bodyguard until now. But why Psinara? And why was his name so feared anyway? He was just a man.

Slingers finally began clambering onto the roof while the square below flowed red. The King's Sword so far lived up to his infamous reputation, not wasting any swing of his blade, scoring necks and thighs with each thrust. His swiftness was so brisk that every time Rufus blinked he missed a kill.

This algus was almost as formidable a sight as Darius, only more controlled, less savage, each slash like a surgical cut no shallower or deeper than required to kill a man.

Too precise.

And then Rufus realised the one who the man reminded him of. *The Magician.* Only she had moved in that well-rehearsed manner.

Rufus had been alive when news of those half-goman children had scattered throughout the Empire. The boys were reportedly executed, yet this man…was no mere man. Could it be?

"Hold until I say," Rufus ordered the slingers. Loosing at will at a half-goman would give the Sword enough gaps to weave through. Only an undodgeable onslaught would do.

But with every passing moment, more algus flooded into the square, and more warriors fell with their blood spraying out to join the pools at their feet. The rakkans rushed in sporadically, no formation, no wits. *Fools.* They should have known what to do. Tight formations. Shield walls. How many thousands of hours had he tried to drill it into these apes? And now they lumbered around like headless baboons.

"Centuries horn!" Rufus called to the hornblower.

The rakkan gave the signal for centuries to rally and get into tight formation.

But as Rufus watched men finally attempt to protect their brothers, he spotted another threat along the rooftops, another group of algus headed straight for him.

Perhaps he should have asked Darius to accompany them after all.

"Protect the slingers," Rufus barked at his Subdued.

They sprang into action and clashed with a spray of blue sparks as algus rushed in. One went straight for Rufus, but he dodged and watched Gorgias leap and stab the woman through the heart. Some slingers began a barrage of the farther rooftops and managed to knock a few incoming algus off-balance enough that they tumbled out of sight. One rooftop even collapsed under the stress of hailing stones and swallowed a dozen enemies.

By then, almost a century of legionnaires had finally made it onto the roof and now formed a testudo, spears sharp and ready. A few algus rushed in and tried to punch a hole in it, but the rakkans finally acted on drilled instinct, bunching together, lashing out with spears from behind shields, leaving no inch unguarded. Those algus that first tried earned a spear point to their guts, ferven breaching the chainmail and sending a trickle of iron rings clanging to the ground.

Behind, Rufus dared another glance below. The legionnaires there had also formed ranks, manoeuvred around the dead, and tossed javelins when any of the surrounding algus lost their footing or paused for too long. *Finally*. This fight was winnable, but one man still gave Rufus a niggling doubt in the back of his mind.

The King's Sword had frozen on the spot and watched from the shadow under his hood, only moving when a javelin threatened his flesh.

But above him, after a few minutes of fierce battle, the Subdued finally gained the upper hand on the rooftops, and a cry faded into the night as the last enemy algus succumbed to Gorgias's blade.

"Slingers, ready!" Rufus bellowed.

The men obeyed, loaded their slings, and began twirling in fiery rings that drew the nervous gaze of the algus below.

"Aim for the hooded one," Rufus yelled. "Loose."

Red streaks filled Rufus's vision as the wave descended like a red flash of lightning. While his eyes adjusted to the brilliance, bodies fell, either dead or leaping behind cover, while the wave became a shower of hellish rain.

Any rakkans there tried in vain to hide under the shell of their shields while the torrent continued, and algus fled the square and into side streets.

But the King's Sword wasn't among them.

Instead, he ripped back his hood, eyes trained on the incoming projectiles while weaving from side to side, slapping away stones with the flat of his flaring sword.

"More!" Rufus shouted. Surely this man had limits.

More slingers, led by Pollio, clambered up to an adjacent roof and joined the barrage from another angle. Still, the King's Sword didn't attempt to run and instead dodged all the more, even batted one stone into the face of an unsuspecting rakkan equally as awestruck at the marvel before them.

Rufus had been wrong. This man didn't rival Darius; he surpassed him. And what did that mean for their campaign?

The King's Sword backed up a couple of steps, teeth bared with the first sign of effort on that aged face. Old men may have had wealth in experience, but Rufus knew they fatigued faster.

If the man could have found a path to safety within the hail of fire on all sides, he would have, so Rufus could only assume they had him trapped.

"Don't give him a breath!" Rufus bellowed, tempted to take a sling and join in himself.

Clashes of steel and kuraminium rang out from the surrounding streets, unseen battles between algus that had survived the square and Rufus's men. But that didn't worry him. In such close-quarter combat, he had the numbers to overwhelm. If the men now kept their heads.

Stones continued flying towards the King's Sword, but they needed more. Rufus scanned below and found Piso and some of his men at the outskirts of the square, fidgeting as if eager to rush in and test their metal against the King's most feared algus but wise enough not to.

Rufus waved a hand to catch his brother's attention, then motioned as if throwing to relay the order to do something bloody useful. Finally, Piso seemed to understand and barked something to his men. They hoisted their javelins and added to the rain.

The King's Sword had backed up so much now he was almost pressed against Psinara's outer wall, which lit up behind him as stones struck and flashed in the darkness. Still, the man didn't tire, didn't blink, but inched closer to the gate.

Rufus still had some men outside but not enough to stop the King's Sword from escaping.

"Don't let him—" Before he could finish the command, the King's Sword darted towards the opening, almost dropping his weapon as a javelin slashed across his forearm. But he didn't slow. With a flash of blue, the algus vanished through the gateway, followed closely by the last of the fiery deluge.

Rufus cursed and turned to his Subdued. "Get your escorts to follow him. I want to know where he goes."

One with a falcon nodded. Hopefully, the bird was fast enough to keep up with an algus.

Meanwhile, the slingers turned their attention to the remaining algus, sprinting across rooftops and calling out when they'd found one below.

"You're one hell of a bastard, you know?" Pollio came up beside Rufus and snorted a laugh. "The King's Sword… Never heard of anyone scaring him away before."

"Don't presume we've seen the last of him," Rufus said. This wasn't time for gloating. He could be back in the city within minutes.

"Still, he—"

"And do me a favour, sort out those damned apes you call men down there. Their lack of formation almost cost us all our lives. Look at them!"

Rufus pointed his spear at the brawling warriors below, now broken from tight ranks and once again smashing into houses, dragging women out by their hair in one hand and looted silverware in the other.

"There are still algus in this town," Rufus said, "and if they get the better of the men again, perhaps this time I won't save their hides." It was at times like these his father had earned his rank of warlord. The fear of Hadrian's wrath had been enough to keep men from recklessness.

Pollio nodded, seriousness finally returning to him, then set off to give the orders.

Rufus tightened his grip on the spear so fiercely it snapped like a twig. Damn these men. He'd known they were bitter after being denied their spoils in the Silk City, but there was a time for relaxing their inhibitions.

He stormed across the rooftop, barking orders at whatever man he spied below getting distracted from their task—which was most of them—until his Subdued confirmed the King's Sword had left the town. That could only mean victory was secure.

Gradually, his fists unclenched, revealing bloody palms where his nails had dug into the skin.

"Brother?" Piso's voice called from behind.

Rufus turned to see the rakkan's insufferable grinning face, helmet off, already cocksure. "Yes?"

"The other algus are fleeing. The town's as good as ours."

"Tell me something I don't already know."

Piso stepped forward. "All right. My men have won you this town with the blood of their brothers, and they'll take what's owed to them. If you stand in their way again, I'll end you myself."

Gorgias and the Subdued around Rufus stirred, drawn swords edging back and ready to swing. But Rufus raised a hand to halt them.

His brother may have been a fool, but he knew enough not to try to stab Rufus in the open. He'd issue a challenge, knowing

Rufus had too much pride to break rakkan law and let his minions kill a rival before fair combat could take place. Only rakkans could fight in challenges, for themselves or as substitutes—always rakkans.

Darius wasn't here to save Rufus now, but challenges weren't fought immediately.

The thought of the Overlord triggered another realisation: he'd be livid once he found out what Piso and his fellow warriors were soon to do to this place, stricken by a worse disgust than that on even Gorgias's face at the moment. Rufus had seen pillaging so many times he was numb to the screams and blood, but the Overlord was still moved by acts seasoned veterans could ignore.

And as much as Rufus would like to run his brother through, a reason occurred to him to keep the fool alive. Who better to take the blame for this when the reprimands came?

Rufus glanced and made sure Gorgias was watching this conversation. *Perfect.* A witness.

"What's the matter?" Piso lifted his strong jaw. "Lost your tongue?"

"You'll give the order that this town is not to be pillaged," Rufus said calmly, almost willing it to be defied.

Piso spat in his face, the wetness creeping down to his lips. But Rufus kept his revulsion to himself and just glared.

"I won't," Piso said. "And what will you do about it?"

Rufus stepped away until no longer breathing in the stale air his brother exhaled and wiped the foul wet from his nose and cheek. "Do you want me to strike you, brother? Do you want me to give you an excuse?"

Piso snorted. "You're not worth it. Do as you please, and I'll do as Father taught us. If you have an order for the men, give it yourself." With that, the rakkan stalked away to no doubt find some widows and daughters to satisfy him.

Many of the Subdued now turned their attention to the streets below. The screams had begun to join the plumes of black smoke in the air. Doors smashed. Walls cracked.

"Won't you do something?" Gorgias asked, eyes pleading like a dog after a beating.

All that Rufus needed to do was ensure this didn't blow back in his face. "My men don't fear me," he said with an authentic sadness. But they were fools not to.

"Then they'll fear me." Gorgias moved towards the edge of the roof, but Rufus grabbed his arm.

"I cannot allow it. If anything were to happen to you… My mother…"

Gorgias grimaced, then scanned the other algus. "And will none of you stop this?"

"What can they do?" Rufus said before any was tempted. "My Subdued have their uses, but can they succeed where a hundred algus, including the King's Sword, failed?"

Gorgias tried to wrench his arm free, but Rufus held on.

"Don't act foolishly," Rufus warned.

The algus didn't stop struggling, but his eyes screwed shut. He knew it was impossible to stop. Hopefully, he wouldn't try.

# 32

## Darius – Menara

The swift thundered between Darius's legs as the birch trees of Silverbark Forest whizzed by. Menara's grey walls hid behind the trunks, but he wasn't far now thanks to his impressive mount. Being overlord had its perks; now he could travel with ease, and only Thestor and his partner algus came with him to give some discreet protection.

It hadn't been easy to leave his army without anyone noticing, slipping away when it was quiet rather than letting word spread of where he was heading. Lex and Lyra would handle things for him while he was in Menara.

Perhaps he was foolish for even going to inquire about what Frida had told him of. Risking his life so that he couldn't have children wasn't something he'd ever thought he'd be doing, but he was a strong man not long from his prime. The risks had to be low.

And Lex had been right. He'd been risking his life every day to slay the King and sacrificed thousands of warriors in the process. But he'd have chosen to be with Lex over vengeance any day. Why shouldn't he be willing to take even a small risk for her?

He tore through the gateway to the town before he'd realised it was close, quickly slowed his swift so that it walked at the pace of a normal horse, then went about finding the medicine man's place. The heavy grey fur and hood covering his body would conceal his identity, and apart from the Twin Blades sheltered under the garment, he hadn't any armour that would betray who he was. Thestor and his partner were similarly cloaked, but as usual, Darius worried the man was a little too recognisable as privileged.

People scurried through the streets about their business with more cheer and smiles than the last time he'd been here. Having freedom seemed to have worked out well for a change, and once the Psilos Bridge was effectively Darius's, this town would be even safer from the war.

After asking a young couple for directions, he finally found the place he sought. Made from a mix of clay and stone with many finger marks remaining, the building itself leaned to its right with cracks like wrinkles stretching across it and might have toppled over had it not been only a single storey. Shutters blocked the windows and the door nailed in place, but a flicker of orange light through the cracks in the wood gave away whoever was in there.

"Are you sure this is the place?" Thestor asked. "This house barely looks inhabitable for rats."

Despite Darius's wariness about the sealed-off building, the sign outside gave him confidence it was.

"Must be," he said.

"And do you want to tell us what we're doing here now?" Thestor asked.

"Not particularly." He dismounted to end the man's questions, then went up to the door and rapped a few gentle knocks.

Soon after, a sound came from inside but so light it could have easily been from a draught.

Then the orange light died.

"I know someone's in there," Darius called out. "I mean you no harm."

Now there wasn't even a draught in reply.

"Stay back," he told the two algus, not wanting to spook anyone inside; then he walked to one of the windows and tried to open the shutter. But that had been nailed shut too. Now closer, he also spotted pieces of dry, decayed fruit stuck in places and rotting on the ground below.

"Guess this person's not too popular." Darius could relate to that.

He gave the shutter a couple more knocks, and the second strike of his knuckle snapped one of the slats. A shadow flitted inside, but when he pressed his eyes to the new gap, nothing stirred in the dark room except for the faintest wisp of smoke from a candle.

Smashing open the thing would have been easy, but perhaps that was a tad rude.

"I saw you," he called through the shutter. Should he say who he was? That might make them more afraid, and if it didn't, he wasn't sure he wanted to meet them.

"We're closed!" a woman's voice called from inside.

"For good, it seems," he replied. "I'm searching for a man named Bijan. I can pay a lot just to speak with him."

"Our definition of 'a lot' may differ."

Darius reached into his pocket, pulled out two silver crests, and tossed them through the gap in the shutter to let them clang onto the floor inside. "There's more where that came from." There were benefits to taking an affluent city like Xavala beyond revenge.

Soft footsteps pattered inside as a figure came forward, and the thin strips of light coming through the shutters highlighted a woman as she bent to retrieve the money.

"A lot of folks mean us harm these days," she said, inspecting the coins. "How can we trust you?"

"Because if I meant you ill, you'd already be dead." He grabbed another one of the slats, flared algor across his fingers, and squeezed until the wood cracked. "This wouldn't keep me out."

The woman stepped back into the shadows again but didn't leave.

"You said 'us' before," Darius said. "Does that mean Bijan is here?"

The woman didn't answer, so Darius looked more closely at the shutters, at the nailheads that poked out on the outside, then he checked the door and other shutters too, all bearing the same features. "Is there another way into this building?" he asked through the hole again.

"No," the woman replied.

Then they hadn't shut themselves in; someone else had sealed them in. The question was, by a friend or an enemy? And why?

"May I open your shutter?" Darius asked.

"If you'll agree to protect us."

"That I can do." He took a dagger from his belt and sent a film of algor down the blade, then began cutting through the nails hammered into the frame. When the last one broke, he eased open the shutter, held up a palm subtly to tell Thestor and his partner to wait outside, and climbed inside the place.

The woman stepped back, now highlighted by the blue of his algor. Her features were sharp and angular, skin loose and wrinkled, sagging over the bones of her face with an age her voice hadn't suggested. Around them were shelves stacked upon shelves bearing dusty pots and jars of all shapes and sizes, some plain and worn, others painted a stark red that likely warned of the contents within. At least he seemed to have found the right place.

"Greetings." Darius lowered his hood and sheathed the dagger.

"Who are you?" the woman asked.

"My name's Philippos," he said. "I'm an algus from Laltos."

The woman's eyes narrowed, head tilted as if searching for falsehoods. "Are you an ally of the King?"

"Certainly not. Is that a problem?" He wondered whether these people were loyal to Toria and that's why they'd been sealed away.

"Doesn't make much difference to me," she said. "I just don't want people hunting you here."

"You're in luck. This is one of the rare times in my life I don't have enemies on my tail."

She murmured, glancing over her shoulder at an internal door that hung ajar and a dark room beyond it.

"Is Bijan here?" he asked.

"Depends on what you want with him."

Darius took another three silver crests from his pocket and brandished them. "For now, I just want to talk."

"That's what they all say." A gruff man's voice echoed from the dark room before his figure slowly emerged, limping with his left leg supported by a thin stick that, judging by the odd green leaves still attached, hadn't long been snapped from a tree.

The man cleared his throat with a few hacking coughs before speaking again. "And what do you wish to talk to me and my wife about?"

"I heard you know of potions and concoctions," Darius said. "I have something I need to take care of."

"Say what you need, and I'll sell you it."

"I don't know exactly." Now that they were getting onto the subject, Darius suddenly felt awkward in speaking of it. "I heard…slaves used to be brought here to prevent them from having children."

The woman stepped in front of the man, face stern. "Do you think we had a choice in doing that?"

Behind her, the man stared with equal intensity but made no move to hold the woman back. He didn't have the look of a coward, so Darius knew there must have been some other reason he was prepared to let his wife protect him and to be the first to greet a strange, harsh-looking foreigner.

"You're an algus," Darius said to the woman.

She shook her head. "I was never ordained, but I know enough to protect my husband from people bent on revenge."

Darius raised his hand and offered out the silver crests still there. "I mean no harm. If you aided the Empire and its gods, is that why you've been locked away here?"

"Indeed. So, are you really here to discuss neutering?"

Darius snorted a laugh. "You make me sound like an animal."

"Well, that's how they treated the slaves."

That was too true. Darius could understand the townsfolk having an issue with the couple, then, but they were hardly alone in doing what was necessary to survive.

"We know of nothing that can reverse it," the man said, finally stepping from behind his wife. "If someone gave you the medicine, we can't be of help."

"That's not it. I don't *want* to have children." But as soon as he said those words for the first time, the reality began to sink in. Being a father had never crossed his mind, but perhaps it would one day, and he didn't want to regret any decision he made now.

"Ah." The man walked towards a wall of shelves and ran a finger across them that left a line in the dust coating them. "Well, we've got the ingredients you need; they're not very popular since the revolt. But the concoction isn't without risk. Do you know that?"

Darius nodded, although he needed more detail before agreeing to anything.

The man scanned him up and down while circling around. "You seem in good enough health. Any maladies?"

Darius shook his head. "Have you had people choose to do it before, or did you only do it to slaves?"

"Some people chose, mostly men. There are concoctions for women, but they're far more deadly."

"... *More* deadly?"

The man exchanged a glance with his wife that Darius couldn't quite decipher.

"How much are you willing to pay?" the man asked.

Darius fished another ten crests from his pocket that lit up the man's face. "Enough?"

Bijan nodded. "The chance of death is overblown, to be honest. Fever is common, as are headaches and bleeding. A good bit of sleep usually helps."

This sounded less appealing by the moment. "How bad will these illnesses get?"

"They're temporary. You probably won't notice them much." The man nudged him and motioned towards the back room.

But before he went any further, he gave a whistle to Thestor outside.

"I hope you don't mind," he said. "I came with a couple of friends."

Bijan looked a little nervous, especially as the pair of algus climbed through the window and peered curiously at the dingy room they'd entered.

"Shall we?" Darius said.

After a last suspicious look at the pair, Bijan motioned again for Darius to enter the back room, and although Darius was still unsure of whether to go through with this, as soon as he moved, the woman began scouring the shelves and removing bottles as if he'd given his agreement.

He made his way into the back and made sure to close the door behind him so that the other two wouldn't overhear the conversation. Apart from a woollen mattress laid in the corner, the room was bare stone-and-mud work, except for some old food and a half-played game in the corner. This was a miserable place to live, and there was a stink in the air masked by lavender but not well enough—the stink of decay, of past failures.

"Tell me honestly"—Darius dropped his tone to a more menacing one—"and do not lie. What are the chances of death?"

The man's lips moved as he ruminated before answering. "I'd guess one in fifty."

That was better than Darius had feared. "And is it guaranteed to work?"

"Of course. If it wasn't, we'd have a lot of unhappy algus barging in here. Don't worry, you'll get no offspring but won't have issues doing the deed."

But he couldn't be sure "no offspring" was what he would want in a few years or decades. His mind was clear that he wanted to be with Lex, and one in fifty odds was probably better than any battle he entered for a cause his heart yearned for less, but would having only her be enough, without a family, without an heir?

"You look unsure." The woman lumbered into the room with dozens of pots balanced in her arms. "If it helps, we've never had an unhappy customer."

*Except the dead ones.*

Bijan helped her put the pots and jars down along with a mixing bowl while Darius once again lost himself in his thoughts.

The measuring and combining took a couple of hours in total, and during that time, his mind often connected to Lyra as she marched with his army. She comprehended the decision before him and made her objection plain without words but sheer terror, but this didn't feel like too great a risk to him when compared with what he'd gain. If only there wasn't that niggling doubt in the back of his mind.

Despite the additional time to ponder this decision, he was no more sure of himself by the time Bijan carefully took a drinking cup and filled it to a precise mark on the side.

"Ready?" the man asked.

Darius murmured, Lyra once again growling in his mind.

"If you're still undecided," the man said, "answer me this, because I suspect you're doing this for a woman."

"What if I am? What if this is the only way I can be with her?"

"Then is there anything you want in life more than her?"

That was such a far-reaching question, Darius first had to pause and list exactly what he did want in life. There was the safety of Lyra, Lex, and all those he cared for. But after only those few things, his mind was devoid of clear ideas or meaning or purpose. In his dreams of the future, it was just him, Lex, and Lyra, resting in safety somewhere away from the horrors of the world. Vengeance was his current intent, but that wasn't an end goal.

"No," he answered.

"Then if there's anything worth risking your life for, it's this." Bijan handed him the cup.

Darius took it, sniffing a mix of fennel and mint among other more noxious things. "Does it at least taste nice?"

The man smirked. "Make yourself comfortable. You and your friends can stay here as long as you like, until you feel like travelling again."

Darius placed the cup down and carefully removed his cloak, taking off the Twin Blades at the same time and keeping them concealed as he laid them beside the mattress.

"Don't mention what this is about in front of the others," he said. If word got back to Sulla, he'd never hear the end of the jokes. "And be careful not to touch my swords. They're deathly sharp."

The man frowned and glanced down at the heap where one of the hilts was partially showing, but Darius quickly covered it as the man's face became ashen.

He wouldn't recognise them, though; even most rakkans didn't until they spied those runes on the metal.

Darius retrieved the cup and gave it another sniff. "How long will it take?"

"It varies," the woman said. "A week at the most until you're back to full strength."

That gave him enough time to be ready to fight at the Psilos Bridge in the worst-case scenario. His army didn't have many carts or wagons, but they had some that he could ride in once he rejoined them.

As he touched the cup to his lips, he thought back to Frida's poisoning and wondered whether he should get one of the others to taste it first, but the chances of it being tainted struck him as low. For one, they'd warned him this was dangerous rather than made it sound appealing, as well as having no way to know who he was or that he would be here.

After taking a few more moments to ensure he hadn't missed any warning signs, he made his decision. "Bottoms up." He downed the cup in one, face twisting at the sudden bitter taste that he recognised immediately. He gasped. "It has the weeping plant's tears in it?"

The man still hadn't ceased gaping at the hilts of his swords.

"A few drops." The woman ushered him to sit on the mattress. "To help with the pain when it begins."

Darius sat and clenched his thighs together. "You never said anything about pain." He didn't dare ask her to elaborate in case he'd just volunteered for the worst week of his life. Although he'd survived torture, at least Gorgias had left his manhood alone in Laltos.

"Of course it'll hurt," she said. "Just try to sleep it off. We'll keep giving you tears until it subsides."

As she spoke, every word seemed to lengthen into a slur, her hair blurred as she moved, then even the walls began shivering of their own accord.

A few drops… That was enough to knock him out.

"You didn't say I'd go unconscious," he said.

The woman grasped his head and studied each of his eyes in turn before smiling. "It's working quickly. That bodes well."

But even her face began to lose focus, spin, and soon he couldn't sit upright. The mattress broke his fall except for his head bashing into a wall, but pain barely registered. He instinctively grabbed for his dagger, but it was buried somewhere so deep in his cloak that he hadn't the lucidity to find it.

The man now edged closer, face an empty swirl of paleness as he leaned over. "Can you believe it's him?"

The woman's reply was high, excited. "The Slayer of Gods himself. We..." Her voice faded away as brightness flooded his vision and all thoughts became dreams.

# 33

## Lex – Silverbark Forest

Lyra's ears twitched and stood upright, as rigid as every muscle in the panther's body soon was.

"What's wrong, girl?" Lex asked.

The cat ignored her and fixated on the shadowed trees of Silverbark Forest by the road, their army's torches the only source of light on the undergrowth. They'd only just entered the dark place, and if Lex had to guess, she'd say the cat was looking in the direction of Menara. What she wouldn't give for rakkan eyesight tonight.

Beside her, Varro and Hera also peered into the distance with similar puzzled looks while horses nickered as they carried on unperturbed, dragging carts full of rations and weapons, joined by thousands of boots flattening the dirty road for miles in front and behind, all currently under Lex's command.

While she searched for the source of the panther's angst, her own escort called out to her and willed her to enter his senses fully and take in what was happening.

Although not a good time, she allowed herself for a few moments and immediately heard voices and saw her men approaching the Psilos Bridge. There were Viridians there, but far fewer than the thousand-strong army she'd been expecting. Thankfully, the rakkans were letting her caravan past to get one step closer to Eluthia. *Take the southern road along the coast.* She'd already instructed her algus to do so, but it was worth a reminder. That road would keep them clear of anywhere Darius's army marched next, and Regent Panorea had already promised to meet her algus along it before they reached Eluthia. Although not usually one to fret even when hunted by assassins, she couldn't help but feel relieved.

But as she returned to her senses, her relief vanished when she saw Lyra still staring into the forest; a disturbing feeling grew in her gut that told her this had something to do with Darius.

"Do you smell—" Lex couldn't finish the thought because Lyra suddenly darted into the forest and disappeared within the trunks before Lex could call after her.

"Where did she go?" Hera's voice didn't sound half as concerned as it should have.

Lex stood there, a thousand possible reasons for the panther's disappearance running through her mind without an obvious best guess, but none of them were good.

And before she could figure out which ones were worst, Sulla came running up. "What the hell did you say to her?"

"She just…" Lex turned to Hera and Varro. "Do you think it means Darius is in trouble?"

"I'm sure he can handle himself," Varro said quietly, the first time he'd spoken to her on the road.

The army around them continued moving and soon nudged them back into motion again, but all Lex could focus on was Darius. The worry threatened to bring up her supper. Her heart pounded. This couldn't be happening. Not again. He had to be fine. This was *Darius*. But Lyra…

Flashbacks of the time when her late husband had disappeared filled Lex's mind. She'd been too relaxed that day, and perhaps if she'd begun the search for him sooner…

A pair of heavy boots stomped up behind her, and she recognised the Branz Warlord's grunts before she'd turned to see him.

"Where did the panther run to?" Warlord Flavius asked.

"We don't know," Varro answered.

"That's the problem," Lex said. Lyra had been separated from Darius a lot recently, and she'd never taken off like that. Despite having two algus with him, all Lex could assume was the man was in dire straits.

"We should go after her," she said. "Who's best at tracking?"

Flavius scoffed. "You can go if you wish. I'm not putting any more of my men in harm's way."

"We're speaking of your Overlord," Sulla said. "You should be willing to do whatever you can."

"My orders are to march to the Psilos Bridge," Flavius said. "If the panther wanted assistance, she would have communicated that."

Lex gritted her teeth. There was some truth to that; although difficult for Lyra to relay messages, it wasn't impossible for her to request aid. But that presumed Darius was *able* to give a message to relay. Was this why he'd left Lex in charge? Had he planned for Lyra to leave, meaning there was nothing to worry over?

But it only took Lex a few moments to reject the thought of ignoring a potential threat.

"Someone needs to go, just to be safe." Lex was only a few moments from setting off herself, but Darius had ordered her to remain here, and it wouldn't look good to the men if both she and Lyra abandoned them.

"Then one of yours should go." Flavius turned to Regent Hera. "Your algus would be fastest, and their escorts can track the cat."

Hera looked down her nose at the rakkan. "Clean the odour from your breath before you speak to me."

"He's right, though," Varro said.

"He's not." Hera turned to Lex. "The panther leaving doesn't change our plans. We march to the Psilos Bridge."

"But if Darius…" Lex couldn't even finish the thought, bile stinging her throat.

"How could Darius be in danger in Menara? It's an allied town, and he has the Blades along with two of your algus!"

It didn't make sense, but Lex's gut told her otherwise, and she'd be a fool to ignore it.

She sighed, realising that she'd thought she'd kept Darius at enough of a distance not to be affected like this again.

"Stop being stubborn, Hera," Varro said in his typical frustratingly calm yet condescending tone.

The Regent scoffed. "Is it—"

"Quiet." Lex's voice was weaker than usual but had enough force to silence the others. "Darius left me in command, so *I* will decide our reaction."

Flavius snorted. "Because you're sleeping with him, not because you're fit to lead."

Lex flared algor in her eyes, reminding the rakkan that she could slay him without Darius's help before any of his wretched legion—or what survived of it—had blinked.

Her display worked, and the Branz Warlord wilted and looked away like the coward he was. Although she wouldn't have ordinarily overlooked such flagrant disrespect, she had to focus on Darius right now.

*Think.* Who was in the best position to help? Perhaps an escort? But her own was still busy, and regardless, she needed not just one but a team to scour the town.

At the thought, she suddenly recalled one man who had potentially unlimited resources at his disposal.

She turned from the others and set off at once back through the ranks of her army, ignoring their puzzled calls of indignation at her back.

Sulla was the only one that followed her. "Where are you going?"

"To find—" She cut off as she spotted the Chief Priest between a pair of birch trees at the side of the road. There, he knelt in the thicket with the gloomy expression of a mourning widower, even more sullen than he'd been on the streets of Xavala, and she couldn't help but fear it was because he already knew something about Darius.

She rushed towards him, and he flinched as she skidded to a halt and knelt next to him in the damp soil.

"Aran, do you know where Darius is? Are any of your escorts with him?"

The Chief Priest stared at the ground and shook his head. "I don't know what he's doing, but Darius is the least of our worries. Psinara is…"

Sulla soon caught up with a huff.

"Psinara can wait," Lex said. "You must know something about Darius or at least be able to get your escort to Menara quickly."

When the Chief Priest didn't react to the words, Sulla stomped over and planted his boots on the spot of soil the man was aimlessly staring at.

"Don't make me slap you out of your stupor." Sulla flexed his fingers. "It's easy for a rakkan to accidentally kill a human."

The Chief Priest slowly lifted his heavy gaze. "Do what you will to me. I don't know whether I can do this any longer."

Sulla frowned. "What? You want me to kill you?"

"I wish it were so simple."

"Speak plainly," Lex warned. "We may not have time."

"I mean I've seen worse than I could have imagined." Aran stood, took in a deep breath, and brushed the dirt from his robes. "You don't know what hell you're about to walk into, but I have just seen… My escort witnessed the horror. I thought the Silk City was bad, but this… In trying to defeat one evil, all I've done is unleash another. And which is worse?"

"Darius may be in trouble," Lex said, not having the energy or the will to worry about what the man spoke of. "Please." She may as well have been on her knees.

But Aran shook his head. "I don't know; my mind is too clouded, and my pleas to the Goddess still go unanswered. If you'd seen the bloodbath I've recently seen in Psinara…"

Lex felt the blood drain from her face. As if she needed more to concern herself with.

Sulla balled a fist and stepped towards the man, but Lex leapt up and held the rakkan back. As much as she wanted to throttle the priest too, they needed his help in the long term, and he wasn't alone in his horror in the Silk City. Without him, they'd probably all be dead by now, and his warning of Psinara didn't take much imagination to understand. The Viridians had attacked the town, which was why her escort hadn't seen most of them at the bridge, and she cursed herself for not questioning the fact earlier.

But although Lex had a terrible inkling of what was to come, Darius was more important. Somehow, they needed to find out what had happened to him.

"Leave him," Lex said to Sulla. "We'll deal with his crisis of faith later." She set off back towards the others, tightening her belt to ensure her weapons were well secured. By now, the warlords and Hera were shouting at a pitch that would have carried to Menara and squared up to one another as algus and warriors watched with their hands ready at their weapons.

"We don't take orders from the likes of you." Warlord Flavius grimaced at Hera.

She bared her teeth and looked ready to cut through his sturdy neck when Lex thrust her body between the pair.

"Stop this!" Lex's shout brought them all to silence. "I've made my decision. We'll march to the Psilos Bridge, then on to Psinara, and we'll send a team to check on Darius in Menara."

"And I don't take orders from you either, filthy human," Flavius said.

Lex whirled until facing the rakkan, breathing in the sting of the Xavalan burwine on his breath. "Do it or I'll make you."

"We outnumber you humans. You think you can give orders?"

Lex waited for the rakkan to blink, then ripped her dagger out and pressed it to the brute's neck before he could react. "You think I won't strike you? You think any of your men will dare lay a hand on me in retaliation?"

Flavius leaned back, but she kept the dagger cutting his skin.

"My men are loyal," he said.

"Loyal enough to anger the Slayer?"

The Warlord's eyes flitted to his men. He was right to be unsure. When conflicted between loyalty and fear, fear usually won.

"Your orders were from Darius," she said. "Obey them." Hopefully, she hadn't betrayed her fear that the half-rakkan had fallen.

A few tense moments passed where the two glared in a test of dominance, but finally, Flavius snarled and backed away. "Fine. But when we're at the bridge, things will be different."

Lex looked at Varro, but the Black Warlord offered her no support. Perhaps he too planned to follow Darius's orders and then do as he pleased.

"Why don't I go to Menara?" Sulla stepped beside her and dropped his voice. "I think you should stay here; you're the only one they fear enough to listen to."

It wasn't fear of her but of Darius. Still, it amounted to the same. Sulla was right.

"But what if he's hurt?" She recalled her last words to Darius, jesting about his death.

"Chin up." Sulla put a finger on her jaw and lifted her head. "Darius is in a friendly town and has two algus and the twins to protect him. What's the worst that could happen?"

It took all Lex's energy to not think of the possible answers to that question, images of Darius's bloody corpse filling her mind no matter how sound and logical Sulla's reasoning was.

"Go," Lex said, then turned to Varro. "Give him any men you can spare."

The Black Warlord gave her a silent nod, but he was fixated on something else on the road ahead of them.

When she turned, a rider galloped towards them, veered off the road to bypass the army, and didn't slow until almost crashing into the group. She recognised the rider as one of Hera's scouts, his face scarlet from the ride.

"What is it?" Hera called.

The algus strode up and bowed hurriedly. "Apologies for the haste, but I've just been scouting over the bridge and close to Psinara..." His last words were almost a wail.

# 34

## King's Orator – Toria

"Lay him down on the bed!" Ophelia hurried into her private chambers and threw back the covers from her mattress while two slaves helped the King's Sword come forwards, one supporting each arm.

"I'm fine," Jason muttered, but Ophelia wouldn't take any chances. All her duties could wait. His health was more important than the reports of her spies that had just come in.

"Call Demetrius," she shrieked to a slave outside. "And if he's not free, I want the next best surgeon in Toria!"

"It's nothing," Jason said.

"They'll be the judge of that." Ophelia took one of his arms from the slaves and eased him onto the soft mattress, but he threw off her hand with a swing of his elbow.

She could tell by the way he moved that he wasn't dying and was annoyed about something. Whilst not surprising after almost being overcome, he didn't usually take it out on her.

His own bed would have been stuffed with the same lush wool and feathers that hers was, but his room was too cold and dark, on the far south side of the palace that the sun neglected for most of the day. He'd be much more comfortable here, with the floor-to-ceiling windows that allowed slits of rays onto the polished wooden furnishing, giving the place a warmth that complemented the fire flickering away at the far side of the room.

The King's Sword winced as he slipped off his cloak and began ripping away his bloody tunic.

"I told the King it was too risky." Ophelia inspected the wounds on Jason's chest and back. "How close was the battle?"

Jason grunted and grimaced at her as if her peeling skin suddenly disgusted him when it never had before. Whatever went on behind those eyes at times, Ophelia wasn't sure whether she wanted to know.

But as uncomfortable as being with him presently was, she wouldn't leave until she was satisfied he would be fine, even if she had reports to pass on to the King and a thousand other tasks to complete.

A couple of spears or swords had opened Jason's skin and left dirty wounds, and another few blackened holes dotted his torso with shards of rock or metal still embedded within. What if the rakkans had poisoned them?

At times, their goman ruler infuriated her. Why not warn Jason of the risk? Their greatest soldier was almost killed again. Her friend…

She touched the scar on his arm, still able to make out the shape of half a skull. What a wretched life he'd had. He deserved better.

Jason seemed not to notice her fingers for a moment, looking down as if ready to scratch an itch, but when he saw her touching him, he yanked his arm away.

"Jason," she said, standing lest his temper grow further. "What's wrong?"

The algus turned his head away. "You should have told me."

"Told you what?"

The algus didn't answer, just froze as if waiting for her to leave, but she hadn't got where she was today by being so easily defeated.

There were many things she hadn't told the man, so he could have discovered anything she and the King had been hiding. This couldn't be good. Usually, in these situations, another visit to the King was inevitable, sadly for Jason.

"This isn't to do with…" She hesitated as he turned and glared again. "With your sister?"

Jason tilted his head much like an animal did when seeing something of interest.

"Did someone say something about her?" Ophelia asked.

"… You said I have no sister."

None of the people he'd travelled to Psinara with knew his true identity, so where was this coming from?

"You don't," Ophelia said. "It's just that you mentioned it before; that's why I'm wondering if someone has been lying to you."

The algus studied her for a while, but she held her expression steady, giving nothing away of the lie until he broke the stare and shook his head.

"Nothing about a sister," he said. "You just said, 'I told the King it was too risky.' If I'd known…"

Ophelia clenched her fists behind her back. It seemed not once but twice in one conversation she'd said something she shouldn't have.

"It was just a hunch," she said. "The King was confident you'd survive."

"… Barely."

Considering the fact Jason rarely got injured, to be in this state told of the actual danger he'd been in.

"Would you have fought any less valiantly if you'd known you might lose the battle?" Ophelia asked.

The man shook his head without pause. "But I should know…if the King knows."

If only the King knew things with the certainty Jason seemed to presume.

Ophelia cursed. "If the King had let you take the Sta—"

Two loud knocks shook the floorboards and cut off her words, and she turned to see the King standing in the doorway, a cane raised in his hand and ready to strike the floor again.

Panic gripped her. How long had he been there? Was Jason about to be touched again?

"Leave us," Ophelia called instinctively to her slaves while straightening her tunic. Blood had smeared on the pale silk, so she covered it with a hand while the slaves began scurrying away.

As they left, the King strode into the room, his long floral robes sweeping the floor as he walked and his masked face still a shock to Ophelia. She hadn't enjoyed such esteemed company before in this room; she'd have had slaves scrub the place spotless that morning if she'd known.

When the last slave exited and closed the doors, the King's glare fixed on her. "*Careless fool.*"

Ophelia shrank away.

"*You speak of our greatest weapon so freely?*"

She hadn't even realised that partial slip given the ones before it. For people like Ophelia, with a higher standing earned in life, slaves faded into the background, no more eye-catching than a painting one found for the price of mangy bread at the market. But they had ears, and Ophelia had used the fact enough to have known better.

She bowed deeply. "I apologise, my king."

"*Perhaps I should rid you of this secret. If only Jason and I know, I'll sleep easier.*"

Ophelia swallowed, feeling the phantom touch of the King's erasing fingers at just the thought.

But what he'd said also relieved her; if he was so focused on the Staff, it meant he hadn't heard her speak of sisters, at least.

"I assure you," she said, "that isn't necessary. I haven't let slip to anyone. Only we know."

The King's dark eyes narrowed but relaxed a few moments later. "*I guess I've trusted you thus far… How is he?*"

"He'll recover with the help of our surgeons, but he could have been victorious if he'd had the Staff,"

The King stalked towards them, scanning Jason's wounds, and finally stopping when within touching distance of the man. "*The odds were in his favour, but it seems the One Mind had other plans.*"

Ophelia nodded to hide her anger. *Don't blame this on higher powers.* The King's recent hesitancy had begun to make her question things she never had before. It had been easy to trust in the decisions of someone that saw the future, but mere possibilities? That was more of a stretch. It even made her hesitant to reveal the latest news from her spies, just to frustrate the goman for allowing her friend to be in peril.

"*You're impatient.*" The King bent and inspected Jason's wounds more closely. "*But there's no need to be. If I'd revealed the Staff, their strategists would have divided their forces and eventually overcome us. Our opportunity approaches, but first, they must cross the Plains of Psilon.*"

Finally, open ground. Finally, the swifts of Alogos would ride. Her spies and scouts had spent weeks mapping the area in detail and had located the best places to harry and rip apart the rakkan forces. Such meticulous preparation had won her and King Medus I victory in the War of the Four, and it would again. Battles were won in the weeks before the clash, not on the day.

"I have the latest maps and notes from my scouts," Ophelia said. "Should I tell Alogos to prepare?"

The King paused and walked towards the tall window, stopping only when bathed in the sun's rays. "*Have* all *your informants sent word?*"

"Yes, my king." And Ophelia suspected she knew who was of most interest to him. "I have news on our hunt too. I have men close to Alexandra now, waiting for their opportunity, and I think I've found the Numbered you seek."

The King didn't react other than to hold out a hand.

Ophelia went to collect a roll of parchment she'd been sent and handed it over to the King. When he unrolled it, a sketch of a young man was revealed, scratched in charcoal with such detail it almost seemed alive on the page. But despite the piece's artistic realism, the man's face was oddly devoid of life, showing a vacuous expression so common amongst the Numbered.

"*That's the one.*" The King whirled around. "*Send him here at once.*"

"Very well." Ophelia bowed. "Am I now to be privy as to why you want him and Alexandra?" The woman was a known traitor, but killing her would have been far easier than capture.

"*... Perhaps, when you've better learned to control your tongue.*"

Ophelia gritted her teeth but hid it behind a smile. "I assure you, my tongue is the most trustworthy in the Empire."

"*That's not saying much.*"

How could she disagree with that? People's proclivity to favour wealth over loyalty had been the heart of Ophelia's success over the years.

"I'll deliver the rest of the parchments to the throne room," Ophelia said. "In the meantime, Alogos needs time to prepare."

The King continued staring at the cold face on the parchment. "*Tell them to muster. The time to ride has come.*"

# 35

## Darius – Menara

Darius eased his eyes open to see candlelight shimmering on the mouldy ceiling above, but even the dim light had him squinting, and he groaned when his skull pounded as if cracking open.

But that discomfort soon paled when the sting from his groin came to his attention. He'd taken many a kick to that region when training with Julius and Brutus in the past, but this pain was something else, like a dog had bitten down and tugged to rip off his manhood.

He cursed and curled his body, tried to move his hands to soothe the area but felt the bite of shackles and cold links of chain across his back. This couldn't be good.

Flexing his arms, he tried to rip himself free, but the metal wouldn't budge—kuraminium. Only a rakkan could have restrained him, but that realisation only raised more questions.

Muffled voices murmured through one of the walls, a deep hum that only magnified the ache of his head. When he tried to sit, not only did his groin punish him for the effort, but he also felt and saw the weight of dark metal shackles binding his ankles. Yet, the sight beyond his feet calmed his building panic—his panther's dark, furry body lying on the floor.

The room around him was the same one he'd taken the hideous concoction in, and at least he'd been laid on the mattress. But the room was battered in a way it hadn't been before, chunks cleft from the walls at either side of him and the floor scarred with cracks and dust like the earth had shaken again.

*Lyra.*

She lifted her head, opened her amber eyes, then gave a wide yawn and stretched as if without a care in the world. At least *she* was at ease.

He opened his mouth and began to cry out and call for Thestor or anyone else around when the door opened and the woman from earlier entered carrying a steaming pot in her hands. She'd reached the middle of the room, placed it down, and took a towel from her shoulder before their eyes met and she gasped. "You're awake?"

"I wish I wasn't." He lifted his right arm as much as he could and shook the chains. "What's this?"

She gave a nervous smile. "Sorry. Your thrashing was destroying our home, and we thought the place might come down at one point."

Darius was glad he didn't remember that if this pain was any clue as to what caused him to be so violent.

The woman rushed to the door and called out, "He's awake. Come and take the chains off."

There was a crash in the next room followed by the padding of footsteps before a familiar yet unexpected scarred face popped through.

"It's about time…" Sulla strutted in with a shake of his head as he looked at Darius's lap. "You're a stupid bastard at times. Makes it so hard to love you."

Darius stared at the woman as she soaked the towel and wrung it out. "You told him?"

"She didn't need to." Sulla took a key and began unlocking the shackles. "Doesn't take a genius to figure out what's happened here." He gave Darius a pat on the groin, a strike as soft as a breath of wind yet that felt as if a sword had run him clean through.

Darius groaned and curled up. "You bastard."

"You deserve it. You know how long you've been out of it? Days. Your army will be at the Psilos Bridge by now and awaiting new orders. I don't care how much it hurts, you're getting on a horse before the sun sets."

Darius wouldn't argue with that.

"He'll do no such thing." The woman came over and mopped his brow. "He needs rest or he may fall under again."

Sulla murmured, "If you'd let me give him a good slap, he'd have been awake days ago."

After having taken a few "slaps" from Sulla in the past, Darius was glad to have been spared them this time.

The woman took a vial from her pocket and handed it to him. "Take more tears."

"I'll be fine." Darius sat up, wincing, finally free of restraints, the stinging wounds on his wrists evidence of how hard he'd thrashed. But that pain was still nothing compared to the main one.

"You're through the worst of it," she said, "but you'll still ache for a while."

Only a woman would describe this hell as an "ache."

Darius checked everything was still physically intact downstairs before he grabbed Lyra and greeted her properly. *Why are you here? I told you to stay with Lex and the others.*

She gave him a nip on the ear along with an annoyed growl.

"By the way…" The woman finished cleaning him, then dropped the rag and folded her arms. "You owe us extra. Not only did you break most of this room, but your thugs smashed open our door."

Sulla shrugged. "Hey, I thought Darius was captive here with the way Lyra was pacing outside and clawing at the door."

"Gave us the fright of our lives," the woman said with a shudder, "to see that hulking cat and his ugly mug barging in here."

"Did they hurt you?" Darius asked.

"Only their hearing," Sulla said. "Me and the men were a little riled up, but we soon found Thestor and your other guard, and they explained what had happened."

Darius shook his head and tried to stand, having to catch Sulla for support when his knees objected to the sudden load upon them. Blood drained from his head and at least eased the headache while making him wobble more, but his groin stung with every shift of his legs.

Shakily, he took more crests from his pocket and handed them over. "That should cover these louts' damage."

The woman squeezed the coins, barely able to stop some spilling out of her hand, and bowed deeply. "Thank you."

Darius gripped Sulla for support and leant to pick up his cloak and the Twin Blades. It was an effort to get them secured once again to his waist, but he just about managed it.

"I've reconsidered the tears," he said to the woman. "I'll take a vial just in case."

She handed one over with a smile.

"Sulla, is my swift still outside?"

"Ready and waiting," Sulla replied. "Want me to show you how to ride side-saddle?"

Darius shoved the rakkan forward, and the pair made for the door. "I'll manage." Although, he might be forced to do as Sulla suggested. "Where's Thestor?"

"Outside, enjoying a rakkan pipe."

"Good. I'll head to the bridge with him. You and whatever men you've brought can help fix up this place, and make sure the townsfolk give them no more grief."

Sulla raised an eyebrow. "When did you become so dictatorial?"

"The same time you learned such fancy words."

Sulla laughed. "I've been around Lex too much. All her highbrow education must be wearing off on me. I'll be a scholar soon."

"That's a terrifying thought." Darius let go of Sulla and finally took some steps on his own, the pain easing enough he could unclench his jaw. "Lyra, let's go!"

The panther bolted out of the door and set off at once, eager to get a head start on his rapid mount.

"I didn't send any word back to Lex," Sulla said. "She'll still be worrying over you… You're welcome."

Darius frowned. "Welcome for what?"

"There's nothing like the fear of death for helping a person realise how much they care."

"I'll be offended if she thinks I'm dead." It was a cruel thing to do to the woman, but Darius supposed Sulla and Thestor hadn't escorts to make use of even if they'd wanted to, and the rakkans' mounts outside were all regular horses; his swift would make the journey to her in less than half the time a rider would have. Assuming the hard ride wasn't too much of a punishment for his delicate area.

"Pace yourself," Sulla said. He must have seen Darius's grimace along with his pondering.

"It seems I don't have the time. Don't be more than a few days behind me."

# 36

## Rufus – Psinara

"I told you to bury the bodies outside the town!" Rufus grabbed the centurion by the scruff of his neck, pushed him towards the burning corpses, and roared, "Who told you to burn them, you lazy cretin? Put them out! The wind's blowing west now; this stink will carry all the way to the Psilos Bridge!"

Piled high in the square, the bodies of civilians had been stacked and were already coated in ash and blackened skin. Flesh burned, but armour and weapons were slower to do so; anyone with half a brain would see that these weren't defeated soldiers or algus but the butchered inhabitants of Psinara.

Rufus turned to Pollio. "How far are they from the town?"

"They'll be here within the hour," Pollio replied. "Darius isn't with them, but Regent Hera is."

Rufus checked over his shoulder to ensure Gorgias was still out of earshot. If the algus caught him covering up the extent of the slaughter and pillaging, his best witness would be as useful as a wooden sword.

But these fires might just have sealed his fate, regardless. Although the morning sun lit up the sky with a joyful summer blue, black plumes spoiled the clear air and betrayed the fire and blood that still coated the town. Buildings fell as their weakened foundations finally submitted, and the red between the cobbles had run so thick it hadn't even dried in some places, despite the heat and sunlight. Every civilian that had survived the pillaging had either fled outside the town or sensibly still hid in cellars or other dark places, which at least left Rufus with fewer witnesses to tell of the real death toll.

A few of the warriors groaned and tried to shield their skin from the sun's rays, but Rufus had no pity. These fools would work until their skin was scarlet.

"The next man that stops work and shelters in the shade will be crucified!" Rufus roared. They'd made this mess. They'd damn well clean it up.

Rufus dropped his voice to Pollio once again. "Have Piso take bodies to the east. Bury them deep and scare away the scavenger birds." Crows and vultures were a mass murderer's most frustrating betrayers.

"Yes, Warlord." Pollio gave a wave to one of his centurions. "I'll keep the Subdued occupied so they don't see."

Perhaps it was foolish to hope that Hera's algus hadn't already seen the full extent of the ravaging of this place, but if Rufus could even halve the apparent casualties, perhaps it would save his neck from the Blades.

The next hour was a frantic one, but warriors marched outside the town with four or five corpses each slung across their shoulders. The fools had to be told not to carry the bleeding ones and leave a trail to wherever they dumped them outside, but apart from that, Rufus left the work to Piso while he made sure the Subdued and his more trusted commanders readied themselves on the west side of the town, ready to receive their guests.

The morning sun poured a heat it usually reserved for midday and had Rufus standing in full armour, his helmet blocking his skin from burning at least. But that wasn't his only reason for being armoured.

Nervous energy spread through the men, one evident in the uneasy silence and restless twitching, the same feeling as before a battle but with an intensity that even the assault on this town hadn't provoked.

And Rufus shared the worry. Leaders rarely feared war, especially ones more inclined to direction than fighting, such as himself. But this was different. When it came to facing blame, a leader was in the vanguard, the head of the army that would be the first to lose his head.

As the army neared the town, two women led from the front, their weapons unsheathed, fury evident without even seeing their distant faces. His scouts told him the rest of the Viridian Legion marched at the rear so would be hours behind, of no use should this greeting become bloody.

Rufus stepped out in front of his men and brought Gorgias and the other Subdued with him for the wait.

"How is your mother when she's angry?" Rufus asked.

Gorgias stared at the approaching people, standing more relaxed than usual. "The same as always. She kills like a leopard."

It took Rufus a few moments to decipher the man's meaning—leopards did not rush towards prey from a distance. They remained calm and slow, getting close enough to be within reach. And when they pounced for the kill, death came too suddenly to react.

The two both rejoined the silence until the army approached with Lex and Hera stopping only a few feet short, and the priest man stood behind them, looking his usual harrowed self.

"What the hell did you do?" Lex said.

Rufus felt the weight of the smoke in the air, the fires burning behind him and the stink of charred flesh that even a warrior never became accustomed to.

"We've taken the town," Rufus said calmly.

"After you were told not to?" Lex replied.

"We were told to defend the bridge, and it became impossible to do so without neutralising this threat."

Lex's sword arm moved and flashed upwards as she lunged forward and sliced towards Rufus's neck.

But three other blades moved swiftly, and the Subdued blocked the strike an inch from scoring a mortal wound while Rufus froze in place, not allowing himself to flinch.

He paused for a moment, stepping back without a trace of fear. Such a death would have been a kind way to go.

"We should speak privately," Rufus said. When it came to throwing his brother and warriors to the wolves, it was best not to let all his men bear witness.

Meanwhile, Hera glared at her son, one of those that had rushed to Rufus's defence.

"You protect him?" she asked.

"He's not to blame," Gorgias said, withdrawing his sword, "and he's right about needing to take the town. He may have made only a paltry effort to prevent the pillaging, but he at least made some. And Lex has no authority to slay a warlord. This is for the Overlord to settle."

For the first time, Rufus realised the boy was wiser than his young looks suggested.

Lex scoffed. "You think Darius would disapprove of me slaying your warlord?" But her voice faltered at Darius's name, almost broke. Her eyes widened a little as if shocked by the unconscious slip, but Rufus couldn't infer why. She was correct; Darius wouldn't reprimand her even for murdering the innocent, let alone a warlord, such was his blind devotion to her. *Fools and their love.*

"Your son is right," Rufus said, directed at the more level-headed Regent. "We should wait for Darius to arrive before rashly taking up arms. Which begs the question, where is he?"

"Don't deflect," Lex said. "We've heard what happened here. Don't think this won't go unpunished."

"Move aside and let us into the town," Hera said. "I'll witness the carnage for myself."

With the weight of the Black and Branz Legions behind her, it wasn't like Rufus could object. His lookouts would have spread the word by now for the rest of the men to make themselves scarce or at least stop whatever they were doing. Even the somewhat sanitised town would spark fury in all the humans, so Rufus would be wise to keep his distance for now.

He stepped aside and opened an inviting palm. "I'm here to greet you, not prevent you from entering."

The army lurched into movement again while the Viridian Legionnaires moved out of the way. As they began entering the town, Rufus made for one of the outer buildings, but Lex thrust herself in his path.

"You think I'm letting you out of my sight?" she said.

"Come with me if you wish," Rufus said. "But I thought you wanted to survey the town yourself."

"Oh, I will." She pushed her forehead into his helmet, only a smidgen shorter than him but carrying an aura of one far larger.

Was it the ever-present shadow of Darius in her wake that made her appear so foreboding?

"Where is your man?" Rufus asked again. "He should be here."

"He will be. And what's happened here will be on your head."

# 37

## Lex – Psinara

Sunny days should have been something to relish in, reminding Lex of the days picking tarnflowers from the fields east of Laltos in her youth. The sun had been a way for Agathos to spare them the worry of rakkans in those days, but now, times had shifted.

The rest of her day was one of mourning, surveying the town with Hera, Varro, Cyrus, and the Chief Priest in a haunting silence. But this wasn't like it had been in the Silk City. Seeing the devastation there had filled her with sorrow, a sea of cruel death that brought both rage and sadness. But Psinara struck her with an emotion more unbearable than any other she'd borne, one whose weight wasn't just a yoke on her neck but an entire town crushing her beneath its corpse. Guilt. This war was hers; this was her fault.

And on top of that, thoughts of Darius plagued her. She still had no answer as to why Lyra had run away, and Tiro was still too far away with her gold wagons to help. She had to constantly resist the temptation to mourn the half-rakkan as she had her late husband.

"Why would Agathos allow this?" a woman wailed as she emerged from her crumbling home and fell to her knees before the Chief Priest.

Aran couldn't even look at her but held out a gloved hand and touched her head. "The God and Goddess must have their reasons."

The woman didn't seem convinced, but she gripped tighter on a wooden figurine of the God and Goddess embracing, like it might strengthen her faith.

And she was just one of a sea of survivors wearing that same despair. Some knelt before the Chief Priest; others just gaped as if expecting a definitive answer to that question or some instruction on how to pick up the pieces of their lives.

But they'd never get answers. For years, Lex had wrestled with that same question—why? It was easy to think of possible reasons for allowing such tragedy, especially when one wasn't an all-knowing goddess like Dianoia, but that didn't make the suffering any less intense, didn't dry the tears of grieving mothers and widows.

"This is our doing," the Chief Priest said, bringing her thoughts back to the surrounding hell.

He was right. Who would dare lay the blame for this on higher powers when it was her that had caused it?

"I can't…" Cyrus shook his head after muttering the first words to leave his mouth all day. "How could we be part of this?"

Lex knew he was speaking on behalf of all the Menarans. Seeing fellow humans defeated like this was enough to destroy anyone's resolve, despite seeing what the raiders of this town had done to the Menaran farmlands. Most of the townsfolk here wouldn't have been responsible for that.

They set off again, let the crowd follow behind, and passed through the shattered door of another building. The altar inside looked like one of the Diagathic Order, and Aran's tear-filled eyes confirmed this had been one of his holy places. But now, it was defiled.

Blood splatters on the walls barely left a stone untainted and told a story of chaotic slaughter where blades had met their victims. Deep stains in the corner marked the final resting places of a woman and her young girls, stripped, bruised, and twisted so violently that tears filled Lex's vision too. She'd held them in until now, but seeing someone's daughters so…

The Chief Priest turned away and retched, but Lex wouldn't give herself any reprieve; she deserved none. Aran was right. This was on her, Darius…all of them. She should have argued more forcefully that the Viridians shouldn't be sent to defend the bridge.

Varro and Hera stood beside her, neither betraying how moved they were by this.

"Will you protect me if I kill Rufus?" Lex asked the room, anyone and everyone. If neither of the leaders there would, perhaps the ghosts of the defiled would.

Varro gave only a frown in answer but at least acknowledged her. She knew that look on his face. He worried over her.

"Need you ask?" Hera said. "You'll need to be quick because my sword thirsts for his blood too, as well as that of his men."

Lex had never needed Darius more than in that moment, but where was he? Surely not among the spirits now listening.

She knew she shouldn't have been worrying over the man when surrounded by such horror, but her mind struggled to focus on much else as if he mattered more than any of it. Perhaps he did. Perhaps she'd failed in staying detached.

"I don't wish to see any more," the Chief Priest said.

"Me neither," Cyrus added with a grimace.

"Aran, you said you knew of this before we arrived," Lex said. "Why come and see it?"

"Because I am responsible." The Chief Priest picked at the gloves covering his holy fingers. "I don't deserve to be spared this sight. I've made some grave mistakes in my life, but this… I will speak with Darius once he returns and will not mince my words."

If the half-rakkan still breathed.

"Us too," Cyrus added, and Lex could tell he wasn't merely following the Chief Priest's lead but was equally appalled. Darius stood not only to lose his army's morale here but all the humans that had supported them thus far.

Cyrus and the Menarans would be a great loss, and none of the others knew how integral Aran was. Lex did, yet, she didn't have the energy or heart to try to persuade any of them to stay at the moment. After this, she was even questioning her own role in this, whether she'd also best stop this pursuit of justice. Because no cause justified what had happened here.

But then what of all the people the King had slaughtered and ruled over? Would cutting out the Viridian Legion, like the festering, malignant growth it was, right this wrong and solve their problems?

One of Hera's algus entered the room, and Lex quickly wiped away her tears. She couldn't appear weak now.

"Regent." The algus bowed. "There's a swift arriving in the town. We think it's the Overlord."

Lex's heart stuttered, caught like a lump in her chest. "You're sure?"

"As sure as our escorts can be. They—"

Lex raced out of the room without waiting for a full answer, almost tripping over the rubble in the street outside as she dashed towards the western gate. She had to verify this news.

And as she approached the entrance to the town, she didn't have long to wait because a swift swept through at that moment, only revealing its rider when it slowed in the centre of the square, next to the steaming pile of corpses.

Darius winced as he surveyed the area for the first time, face pale as if about to vomit, but his lips shone red with a life they'd lacked in Lex's deepest fears, and he stared wearily but with that old fire within. He snarled as he dismounted and had barely planted a foot on the ground when Lex rushed and leapt at him, wrapped her arms around his back and pulled him into an embrace as tears filled her vision again.

His body was warm, tense in reflex to the sudden impact but relaxing in moments when he recognised the caring arms he was within. For a moment, the surrounding tragedy faded to a lesser worry, along with a sense of relief that felt alien to Lex's mind, now too used to spiralling.

As she clung to him, she imagined never letting go, never being parted from him again. Nothing felt more right, but in many ways, nothing felt more selfish too.

"Lex?" he asked as she buried her head into his cloak, glad the only thing separating their bodies was layers of soft, warm fabric rather than the usual hard chill of armour.

"What the hell happened?" She ensured his cloak dried her tears before allowing her head to break away until face-to-face.

"Came down with something rough," he said. "Had to sleep it off for a few days."

The man was a terrible liar, but she didn't care right now. He was breathing, although those breaths betrayed the scent of the weeping plant's tears.

"I should be asking you what the hell happened *here.*" He scanned the square while keeping their embrace, though his hands gripped her so tightly by the end that she almost cried out in pain.

After subtly squeezing different parts of his body, verifying he had no injuries on his torso at least, she pulled herself free with a gasp.

"Sorry," he mumbled before readjusting his belt with yet more wincing, like a man trying to hide something. Surely he couldn't be having those kinds of urges amidst this show of slaughter.

Lex filled him in on everything she'd seen and all that Rufus had told her, as well as the testimonies of those algus that had been present for the ravaging. Every word she uttered built a rage that soon consumed any relief she'd felt at their reunion, and by the end, Darius too was growling a sound akin to coals within a furnace. The worst of it was that the Viridians still walked around the town, strutting with pride and not giving a second glance to the humans that scurried out of their way in the streets.

"We should call the assembly," Darius said. "Whatever the Psinarans did, it doesn't warrant this. There'll be hell to pay, and everyone should witness the punishment when it's meted."

Lex couldn't even think of a punishment harsh enough. "That's wise, but Warlord Quintus is still at the Gap of Aphatos. We can't afford to wait."

Darius sighed, pulling his dirty hair back from his striking face. "I know; *I* cannot wait. Are Hera and the other warlords here?"

Lex nodded and felt a stray tear fall and expose her.

Darius's gaze latched onto it, but he said nothing for a while as if no words could express his emotions.

"I think you'd best speak with Aran and the Menarans too," Lex said. "They're in one of the Order's gathering places."

"Later. I can't face them until I've digested this and spilt the blood of whoever's responsible. Now, let's go call the assembly."

# 38

## Lex – Psinara

There was definitely something off with Darius since his return, an odd gait that one usually saw of a wounded man, and curious glances he gave her when he thought she wasn't looking. Whatever had happened in Menara, she'd find out once their more pressing matters were dealt with.

As they set off about the town, her falcon called out to her from afar, so she allowed herself to share in Tiro's senses completely and saw her caravan stopped and the wagons being inspected by foreigners. They weren't so bold as to wear Eluthian colours, but her men looked at ease with them and began disconnecting oxen from their wagons ready for the handover. Finally, her debt was settled. If only she could take any pleasure from the fact given where she was.

"My gold problem is solved," she said.

Darius turned to her, mouth twitching as if trying to smile yet unable to. "So, there'll be no more assassins after you?"

"For now," she said.

With a sigh of relief that didn't last, he turned his attention back to the town, and they carried on surveying the full extent of the horror. After taking more and more in, Darius became all the more laboured, and speaking with the survivors, warriors, and Subdued under the darkening sky only fouled his mood further, so much so that when the time came for the assembly, both of them had nothing but retribution on their minds.

The warriors found a suitable place to hold the gathering without causing yet more disruption to the locals, and the pair met with the other warlords and entered what must have been old barns. The wooden sides of the building shuddered as the winds of a storm gathered strength outside, and shutters bashed back and forth despite being latched shut to blot out the evening light. Oil lamps had been scattered across a large table at the centre, flames flickering and threatening to die, and around were the precise number of seats required for both the leaders and their most trusted advisors.

Darius took his seat at the head and motioned for Lex and Gorgias to join him at either flank, then the other leaders filled each side and left the foot of the table empty for the ones to face the gauntlet about to ensue.

Warlord Rufus entered last, limping with a heavily bloodied bandage around his leg and a face marred with scratches likely from flying debris rather than battle. As usual, he bore no weapons or armour and hobbled without any of his rakkan commanders, a lonely figure treading to wrath without any apparent fear or guilt over what had happened—nothing but vacuous indifference written on his face.

As he sat, the storm howled and slammed the doors to the place shut, leaving an echo that lingered before it joined the hush of everyone there.

Lex gripped her dagger under the table. What was Rufus's play here? The rakkan was too smart to submit to execution so willingly, so he must have had many excuses prepared. Although his wish to remain unthreatening was obvious, there had to be another reason he'd come alone.

Darius cleared his throat and waited until everyone gave him their full attention before speaking. "I've been told what happened here, Rufus, and why you attacked the town. I'm prepared to grant you the fact you had no other option and that the Torians were the aggressors, but what happened after… I have no wish to hear the details repeated. Just tell me what you have to say in your defence."

The Viridian Warlord took time to consider his response, so long as to be suspicious. "I will give no defence."

Of all the answers Lex had expected, that hadn't been among them.

"So, you accept your guilt?" Darius asked. "Should I call for the executioner now?"

Rufus became so still it was transparently deliberate. "I accept I am responsible—as the Viridian Warlord—for what my men do, but I will say why I think it would be a mistake to replace me."

"I thought you might. Let's hear it, then."

Before the Viridian Warlord spoke, Lex pondered his plan again and soon realised what he intended; his commanders weren't here because he was about to turn on them and divert the executioner's sword onto their necks instead of his own.

And why should Lex let him get away with that? The Viridians turning on themselves could be used to her advantage. After all, betrayed brothers were prone to spilling many new and old secrets when given the chance.

"Should we not call witnesses?" Lex asked. "He may have admitted guilt, but the depth of his involvement should be ascertained."

Rufus frowned for a mere moment before seeming to collect himself. "My best witness sits next to you. Gorgias was with me throughout the battle."

Everyone turned to the youthful-looking man at Darius's left, who shrank in his seat. "I've already told Master what I saw."

"If it's true he was forced to witness this barbarism," Hera said, "I must insist my son is returned to me. It's unconscionable that he be made to remain with such animals."

The other two rakkan warlords murmured their disgruntlement at the all-too-common slight against rakkans. But Lex knew Hera had directed the insult solely at the men that had laid waste to this town and its people.

"Gorgias doesn't need your coddling," Darius said. "And that's not the matter we're discussing here."

Hera scoffed. "You dare call—"

"Enough!" A tint of red surfaced in Darius's pupils. "Rufus, give your excuses and let me decide your fate."

"Very well," Rufus said. "I took this town with only a thousand men pitted against a stubborn enemy bent on driving us away from the bridge. Not only were Psinara's battlements heavily equipped, but the King's Sword led an algus army against me."

Mumbling spread throughout the room. Lex had heard whispers of Jason showing his face here but had wondered if they were really true. She hadn't seen the man fall on Mount Psilos, but Darius had assured her he'd knocked him from the high ledges. Jason's survival only highlighted their failure to infiltrate Toria's highest places and learn of such things.

"I do not wish to sound arrogant," Rufus continued, "but few others could have survived such a foe, let alone secured the town and freed Menara's farms from further raids."

"Do you think being a good tactician absolves you of these crimes?" Darius asked.

"No… But it might make me worth keeping alive."

"Justice will not be sacrificed for practicality," Lex said.

"Forgive me, Overlord," Rufus said. "Does she speak for you now, or do you still have authority here?"

Lex squeezed the dagger in her hand, tempted to fling it towards the rakkan's head. What a satisfying thud it would make.

"She does not." Darius avoided looking at her. "The assembly will refrain from speaking out of turn."

The half-rakkan may as well have given Lex a slap; she'd have been no less insulted.

Sulla hid a grin poorly behind his hand, but no one else reacted, including Rufus. The bastard must have been pleased with himself, though. He knew that when it came to sharpness of wit and observation, Lex was the most dangerous person there and was now hesitant to speak out again.

"The Viridian Legion is the most veteran among your armies, Overlord," Rufus continued. "For decades, our warriors have lived and breathed war, and with experience have come ingrained habits that warlords of old encouraged and used to make our enemies cower."

"Most of them," Darius said. "Some enemies, you just enraged."

Lex supposed some benefit had come of it. Without the sight of such horror, Darius would never have joined the war or become the titan he now was.

"But recently, I demanded they change," Rufus said. "Under your orders, I demanded they stop pillaging and taking the hard-won spoils that they've enjoyed for decades. And old habits are hard to slay."

"I don't know…" Darius rapped his fingers on the armrests of his chair. "Wouldn't my slaying the men slay their habits?"

For the first time, Rufus's expression betrayed him. His jaw dropped a fraction, eyes became hollow and fearful. "… Slay the entire legion?"

Darius remained quiet and threatening, having even Lex clutching her dagger no longer in anger but for comfort.

The gales outside howled again and inflated the silence inside. Even without Darius's prior edict on speaking out of turn, Lex doubted any would have so much as breathed loudly.

"But…" Rufus dared utter, "but most of the legion wasn't here. You shouldn't punish them for the crimes of their brothers."

"Their guilt isn't only in Psinara," Darius said, "but the entire west. Laltos still lies in ruins, and if I hadn't been with you in the Silk City, the same pillaging would have happened there. Whenever my back is turned, your men defy me!" With the roaring words, a new presence seemed to fall upon the man, as if he'd grown in size and might, filling the room with the aura of not only an infamous warrior but a true overlord. He emanated a heat in the air that made one want to both flee and fall to their knees.

"Darius," Lex whispered. "May I speak?"

His eyes flitted to her and immediately softened, pupils widening as if to better take in the sight of her. Then he nodded.

She cleared her throat only to give her a moment to shake whatever feelings had just arisen and to summon the will to argue something she never thought she would. As much as the Viridian Legion deserved to die in the frozen grip of algor, defeating the King was a priority they couldn't disregard.

"Armies can be disciplined without destruction," Lex said. "There are other methods, such as decimation."

"And many more," Rufus hurriedly added.

Darius digested her words, then looked to the others at the table. "And what say the rest of you?"

"Decimation won't cut it," Sulla blurted out as if he'd been holding his breath the whole time. "The whole point is to get the warriors to kill their brothers, and it won't work when it's the whole legion."

"I agree," Warlord Varro said. "And decimation isn't punishment enough."

"Then why not execute two in ten," Hera said, "instead of one in ten."

"Or five?" Sulla added.

The discussion continued on various methods of punishment while Rufus remained silent and watched the theatre unfold around him, likely calculating his best strategy to lessen whatever hammer of judgement would fall upon his men.

Only after the discussion had droned on for more than an hour and repeated itself more than once did Darius stand and still the room.

"Rufus," he said, "you've still not given me a good reason to spare your life."

The Viridian Warlord nodded calmly. "After listening to you all, I can say that none of your ideas will work. You can try decimation, you can try beatings, you can try dispersing Viridians in the other legions…none of it will work. You all know the anger that festers when battles drag on for days and weeks, the hatred of the enemy that instils, and the difficulty in controlling such rage within feral men once it has an outlet. There's barely a warrior under eighty years old in my legion. Their habits won't be easily broken, and their loyalty to Viridia will survive much longer than their bodies. You will end up slowly whittling them down until there is nothing left."

Darius raised an eyebrow. "So, you're saying I should slay them all now and be done with it?"

"Or leave it to *me* to instil discipline."

Darius scoffed. "If you haven't done it by now, you never will. Your men do not fear you."

"Then I will make them." Rufus stood, his slim frame hardly giving weight to his words, but the steel in his glare more than made up for it. "My legion will only be obedient to a Viridian they respect, and I now have the support of enough of my brothers to act. Allow me to."

"And if you fail?"

"Then bury me along with my legion."

Curiosity was getting the better of Lex. Before this meeting, she'd considered no circumstances under which she'd be content to let him leave alive. But if there was anyone shrewd enough to straighten out the Viridians, it was Rufus.

"What will you do?" Darius asked.

Everyone there edged forward a little in their seats.

"You will hear of it before you see it," Rufus said. "And the terror I'll inflict will not only cow my Viridians but every man, woman, and child, whether under your dominion or not—even rats and mice won't dare cross you again. Do I have permission to do as I wish to my men, everything from a slap to death?"

Darius paused, then leaned across to Lex and whispered in her ear, "Is this man too smart to give such freedom?"

"Undoubtedly," Lex whispered back, "but if he fails or betrays you, you can slay them all. And I suspect his idea of punishment surpasses even our darkest intentions. He's more heartless than any man or woman here."

Darius sat back upright and chewed on the problem for a few moments before giving Rufus a nod. "Fine. You have my permission. Take your legion out of Psinara at once and back towards the Psilos Bridge. When you're done, whatever's left of your men will be lugging supplies from the west to the war front until I can trust them in battle again. Your men should be able to carry more than mules and oxen anyway. And Rufus… This is your last chance. Do not disappoint me."

# 39

## Darius – Psinara

After his decision, Darius called the assembly to a close, and the various leaders left to find whatever food and lodgings they could. Darius, however, remained seated, deep in thought with fingers idly grazing the stubble on his chin. Lex lingered with him and stayed silent until Gorgias left into the storm outside to leave the two of them alone.

"What ails you?" she asked.

He grunted, sank in his seat. "What doesn't?"

"Are you still troubled by whatever illness you had?"

If only the discomfort in his groin was his greatest problem. "Pain I can live with. But that's not what I'm dwelling on."

"Will you tell me what happened in Menara?" she asked.

He murmured to himself, not sure whether this was the time or place to get into what had happened like he'd originally intended. "I'll tell you later; I suppose I owe you an answer. I'll have my men find me a place to sleep and plenty of firewater.

Meet me in an hour." That would give him some much-needed quiet time to clear his head.

"… Meet you in a bedchamber? I hope you're not getting ideas."

"… Is that really your first thought at the prospect of us being alone together?"

"Don't read too much into it," she said. "You've made your intentions clear to me, that's all."

"Ah. So, now that I've confessed my love, you're afraid to be alone with me?"

"Should I be?"

"Only if you're afraid you can't control yourself. I invited you to talk, nothing more." He stood and stretched his limbs after the long meeting. "I'd better see the Chief Priest before the night's over too. Where is he?"

"Still in one of the Order's ceremony rooms, I think," she said. "Although whether that bloody place could still be called such is a stretch. I'll take you."

He didn't relish the state of the place she'd just alluded to, but they left to head through the town and soon found the building where the Chief Priest and Cyrus were sitting alone, eyes closed in dead silence as the wails and laments of the ravaged town echoed like a dark harmony outside. The stink in the room was so putrid Darius practically tasted the blood in the air, concluding that the two men must have been punishing themselves by remaining here.

He swallowed deeply, then went to sit beside the Chief Priest, facing what had been the altar.

"And so our hero returns…" the Chief Priest said before he'd moved to look at them.

Darius frowned. "What's that supposed to mean?"

"I call you what I held you to be—a hero. But is this the work of a hero?" Aran threw out a tired breath.

"I've never called myself that," Darius said.

"I didn't claim you did." Aran let the words sink in, then shook his head. "What next, Slayer?"

Darius had avoided asking himself that question so far. All he'd brought to this land was chaos and destruction, but at least before it hadn't been at the hands of his own men. Now…

"I don't know," he admitted, "but the King gave us a taste of what he's capable of in the Silk City. As vile as the crimes in Psinara are, can we forget everything that led to this point?"

The Chief Priest nodded. "My part in that tragedy is not lost on me. I ask myself that same question. At what point do I stop? At what point do I admit I no longer know what the God and Goddess wish me to do? We've failed to bring justice here."

"Our failures would have been worse if not for you," Lex said. "Overlord Hadrian would rule the Empire."

"Hadrian is gone," Aran said. "Stopping him doesn't justify anything I've done since his death. For many hours I've prayed on this question, but I think this town has given me my answer."

As cryptic as the man was being, Darius suspected he knew what that answer was. "You're leaving?"

At that, Cyrus opened his eyes and glanced at the holy man as if also seeking his response.

And unfortunately for Darius, the Chief Priest nodded. "At once. I don't know how long it will take me to discover the answers to the questions I must ask myself, but I know I cannot aid you anymore until my mind is clear. I've helped you so far because I wanted this war to end. I thought the toll on the people would be less in the end than the alternative. I thought your cause was a just one, but now I doubt my assumptions."

"The King should meet the God of Justice," Darius said. "Don't we agree on that?"

"In theory, but will you achieve it? The King's Sword lives and was here, and based on what Warlord Rufus told me of the encounter, it seems my fears about him were true. The man that killed the Waif Magician is none other than her brother."

Lex walked in front of the man and studied his face before saying, "That cannot be… The Magician's siblings were killed."

"Apparently not. What I've heard in the Empire only confirms it."

Was that revelation from the spies he seldom spoke of?

"Should I fear the King's Sword?" Darius asked, currently not doing so with the Blades at his side.

"Yes, if you wish to survive him," Aran said. "But there are much greater evils you should fear beyond one man, those which you will bring to the Empire if you continue."

Darius wasn't even sure how someone could conclude what means were just and what weren't. Would another Psinara be too high a price? Would another Xavala?

"I have no doubt that you will continue this campaign whether I'm here or not," the Chief Priest continued, "even if I dropped to my knees and begged you to cease your march and return home. So instead, all I can do is implore you to keep the truth in mind."

"What truth?" And how was the man so sure of a decision Darius hadn't even made yet?

"You mentioned the God of Justice," the Chief Priest said. "Do you still wear his symbol?"

Darius reached to his neck, but there was nothing there but the memory of where he'd treasured his pendant. Now it was nestled within Lex's bosom, a trinket that he considered as much a part of him as it was her.

"I don't," Darius said. "Don't tell me that's why this has happened."

"No," the Chief Priest said. "Both of your obsessions with that thing only illustrates your problem. You speak of justice when all you lust for is revenge."

"Can we not have both?" Lex said. "Wasn't the death of Aristippus just? Or Archimedes?"

"They are not the same," the Chief Priest said. "Revenge is evil; retribution is just." He reached into his pocket and withdrew a necklace. "I have a gift for you, Darius, something I feel you've been lacking."

Darius took it and inspected the small figurine hanging from it—a silver, winged idol of the Goddess.

"Dianoia," Darius said. "Looks like the statue that was in the fountain in Laltos." The tiny woman reached out a hand above her head like the statue had, wailing in grief at the evil in the world, calling for the axe of her husband.

"I'm glad you remember it," the Chief Priest said, "because clinging to your hopes in the God of Justice alone is like trying to survive only on water. You need food too for nourishment, and the Goddess of Mind cannot be separated from her husband."

"But what has she to offer for our pain?" Lex said. "Can she heal the wounds of our murdered brethren? Our murdered children?"

Darius had only ever heard Lex take hope from Agathos, so her questions made sense to him.

"Look at Dianoia's figurine," the Chief Priest said, "or remember the fountain. Does she not weep along with you?"

Lex scoffed. "Does that cure my pain?"

"Does revenge?" The Chief Priest's voice sharpened. "Tell me, when you see Dianoia reaching for the heavens in anguish, what does she call for?"

"Justice," Darius answered quickly. "But Agathos doesn't answer."

The Chief Priest shook his head and breathed out until he deflated to the stature of a frail old man. "How have my teachings been so misunderstood? Am I that poor a preacher?"

"Then what does Dianoia plead for?" Darius asked.

The Chief Priest stared at him as if measuring whether he would accept the response before answering. "Mercy. If the axe of the God of Justice falls, *all* her children will feel its edge, you and I included."

As if any of the rulers of this world deserved sympathy, let alone mercy.

Darius's face twisted. "What are you suggesting? That I stop fighting my enemies? Let them be free to ravage at will and make my life hell again?"

"There's a difference between defending yourself and what happened here. If you're so blinded you will lay justice on the altar of revenge, then I truly did misjudge you."

Darius scoffed. "I do no such thing. The crimes you've seen here will be punished, rest assured."

"Punishment is not enough. Do not repeat them." For the first time, the Chief Priest's tone became threatening, more ominous than a warning originating from him alone, one seeming to have the might of the God and Goddess behind it.

Surely, the man couldn't be speaking of mercy for the Viridians.

"And which of our enemies deserves mercy?" Lex asked.

"Any that rue their crimes and sincerely ask for it," the Chief Priest answered.

It was a good thing none did; that saved Darius from breaking the edicts of the Order. But although his instinctive reaction was one of disdain, the priest's reasoning gave him pause. There was a ring of truth to it.

"I'll say no more." The Chief Priest stood and straightened his robes. "Perhaps we'll meet again. I'll continue to pray for you and those at your mercy."

"Us too," Cyrus added, standing in support of the priest. "We Menarans are still prepared to sell you what supplies you need, but to be a part of something like this… I know you disapproved of this, but we cannot stomach it, whoever is to blame."

As difficult a position that left Darius in, he considered it generous of the man to offer support.

"Very well," he said. "In return, be assured we won't allow any more Torian raids on your lands."

Cyrus gave a bow of respect, which Darius couldn't feel was fully deserved.

"I should go with you back to Menara, Cyrus," Lex said, "to ensure your safe travel."

Whatever her reasons for offering, Darius wasn't sure, but Cyrus accepted the gesture.

"Then I'll call for you when we're leaving," the man said, and with that, he and the Chief Priest left them.

"Aran's right, you know," Darius said. "We all deserve the axe of justice after this."

"Yes, but some more than others," Lex said.

"Did we at least recover any of the stolen supplies?"

Lex nodded. "Enough, but not all of them, so this attack wasn't completely pointless. But Aran's right. That doesn't justify this."

Darius sighed, still staring at the doorway the man had left through, wondering if he'd see that silver hair again. "He's guided us wisely in the past. I fear we'll suffer without his counsel."

"I doubt we've seen the last of him. Whatever crisis he's enduring, whatever mistakes we've made here, I still believe our cause is just. Hopefully he and the Menarans see that before long."

Darius grunted. "I'm not surprised, to be honest. Why did you offer to see them back?"

"I should make sure our relationships aren't permanently destroyed."

Darius nodded but was still taking in every broken and cracked piece of furniture in the place. "How could we let this happen?"

"We've been too reckless, and we mustn't make this mistake again."

"I hope we don't." At this point, he'd seen enough and was ready to wash away the dirt and blood. Plus, if Lex was soon leaving, he needed to speak with her about what he'd done in Menara too, lest she find out from Sulla first.

"I'll have the men find me a room," he said. "Meet me in an hour."

# 40

## Darius – Psinara

There was something relaxing about a warm bath while a cold storm tore at the shutters. Not only did it soothe the aches and pains, but it made a man feel oddly safe, like nature couldn't harm him despite its fiercest efforts, like he could even curse the gods with impunity for these fleeting, restful moments.

Warm water may not have washed the horror of this town from his mind, but the bottle of firewater beside the tub was doing its best. Seeing so many devastated families and parents, both slave and civilian, only drummed into him how brief his time in this world could be and how important it was to make the most of it.

Which had him thinking only of Lex and how much time he'd already wasted.

Would he be able to tell her what he'd done when she came to see him? Given what had happened here, he was hardly in the mood to have the conversation, but he'd put this off for too long and delaying it would do nothing to help the Psinarans and might leave him with more regrets.

The hour was almost up, so he hauled himself from the tub and dried himself off, looking at all the old scars on his belly that he mostly didn't recall getting. How did Lex's look now? Had these wounds once brought him close to death too?

Lyra was still making her way to the town but had sheltered under an uprooted tree to avoid the storm. It was a cold one, tossing thin rain that refused to be halted by roofs and instead whipped up into your face, your eyes, your throat—much like when he'd stood too close to the coast as waves crashed and frothed. He missed that sight and the feel. Compared to the might of the sea, his issues always shrank and felt insignificant.

He placed the Dianoia pendant the Chief Priest had given him around his neck, then dressed in the clean clothes his men had brought him. His hair hadn't time to dry, but perhaps the rugged look would suit him. Or would tidy be best?

Unsure, he took a comb left in the room and began neatening his mane as much as his naturally dishevelled locks allowed. If only Psinara could be fixed so easily.

Although the town had been defiled and ruined in many places, his men had found him an empty room. It wasn't fit for an overlord, but Darius wasn't one to demand luxury. Besides a mattress, there wasn't any furniture in there, and Darius's bottles of firewater had been laid on the floor near the door, the smoothest on the left, which were always best to start with, then the cheaper, tangier ones on the right for when he'd lost enough of his senses for the good stuff to be a waste. At the moment, he was drinking the bottles in the middle.

Although his groin still ached, he paced, wearing away the floorboards as he waited, and when a knock finally came, it took him a few deep breaths to calm his inclination to fidget.

"Come in," he said.

Lex entered slowly, took in the room, and seemed unimpressed.

"It's the best they could do," Darius said. "At least it has no bloodstains."

"My, my. How our standards have fallen." Lex unfastened her sword belt and tossed the weapon along with her bag beside the mattress. Then, looking at him properly for the first time, she added, "You bathed?"

"Yes. Why do you sound surprised?"

She shrugged and peered into the next room where the tub still steamed. "Wouldn't have thought you had the time."

"I've got nothing but a long night ahead." And her reaction to what he'd reveal would determine whether that was filled with curses or blessings. "Do you want to wash too? I can wait. There's dry cloth still in there."

"All right. I'd feel better without this blood under my fingernails." She slipped into the next room, leaving the door temptingly ajar while she stripped and eased into the waters with a slosh.

Meanwhile, Darius lay on the bed, trying to avoid the urge to peer and instead think of something else, but every swoosh of water had him imagining the droplets slipping down her neck, down her exposed chest… And the sudden thoughts only magnified the pain below his belt.

After a long wait, a large fall of water announced Lex had finished, and when she came back into the bedchamber, her skin had a clean, soft glow to it. The ends of her raven hair were damp and curled, clinging to her neck, and she hadn't put her armour back on, instead wearing only a tunic that, despite being loose, showed him enough of her figure to magnify those pains.

"Can you do me a favour?" she asked.

"It's a bit late to scrub your back."

She rolled her eyes, then pointed to her bag. "My tea leaves are in there. Can you brew me some?"

"Of course." He grabbed a cup along with some clean water, stuffed in the mix of leaves she needed—which by now he knew by heart—and began warming the water between his hands. Once it started to bubble, he handed it over.

"Thanks," she said. "I guess hot men have their uses."

Unsure how to respond, Darius just sat and wished they had a lighter mood that might have allowed him to feel some humour at her remarks.

She drank half the cup, then held it out again. "Throw in some fire while you're at it."

Judging by the whiff of her breath, it wouldn't be her first or even second stiff drink of the evening, but he obliged. He grabbed his strongest bottle of firewater and began pouring it in, only stopping when she nodded as it reached the brim of the cup.

"So, what did you want to discuss?" She sat gently on the bed beside him and pressed her hair in a linen cloth to dry.

"Us."

She froze, whether allowing her cloth to soak the dampness or because of what he'd said, he couldn't tell.

"But I think we should agree to something first," he added.

She turned her head a fraction, gave him a taste of those alluring eyes. "Agree what?"

"For once, I want us to be honest and not hold back. So, for however long this discussion lasts, let's agree to be truthful."

"You think I usually lie?"

"Not lie, but I fear you omit most of your thoughts."

She turned away again and ran the cloth through her hair, but it got stuck in a tangle of knots. "And you want me to agree to tell you everything?"

"Here." He slid behind her, took his comb in one hand and a few of her locks in the other. "Let me straighten it for you."

At first, her body visibly tensed at his touch, but soon it eased until so relaxed it rocked with every glide of the comb through her hair.

"Fine," she said. "I'll swear to be honest."

He took a breath, knowing how great a promise she had just made to him and how difficult that must have been for her. He'd rehearsed many of the things he wanted to say when alone on the road, but now that the time had come, his throat almost closed and refused to utter more than a grunt.

"I feel like I've known you my whole life," he forced out, each word thankfully becoming more natural than the last. "Ever since Archimedes stole my mind, you're the only one that's always been there for me."

"You have others that have been loyal to you."

"But they weren't always able to help me, for whatever reason. You've been beside me the most, you taught me how to be more like who I once was, to embrace my power, to listen to the instincts of my gut rather than question any inclination that didn't benefit me. Well, those same instincts have been telling me something I've ignored for too long." By now, the comb was gliding smoothly through her straight hair, but he didn't stop sweeping down. "What am I to you?"

She sighed and dropped her head. "You really want me to be truthful, even if it hurts me?"

Was it so painful for her to admit the truth just this once?

Perhaps he would be better facing her to gauge her feelings best. Sure, it was easier to say these things to the back of her head, but it was also easier for her to deny her feelings.

So he placed the comb down, stood from the mattress and moved in front of her, where the blue of her eyes glinted with a light of their own.

"What am I to you?" he repeated.

"You're…"

When she hesitated for too long, Darius added, "You promised honesty."

She breathed deeply before continuing. "You're the man I trust the most, the man who I never worry will cross me, the only man who makes me feel safe."

It wasn't often she showed him vulnerability or kindness. If he'd had to guess what she thought of him, those things would have been far from the first he'd utter.

"Hearing you say that," he said, "pleases me more than you know. It's what I'd expect of a true friend, one I trust… But is there nothing else? When I came back from Menara, you embraced me as you never have before, like a wife does when her husband returns from months at war. Am I wrong in feeling that?"

"What do you want from me, Darius?"

"I want *you*," he said, "more than I want riches, more than I want the Empire, more than I want the King's head."

"Do you think we all get what we want in this life? Do you think I deserve that?" She slumped. "I have to listen to my head over my heart. I don't want any more children, and I don't want to risk loving another man I'll probably have to bury."

"And what if we walked away from the war? What if there were no more fighting?"

She paused for a moment as if daring to imagine such a future, but soon shook her head. "Wishful thinking. As long as the King lives, your enemies will hunt you. And it's beside the point."

"Because you don't want any more children? Because they might suffer in this world?"

"Yes."

"… And what if I told you I cannot have children?"

She frowned, then her gaze slipped down to his belt line. "Menara…" As if finally understanding, her eyes lit with a new angry fire. "You didn't."

"I did."

She buried her face in her hands, ran them through her hair and squeezed, spoiling the neat lines he'd stroked through it only moments ago. As tempted as he was to defend what he'd done, he remained mute and let his news sink in, the risk he'd taken for her, the destruction of a barrier that kept them apart—at least, that's what he hoped she was thinking.

Groans, or perhaps growls, came through her tangle of fingers and hair, for how long he couldn't say, but after a long wait for her to break the silence, she instead moved and flew up so quickly they almost butted heads.

"Are you a fool?" she yelled an inch from his face. "That's what you were doing in Menara?"

"Yes."

She drew back her hand, jaw clenched, ready to crack him. But she paused instead, shaking. "How could you be so foolish?"

He wasn't fazed by the threat of her striking him. That was probably the least hurtful thing she could throw at him right now.

"It wasn't foolish," he said, tiring of people accusing him of such.

"You could have died!"

"And? You were worth the risk."

"I…" This time her hand balled into a fist and hammered him in the chest. "What would I have done if you'd died? What about the throne you'd have left?"

"I have no 'throne,' and what good are the Blades if they can't get me the one thing I want most?" He caught her arm.

There was fear in her eyes now as he gripped her, as if he weren't a lifelong friend but a strange man ready to overpower her and worse.

"Why are you afraid?" he asked.

"Because you could have died!"

"And why does that make you afraid?"

"Because…"

"We agreed to be truthful," he reminded her again.

"You really want me to say it?" Her voice wasn't much louder than a breath.

Although he could guess her meaning, this time, he wanted no doubt. "You said you wouldn't risk loving me lest I died. So if you don't, surely my death wouldn't have troubled you for long."

She pushed past him and buried her hands in her hair again. At this rate, she'd rip clumps out.

"Or have you failed? All I want is the truth."

She stopped an inch short of the shutters to the window, letting the gales breaching the cracks brush against the hairs now falling across her face.

Another silence fell between them while he braced for the next words from her lips. But whatever they were, he needed to hear them.

"Of course I've failed," she finally said. "Except for my children, there's no one I love more than you."

Her words finally gave him some relief, abated the fear that he wasn't even worthy of such in her mind. It didn't remove the obstacles between them, but at least he knew where he stood.

"I'm glad you told me," he said. "It seems love's jaws have caught you as unwillingly as they have me."

"…'Love's jaws,' really?" She snorted a laugh. "You never were good with metaphors."

"I'm glad my clumsiness with words amuses you. You know, you're no poet yourself."

"Better than that, at least."

"Go on, then, give me a better turn of phrase."

She thought for a while, breathing in with every gust hitting the slats. "Love's shadow."

Perhaps he was too foolish to comprehend, but he preferred jaws. "You'll have to explain that one to me."

"Sometimes, it falls on you without you realising and darkens the world around you."

If that was how she looked at it, no wonder the woman avoided love.

"You have a strange take on things at times," he said.

"There's only one way to escape the shadow—to stand beside the one that's casting it." She turned to him, fear now etched into the weathered lines on her face. "But if you died, I'd never reach you. I'd be forever mourning in your shadow."

"Forgive me for saying, but you already look like a woman lost in shadow. Isn't it better to at least try to stand next to me?"

Her stare intensified. "But how long will it be before I'm back in darkness? If anything happened, I fear I'd lose myself."

"Isn't it better to enjoy the light when you can? I'll give you no more children. I'll protect you, your daughter, and myself with all my might."

"And if it's not enough?"

"Then we'll die at peace, knowing that we've enjoyed the light beside each other, knowing that we didn't let fear rule our lives."

"That's what you think I'm doing?"

For all of Lex's outward strength and drive, he knew deep down she was a woman not only controlled but consumed by fear. "You've been through hell." He released her arm and ran the back of his finger down the softness of her cheek. "We're always afraid of history repeating itself, but the future is never as we imagine. Perhaps it's better; perhaps it's worse, but it never plays out as it does in the terrors of our imagination. Will you let what-ifs defeat you?"

Her gaze slipped down to his lips, her own parting a fraction before a pause. "Every day, the fear becomes greater. Your shadow… But we cannot run from this war. It must be finished."

"And when it is? When our enemies' bodies lay dead at my feet, what then?"

"Then… Then you rule an empire, forever a target to whoever holds grudges, forever embroiled in politics and treachery. That isn't a life I want, a life lived in fear."

"Me neither." To be honest, he hadn't given much thought to what he'd do if he defeated the King. Not once had he imagined ruling the Empire or dealing with the hassle he already dealt with as overlord but a hundredfold worse, not to mention the backstabbers and politickers whose only aim was to flatter him and enrich themselves.

He didn't want a throne, politics, power, treachery or anything else. "What if I leave the throne empty and bloody, let the cities rule themselves, as they once did? What if we escaped once justice is delivered?"

"You shouldn't promise that. I've seen men seduced by power and seen them—"

"Have I been? I'm not saying this to please you but because I want no life like that. Tell me, is the Darius you know a man that wants a crown?"

She studied him in silence for a while before answering. "I guess not. Such a man wouldn't take potions to eradicate his legacy, for one. Did you really take it? Are you sure it worked?"

"It bloody hurts enough. Unless they gave me a kicking while I was passed out, I'd say the deed's done."

She closed her eyes and sighed. "Why?"

Did there need to be another reason? Wasn't love another one of those irrational urges that you either ignored or followed without understanding the "why"?

"My life has had little joy," he said, "from what I remember of it. I've been hunted across the Empire, tortured and starved for weeks until reduced to a shrivelled corpse of a man, and betrayed by someone I loved. But, despite it all, I've only ever prayed for death once."

She winced as if understanding his pain.

"Do you know what made me give up hope?" he asked.

"What?"

"Gorgias said something to me during the torture. Up to that point, I'd desperately clung to faith, forced all my thoughts to focus on one person who was worth clinging onto life for—you."

As his words sank in, he saw his own despair reflected in her eyes. She knew that pain too.

"But Gorgias told me you'd left Laltos," he said, "run away, and left me to face my doom."

"I'd gone to get help," she said.

"I know now. I didn't then. I gave up. If I didn't have you, life wasn't worth it."

She looked almost ready to shed a tear, and he prayed she didn't or else he might break too.

"I don't trust anyone in this world like I trust you," he said. "Who else could I love but you?"

She didn't answer, just let the question hang with the draughts eddying in the room. Despite the difficulty of this topic, airing their true thoughts felt like something that should have begun a long time ago. Some of what he'd said hadn't even occurred to him before the words had left his mouth, but now it all made sense. That's why he felt so strongly for her.

"Why do you love me?" he asked. Perhaps she needed the same chance to clarify her feelings.

"I'm…drawn to you," she said. "I'm not sure what it is, but I feel your loyalty to me. I trust you. And we share wounds—losing a boy too young for his time, and losing a partner we loved most." She paused again as if unsure whether to continue. "And there's something alluring about a man with the strength to tear apart our enemies with his bare hands."

Were his now clean hands that had slain so many such an attraction? It said more about her than it did about him, and he wondered what her feelings would have been if he'd never regained his rakkan strength.

"Drawn to me…" he said. "That isn't saying much, like men are drawn to whores."

"Or otters are drawn to water. Without it, they'll die."

That was a little clearer. "And what if I wanted you to be mine, for us to retire to a quiet place near the sea, live our lives in peace with each other?"

She smiled, but it was wistful, like imagining a future never to become a reality. "I fear I can never feel peace again, but if our enemies are dead…"

Not for the first time, he sensed indecision in her but also saw she was entertaining the idea. But he also realised words would never sway her. He could have laid out an argument worthy of the greatest minds in the Empire, and she would have found an excuse to deny and punish herself.

The only way to see what she truly wanted was to forget words. He had to act how a lover acted and see whether she returned his passion.

So he took a step closer, slipped his fingers through the hair on the side of her head, and when she didn't resist him, he turned her head until their eyes met. And what he saw wasn't revulsion or even surprise. It was desire.

Without him moving further, her head leaned back slightly, invited his lips, and what she truly wanted had never been so clear.

He eased closer. First, their noses grazed, then her eyes closed and his mouth found the softness of her lips. The kiss began so gentle she barely shared her warmth, but as she leaned deeper into him, as his fingers kept sliding to the back of her head and across her neck, her heat was all he felt.

And never had he felt so alive, the butterflies in his stomach, the excitement that even the growing pain in his groin could do nothing to dampen. This is what he wanted more than war and victory.

But however long the kiss lasted, it wasn't long enough, and she broke away and met his eyes with a breathlessness he'd never seen arrest her before.

Only a few beats later, she looked away and composed herself. "That was—"

"Don't say it." How hurtful it would be to call that a mistake. He'd made many in his life; that certainly wasn't one.

"I don't think you know what I was going to say," she said.

"I'm not sure I want to."

"Do you think it's been easy for me to keep my distance? Do you think this helps?"

"You torture yourself for no reason." His voice grew deep, bitter. "When I sat beside you as you lay dying, I felt no less pain because we don't share a bed. Tell me you feel less. I know by the way you greeted me that you feared over me in Menara. Tell me my death would have hurt less because we've denied ourselves."

The sheen of algor finally left her eyes and she let tears flow. "It didn't."

"Then why deny yourself? You said no children; that is done. You said no throne; I will burn it. What other excuses have you?"

She wiped a hand across her cheek. "None."

Only then did he realise red ferven coloured his sight. He banished it as quickly as he could, reached down and took her hand, then ran his thumb across the calluses her bowstring had worn into her fingers.

"Then be mine," he whispered.

She regarded him with who knew what running through her mind, as if paralysed by indecision. But he gave her time, however long it would take.

And sooner than he'd expected, she moved towards him and pulled him into an embrace. "If we win the war."

Had she really agreed? Had he misunderstood? For a few moments, he stood frozen in her arms, not squeezing for fear of breaking her, not speaking for fear of changing her mind.

"Forgive me," he said, "but was that a 'yes'?"

"Do you really need me to say it again?"

"Well… I am a fool."

She pulled back and slapped him across the chest. "Yes, you are; don't think I'm still not furious at what you risked. But what's done is done. If we win the war, if we leave all this behind and find our place of rest, I'll be yours."

Even she wasn't cruel enough to lie about that, but it still didn't feel real. Good things like this didn't happen to him. "I fear I'm dreaming."

"Well, you're not. Here." She reached to her neck and unhooked her necklace with the Agathos pendant hanging from it. "Take this back so you'll know my promise is real."

He took the intricate thing, never thinking it could have had more significance than it already had, but now he wouldn't take this off for the rest of his life.

"Thanks" was all he could mutter while hanging it around his neck where it belonged. He would have smiled but still couldn't bring himself to, given all that had happened in this town. Still, he was more content than he ever recalled before. He'd somehow won the heart of this sharp, brave, stunning woman.

"You know," he said, "you missed out one reason you're drawn to me."

She raised an eyebrow. "Did I?"

"Yes. You said nothing about how handsome I am."

"I see. And who says you are?"

"No one, but it's obvious. Only a handsome man would attract someone like you."

"Well, I did agree to marry the Silk Regent."

"True. But while the man may have been a weasel, he was good-looking, at least."

She retched. "Trust me, he wasn't. Women see through shallow beauty, not that he ever hid his personality."

Although Darius hadn't known the man, his reputation and the art on his walls were vile enough. "I wish you'd heard his screams of pain before the end."

"Just make sure I hear the King's."

Darius wouldn't make any promises but would do his utmost to ensure the reprobate didn't take the coward's way out like the Silk Regent. But first, they had this town and an unruly legion to sort out, which probably meant he should get some much-needed rest.

"Sleep here tonight," Darius said. "There aren't many clean rooms left. I'll go and sleep with the men and see you in the morning."

"All right. But the Menarans are planning to leave soon, so I may not see you for a while."

"Very well." Darius was unsure whether to give her a kiss farewell, so he instead offered an awkwardly forced smile and began walking towards the door.

But she grabbed his arm. "Aren't you forgetting something?" Her eyebrows were raised, expectant.

"Oh. You want me to stay here with you?"

The fall of her expression confirmed he'd guessed wrong. "No. I just swore to you that if the war is won, I'll be yours. Don't you want to do the same?"

"Ah," he said, mulling the question. "No."

She clenched her jaw. "No? You don't think I'm worthy of that? You won't promise to be mine?"

"Lex, you fool. I already am yours."

# 41

## Darius – Psinara

A couple of weeks later, Darius sat in a busy room and tried to calculate how long an army marching from here to Menara should take. No matter how many times he ran over the journey, two weeks should have been enough, so he couldn't fathom why Lex hadn't returned yet. He'd made sure she'd taken a swift with her.

Never had he woken with such joy than the morning after that conversation with Lex. The birds soaring across the murky sky had never been so majestic—even if they were crows and vultures—and despite the score of horror still playing throughout Psinara, life had rid itself of a smidgen of the usual toil and labour. It didn't lessen his burden, feeling like only a single brick falling from the sacks on an overloaded mule, but it helped a little and gave him a little more energy to help those remaining in Psinara however he could.

That task became harder when the Menarans had left, but despite his regret at the loss of good people, he couldn't blame them. His rage at the Viridians was ever threatening to grow out of control, and it was fortunate they weren't in Psinara anymore.

Lex had said she needed to journey with the Menarans but hadn't given details on why that he fully believed. Meanwhile, the demands of being Overlord had kept him from ruminating on it too much. Every day since that evening with Lex had been spent as the current one was, crowded in a windowless room that veiled the passing hours of the day until one's stomach growled for food, surrounded by men and rakkans with more opinions than teeth. Dealing with the surviving Psinarans—who mostly hadn't been part of the raids west of the river—made Darius's mistakes all the more clear, and they were here to be repaid for crimes that no gold or riches could make right.

That day, he'd finally continued discussions focused on protecting the town, talking around maps scratched into the stone floor. They showed three deep chasms that blighted the eastern landscape, known to the locals as the Great Scars, shaded in a mass that was almost beyond belief, large enough to fit many entire cities within. If so many hadn't sworn to their scale and depth, Darius would have doubted even the axe of a god could have split the world so deeply.

But now the various commanders and warlords simply trod over the illustrated fields while making rude gestures to each other. Well, that was mainly Sulla.

"If the river to the north isn't wide," Sulla said, "we could cross it, then we're almost in Toria."

"But it's unfathomably deep," Hera said. "The fact you show no trepidation after witnessing the Branzians massacred by a leviathan in the river is frankly baffling. Must we continue to entertain your misbegotten ideas?"

"The only thing *baffling* here is you speaking like words less than four syllables don't exist."

"Enough," Darius said. "We're discussing Psinara right now, not our campaign against Toria." Which they'd gone over many times in the last few days, suffering from the absence of Rufus's shrewdness while he sorted out his legion. Darius still hadn't decided what they would do next.

Psinara's highest-ranking surviving algus stood before them, a boy not a day over sixteen but adopted by a family of importance, which seemed to be all that mattered to some of these human towns. Although rakkans fighting for their ranks often left Darius lamenting the practice, at least they didn't end up with people in positions far beyond their years.

The boy's mop of blond hair was like an unkempt version of Varro's, and his long chin pointed out as if determined to be longer than his nose.

"What other places were raided to the north?" Darius asked.

"I found a few farmers whose stores had been taken," the boy replied.

"Very well," Darius said. "My men will verify their losses and compensate them." At least the fall of the Silk City had left some valuables to be distributed, but his war chest was already running low.

The boy gave no thanks and instead bit his lip nervously.

"What else?" Darius asked.

"There's one issue. The people will still not renounce the King. They will not swear an oath to you."

That wasn't all too surprising. "Did you tell them we're compensating people for their lost produce?"

The boy nodded. "But their daughters were taken."

Darius cursed. *Damned Viridians.* "I'll speak with these farmers personally too." At this rate, he'd be meeting half the town to assure them the crimes committed here would be punished. But how he'd prove that was a mystery. Whatever Rufus was doing, he did only at night, when Darius collapsed from exhaustion from a solid day of untangling the web of horror in this town.

As he dismissed the algus and decided whether his body needed food or rest most, the door to the place opened and in strode Lex, dressed in algus battle attire and with windswept hair as if she'd been on horseback moments ago.

"Welcome back, stranger," Sulla said.

But her eyes fixated on Darius, blank and unreadable, so different from when they'd reunited after the last period spent apart and enough for him to know something was amiss.

"It's nice to finally see you again," he said. "How was Menara?"

"Fine," she replied. "I spent a day collecting some supplies, but I was delayed on the way back. I think there's something you should see. All of you."

When people said that kind of thing, it was never good, and he didn't quite believe her "collecting supplies" story either.

"Very well," Darius said. "I think we're done for the morning here." He stood and followed her out of the door along with Sulla, Varro, and Hera. But instead of being bathed in the afternoon sun as Darius had expected, he found himself in the depths of night without the moon or a star breaking the dark veil above. How many hours had he been in there?

"Where are we going?" he asked as he followed Lex through the street.

"I passed Rufus on the road west," she said. "He's begun his punishment."

"On the road?" Darius had expected a public spectacle in the town square: lashings, beatings, executions, or all three.

"You'll see." Lex led them to the stables, took a quick glance around the empty place, then pulled a rolled-up parchment from her pocket. "And there's another thing. The King has sent you a message."

Darius wouldn't ask why *she* had it, then. He took it, broke the wax, and read it while the others craned to see too.

*Slayer,*

*You may think highly of yourself considering how far you have reached, how many of my towns and cities you've taken, but by now, it must be known to you that I have a goman at my right, and anything you have achieved thus far is only because I have allowed it.*

*I let you take the Silk City and Psinara so that you could witness not only the horror I can inflict but that which you bring to those I know you pity. This is but a taste of what you could unleash on the Empire should you attempt to continue.*

*But know this: I shall not yield a yard more. My armies are ready, and my goman sees all.*

*Surrender now, return to the west, and I may allow you to keep the lands you've won. If you do not, you will bring ruin upon yourself and your people. You will force me to act.*

*And if my armies march west, they will not leave a building untouched or a field untrampled. Only a desolate waste will remain, with earth salted until not even a weed will sprout.*

*If my armies march west of the River Toras, they will leave no human or rakkan with breath.*

*King Medus II*

Below the name was the official seal of the King, one Darius had only seen a couple of times for the most important of commands. Did the reprobate think that would influence him?

When he'd finished, he handed the message to Varro for a better look. Some of the words had struck a nerve, the chaos and death he'd brought to people after cursing the King for far less. But the King couldn't be trusted to honour a truce.

"What a waste of ink," Darius said. "Am I supposed to be afraid?"

"There's some truth to it," Lex said. "The King could have mounted a fiercer defence. Our path farther east won't be as easy."

"We already knew that. Don't tell me you're considering surrender."

Lex scoffed. "Of course not. The King would never allow such a lenient surrender. It's a ruse."

"Then what? Do you think he has his sights set on the Psilos Bridge? That's the only route west."

"I'm not sure. Perhaps he plans to cross on boats or on that monster of his."

Darius murmured to himself. The Azure Legion was still defending the Gap of Aphatos, and the Silk City hadn't much of value left there, but he'd have plenty of warning if anyone tried to cross the river. There was little cover on the eastern banks to hide a preparing army or boats coming into position.

He wasn't worried about them crossing the river and even wondered whether he still needed the Azurians back at the Gap. With the departure of the Menarans, having an entire legion sitting so far back from the front line was a luxury he couldn't now spare if he wanted to press on towards Toria.

He read the note again, imagining how twisted the mind that penned it must have been to threaten such death. *This* was a man—or goman—the Chief Priest had told him to show mercy to?

The more times he reread the message, the more clear his decision became.

"We should have more scouts patrol the river," he said.

"You're both worried?" Sulla turned from the parchment with a roll of his eyes. "Isn't it obvious? The King's afraid. Why else would he try to intimidate us?"

"I hate to agree with him," Hera said, "but that was my first thought. The last time a human king wrote to threaten a rakkan was before the Denehill Massacre."

Darius grunted. "Can we please stop calling it a 'massacre'? I slew an army, but you make it sound like I cut the throats of women and children."

"Typical ruler," Sulla said. "Rewriting history already."

"This note…" Varro moved between the group and gingerly held out the parchment like a cursed object they should fear to touch. "Does it make sense? He wouldn't allow us to surrender."

Darius stared at the ink marks again, dwelling on what they actually knew of the man that wrote them. And conversely, how much did the King know about *him*? For the last few years, Darius had been discovering himself, becoming the man he now was. Only those closest to him knew his temperament, his sore spots, and his flaws, so the King couldn't know much.

"I think Sulla's right," he said. "The King is afraid. This message reeks of desperation."

Lex's frown betrayed her scepticism, but she didn't voice an objection.

"I'm not surrendering," Darius concluded, "and I'm not waiting for him to attack. Lex, is Tiro near?"

She nodded.

"Good. Send word to Warlord Quintus; the Azure Legion will leave a small force at the Gap, then march here."

"I think that's the right call," Varro said.

Darius was grateful for the support. As for the King's message, they had time to ponder what their reaction should be.

He went to a swift and grabbed the reins. "Now, are we going to see what Rufus has done or not?"

Lex nodded, and soon after, they all mounted swifts and began to tear along the road west.

# 42

## Darius – Psilos Bridge

Atop swifts, the ride to the bridge wouldn't take long, so they set a sensible pace. Darius rode alongside Lex, still unsure how to begin a conversation on what they'd discussed in that quiet room a couple of weeks ago, but he concluded anything would be better than awkward silence.

"So, you stayed in Menara for a couple of days," he said. "Any reason?"

"Of course I had a reason," she replied, followed by nothing but a slight grin.

"Do you enjoy making conversations difficult?"

"Only with you. You think I went to check with the medicine man, don't you?"

Darius admired her habit of cutting straight to the point. "I'd be surprised if you didn't."

"Then colour yourself shocked; I didn't."

He wasn't sure exactly what that meant. "You mean you trust me?"

"It would be a wicked thing for you to lie about, so yes, I do."

He couldn't help but feel a little pride at the fact. "Then what were you doing?"

"I told you. Making sure to keep good relations with the Menarans and their farmers, as well as collecting supplies to make more of the powder we tried using to disable the Waif Magician. If Rufus and Aran are right, then Jason will share her powers and weaknesses. It'll help you defeat him."

Which meant helping him defeat their enemies and being together at last.

"You could have told me you'd be staying for a while before you left," he muttered.

"Why? Do you need to know my every intention?"

"Of course. You expect a man not to worry when a woman doesn't return when he expects?"

The sternness of his answer saw her grin fall, replaced with a hint of embarrassment as if she didn't know that he worried over her like she had over him.

Dropping the subject, they continued chatting, and it wasn't long before they neared the Psilos Bridge and something caught Darius's eye, pulling his mind away from Lex's absence and the King's message and back to the matters of the present day.

At each side of the main road, lines and lines of structures ran as far as he could see into the west—hundreds of wooden stakes stabbed into the ground at regular intervals with a crossbar at the top, like lantern posts but without a flame.

They looked like banners from a distance, pale flags hanging undisturbed in the windless night, but as he neared, he realised what they were. Attached to the beam across the top of each stake hung rakkan bodies, stripped to their undergarments to let the sun parch their pale skin when it rose, and arms nailed outstretched as if awaiting the embrace of death.

The closer they drew, the more it was apparent over half weren't dead yet, pushing with their feet and breathing hoarsely before slumping back down every few seconds. Crucifixion was an ugly thing to witness. Unlike with the blood eagle, the condemned lasted for days.

"Where's Rufus?" Darius asked.

"Near the bridge," Lex answered.

Whipping the reins of his swift, Darius tore past the parade of bodies until he reached the Psilos Bridge and found the Viridian Warlord overseeing the nailing of another rakkan to a post—and not just any rakkan, but his brother Piso.

The other rakkans around were lined up in silent respect, as was more often seen at a burial or memorial. Unlike most executions, the Viridian Warlord and his party spat no curses or condemnations of the crimes that resulted in justice being meted; they only kept quiet observance.

Darius leapt off his horse before it had come to a stop and approached. "This is your punishment?"

Rufus's brother howled in pain as a nail was hammered into his right wrist while the Warlord watched. Next to him, a couple of other Viridian Commanders stood as fearfully as Darius had ever seen them, and it wasn't through dread of *him* for a change.

"Indeed," Rufus said. "Piso here will be an example to all my commanders."

"I'm less concerned about your commanders and more about how many of your men are dead."

A rakkan hammered a nail into Piso's second wrist while Rufus regarded the sight as casually as a friendly game of katakto.

"Soon, all of those that took Psinara," the Warlord said.

Darius scanned the road again, trying to estimate the count. "A thousand?"

"Bar a few," Rufus said. "They will line the road all the way from the farms to Psinara, a spectacle for both the locals and my remaining men."

How had the Viridian Warlord even convinced his men to crucify their comrades? Did Darius dare ask?

"Are you displeased?" Rufus asked, finally granting Darius the respect of looking at him.

"More surprised," Darius said. The truth was, he wasn't sure what to feel. After seeing Psinara, it was hard to feel pity for any of these wretches. But hadn't there been any men that hadn't partaken? And what about Rufus and Darius himself? They bore some of the blame for this too, so he couldn't shake the feeling that they too should be letting out the agonised screams that pained the ears.

While more questions ran through his mind, Lex, Sulla, and Warlord Varro finally caught up and came to join them.

"Were my men of use?" Varro asked.

"I didn't need them in the end," Rufus said. "The threat was enough."

Darius's attention shifted to the Viridian Commander behind Rufus, the twin of the wailing brother being crucified before his eyes. Despite the helmet hiding his face, there was more than pain in there, more than fear.

"Why the road?" Darius asked.

"The farms west of the river will need to feed our armies," Rufus said. "My men will journey along this supply route many times, and when they do, they will be reminded at every step of my authority and power over them. The rest of my legion will obey whatever I command lest they wish to suffer the same fate."

How similar that was to what had happened with the slaves in the Silk City, a thought enough to make Darius retch. He couldn't argue with the results, but the methods… This was what happened when giving such a merciless rakkan a blank slate, and he'd be sure never to give Rufus such power over anyone he cared for the welfare of.

"Is your punishment finished?" Darius asked.

"It will be in a few days." Rufus sighed, seeming regretful. "Then we must plan for the march east."

"Who said we're marching east?" Sulla asked.

"Apologies. I just assumed." Rufus frowned, a return to that calculating expression. "Crossing the river to the north is too dangerous with that beast, and the Great Scars cannot be bridged. There is no way to Toria but to go east through the Plains of Psilon, north through Alogos, then back west through the Arid Gorge."

That matched Darius's opinion after days of deliberating. "But the plains. What shall we do about the swifts of Alogos?"

"Try not to lose too many men," Rufus said. "And our greatest problem will be if they get behind us and cut off our supply routes."

"I hope you have ideas on how to prevent that," Darius said. "We just received this."

He handed Rufus the King's note, and the Warlord took it in as impassively as everything else. When he'd finished, all he gave was a slight raise of his eyebrows.

"Will you respond?" he asked.

Darius hadn't really considered it. "I won't surrender, so what's the point?"

"I can respond on your behalf." Lex took the parchment. "I'll be brief in your refusal."

"Fine. And what of the threat of the King's army marching west?" Darius turned to Rufus. "Do you think we'll have early enough warning of anyone crossing the river on boats?"

"I'm far more worried about the swifts of Alogos," Rufus said. "The King would be a fool to send his armies west when his enemies will approach from the east, after we've laid waste to Alogos."

The Warlord's pitiless phrasing sent a cold shudder through Darius. Never would he leave this rakkan alone to lead again.

"If we use the roads and defend them," Darius said, "will we be able to survive the cavalry?"

"No," Rufus said. "My Subdued scouted a little weeks ago, and the plains are firm on either side of the road, perfect for cavalry. They're more uneven and wet to the south, so we should march there."

"And what of our food wagons?" Darius asked.

"Food can be carried," Lex said. "Rakkans have the strength of oxen, and if we don't rely on the roads, it's that much harder for them to disrupt our supplies."

Rufus nodded in agreement.

That plan made the most sense, but uneven ground would only hamper cavalry, not halt them.

"We'll make preparations to march at a few hours' notice," Darius said. "Once Psinara is sorted, we'll set off after the first day of heavy rain." His own scouts had noted how boggy the plains had become after the storm had eased days ago. That combined with Rufus's intelligence would give them a fighting chance.

"Does that mean," Rufus began, "that I shall be marching to battle with you?"

"Only you," Darius said, "and perhaps a few of your men. I want your mind, but your legion will still be our workhorses."

The Viridian Warlord and other leaders all bowed their acceptance of that and the other orders.

"Then pray to your God and Goddess," Rufus said. "Pray for storms and floods that hamper hooves but not boots."

# 43

## King's Orator – Toria

Ophelia rushed into the throne room, but as the slaves opened the doors and she stepped inside the familiar place, she was surprised to find the King absent from his throne and a cold bite in the air. He couldn't have been here for a while because he always had fires warming the place when residing here.

"Where is he?" she asked one of the guards.

"The Pool of Toriamas."

*What would he be doing there?*

She set off at once, trying to recall the last time she'd seen the pool. Legend had it that Toriamas had founded Toria around that very spring, using its endless water to sustain the tribe and eventually built his home around it, a monument that later kings had turned into this very palace.

She followed the winding corridors deeper, descending with every step but without any stairs, and eventually reached a pair of metal doors gilded with symbols from the language of their forefathers.

She passed by the guards there and entered what was more like a cave than a room, with a dirt floor lacking even a hint of green. Only clay lamps granted the windowless room light, hung on the walls all around the vast perimeter.

In the centre, the ground sank into a pool that was barely large enough to swim in and held crystal water without a ripple disturbing the glassy surface. And standing statuesque next to it, the masked King stared into the depths.

"*What news from the city's algus?*" the King asked.

"Tales of Darius's victories seem to have spread fast. They're not happy with us."

"*I sense you're concerned, but you needn't be. My motives are towards success, not popularity.*"

"I didn't question you, my king." Not out loud, anyway.

"*Nevertheless, it's time to show Darius that he will need untold force to defeat us, to keep his army unified. Are the swifts of Alogos mustered and fed?*"

"Yes, my king."

"*Good. Then send your best algus to lead them.*"

Ophelia had a sinking feeling about what that meant. "Jason has barely recovered. If we send him out, is he to take the Staff this time?"

"*There are too many routes of escape on the plains. Their armies would scatter, and we'd barely kill a few hundred rakkans. The Staff stays with me.*"

Ophelia lowered her head, beginning to share the resentment of her fellow Torians but feeling shameful for the fact. Sitting on such power made little sense without the King's foresight, but now she doubted they'd ever reach the point of this devastating blow the King oft prophesied but that was still no closer to the present.

"*I know your thoughts.*" The King finally looked at her, and chills ran down Ophelia's arms as if the goman were touching her skin. "*They're written on your face. Do not fret. We are but a prelude to the war. We have achieved much in delaying the rakkans until the gomans arrive. It won't be long until the sea calms.*"

As reassuring as the words were intended to be, Ophelia couldn't imagine more gomans in the Empire, let alone what they might achieve. She'd seen nothing to suggest such a future was even possible, let alone probable.

"Are you sure they're still waiting?" Ophelia asked. "It's been almost fifteen years since you left."

The King's glare intensified and pierced her. "*If I have foreseen the calming of the sea, then the Council surely has. Our army will be ready to sail and wipe out the rakkan threat once and for all.*"

"Then, have you seen them arrive?" Ophelia asked.

The King remained silent for a moment, but his eyes weren't clouded and viewing the future; they were still fixated on Ophelia with what she knew was quiet fury.

"*No.*"

Then Ophelia had no confidence in his prediction, having heard much the same for years. And one thing had always puzzled her. "Why are you so sure your people are intent on invading?"

"*You make it sound like we are the aggressors.*"

Ophelia didn't dare voice her opinion on that.

"*Back home, we're a peaceful people and are able to trust one another. You can't imagine how a society works without lies and where people know what you intend to do in the future. There's no hiding, and quarrels are often resolved before they've begun. But then, those with the greatest foresight began to prophesy our ruin… Demons arriving on boats with fire in their veins and blackness in their hearts. Immune to our powers. Too strong to resist. This is a quarrel we must not allow to begin. We're defending our people. We'll fight the war here.*"

Although rakkans seeking domination was easy for Ophelia to believe, they had no sailing knowledge within them. It would have taken years.

"Who would lead this rakkan invasion?" Ophelia asked. If they killed them, surely that ended the threat.

"*There are many that could. Hadrian was one.*"

"And is Darius?"

The King shook his head. "*I could not say. I'm not the one that foresaw it, and I don't know all the names.*"

Apart from Darius, Ophelia struggled to think of anyone capable of leading the rakkans. With what her spies had told her, the only one with the will and the smarts to pull it off was Warlord Rufus, but she didn't expect him to breathe long after Darius was killed.

"What if Darius surrenders?" Ophelia asked. She didn't expect it, but they had given the Overlord the option in their threat.

The King turned back to stare into the pool. "*Then we continue as planned. The rakkan risk is too great. Whatever happens, they must be wiped out, and Darius along with them.*"

So much for a "defensive" war.

"Then send Jason with the Staff," Ophelia said. "Forget Darius's armies. Remove the head of the beast rather than trying to destroy the whole thing."

"*Darius is one man; his army is a much greater threat. You know well that heads have a habit of growing back.*"

Of course she did, having made that mistake with King Medus I early in her career. But this was Jason's life they were talking about.

As if reading her thoughts, the King added, "*I know you fret for Jason, but this time, I do not send him to battle.*"

"Then why send him?"

"*I won't reveal the Staff until it's time, but you're right about cutting off the head. Darius is about to leave us an opportunity, and Jason will seize it.*"

A rush of excitement stole Ophelia's breath. Would the half-rakkan finally sleep outside the safety of his army or overstretch himself?

"When?"

"*After they reach the town of Chiva. The One Mind is ready to intervene and shake the world again. This time, we'll use it, but Jason will need to follow precise instructions.*"

If there was one thing the King's Sword was good at, it was following guidance to the letter.

"*And send word to the sailors: when the fires start, ready our ships to ferry men across the River Toras.*"

Ophelia frowned. "What fires, my king?"

"*They will know when it happens. Darius's information channels will be severed and his armies destroyed soon after. We need to be ready to march west to take back our empire.*"

Transporting that many soldiers would take more ships than Toria currently had, so Ophelia would order new construction to begin at once. Finally, the victory the King had promised all along was coming to fruition.

As Ophelia opened her mouth to laugh in both glee and relief, the doors to the room opened and an elder slave rushed in with something clasped in his hand. He only stopped when before Ophelia and bowed deeply.

"What is it?" she asked. Slaves shouldn't ordinarily have been in here.

"We have a reply from the Slayer." The man held out a roll of parchment bearing the broken seal of the King.

"So quickly?" Ophelia snatched the message, but the King held out a hand, waiting to read it first. She handed it over while the slave rushed out.

Messages to one's enemies were things that should have been meticulously thought of and took days or weeks to craft for even a skilled woman such as her. What scrawl had Darius sent back so quickly?

The King's eyes scanned down the parchment until lingering at the end for a moment. Then he shook his head.

"*So arrogant. The warning worked better than I thought.*" But there was anger in the King's eyes as he tossed the parchment to Ophelia, who at first only saw the message she had penned until arriving at the response at the end.

...

*If my armies march west of the River Toras, they will leave no human or rakkan with breath.*

*King Medus II*

*If.*

# 44

## Rufus – Plains of Psilon

"Cavalry sighted to the northwest!" a Subdued called.

"How far?" Rufus asked.

"Minutes away from being in range."

The rains had mocked them, pouring for two days and nights to give them the courage to begin the march, only to desert them and leave them baking under a cloudless sky usually seen in the height of summer.

Rufus adjusted the hood of his cloak until it cast his face in shade again. Marching in the vanguard wasn't what Viridian leaders did, but Darius demanded it of him and all the other warlords and regents, probably thinking his presence was enough to save them from danger. Of all the things that killed men, overconfidence was one of the most potent.

Dried mud cracked underfoot as the jagged mountains to the south watched over the foolish rakkans that decided it best to march in such conditions. To an escort, lands this soft and potholed were a breeze to skip across and recommend to others, but the reality of thick-boned rakkans wearing kuraminium armour was another matter. They'd marched at night at first, but too many broken ankles of humans and mules had forced them to do the next few miles burning in the day.

If some of the Psinarans had been made to help guide them, the experts on this terrain, they'd have fared better. Rufus suspected there was a safer route through, but he was hardly surprised they held their tongues.

"We need more rain," Rufus said. Hopefully, any gods around heard.

"We'll have to make do with what we've got," Darius said. "I'm not turning back."

Rufus hadn't been suggesting such an un-Viridian thing. He turned to Warlord Varro. "I suggest you ready the shield wall and slingers."

"Indeed." Varro sent one of his commanders off to organise his men at once while Warlords Quintus and Flavius gave similar orders to their warriors.

It was so foreign for Rufus to be without his army, having to give suggestions rather than orders, but at least the Overlord and warlords listened to him, unlike his brothers in decades past.

"No pikes?" Darius asked.

Rufus shook his head. "The swifts won't engage us. They'll toss their javelins from a distance."

"They'll have horse archers too," Lex said, "more skilled than you'll have seen before."

Rufus had heard the stories, and the combined strength of the Azure, Branz, and Black Legions made for a large target easy enough to hit for even an inexperienced man on horseback. The sooner they could march in darkness again, the better.

"I suggest we set up camp within the hour," Rufus said.

"Very well," Darius replied. "Are you sure it's a good use of our time building ramparts and palisades every time we stop? Even the Viridians are tiring from carrying those logs behind us, and it's hard work for the diggers in both the bog and hard ground."

"It's the best protection we'll have from the cavalry," Rufus said. Plus, his men were so drilled in erecting the small forts that it was almost automatic now because for decades, his and his father's plans had included marching far into enemy lands.

"You should join the Black Legionnaires," Rufus added. "And be aggressive. Swifts are not reared as warhorses; they can be spooked."

Darius nodded as the Blades at his hips let out a whisper and a glint. He touched them, like a father asking for his children's patience, before stomping away to join the men forming an offensive marching formation on their flank.

As he left, Rufus caught Lex's eye and knew it was so rare to get her away from Darius that he'd best seize this chance to speak with her.

"We should discuss Alogos," Rufus said.

Lex glanced sideways at him as one did a disease-ridden leper. "Should we? I thought you wanted to deal with Chiva first."

"I do." Any siege on Alogos could be thwarted by an army from that small town to the south. "But Alogos is the true test, and we may need to begin planning now."

"I see. Planning what?"

Rufus needed to choose his words carefully, as this idea wasn't exactly palatable after recent events. "How many slaves does Alogos have?"

"I'm not sure, but I don't think as many as Xavala had. Why?"

By now, the swifts of Alogos were not only visible but the thunder of hooves reached his ears. Their numbers looked only a fifth of their rumoured full-strength army, but that was more than enough to give Rufus pause.

"Get me a shield," he called to one of his men.

As the man ran off, Rufus gave Lex his attention again. "I've thought much on what happened with the slaves in the Silk City. Our strategy had promise, but exactly where the fault lay wasn't obvious to me. Have you any thoughts?"

Lex's narrowed eyes were those of a suspicious woman, but she replied nonetheless. "The slave revolt was quashed because that's all we relied on."

Rufus smiled, her thoughts mirroring his. He waited until his man brought a large kuraminium scutum before responding. "If my legion had attacked the city first, perhaps it wouldn't have been as clear to the ever-watching goman that a significant number of slaves had assisted us."

"A mistake you do not wish to repeat in Alogos, am I to presume?"

A sudden disturbance in the air set the hairs on Rufus's neck on edge. He whirled around and brought up his shield to cover his and Lex's bodies before three arrows crashed into the metal. Hundreds of metallic thumps followed as the first volley from the horse archers hit, followed by a cloud of dust as the swifts wheeled and rushed back out of range with fiery slinger shots chasing them, albeit too slowly.

"Thanks," Lex muttered somewhat reluctantly.

"Get used to it." Rufus did a quick count of how many nearby had been injured—half a dozen. "We've got weeks of this ahead of us."

A roar erupted from the fields at their flank, drawing everyone's attention to the swirls of red flame that followed in the wake of the Overlord. He charged at a group of riders approaching with their javelins ready, dodged one with an algor tip at the last moment, then leapt and hacked the rider's head off with a red thrust.

The corner of Lex's mouth curled.

"I see you have a new pride in him," Rufus said. "Did your relationship change recently?"

Her pleasure vanished. "Don't ask about what isn't your business."

"Noted. I only ask because I hope that he will listen to you about matters that he may be instinctively averse to."

"Ah, you're speaking of Alogos again? A slave revolt, perhaps?"

"I'd avoid calling it that. I prefer to think of it as building support for our cause before our eventual assault."

Lex shook her head. "If you were as skilled with a sword as you are with words, you'd be a dangerous man."

Had she meant that as a compliment? Because Rufus *was* a dangerous man, and only fools thought otherwise.

"Do we have any contacts in Alogos?" Rufus asked.

"I don't, but Hera may. Do you wish to send someone in?"

"It would be wise. At worst, we may get some new information on the city." So far, the few Subdued that Rufus had sent ahead to spy had been killed. Whatever was happening in that city, the King was going to great lengths to ensure no one discovered it, and Rufus couldn't afford to let more of his limited supply of algus die given he couldn't replenish them.

"And why ask me?" Lex said. "You know Darius will need to give the order to begin anything with the slaves in Alogos."

Rufus sensed the air shift again, but this time Lex caught the movement, and she skipped aside as a javelin speared the dirt behind her.

"To speak with slaves risks a repeat of Xavala," Rufus said. "Darius hasn't the stomach for such an outcome."

"And I do?"

The two shared a look, one of two grizzled war veterans with so much blood in their past that their future wasn't anything but red.

"You've risked much to get this far," Rufus said. "I'm willing to bet the lives of thousands more slaves are a risk you'll take."

She offered no contradiction, only a subtly shameful glance at the Overlord, who was chasing away another group of riders only for more to travel farther and aim for the rest of the army behind.

"If we can arrange a simultaneous revolt and assault," she said, "it could work. I'll convince Darius."

Rufus gave a nod, then left her alone for the rest of the march. The journey only lasted another hour before the cavalry took a greater toll than he was prepared to absorb, so he ordered they make camp.

How different the last few days had been. Whenever Rufus issued an order to the Viridians handling the army's logistics, men now saluted and rushed to fulfil it. No more hesitation. No more looking down their nose at him. Finally, the respect he deserved. And it had only cost a thousand crucified comrades.

Digging trenches and erecting the palisades for the camp took even longer than usual with clusters of projectiles constantly battering the men's morale, but the Overlord was unrivalled in quelling their fears, a titanic symbol they'd need to steel their nerves for the rest of the march to Toria.

And, true to her word, Lex had Darius sending escorts and algus straight away to Alogos via a long, indirect route that would hopefully avoid the swifts.

Evening had barely come when Rufus called on the army to march again. Back to travelling in the night, and so it was for the next few weeks, weary nights with ever-thinning numbers and resolve, like wild deer being hunted by a pack of rats taking one bite at a time, making the possibility of surrender more appealing by the day. Sleep was difficult to steal with even more attacks during the day, and soon the humans complained at the night-time travel as their bodies struggled with the unnatural pattern.

Rufus kept track of the hundred or so men lost every night, but only a few others outside the warlords were allowed to know the number lest morale further suffer.

It was almost two weeks until they were granted a night without an attack, not long before scouts spotted the town of Chiva in the distance along with the Tar Sea at its side. The next hill they crested gave them a perfect view of both that and the rest of the plains to the east.

Nestled into a small valley between a few hills, the town looked sparsely built and mostly of wooden construction. Its streets were uniform and wide, all crossing together in a way that made trade and transportation easy, and the lack of any natural rivers or springs made sense given this town had been purpose-built for mining the nearby mountains, a perfect place for travellers to take respite rather than being a town settled by the early human tribes.

Opposite the hills, the town was built on the banks of the Tar Sea, a sight that had Rufus suspicious he was hallucinating. It was so common for humans to label the thing a "wonder" that he'd considered it a trite exaggeration that doomed him to suffer disappointment when he finally saw it. But the sheer scale before him was almost unthinkable, stretching as far as the rakkan eye could see into the horizon like an ocean, but without a ripple, without a wave, just an unending black inkblot on the landscape, so perfectly level it was almost unreal, like the gods that had painted the world had simply left that part of the dark canvas blank.

Whatever stained its waters or however it had come to be was a question Rufus knew would only frustrate him, so he turned his attention back to the present and came alongside Darius.

"We should make camp," he said. "We can launch our attack from here, so we'll set the palisades deeper this time."

Darius nodded as he always did now with Rufus's suggestions, but his attention didn't leave the town.

"You say attack…" The Overlord waved over Lex and Hera. "How many soldiers and algus will Chiva have?"

"A few hundred soldiers at most," Lex replied.

The Black Legion had already sent a few centuries to cut off the road to the sulphur mines to the south.

"Then why attack?" Darius asked. "They'll probably surrender."

"We should assume the King will have bolstered their defence," Rufus said, "as he did in Psinara."

Darius frowned. "But our scouts report nothing like that. I'm willing to give them the chance to let us by peacefully."

Even if they did, Rufus knew better than to trust the word of humans who would be able to cut off their route back home once the rakkan army made its way towards Alogos. Even the former people of Laltos weren't ones Rufus trusted with anything of significance.

"I will plan for an assault regardless," Rufus said.

"Fine. Varro, send an envoy to begin discussions."

Hera cleared her throat in her usual way to get attention. "Shouldn't my people do that? Negotiations would be better human to human."

Darius ruminated on the thought for a moment. "No. They'll have heard what happened in Psinara. May as well make use of the fear."

At the somewhat harsh decision, both Lex and Hera pinched their cheeks as if sucking a lime but said nothing more. Varro sent one of his commanders as an envoy while they began setting up camp, ensuring the Overlord's tent was erected first where they could call the assembly to discuss their plans. Varro's man was only gone a few hours before he returned with good news but a discontent face.

"They say they won't resist us," the Black Commander said to the seated leaders around him. "There are only a handful of algus at the town that we saw."

Darius smiled, more from relief than pleasure, it seemed. "Then we'll march in tomorrow night and take respite."

"But they have conditions," the Black Commander continued, "among them, they want reassurance they'll not be treated like the Psinarans were."

"I hope you gave them that reassurance," Darius said.

"I did, but I may as well have offered them a polished turd. They want your word in person."

*Strange.* Usually, a town would want the Slayer of Gods as far away as possible, not in the midst of them, even if promising not to begin a bloody massacre.

While Darius scratched at the stubble on his cheek and contemplated it, Hera responded first. "Perhaps it would have been wisest to send a human envoy after all."

Sulla groaned and massaged his temples. "I'm too tired for 'I told you so.'"

"All of you, give it a rest." Darius stood, the tent stilling around him. "If they want to hear it from my mouth, fine. I'll go there at dusk."

"And how many warriors will you take with you?" Lex asked.

"Hera's right; they'll probably be more reassured by humans. I'll take a dozen algus."

"That's all? What if it's a trap?"

The Overlord scoffed. "And what can they trap me with? Kuraminium restraints they can't even lift? I'll be fine; I'll even take a swift to be sure, and I'll leave a few centuries not too far away."

"Still… I'll go with you too."

He shook his head. "If it is a trap, I'll want you nowhere near. If it isn't, I'll have no need for you."

The woman's face flushed in frustration, but she gave a reluctant bow of her head in acceptance.

Whatever this town wanted to hear from Darius, something told Rufus he should continue his plans for an assault. Not that it would be much trouble. Reports said Chiva had no town walls, and the townsfolk's only escape once an attack ensued would be to run and drown in the Tar Sea.

"You should take some of my Subdued with you," Rufus offered. "Perhaps Gorgias?"

Darius's reaction was one of suspicion, but after a pause, he simply shrugged. "If you wish."

"And if you want to have centuries close by," Rufus said, "I'm happy to lead them."

Again, Darius looked suspicious but gave no objection. "Very well, but you'll be the only Viridian there. Be ready to leave within the hour."

The assembly then came to a close, and the various leaders left while Rufus began his plans. Gorgias was there, so he first went amongst the camp and found the algus watching over the construction of some of the palisades. He quickly relayed where the man was to go.

"Why did you request I join them?" Gorgias asked.

There were times when having Darius's spy around came in useful, but this was not one of those times. Plans for an assault after Psinara were best left behind the Overlord's back.

"You were in Psinara," Rufus said. "I thought you'd be of assistance in assuaging their fears."

The dark-haired algus didn't look convinced.

"There is one thing, however," Rufus added. "You must leave your escort with me, given you're supposed to be my hostage."

Gorgias's eyes narrowed. "I never told you I have an escort."

"I never said you did." Rufus smiled. "But your mother has been taking good care of her. Have the badger brought to my tent."

The algus stomped away without reply like a petulant child, but Rufus knew he'd obey. Now that Rufus had rid himself of one problem, he had another to tackle. Without Viridians to call upon, a quiet word with the Branz Warlord was what he'd need to get some troops unafraid of action, and he'd begin preparation of the rakkan's legionnaires.

# 45

## Darius – Chiva

The night was at its brightest, with a full moon bathing them in a cool light while supported by an army of specks in the sky. There couldn't have been a more peaceful, starry night, with the clanks and thumps of his legions left safely behind, and for the first time in weeks, the buzz of insects and calm treading of hooves were all that filled his ears.

"Bloody swifts," Sulla grumbled. "What good is a horse that moves too fast to see where you're going?"

Too fast for everyone except someone with algus reflexes.

"Just don't kick it again," Darius said. "It's only when it gallops you're helpless."

Although rakkans would scare the locals, he'd decided it was best to have at least one. And when tensions grew, Sulla was the only man that could cut through them and bring back a jovial mood. At least, that's what Darius was hoping.

Sulla and Gorgias guided their mounts beside him while the rest of their party followed behind, almost three dozen algus from Hera's ranks, not all men and women he knew and trusted, but so far, he'd yet to meet an algus of Laltos that wasn't skilled in battle.

The town ahead burst with the glow of torches, braziers, and lamps, so much that as his eyes adjusted to it, he barely discerned the stars anymore. The entrance to the town had no gate or even walls, just a dirt road leading down a main street flanked by wooden buildings all boarded shut. And despite the bright lights, not a soul stirred, the only thing disturbing the streets being the rustle of dust in the wind.

Flying escorts had said the town was shaped like a giant cross composed of two main roads north to south and east to west, and at the town centre, what used to be a market was now nothing more than deserted stalls and tables.

Darius brought the group to a stop a few hundred yards away, focusing his skin on anything moving; but there was nothing.

"We'll wait here," he said, dismounting. Something about the town centre ahead put him off. "I'm here!"

No reply came, but rather than look around further, he decided it was best to wait.

And the wait was a long one, lasting an hour or two of his constant announcement and growing temper before he finally caught sight of life ahead of them.

A group emerged from a building at the far side of the town and made their way into the centre where they stopped. At first count, there were over a hundred rough-looking people huddled together with a group of three at the front who seemed to be in charge, one wearing a cylindrical hat almost comically tall and a golden chain at his neck that hung so low it would bash his groin if he ran.

The algus with Darius wouldn't see as well as he did, so he studied every person there. The inhabitants looked to be miners, with faces smeared in dirt and grime as well as keeping to the shadows, but there was something a little too dirty about them, almost too uniform and too alike.

Darius climbed back atop his steed, and soon after, so did the rest of his men.

"What's wrong, master?" Gorgias asked.

Scanning the distant faces of the waiting townsfolk again, Darius saw no youngsters, which perhaps wasn't surprising given his reputation, but the thing that did unnerve him was that there was only one man there that looked to be aged over forty.

"They're not townsfolk," Darius said. "They're an army, probably algus given how many women there are." This was some sort of trap, but a pretty poor one. "Do your escorts see swifts anywhere?"

"No," three algus said in reply.

How odd. Did algus think they could outrun swifts now?

"Should we turn back?" Gorgias asked.

Before Darius could answer, the man sporting the huge hat and chain began walking forward with only an older gentleman accompanying him. As they approached, Darius sensed something about the older man, the smoothness of his walk that barely disturbed his loose grey tunic, and his unrelenting stare was that of a man focused and ready to fight.

But what threat could they pose to men on swifts?

Not much, Darius concluded, so he allowed them closer until within range of hearing.

"Stop there," Darius called. "I don't like to be kept waiting! Do you take me for a fool?"

The hat man frowned. "I know not your meaning. Are you Darius, Slayer of Gods?"

Darius ripped the Twin Blades from his waist, wreathing the swords in ferven until the runes hissed their deathly rasp.

The hat man took a step back, but his old friend was unmoved by the display.

"Why are you hiding algus?" Darius yelled. "Do you not think my army will continue its march even if you slay me?"

The hat man glanced at his friend before answering. "We're not hiding. We've been abandoned by the King and are ready to surrender. But we do not wish for our families to be—"

"Oh, save the lies!" Sulla shouted with such force his swift wobbled nervously.

"We should head back, master," Gorgias said. "There's no sense in engaging without your army."

As much as Darius loved a scrap against uneven numbers, Gorgias was probably right. But hadn't this situation been the same in Psinara? Hadn't the people there suffered more than the algus army stationed to supposedly protect them? Darius owed it to whatever civilians were left hiding here to at least try to negotiate a surrender.

"Who are you?" Darius asked the pair.

"I'm the steward of this town," the hat man replied, "by authority of the Regent of Alogos and the King of Toria."

"They no longer have authority here," Darius said, now watching the stationary aged man more than the supposed steward. Most male human leaders Darius had met were advanced in their years, so he suspected that man was the true leader in hiding.

"And who are you?" Darius shouted at the man.

No reply came, and the hat man grew all the more twitchy, scratching his heels back inch by inch.

First, they'd kept Darius waiting for no apparent reason, and now, they refused to speak candidly. It was clear they were wasting his time for some reason, and he was done allowing it. These talks would continue on his terms, not theirs.

"You have until sunset tomorrow," Darius yelled. "If you wish to surrender, you will not be harmed. If not…"

As if in reply, a murmur came from the ground, a low thrum that sent a tremor through his steed's legs and to his thighs.

"What the hell." Sulla cast his gaze at the street, and Darius's swift shifted uneasily.

"Calm, girl." He gave the mare a pat on the neck.

None of the townsfolk, however, seemed perturbed by the rumble, and this was eerily similar to the feeling he'd had near the Gap of Aphatos when the ground had tried to swallow his army.

"I think we've overstayed our welcome," Darius said to the others. "Let's head back to camp."

The algus behind him turned their swifts around and set off, but the older man arrested Darius's attention for a few moments. There was something familiar about him, but without being close, it could have been a trick of the eye.

"You coming or what?" Sulla asked, hanging back with Gorgias.

"Do you know that man?" Darius asked, more to his human friend than Sulla.

Gorgias squinted. "I can't really see him."

"All old men look the same to me," Sulla added.

"Never mind." Darius grabbed the reins of his horse, but before he could whip the swift into action, the older man began walking forward as casually as if taking a morning stroll.

His steps were slow and calm but long and with purpose, and once a little closer, Darius spied the hilt of a sword occasionally peeking from behind his neck.

What was this? One man coming to face the Slayer of Gods?

Anyone that would dare wasn't someone Darius wanted to meet, and there was an unsettling look about his face, an iciness, a man that had faced and slain foes as fearsome as Darius a hundredfold.

"Gorgias." Darius began wheeling his swift around. "Isn't that the King's Sword?"

The algus's eyes widened. "By the Goddess."

That was enough confirmation for Darius. Although he had no reason to doubt his ability, the Chief Priest had warned him of the danger the King's servant posed. And only then did he recall Lex mentioning the powder she'd bought, which he'd stowed in the bag attached to his swift.

He pulled the reins to steady the horse and reached down for the powder, but as he did, the ground lurched, and a sudden thunder filled his ears, a rumbling like a thousand wooden wheels coursing down a cobblestone road. His swift reared too quickly for Darius to grab anything but the reins as he fell back and instinctively pulled to save himself from the fall.

His backside fell clear off the horse before the reins tightened and yanked the swift's head back with a force that snapped its neck. He hit the shuddering ground, and the swift's mass fell on top of him, pressing the air from his lungs and coming to rest without a twitch.

It took Darius a few beats to get his hands under the thing's muscle and shove it clear enough to slip away. But as he did, the Twin Blades caught on something and tore free of his belt.

"Darius!" Sulla called while he got to one knee.

Before Darius saw anything, the air behind his neck shifted, betraying something hurtling towards him. He ducked, and sharp metal cut through his hair from behind with a speed that only an algus could summon, confirmed as the blade next screamed in front of him and left a bright blue arc in the night.

He rolled forward, grabbed one of the Blades, and felt the initial coldness in his palm cease as fire ignited without will or effort from him.

Before he'd regained his feet or turned his head, the air shifted behind him again. He ducked and brought his sword up above his head, parried his enemy's chop, and left a haze of sparks sprinkling across his hair. His enemy pushed down, but Darius's strength reigned even in such a weak position.

He spun on his heels, then leapt, forcing his enemy backwards, and would have taken the algus's head off with his flying knee had the man not weaved to the side, out of the way of his thrust, and retracted his sword. Now soaring through the air, Darius watched as the man's flaring blue sword swung around and came at his back. It slashed through his clothes and skin as he twisted and only just avoided it severing his spine.

Darius landed and skidded to a halt on the still-quaking street, turning to see his opponent now motionless and brandishing his sword above Darius's dead horse. The man's eyes shone an icy blue, yet there was no anger, no hate, no fear in them, only a fixation on his quarry, one more neck ordered to meet the edge of his sword.

"Jason," Darius said, but his voice was lost as a building to the side split in two, wood rupturing along with the ground beneath it.

The King's Sword turned his head a fraction as two others appeared behind Darius—Gorgias and Sulla struggling to stay atop their frenzied mounts.

"Master!" Gorgias shouted. "Come on!"

Darius glanced behind Jason. The algus in the square were coming, and Jason was too close to his horse to retrieve the powder. His best hope was to run.

But as he turned to flee, the air shifted again, and he knew the King's Sword was attacking. He pretended not to notice, mapped out the algus's position using only the air on his neck and hands, then turned at the last moment and swung the Twin Blade.

His weapon struck Jason's, but only with a glancing blow. The algus had adjusted his strike at the last moment and now brought his sword down towards Darius's abdomen.

Darius pulled his other arm across, flared ferven across his armguard, and let the sword strike the metal. Before Jason could react, Darius thrust forward, aiming to slam his arm and shoulder into any part of the man and shatter bones. But Jason had already moved. As if spinning in a dance, the algus was now at his side and brought his blue sword down again in a stab.

Darius dodged to his side, but Jason's leg moved too and tripped him to send him crashing to the street and almost into a yard-wide fissure that had opened up.

It was no use. Every move Darius made was no surprise to the algus, and Rufus had been right. This man was undoubtedly half-goman.

Behind Jason, one algus ran up to the other Twin Blade Darius had lost. She flared algor across her whole body as she bent and touched the hilt, but in an instant, fire raged from the sword and shot into the sky like a column of fury. The algus's teeth were bared, blue from algor, but soon she began to scream with such pain even Jason stole a glance.

After a few seconds of resisting the fire and trying to pull the sword from the ground, the algus keeled over and was swallowed by the flames, her algor evaporating in an instant to leave nothing but floating ash as the ferven eased and swept back into the runes on the blade.

Once again, it lay still and lifeless with only a subtle glow.

The pounding of hooves brought Darius's attention back to his enemies and came skidding to a halt behind him.

"Master," Gorgias said. "Get on."

But he only had one of the Blades. Could he leave its twin?

The air stirred again, this time in too large a mass to be just the King's Sword, and he turned to see the algus in the centre of the town release their bowstrings and send a wave of arrows at them. Without a shield or kuraminium armour, he was helpless, so he rolled and plunged himself into the nearest crevice, digging his fingers in until hanging over the black hole as the arrows sailed overhead.

The shaking of the world eased a little, enough for him to hear the shriek of Gorgias's swift. Hopefully, its wounds weren't severe and the man hadn't taken any either.

Once the arrows had eased, Darius kicked and leapt out of the crevice to see Gorgias on the ground, his swift pierced with a dozen arrows and its neck, legs, and body spoiled with blood.

"Are you hurt?" Darius called.

Gorgias shook his head, not taking his eyes from the enemies behind Darius while Sulla leapt from his swift to join them.

"I told you I should have brought a shield!" the rakkan roared as he unsheathed his gladius, his one piece of kuraminium.

The swifts wouldn't have borne the weight, and this wasn't the time to argue.

"Get back on your horse!" Darius shoved the rakkan.

But Sulla resisted. "I'm not leaving you."

"You can't outrun algus! We at least stand a chance."

Hairs bristled on Darius's arms again and told him another barrage was incoming. Sulla leapt first, through the fractured wooden front of a building while Darius sprinted in the opposite direction after grabbing Gorgias by the tunic. The building directly in his path hadn't split and remained a solid wooden wall that Darius's run had committed him to breach.

Gorgias gasped as Darius leapt and twisted his body in the air until his back hit the wood as he flared ferven across it. The planks shattered on impact, and the two fell inside, his fiery back saving him from splinters and sharp spikes of wood as they landed on the floor.

Arrows sailed past the gap, and it would only be a few moments until the King's Sword made it to them.

But as Darius watched the charred hole in the wall smoke and spark the odd flame, a new fire filled the area, one in the street outside. Balls of flame hailed from above and crashed into the street, the roof, the walls, bouncing with the unmistakable thump of slinger shots.

Rufus.

Whatever the Viridian Warlord had planned next, all Darius could focus on was surviving because stones didn't differentiate between friend and foe.

Darius and Gorgias got back to their feet, and the town finally ceased its tremors but rumbled under the continued onslaught of stones. Soon, the roof above them cracked and split as flaming stones breached the wood, making Darius feel all the more naked without kuraminium armour and instead having only melted remnants of his mail hanging from his shoulders.

Thankfully, this building was empty, but were the rest?

"Master," Gorgias said, pointing. "There's a back door. We should head towards the slingers."

"But Sull—" He hadn't finished the word when a figure rushed from the building opposite and leapt across the street with what Darius swore was a grin on his face. The rakkan crashed through the floorboards as he landed but continued his run and smashed apart the wood like a man running through water.

"Are you coming or what?" Sulla shouted as he hurtled towards the back door.

Darius and Gorgias followed at once, reaching the exit before the slower rakkan and emerging in a new street only to be almost peppered with falling stones. The three fell back and paused in the doorway.

"Do you think they know where we are?" Gorgias asked.

"Rakkans have good eyesight," Darius said, "but not *that* good." Still, Rufus was smart enough to know keeping Darius alive was in his best interests.

The building above moaned again, threatening to crush them.

"Looks like we'll have to risk it." Sulla tried to step outside, but Darius caught him.

"Wait," he said. Slingers couldn't keep up this rate of fire for long. Even if they didn't cease, they'd need to even their pace soon. And surely Rufus would give them a chance once he'd scared the algus and prevented them from advancing.

But as Darius watched, the molten hail didn't ease, and a crash behind made him turn and see a new threat.

The King's Sword rushed into their building, slowing as the shattered floor beneath him barely gave a secure foothold, but he somehow danced from one spot to another and left Darius sure it was better to face the molten rain than this enemy.

"He's after me." Darius shoved his two companions outside with a force that threw them to the right, towards the source of the slinger fire. "Don't follow me!"

Then he sprinted out to the left, back towards the heart of the town through a narrower street with buildings at either side but without a door or window that wasn't nailed shut.

Glancing over his shoulder, he saw Sulla—like the fool he was—had ignored his order, but Darius's push had done enough, clearing him out of the path of the King's Sword as the algus bolted out of the building and straight after Darius.

At least Gorgias was obedient and didn't move to follow.

After a quick run with lots of ducking and weaving, Darius saw that the slingers had mercifully eased their barrage until he only had to use his Twin Blade a couple of times to bat away a stray stone, but with the pace he'd set, the end of the street was only moments away, leading him back to a town centre swarming with algus.

Whatever he chose to do, he'd have to face the King's Sword, and it was surely best to do that without alerting anyone else to where he was. Although Jason had proven he could match Darius's pace, there was one skill the algus couldn't hope to replicate—his rakkan leap.

Darius skidded to a halt, turned, and dug in his feet ready to jump over the King's Sword and head back the way they'd come.

But Jason was already slowing and stopped at the point Darius would land if he leapt. In the heat of the moment, Darius had forgotten the bastard knew what he'd do before he'd even done it.

Darius dodged a last slinger shot as the rain all but ceased, and the two stared at each other while Sulla lumbered towards them, albeit too slow to reach them in time.

"Come at me," Darius said. Just a few yards forward, and he could use his rakkan legs.

The King's Sword cast his gaze up at the smoking rooftops on either side of them, only a couple of storeys high and within Darius's reach.

"Thanks," Darius said. "I hadn't thought of that yet."

Jason's glare snapped back to him for a moment, then without warning, the algus sprinted forward.

# 46

## Darius – Chiva

It was a good thing Darius's feet were already planted because Jason was so fast Darius sensed the movement before he'd processed the blur ahead of him. He leapt and soared over the blue streak Jason's sword left as he continued down the street, and Darius didn't even look back as he landed behind the algus and readied his blade to fight.

Sulla finally reached him with a frown. "What did you say to him?"

Darius shared his confusion. "Nothing. He was looking at…"

Before he'd looked back up at the rooftops, the buildings on either side of him began to shine with an orange glow. The air above lit up with streaks of fire again that soared and dipped towards them like a flaming tidal wave about to drown them.

Sulla cursed as Darius set his sights on the closest building, surged forward shoulder-first and crashed through the door before immediately searching the room for whatever would shield them. All he found was an old, empty kitchen with clay ovens at one side and a thick wooden table at the centre stained with blood and burnt rings. It'd have to do.

Sulla followed, and they both dove headfirst under the table, landing with a thud that cracked the stone ground but that was soon swallowed in a colossal roar as thousands of slinger shots struck wood, dirt, stone, bones—anything in that town that could see sky and much that couldn't.

The initial crack of impact set Darius's ears ringing and a dust cloud from outside that choked every breath, and many fiery shots breached the roof, floors above, and the table. But every one that struck had been deprived of its lethal force until without the power to break Darius's bones as they hit.

Sulla cursed loudly as a large stone thumped into him. "Right in the liver."

The torrent continued and left Darius in no doubt that this town would be reduced to a smouldering wreck. Had the first wave been a warning to Darius to take cover? Hopefully, the townsfolk had already left, otherwise, how many more innocent bodies would litter the ground because of Darius's doing? He hadn't seen civilians so far, so he wouldn't curse himself just yet.

After Darius had been lying there a while, smoke joined the dust and forced him to breathe through what remained of his tunic. He wasn't sure how long he could survive on such tainted air, but when every breath began to burn his lungs, he reckoned his chances of weathering slinger shots outside were better than drowning in the smoke here.

He and Sulla crawled out into the now dark, smog-ridden street. Fires ravaged buildings and threw off a heat that had Darius conjuring algor to ease, and the stink wasn't just of burning wood and charcoal—there was something else, something putrid he hadn't sniffed in a long time. At least the slingers had stopped again.

"Let's head towards our men," Darius said with a cough.

Sulla had already set off. "Smell that? Sulphur." The rakkan bent over with a hacking cough. "Whose idea was it to burn a town that mines sulphur?"

Darius wasn't going to complain, although his stomach sure was.

The two made their way to the edge of the town without another algus in sight, but the smoke didn't ease, instead becoming blacker and fouler as the fires brought more buildings down and almost exhausted their fuel. Only when they were several hundred yards outside the town's perimeter did the smog thin enough for them to see new figures ahead in a rakkan formation.

Darius ignited ferven on his hands and waved lest they think them hostile, and they soon got close enough to make out their coloured bands marking Branz Legionnaires.

"Overlord," a centurion said as Darius reached him. "You're alive, then."

"Barely." Darius coughed and spat up a black wad of phlegm. "Where's Rufus?"

"I'll take you to him."

They set off, and he led Darius to the Viridian Warlord, Darius glad when he saw a dirty-faced but alive Gorgias standing next to the rakkan.

"Look at him, Sulla"—Darius pointed to the algus—"and learn from him. That's a man that listens to his superiors."

Gorgias gave a nervous smile while Sulla scoffed.

"He's lucky his superior is alive," Warlord Rufus said in the stern tone fathers used with unruly sons.

Darius would let him get away with that just this once, given so much else was going on.

"I said to bring a few centuries," Darius said. A whole legion would have been needed for the onslaught he'd just witnessed, and the numbers in the smoke around him confirmed many more than "a few" centuries.

"I thought you might need more assistance than that," Rufus said.

It was a good thing the rakkan was so cautious. Now that Darius had a few moments to think, it made sense that his enemy had made him wait and wait until just before they knew when the quake would happen. If not for that, he could have galloped away with ease.

"You're lucky you didn't hit us," Darius said.

"I do not rely on luck," Rufus said. "My Subdued's escorts kept a close eye on you."

"Then I guess I'm the lucky one for having you," Darius said. "Where's their army?"

"In retreat. They headed north towards Alogos as soon as we unleashed hell, the King's Sword among them. I take it he gave you some troub—"

"Nothing I couldn't have handled," Darius interjected. The last thing he needed was word getting around that he was no match for the King's Sword and morale suffering as a result. "But your intervention helped."

The sound of running footsteps came from behind, and Darius turned to see Lex rush up to him while scanning every inch of his body.

"Are you hurt?" she asked.

"Just a few bruised ribs," he answered. "The town looked like it had been evacuated. We should move forward and take it, put out some of those fires before there's nothing left but ash."

And his Twin Blade was still lying in a street somewhere, waiting for its master to return.

Lex didn't answer but had the unease of someone with more to say.

"What's wrong?" Darius asked.

"I just came from the camp; the quake ruined most of our ramparts and palisades, and our algus with escorts still in Psinara report that the tremors originated from the River Toras."

"Is Psinara still intact?" Darius asked.

So far, Lex hadn't blinked. "Mount Psilos is spitting ash and fury. Plumes have blackened the sky into endless night nearby, and rivers of fire are spilling from its top. The Psinarans are fleeing towards us, but we're not much better off here."

Darius cursed, looking back at the smouldering town he'd just left. "These fires will ease, at least. Then the sky will clear."

"No," Lex said. "That's not all; there's a reason there's so much smoke from such a small town. I had Tiro surveying while you were there, and Rufus's last onslaught…" She trailed off with a troubling look about her.

"What?" Darius urged.

"… The stones reached the banks of the Tar Sea. It's aflame."

The whole group fell silent while Darius tried to infer what that meant. He'd seen the scale of those black waters from afar, and surely the entire mass couldn't catch alight.

"Have any of you seen or heard of something like this before?" Darius asked anyone there, even the legionnaires.

Everyone shook their heads with the same numb, mute expressions as if such a fire was beyond imagination.

"Old songs," Rufus said, "sometimes tell of mountains belching fire. But that seems to be the least of our concerns. If that sea is made from oil…" The Viridian Warlord stared at the ground in a way he never had before, the same look commanders had when the jaws of defeat clamped down.

And what could they do? The algus wouldn't be able to conjure enough algor to put out the sea, even if they could approach it safely. Darius and his army were about to smoke themselves out, locked in with no route of escape—enemies to the north, fire to both east and west. Thank the God and Goddess there were no other towns close by that he'd also unwittingly blighted.

At times like these, Darius found it best to focus on what he could control, not what he couldn't. What was done couldn't be undone.

He watched the smoke drift in the sky for a while and noted that the clouds gently floated towards the north, carrying away the smoke from the sea.

"The wind is in our favour, for now," he said. "We'll march to the town and put out whatever fires we can."

Rufus nodded and began issuing more specific orders to his commanders while Lex took Darius's hand, meant for comfort but only reminding him that he was missing a blade.

He pulled her to one side and lowered his voice. "Do you think this is a bad omen?" Was this the beginning of the "ruin" the King's message had warned Darius he'd bring onto himself and his people if he continued?

A thin coat of ash highlighted the white furrows on Lex's brow. "I don't know. It seems bad, but how could the God and Goddess let us fail against the King?"

How could such a lowly person as Darius think he could understand the will of gods?

He dared not voice the question. "Whatever the reasons for this, we need to head away from the Tar Sea as quickly as we can. How far to Alogos?"

"A week's march if we're quick and if there are no swifts to harry us."

Which there definitely would be. "Then we'd best hope their horses can't tolerate this smoke for long."

# 47

## Lex – Chiva

The rakkans and algus of Laltos that marched into the town had most of the fires out by morning, their only battle being with the stench of sulphur as the townsfolk seemed to have abandoned the place. For that, she thanked the Goddess and was sure Darius too mouthed words of blessings as he clutched the aeternus hanging from his neck.

But the extinguished buildings and lack of bodies only drew more attention to the inferno blanketing the sea, a forest of red flames spitting thunder and smoke as black as the waters beneath. It was as if the quake had opened a portal to hell, one that both emitted a light bright enough to rival the sun in spots yet darkened their vision and threatened to shorten their daylight hours. All that saved them from being consumed by the clouds was the fortunate wind, which wouldn't last.

"What does this mean?" Darius asked as he gaped at the inferno. "Will it ever go out?"

"Surely it must," Lex said, but when it came to repercussions, his guess was as good as hers. Anyone close by would have to evacuate, but thankfully, there weren't any other towns as close as this one.

"I hope the King's head is worth it in the end," he said.

Of that, she couldn't be sure, but they had no option but to keep going.

Wasting no more time than they had to, they trudged on through the town while Lex had Tiro head north, away from the worst of the smoke, to scout more of Alogos. The peregrine first delivered a message to a sympathetic slave owner there she'd contacted before. So far, the man had relayed some appetite among the slaves to assist in any assault on the city, but the same fever gripping her soldiers in Chiva was beginning to take hold in Alogos. Smoke from the sea had already reached the city, and the bird soon struggled to make out anything as he flew without actually landing on every building.

*Tiro. Head west.* The peregrine only had tiny lungs. He'd be dead long before any humans there unless he fled.

Once her escort was on his way back to safety, she turned her attention back to Chiva and noticed Darius was more alert than she'd ever seen him before, eyes hardly blinking, sleeves rolled up to better feel the air. If she didn't know any better, she'd say whatever happened here had scared him—after all, it had caused him to lose one of the Twin Blades. But she wouldn't question the man, not even when he found his lost weapon and retrieved it as discreetly as possible.

A brief time later, the town was verified abandoned and everyone was spent, coughing and spitting from dragging in so much smoke, despite them all now having cloth wrapped multiple times around their mouths until breathing anything became laboured. Lex's lungs began making noise with every breath, like a cross between a groan and rasp that hurt more than the soft sound suggested.

Then the wind turned against them, and the black, turgid billow smothering the sea began to drift inland.

"We need to get moving," Lex said.

"Yes," Darius said, coughing. "Lyra's already told…the Black and Azure Legions to head…directly north from the camp."

Most of the other commanders and algus needed no instructions to begin evacuating the town, and soon they were rushing as quickly as their air-starved lungs allowed. She prayed Alogos wasn't this severely smog-ridden, although part of her couldn't help but wonder whether this would make a slave revolt easier or harder. The city's authorities would be distracted, and sneaking around would now be much easier for both her spies and warriors such as Darius.

She still hadn't broached the subject of another slave revolt with him, but now that they were on their way to Alogos, she needed to, and although this was hardly a good time, when would be? Plus, it would take their minds from the constant struggle for air.

"I've had a message from a friend in Alogos," Lex said. "He says there may be some…slaves that can help us."

Darius's ash-coated face contorted. "Don't even suggest it."

"I'm not." Lex looped her arm through his, not above using his feelings for her if it would have him make the necessary decisions. "But their help may come in useful. They can assist us from within when we assault the city. The King will never…" Her voice withered away to a rasp as she coughed hard, feeling the mucus thick in her throat.

"Save your breath," Darius said. "I have my own plans for Alogos. I want this city to be different."

She couldn't blame the man for hoping. The last three places they'd taken had been disastrous. All Lex could do to live with herself was to remember the ends this conquest was to achieve, of the peace that Darius would deliver to the Empire, the end to the war that could see many more future lives saved than had been devastated thus far.

But what could they plan for? With the air shrouded, escorts couldn't spy and scout, meaning they were walking in blind.

"What plan?" she asked.

He shook his head. "Later, when I can breathe."

# 48

## King's Orator – Toria

"*The sea has calmed.*" The King's eyes had never been so alight with glee, shimmering golden-brown even as they misted over once again as he leaned back into his silver throne.

"Which sea, my king?" Ophelia had to be sure, although this wasn't what she'd come here to discuss. What about Chiva? The swifts of Alogos? The fact that Jason had failed to kill Darius, something that should have made the King feel as defeated as she did. Why wasn't the King focused on their short-term plans?

"*The Aretean Sea, of course. My fellow gomans can at last depart.*"

Ophelia's entire scalp began to itch, flaking away as she dug her nails in and shifted herself closer to the dais the King sat upon. This soon? It must have had something to do with the quake.

"How?" she asked.

The King shrugged. "*Does it matter? I haven't seen it, but the Council has been proven right after so many decades.*"

"Still, even if they wish to come, it would take them weeks going on months to cross the Aretean Sea. We need to discuss Alogos. The swifts are waiting there as commanded, but I think—"

*"Have I not made myself clear?"* Darkness returned to the King's eyes.

He had, but it had been such an absurd suggestion Ophelia had thought it but a test. "Circumstances have changed. Mount Psilos roars in the south, and the road to Alogos cannot be scouted. This is our chance to attack, not abandon the city to our enemy."

The King stood and towered over her all the more. *"I respect your insight, Ophelia, and I've left your conniving mind untouched because of its sharpness. But must you test my patience by questioning me? Do you see what I see?"*

"Do you see the gomans arriving?" She knew the answer was still "no."

And predictably, the King's eyes narrowed. *"That doesn't mean they won't. You wouldn't understand. You don't read all that I read."*

"I do read." Ophelia straightened her back and looked across all the scrolls piled in the throne room that she scoured whenever she had a free moment. She'd only begun doing that recently, frustrated by the lack of answers, and although the King's scribbles were often impenetrable, she'd gleaned much insight while he wasn't around.

"I know how you plan to trap Darius and his army," Ophelia continued, "and I saw your future reports that his army would flee in the smoke if attacked now, and we'd lose our advantage with the Staff of Arria. But need you use the Staff? Send the swifts as you have already. We killed hundreds from their army in just the last week!" How much more effective did the King wish to be? Such losses sustained over time were enough to devastate an army's morale.

The King paused for a moment before leaning down and extending a gloved hand. "*Come up.*"

Despite having been a loyal servant for many years, Ophelia was hesitant to touch even the hem of the goman's cloak, let alone his gloves.

"*I swear I mean you no ill,*" the King added before Ophelia could persuade herself to prove her loyalty.

By conventional wisdom, gomans couldn't lie, but over the last few weeks, Ophelia had begun questioning things she never had before.

Still, rather than snub the most powerful being in the Empire, she obediently took the King's hand, half expecting to be suddenly paralysed by goman cogi but instead shocked by the heat from beneath his glove, burning as if it had been in front of a fire for the last few hours. He helped her onto the dais—not a simple feat for an ageing woman such as her—then released her when they both stood eye to eye.

This was the first time Ophelia had ever dared venture so close to him. At roughly the same height, nothing physically about him intimidated her beyond the powers possessed under those soft, quilted robes. But such terror was enough to reduce veterans to their knees.

"Is something wrong, my king?" she asked without the famous power her voice usually held.

"*The time has come when we can drop the pretence. Call me by my name.*"

It had been so long since Ophelia had dared utter or even think it that she'd forgotten.

"Forgive me…but—"

"*It's Ipu.*"

Ophelia dared not meet his gaze again. "Very well, Ipu."

"*And do not avert your eyes as if I'm a man. Speak to me as a woman, for soon you will sit atop the throne I have kept warm for you.*"

Without meaning to, Ophelia looked the goman straight in the eye, seeing that glee light up again in response to what must have been shock written on her face. "I don't understand."

"*I was not destined by the One Mind to be King—or rather, Queen in disguise—here forever. I will ensure this is the end of Darius and the rakkans, then I will return to where I came from.*"

No wonder the man—no, woman—was so radiant. After living for over a decade in hiding, who wouldn't want to return to a home where they could just be themselves?

But Ophelia dared not even imagine herself sitting on the throne. "But if you leave…surely the Puppet King will retake his throne." After all, he was the rightful ruler of Toria and had been a fine king before Ipu's arrival.

The goman shook her head. "*I've already ordered his death.*"

Ophelia's first instinct was to argue for the man she'd once been loyal to, but the silver sheen of the throne silenced her, seduced her. Dare she imagine taking Medus's place on it?

She certainly wasn't in for a smooth ascent if that's what she wanted. But she had the connections and the dirt on the people that mattered. Already, schemes for her grasp on power began to form.

And the longer she dwelled on the thought, the less she wanted to argue against Ipu, and she realised that if Medus was dead, Ipu's impersonation could no longer be sustained; the end was in sight.

But who knew what that end would look like; they were still so far from victory, and by all appearances, they were losing and needed to plan their next move, not dream of a future not yet secured.

"Must we abandon Alogos?" she asked, still loath to lose what had been a hard-won city by King Medus's father in the War of the Four. It was the largest major city in the Empire besides Toria, and they shouldn't discard such a jewel in their crown.

"*It blocks their path to Toria,*" Ipu said. "*Once they're through it and in the Arid Gorge, they will have no escape.*"

*And a direct path to our capital.* But what use was there in arguing with cogi?

"If that's your final decision," Ophelia said, "I'll have my algus relay orders to the swifts. They'll head northeast and hide in the smoke." Those fertile lands just north of the Tar Sea fed both the city and their armies. The swift riders knew them well and should have no trouble evading Darius's spies with the cover there.

"*Make sure Jason returns here. We'll need him.*" Ipu's voice was as baritone as ever, adding a further ominous ring to the confusing words. Ophelia couldn't think of a reason to keep their greatest warrior out of the impending battle and had many other objections to the recent edicts.

"And what of Alogos's slaves? My algus have kept our plans quiet, but thousands of horses heading east won't go unnoticed."

"*Anyone that is needed shall travel with the army. Everyone else will be under curfew. The chances of a leak are slim.*"

Finally, some comforting news.

"*Would you like to sit?*" Ipu opened a palm towards the vacant throne, its metallic wings shimmering in the sunlight.

Ophelia stared at it. Dare she? Before she could decide, she shifted closer as if drawn towards it by an invisible force and began turning until her backside hovered over the single cushion that broke the monotonous steel the colossal seat was forged of.

Ipu nodded, and Ophelia bent her knees, skin itching with excitement.

At the first touch of her backside, a shudder ran through her, then her weight finally rested where she'd never imagined it would. The armrests bit her arms with coldness, but the hard metal felt powerful, the wings behind her own, and she cast her gaze across the grand room and everything below her for the first time as a ruler, not a servant.

"*Intoxicating, isn't it?*"

The pleasure must have been oozing from every pore as Ophelia grinned. "One could grow too comfortable here, my ki—Ipu."

The goman nodded, such a powerful woman that would give up this position. It brought a thousand questions to Ophelia's mind over who the person she'd spent so many years with really was, ones she'd never dared ask before.

"Forgive me for asking," she said in as gentle a voice as possible, "but will you be marching with our army to face Darius?" After the display at the Great Bridge, Ipu had proven she had the heart of a warrior, and the fact she bestowed such kindness on Ophelia now was almost like a person gifting their treasures before venturing into unknown dangers.

Ipu's mask shifted a little, and for the first time, her mood seemed to become foul. "*Yes and no. The smoke will shroud the battle when it falls, so I wouldn't see much of importance, and my presence would be of limited use. But since we failed to eliminate Darius, I must face him.*"

"I don't understand. How will you face him but not battle?"

"*With the Staff of Arria, the battle will be easier, but our victory is not assured while its nemeses rest in the hands of the Slayer of Gods. We cannot allow the Twin Blades to negate the Staff's power in battle.*"

Suddenly, Jason being recalled to Toria made sense. "You want to lure Darius here."

Ipu nodded.

"But what of the Twin Blades? If he brings them here…" The consequences could be unthinkable.

"*They must be here, for it is here they will be eliminated, never to menace the Empire again.*" Ipu had a look of supreme confidence about her.

"And how will you lure him here?"

The goman leant and took one of the scrolls piled by the throne, unravelled it, then pointed at a line of text halfway down while presenting it to Ophelia.

*Darius must be lured to Toria. Ophelia will bring Alexandra.*

Ophelia swallowed. Was she supposed to have captured the woman already? Some of her spies were in place, but they'd still failed to find an opportunity.

"*You'd be surprised how many times I've written that to myself in my visions over the years,*" Ipu said. "*I've never regretted leaving your mind undisturbed, for it has triumphed many times.*"

Ophelia felt a flush come to her cheeks, and she would have bowed in gratitude if not seated on the throne. "You're too kind." But no sooner had the joy risen than it was replaced by the thought of the Slayer of Gods coming to take revenge for what Ophelia had instigated in the Silk City. Did the half-rakkan know of her part in that?

"I must confess," Ophelia continued, "I'm a little uneasy at the thought of Darius coming here. Will you and Jason be able to protect us from him?"

Ipu gave a long pause before answering. "*My cogi is not as suited to combat as my husband's was. Algus move too quickly, with too many possible attacks when viewed so far in the future. That's why Jason must remain here. There's still a risk, but my life would be worth the sacrifice if it means his armies are devastated. My brothers and sisters would soon finish what I started; perhaps that's why I don't see them arriving.*"

But didn't that mean it was impossible?

And while Ipu might have been prepared to sacrifice her life, Ophelia wasn't sure she was willing to do the same. Half of her was tempted not to bring Alexandra here to thwart this plan, but despite her qualms, after devoting so much of her life to serving the Empire, she just couldn't bring herself to give in to selfishness now.

"I'm still not sure I can capture her," Ophelia admitted.

"*My note was confident.*" Ipu's eyes lit up as if she were smiling beneath her mask—if she'd had a mouth, that is. "*That's why I asked you alone to find her and that man.*"

Ophelia leapt up from the throne, so distracted since arriving she'd forgotten her reason for coming. "Yes, the *man*. My algus brought him to the palace this morning. Would you like me to take you to him?"

Ipu shook her head. "*Later. First, tell me how close you are to Alexandra.*"

"She's one of his inner circle so is always in the middle of the camps. Some of my spies speculate that she and Darius may even share a bed."

"*After seeing her, I'm not surprised.*"

But Ophelia had other worries now that she knew Alexandra's purpose. Capturing the bait for a trap was only the beginning of what would require meticulous planning. After getting the woman, they needed to ensure that Darius knew of the fact without making it obvious they were using her as bait; that meant not only coming up with valid reasons for wanting to capture the woman but also having Darius become aware of them in an organic way.

"*I can see your mind is at work.*"

"Besides her being a traitor, are there any other reasons we might take Alexandra?" Ophelia asked.

"*. . . I suspect she was the one responsible for Khayu's death.*"

Ophelia searched her mind for the foreign-sounding name but came up blank. "Khayu?"

Ipu's eyes grew fierce. "You knew him as Archimedes."

Ophelia winced at the detail she should have remembered, sympathetic to the goman's loss of her husband and still unsure what had happened that day. Alexandra being responsible for his death made sense; even Ophelia's spies didn't know how Archimedes had fallen, but they knew at least one traitor had played a hand in it, someone that had waited by Archimedes for years before that. Darius's closest human companion was their best guess.

"That gives us a good cover story to capture and torture her," Ophelia said, "and she's no doubt the human who knows most of Darius's plans. Bringing her back to Toria makes sense if that's where our goman is."

Ipu nodded. "*You need Jason, don't you?*"

Ophelia tried to think of ways in which they could avoid using him, but her months of failure only underlined how difficult a task Ipu had set for her.

She nodded.

"*Then send him. With the haze, he'll have a short window to get her out of their army when they're in Alogos.*"

Which sounded like it meant no witnesses, and Darius wouldn't know where she was being taken. Luckily, Ophelia had her roots throughout the Empire. "My spies can leak her whereabouts."

But spreading the fact far and wide was too transparent; this needed to come from a voice Darius trusted had special insights into Toria's plans whilst also being from someone Ophelia had access to.

After a quick run through her options, one man came to mind, so perfect that she smiled. *The Chief Priest.*

# 49

## Darius – Alogos

Alogos would not see a repeat of the ravaging of the last human settlements. Tonight, before his armies even decided on a plan to defeat the smoke-filled city he'd sneaked into, the first head to roll would not be a slave's but the Regent's—unless they surrendered.

Darius stepped carefully through the hole he'd melted into the Alogos palace walls, unsure exactly where he was or where he was heading, but most regents liked to reside in the highest places, so he bet Regent Berenice's quarters wouldn't be hard to find.

"I don't like this," Lex whispered beside him. "There should be more guards."

They'd been careful when entering the city, all the easier with the haze, but it had taken him almost an hour to get through that last wall even with the Twin Blades, an hour without seeing a soul. Rufus hadn't loved Darius's assassination plan, but the

Viridian Warlord's methods had too much of a habit of becoming bloody or setting seas on fire.

Wandering within a foreign city with smoke blighting his nostrils had become an all-too-frequent event of late, but at least this time the smoke wasn't from another slaughter added to the list. Still, he hadn't thought a disaster worse than Psinara was possible. No one knew how many people the burning sea would affect or how far the destruction would spread. All this because he sought justice.

For now, all he could do was keep going and help his army escape the plumes they'd set off. The city of Alogos sat with mountains on every side, a valley in the shadow of towering peaks that made one feel more like in Margalvia than other human cities like Xavala. Unlike the rakkan city, however, this one had been ornate and artistic enough that even someone as uncultured as he could see its beauty at a glance. Marble not only plated the lavish interior he now spied but made up the outer walls too, with columns in front similar to those Laltos had, chiselled into perfect smooth cylinders.

Lex moved in front of him into a wide corridor, but he grabbed her arm.

"Stay behind me," he said quietly, biting back his frustration that she'd insisted on coming with him. At least there was no one else with them for him to worry about.

She slipped her arm free. "What did I say about speaking to me like a servant?"

Not this again. Darius took another look around to check the corridor was deserted with not a guard in sight before muttering, "Sorry."

When he turned back to her, she had an eyebrow raised and a grin.

"What?" he asked.

She bowed. "I'm honoured that an overlord would apologise to such a lowly servant as myself."

He snorted and quickly regretted the loud noise as it echoed down the hallway.

"Come on," he said, lowering his voice again. "We'll find the Regent's quarters."

He set off but paused when Lex didn't follow.

"It's this way," she said before heading in the other direction.

With a grumble, he followed her, Blades ready, as they wandered through the deserted hall, into a deserted kitchen, then through to a deserted staircase that was so simple and bare it must have been for slaves. But there were none, and even though it was the dead of night, Darius knew a palace was never this quiet.

The pair matched the silence of the place as they sneaked, and despite Lex taking more than a few unnecessary turns that made Darius suspect she didn't really know the way, they eventually came to a set of grand oak doors, gilded around the edges with golden script etched in.

This time, Lex fell behind him of her own accord.

He eased the door open slowly, the hinges not making a whisper. The inside was devoid of any light, but his rakkan eyes saw it was as lavish as the door suggested, everything from windowsills to curtains, ceiling, and bedding an assault of gold. And underneath silk sheets in the bed, a figure lay curled up in a foetal ball.

One of Darius's swords let out a breath of hot air, its runes preparing to fire. *Easy.* He was still unsure whether the Blades could understand him or not, but they always seemed to bend to his will and restrain themselves when commanded.

He crept closer to the bed, the figure's body rising and falling with slumbering breaths. When he reached the bed, he saw a woman's face for the first time, striking features with curls of fiery-red hair matching the description of Regent Berenice he'd been given. She clearly lacked no wealth or luxury, so why no guards? He could have taken her head without her waking to notice, but something about this wasn't making sense.

A quick check near the bed and under it revealed no weapons, so it wasn't like she posed a threat, and he had too many questions to kill her in her sleep.

He signalled for Lex to leave the room and listen from outside. Backup often came in useful. Then, once Lex had obliged, he nudged the dozing woman until her eyes lazily opened and fixated on him.

The woman frowned, tilted her head, and it was only then that Darius realised the darkness of the room made him invisible to her.

So he flared ferven on his scowling face, seeing her skin light up red with the reflection and her expression twist in horror.

She scrambled up and clattered into the headboard, pulling the silk sheets up around her naked body as if they'd do anything to protect her from the Slayer.

"Do you know who I am?" he growled.

The woman trembled and gave no answer.

"I'm Darius, enemy of King Medus. Your cavalry have taken many warriors from me." He inched closer, the Twin Blades beginning to glow.

Still, the woman only shook with wide eyes. Regents were often cowardly, but even the caitiff Aristippus hadn't been so paralysed.

"Are you Regent Berenice?" he asked.

She nodded, pulling the covers tighter around her.

But he wasn't sure he believed that. "Then find your tongue, or I'll have no reason to delay justice for my slain men."

"Do as you will," the woman said, each word stammered, "for the King has already abandoned me. He took my armies west to Toria."

Her pale, untarnished face and arms certainly had the look of a noble woman, but given her beauty, she could easily have been a slave that worked mainly in a bed. He grabbed one of her hands, pulled it closer with the ease of his rakkan strength as she tried to wrench it free and found her fingers soft and delicate, nails long, clean-cut, and unchipped—nothing to suggest she was a slave.

So he released her with a murmur. There were no tells of her being a liar, and he knew genuine fear when he saw it.

"Why would the King abandon this city?" he asked.

"Because of the smoke," she said. "Because he knew it would fall. You have four legions of rakkans, and our city is surrounded by mountains. Our cavalry would be of little use here, but defending Toria, they'll be insurmountable."

Usually, a regent would have had a tinge of pride when declaring her army's superiority, but this woman showed nothing but cold fear.

"Lex," he called. "Come here." It was time to get confirmation.

Lex slowly came in again with her sword ready and flared algor to give herself a better view of the room. The woman in the bed winced at the brightness and tried to shield her eyes—or perhaps shield her face from clear sight.

"This isn't Berenice, is it?" he asked.

Lex scrutinised the woman closely before shaking her head. "She resembles her, and I only met her a few times. But her chest wasn't so full, and her stare was fierce in any situation, not timid."

Darius turned to the woman and saw the growing dread written on her face that confirmed Lex's conclusion.

"Tell me who you are," he said, "and I may spare you."

"I'm…" The woman's head dipped. "I was a slave here in the palace. They left me because I resemble the Regent, but as soon as the algus left, the guards that were supposed to protect me and sell the ruse instead deserted and fled to Toria."

That made a lot more sense to Darius than a regent remaining unprotected.

"And where's the real Regent Berenice?" he asked.

"In Toria. Our armies really did leave to where they could breathe easier. Only some of the slaves were left behind."

Darius prayed they were still alive. At least he hadn't seen a hint of blood, but smoke was a silent and bloodless killer.

Only a fool would believe what the woman was saying, but some of it did make sense. The human leaders under his command had spoken of the plains outside Toria as well as its formidable defensive lines. The cavalry would be far more effective there than here.

Lex went on to question the woman further, check whether she was connected with those whom Lex had been liaising with in the city, while Darius searched the room and found nothing of value had been left other than a single silver crest placed on the dressing table with the King's ugly head facing up.

*They taunt me when gifting me a city?* People were strange sometimes.

"You can go," Lex said after finishing with the woman.

She didn't look like she believed it as she slid from the mattress, still clinging to her silk sheets, then hurried out of the room without taking her gaze from both of them until she'd disappeared out of the door.

"What do you think?" Darius asked.

Lex didn't look at him, lost in thought. "It's not what I expected, but they did practically abandon the Silk City, so I guess it's not too far-fetched."

And Alogos had had far more opportunity to flee, especially with the smoke that had penetrated even the room they now stood in. After so many days of breathing it, he'd forgotten what fresh air smelt like.

"It doesn't make any sense to leave that woman," Darius said. "Do they think I'm that foolish to have believed it was Berenice?"

"I don't know. But I'm struggling to think of what else they're planning. Pulling the swifts back to Toria makes the most sense defensively."

And for the King, there was no path back to Darius's lands except through Alogos now that the Great Bridge was in ruins, so Toria didn't pose an imminent threat to the rakkan homelands.

"We'll proceed cautiously," he said. "Part of me wonders whether the goman has foreseen the land will open up again and this time swallow a city whole."

"Don't tempt fate."

Why not, when all it did was torture him?

He retreated into his mind to connect with Lyra, who was sat beside Rufus and Gorgias a few miles outside the city. The algus had turned out to be the best at communicating with Lyra, which came in useful now that their flying escorts might not survive so close to the flaming sea.

*Tell them to expect light resistance, but march with caution. The Black Legion is to advance first.*

As his panther began relaying that as best she could, he focused on everything she felt, heard, and saw, especially her breathing, her fatigue, her sharpness. Smoke was too much for small-lunged creatures like birds, but he had no idea how a big cat would fare, or even humans or rakkans if he were honest. The sooner they headed west towards the cleaner air nearer Toria, the better.

"The others will march into the city soon," Darius said. "We may as well wait here. Lyra will go with Rufus and let me know if I'm needed."

Lex nodded and sat on the bed with a sigh, grasping her chest. "Waiting sounds good to me."

"Is the smoke getting to you?" He sat beside her, wishing there was anything he could do for her and the odd pains that sometimes prickled his chest too.

She nodded. "I miss clean air."

"We'll be in it soon." Hopefully, the smoke hadn't reached as far as the plains outside Toria.

He took hold of her shoulders and began a gentle massage that seemed to relax her muscles along with the tension in his own body. What a mess this was turning into, but they were almost at the end now, one last push left until they reached his target. Whether all this had been worth it was a question he couldn't answer, perhaps never would be able to.

But he did realise one thing—if not for Lex, he might have given up long ago. Since the disasters, it was like she was the only thing that kept him going at times, a reminder of all he fought for and why he had to push on no matter how hard it was. Both of them, and most of those under his direct command too, had lost at least one person they loved because of the King. Until someone stood up and said enough, it would never end.

Lex sniffed repeatedly and wiped her nose, the rag she used coming away stained. He dared not to think what their lungs looked like inside.

"What have we done?" he whispered gently, in two minds whether he wanted her to hear his troubles again after discussing them for days already.

"We're doing what we must," she said.

But that did nothing to absolve him. Although some of the devastations the Empire had suffered were acts of the God and Goddess rather than him, he'd certainly added to the people's woes.

"It'll be over soon," Lex added with a confidence that gave him hope.

And when it *was* over, all he wanted was that quiet life by the sea with her, Lyra, and Cynthia, safe from the machinations of kings and warlords.

"We should find some way to keep ourselves occupied," he said before his mind drove him to madness. "There must be something in the palace."

"I don't have the energy." Lex fell out of his hands and slumped onto the mattress, staring up at the golden ceiling. "Let's rest."

That sounded appealing. He began undoing the straps of his armguards, getting comfortable, when Lex sat up.

"What are you doing?" she asked.

"Just getting naked."

"What?"

He smiled weakly. "Relax. I'm not serious. I'm just taking off my armour."

With a relieved nod, she unfastened her sword belt and stripped her armour too before returning to the bed. Meanwhile, Darius did the same until in just his tunic and trousers, a few hours' slumber never sounding more appealing.

But it would be foolish of them both to sleep.

"I'll stay awake," he said. "You get some rest."

She murmured to herself. "I'm too used to being awake at night to sleep properly now."

"Well, in that case, allow me." He came to the bed and dropped down onto it, almost bursting a hole through the mattress with his weight.

"Careful," Lex said.

"Doesn't matter. Not like it's my bed…although…maybe it is now that the city is technically mine."

"I think I claimed the bed first." Lex's eyes half closed.

"That's not how it works. An overlord claims anything he wishes."

"Great…so, what can I claim? Your rejects?"

He waited until she opened her eyes again and looked at him for an answer. "Me."

She didn't blink, her stare more intense yet unreadable than before. Although he'd not been serious, there were no longer any playful looks between them.

"We're only one step away from Toria," he continued.

"But we've still got to…" She mouthed a few more words, but all that came out was a hot breath.

What ran through his mind now should have been far from it given the gravity of the events around them, but he couldn't help but give in, to submit to desires that promised to help him forget the guilt and pain.

He leaned towards her, lowered his head, and expected her to recoil and continue denying him. But she didn't, and it was him that stopped an inch from her lips.

"You know I jest with all the 'overlord' nonsense," he whispered. "I'm still just Darius."

Her lips parted. "You were never 'just Darius.'"

He sank further and met her with a kiss that tasted of ash and smoke but that bothered him no longer. Her touch was soft at first, gentle, and so warm a shiver almost ran through him. But it soon heated as they gave in to desire, let go of whatever restrained them and entwined their bodies together.

The weight of everything on his shoulders still lingered at the back of his mind, but Lex now commanded his thoughts, his drive, and made everything else pale in comparison to his urges.

But when he reached up and ran a rough hand through her hair, she broke apart with a gasp.

"Stop," she breathed.

He slowly slid his hand away, wondering whether he'd inadvertently ripped out hair with his rakkan strength, but he felt no parted locks.

"Something wrong?" he asked.

"We shouldn't do this."

But he felt the lust in her fingers digging into the tense muscles of his back.

"Why not?" he asked. "It's just a kiss."

She pushed him away, and he let her.

"It's not," she said.

He knew that was true, knew that kissing her wasn't like kissing any other woman and that carnal desire would soon have taken over his mind.

"Perhaps we should rest apart," she said.

"No!" He winced as the word came out more forceful than he'd intended. "I mean, I want you to stay where I know you're safe. I'll leave you be if that's what you want."

Every ounce of his body willed her to say it wasn't, but she nodded.

"Very well," he said in a low, defeated tone.

"It's not that I don't want to." She almost looked apologetic. "It'll make things too difficult, and if you die, I'd rather we hadn't—"

He silenced her with a tender kiss on her forehead. "You don't need to explain again. Rest and gather your strength."

As good as a distraction as being with her would have been, he should probably concentrate on Alogos and what exactly was going on here. As much as he trusted Warlord Varro to secure the town peacefully, they might be in for another unwelcome surprise.

# 50

## Lex – Alogos

A few days after Darius and Lex's arrival in Alogos, the assembly gathered in what was once a large banquet hall as their armies filled the city. Resistance had been null, and the few slaves they'd found holed up in the city knew little of anything other than their masters had left.

Sulla sat beside her, a pipe hanging limp from his mouth, and raised a fiery finger to light it.

But Lex snatched it from his lips. "Seriously? You've not had enough smoke?" A grey haze still filled the hall.

Sulla shrugged. "At least this smoke would taste nice."

"Well, I'd rather do without the smell."

"Suit yourself. Can I at least have my pipe back?"

She handed it over, half expecting him to light it regardless, but he slipped it into his pocket, slouched in the chair, and put his feet up on the table.

"Does nothing faze you?" she asked the rakkan. Even he must have been suffering the chest pains, the feeling that each breath never quite satisfied the lungs, the wheezing and coughing.

Sulla twiddled his thumbs for a few moments in thought. "Not really. I used to work in the furnaces back in Margalvia, and if you didn't grow used to smoke there, you didn't survive."

They were interrupted when Darius tapped his fingers on the table and brought all the warlords and regents to silence.

"I'll be brief," he said. When wasn't he? "The sooner we're out of the smoke completely, the better. Unless anyone has objections, we should march west towards Toria at once."

Warlord Rufus cleared his throat while scanning some maps he'd found in Alogos. "There seem to be two routes to Toria from here. One takes us through the Arid Gorge, which we knew of, but there's another that follows the top of the Great Scar to the south. It passes through another town before leading to Toria's southern farmlands."

Lex had never travelled on this other path, but the thought of leaving another town like Psinara or Chiva was too foul a thought to contemplate.

"The Arid Gorge is vast," she said, "and our army will have no issues travelling through."

"But its river is dry," Rufus said. "We'd have to carry the water we'll need."

"Then it's good that your men have rakkan strength."

The Viridian Warlord gave no response, but everyone there knew his frustration at his warriors becoming the oxen of the army, carrying huge loads over hundreds of miles.

"The sides of the gorge could help protect us from cavalry," Warlord Varro said, "which we need to be mindful of. The King will not wait for us to reach Toria before attacking again."

"That's if the swifts of Alogos are there." Rufus still studied the map while everyone turned to him.

"What do you mean by that?" Darius asked.

"It means I don't trust what a slave girl said to you. We shouldn't make assumptions."

"Do we really have time to deliberate? We already have people falling ill from this air. We must push west."

Rufus nodded. "But if the cavalry went via the town rather than the gorge… We'd be better off taking both routes to keep our enemy from circling behind us."

"I'd rather just traverse the gorge," Darius said.

"Indeed. But that isn't because it's in our strategic interests, is it?" Rufus's expression was flat and unthreatening, but nothing could take the sting from those accusatory words.

"Be careful," Lex said. "There's—"

"It's fine," Darius interjected. "Everyone here is free to speak their mind, and Rufus is right. I won't level another town if I can avoid it, even if it puts us at a disadvantage. We'll travel in the gorge and watch the town as best we can to ensure the cavalry don't take that road back to Alogos."

Lex felt the tension ease from her muscles, and Sulla murmured to himself at the decision while Rufus turned back to the map.

"I fear the King knows your mind," the Viridian Warlord said. "We may not make it to the other side of the Arid Gorge."

"I have faith you can ensure we do," Darius said.

"I could if we had more information. Perhaps the slaves know more than they're letting on."

"We've spoken to many that can be trusted," Lex said. "Regent Berenice was very effective in keeping them in the dark, but everything we do know suggests the cavalry went to Toria. There are countless hoofprints leading from here into the gorge, and the little our escorts saw have shown there have been horsemen travelling west."

"But perhaps we can…" Rufus eyed Darius for a moment before shaking his head. "Never mind."

As difficult a rakkan as Rufus was to read, Lex had discerned one or two of his tells in the last few weeks: whenever he was keeping something from them, his brother Pollio seemed to know first.

And right now, that rakkan betrayed a sideward glance at another commander as soon as Rufus had stopped himself talking.

No one else seemed to notice, and she could have drawn Darius's attention to it, but something gave her pause. Maybe Rufus had a point.

After some more quick back-and-forth, the assembly finished and each warlord and regent began planning their marching orders and formations.

Lex left them to it while still watching Rufus, who slipped away from Gorgias during the discussions and spoke to some Viridians in a hushed voice. The commander Pollio disappeared soon after, up to no good, Lex suspected, so she moved to follow him.

But as she did, Hera came beside her.

"Are your algus and soldiers to march with mine again?" Hera asked.

"If that's all right with you." Lex had other things to worry about.

"I suppose, but you should march with us this time. Morale is getting low. We need as many algus as we can get."

Lex wasn't sure what she could do. Inside, her lungs were as raw and battered as the faces of everyone else. But a life of pain had made putting on a brave front second nature to her.

"All right," she said.

With a relieved smile, the Regent left Lex to return to watching the Viridian Warlord, but as she scanned the room to find him again, he was nowhere to be seen, and the rest of his brothers were also absent.

Wherever they'd gone, she suspected she needed to find out.

# 51

## Rufus – Alogos

There was a stink to this city, and it had nothing to do with the haze. A city abandoned in a hurry due to natural disaster bore far more clues than this, such as hastily packed belongings with cupboards and boxes still hanging open in people's homes, or fallen items in the gutters where people in a rush hadn't bothered to take a few steps back to collect them. And slaves. Since when were slaves left behind when they could carry valuables?

Rufus entered the front door to a building that the small contingent of men he was allowed to travel with had smashed open earlier. One realisation wouldn't give his suspicious mind rest: if the King had planned this retreat, he must have planned something else, some kind of traps to hinder their progress. But, despite searching through this city for hours, they hadn't found so much as a rabbit snare.

To Rufus, that meant the traps would be sprung later, in the field, where the smoky haze prevented him from scouting or mapping out the land ahead. He felt like a human entering the arena blindfolded or without rakkan senses to know what was coming. Being in such a position was intolerable and unacceptable.

While numerous potential scenarios played out in Rufus's mind, he was disturbed as Pollio came jogging up from behind and gave him a tap on the shoulder.

"We found her," Pollio whispered.

Finally, some good news. "Did you secure her?"

Pollio nodded.

"No one saw, did they?" Rufus would have lost his head if Darius found out, but too much was at stake not to risk getting more information. If his army marched into trouble, he was dead anyway.

"She was alone," Pollio confirmed. "We've brought her into the kitchens here, where they won't hear her cry."

"Take me."

His brother set off and Rufus followed. Usually, he would have stopped to marvel at the exquisite sights he'd conquered in this place, with its interior shining enough to blind a person. But he took no pride in this. Taking abandoned cities wasn't the glory he wanted recorded on the tablets of his history.

They entered a kitchen where a red-haired woman sat tied and gagged in a corner with Viridian warriors eyeing her hungrily. Her tunic was torn and ashen, much like her face. Thankfully, his men had shown restraint for once, and she seemed unharmed except for the terror in her gape.

Rufus wasn't wearing his fearsome helmet or he would have removed it as he slowly eased up to her, knelt to her level, and pulled away the gag.

"I didn't tell you to mistreat her." Rufus shot his warriors a glare of false anger before calmly turning back to her. "I'm sorry if my men were rough, but the Overlord asked us to find the woman who'd impersonated Regent Berenice. Is that you?"

The woman nodded but was trembling so much that it was hard to discern.

"You met the Overlord before, didn't you?"

She nodded.

"So, you know he means you no harm." That's what Rufus was hoping, at least. The man's kindness had its uses.

The woman nodded again.

If she didn't start opening her mouth, this was going to be a frustrating conversation. A year ago, it wouldn't have taken him long to begin torture methods, but perhaps Darius's influence was rubbing off on him, because his only intentions now were to win her over with kindness while using the mean reputation of his men to stoke her fear.

"He'll be along at some point," Rufus continued, "but I'll keep you safe until he arrives."

That seemed to slow the quivering of her lips.

He shifted from his knees to fully sit beside her, a rest he needed after such a hurried march. "I think he wants to know more about where the swifts of Alogos headed." Rufus kept his tone polite and conversational. It wasn't always enough to fool people into thinking he was compassionate, but sometimes it was.

"They l-left via the western gate, to Toria," she stammered.

"I see," Rufus said. "And does the western exit to the city lead anywhere else?"

"Well… You can head anywhere, I suppose, even circle outside the city or take paths through the mountains to the south or east, but there w-wouldn't be much point."

Just because she couldn't think of one didn't mean Rufus couldn't, and hard mountain ground left fewer traces of a marching army. "And besides the two paths west on the map, are there any other places the cavalry could go?"

She shook her head. "It doesn't matter. They'll be in Toria by now."

A tension born of frustration built in Rufus's head. The only other routes out of the city on the map were east and south. He'd come from the south so knew they hadn't travelled there, and he presumed the east would be blighted with even thicker smoke, making it doubtful many horses or people could survive. Plus, there was no path to Toria from the east except to come back through Alogos. It made no sense. The only logical thing for the swifts to do was to head west.

But the fact they left this woman to say that meant it couldn't be true.

Had he missed something in the east? Rakkans had never mapped the area, and the charts he'd found here didn't give much detail on how large an area there was past the mountains to the side of Alogos.

Rufus grasped his head and let his voice fall to a natural pitch. "Just tell us the truth. It's in your best interests."

The woman slid on her backside away from him a few inches. "I am telling the truth."

Rufus sighed. "I believe you. Why would they leave someone that knows anything of worth? … But I've been wrong before." He gave Pollio a subtle nod.

His brother stepped forward, cracked his knuckles, and prepared himself to work. "I'll get the truth out of her." Humans liked to use tools to torture, but Viridians didn't need steel when their bones were stronger. Plus, there was something more intimidating about doing it with your hands, something that bonded the tortured and torturer in a most fruitful way that Rufus could already see building in the woman's eyes.

He held out his hand to stop Pollio as the rakkan reached the now cowering woman, but before he could speak and defend her as planned, another woman's voice came from the doorway.

"I knew you'd be up to no good." Lex stood grimacing as she scanned the room and focused on the woman surrounded by grim warriors.

Rufus froze in place, paralysed in a way he'd rarely been in his life, and every other rakkan there turned to the door with the same dumbness that struck him.

This looked far worse than it was, and she'd never believe he hadn't intended the woman harm. Usually when caught, Rufus had an out, some tall tale to spin and excuse his own behaviour, at least. But try as he might, now, his mind only told him he was doomed.

He opened his mouth to force some words out, but Lex quickly disappeared in a blur. He bolted up and out of the room after her, wishing he'd brought a Subdued down here, but it was only rakkans, and as he ran, he continued trying but failing to think of any way to convince her that what she'd just seen wasn't as bad as it had looked.

He followed the path where he felt the air shifting as she sprinted down a few corridors until he heard a scream that silenced almost as quickly as it had sounded.

Had it been their captive in the kitchen?

He wasn't sure; it seemed to have come from in front of him, and why would they have hurt the woman after being seen by Darius's closest ally? Pollio would know better, a level-headed rakkan, unlike his late twin.

Rufus carried on at a slower, more silent pace, the air ahead now dead and lifeless, and when he reached the end of the corridor with only a few closed doors on either side, he knew he'd lost her.

*Think, Rufus.* He had to assume the worst—that she'd get back to Darius and inform him. Would one apparent human victim be enough for Rufus's neck to meet the Blades?

Probably.

The only way to excuse taking this woman was if he could justify it. Suppose they gleaned some secret from her, which gave Darius a reason to want to believe no harmful methods had been used… The Overlord would find it harder to condemn him if he got results.

So, giving up on Lex, he turned around and headed back to the kitchen, hoping this woman had something useful to say.

# 52

## Darius – Alogos

The haze shrouding the city faded from orange to red as the sun set behind it, marking the end of a whole day of waiting. Darius waited atop the walkway above the western gate to the city, watching the empty streets as if a woman or ghost would appear and end his wait.

"We should go," Sulla said gingerly.

But if even he was concerned enough to be quiet, Darius should have been panicked. It was all he could do *not* to panic.

"Why would she leave?" he asked for the hundredth time. Lex wouldn't have gone without talking to him, even if their kiss made her feel awkward.

"Maybe she's with Hera," Sulla said. "She and Warlord Varro were the first to march for the Arid Gorge."

"She wouldn't just leave like that." They'd left in the early morning. By now, all of Darius's army was marching, and communication without flying escorts was difficult. Lyra was already searching the ranks of the army, but finding Lex while still within the smoky haze was like trying to find a hair on a beach.

Sulla's hand touched his shoulder. "Wherever she is, she isn't here. Your warriors need you."

Like he needed reminding of the weight of his responsibilities now.

"Fine." He made his way down to the street where his and Sulla's swifts were, and he was waiting for the rakkan when thudding within the city caught his ears. He turned to look as the sounds grew louder and clearer, the pounding of hooves on the cobbles, and he watched the vacant haze as it began to shift, prickle his ears, and the blurred shape of a horse and rider emerged from the darkness. Sat on top, a young man rode with his wild, jet-black mane stuck up at all angles, and his face was as red as the rumbling sky. Although the man was unfamiliar, Darius could have sworn he'd seen him before.

"Thank the Goddess," the man said as he brought his steed casually alongside Darius's.

Darius grabbed one of the Blades. "Who are you?"

The man gaped for a moment before nodding in realisation. "Ah…the disguise. It's me, Aran."

Suddenly Darius recognised those eyes, but how the hell he'd made his face look younger was a mystery.

"Aran," Darius said. "What are you doing here?"

The man's expression fell. "You mean…my pteron didn't make it? You didn't get my warning?"

"I'm afraid not. All the birds that spent too long within this haze have perished."

The man blinked rapidly, wetness building in his eyes. "I see. At least tell me Lex is safe."

Darius's stomach dropped so suddenly his horse must have felt it, because it shifted uncomfortably. "I'm not sure. No one has seen her since we all met this morning."

Although Aran had looked fearful before, his face now paled to that of a petrified corpse. "Then the King already has her."

It took a moment for the man's words to register.

"Why do you say that?" Darius asked.

"Because I know it's true."

At first, the suggestion struck Darius as absurd. How would the King have her? And why?

But the Chief Priest wasn't often wrong about these things, and there were many times Darius had regretted not listening to the man.

"How do you know?" Sulla asked.

"I have spies throughout Toria," Aran replied. "Lex knew a secret of mine—that I have many escorts, and although they can't get into the Torian palace itself, they can get close to people in the know. The King has been looking to capture her for a while, and they sent Jason to complete the task."

The revelation of such a secret would have ordinarily been a shock, but all Darius felt was numbness.

"Are they taking her alive or…?" He couldn't finish the question.

"Alive, but there's worse," the Chief Priest said. "I wish I'd known sooner, wish I'd stayed with you so that I could have warned you immediately. If only I'd—"

"Spit it out, man," Sulla said.

"Yes, apologies. They're blaming her for Archimedes's death and will torture her for information, but something about it seems off to me. It's almost like they captured her just to lure you there."

Whatever the reason, Darius wouldn't let that faze him. Lex was in danger, and under torture or the hand of a goman, she'd give up what she knew about Cynthia too.

Without a pause, he asked, "Do you know the way to Toria?"

"You can't be serious…" Sulla grabbed the reins of Darius's swift and clutched them tightly. "Don't tell me you're that foolish."

"If we go by swift," the Chief Priest said, "we can be there in two days at a push."

"You're encouraging him?" Sulla screamed. "You just said this was a trap. Has this smoke driven you both mad?"

"This could spell the end of the war!" Aran said. "I've done much soul-searching, and while I doubt the God and Goddess approved of what you or I have done in the past, I believe they wish for me to intervene here."

"Is that it?" Sulla said. "Or does Lex know too much about you?"

"She does," Aran said. "I can't afford for the King to find out about my escorts. And even if he wants to lure Darius, he's leaving himself open and has underestimated the resources I have at my disposal to assist you. Oh, if only I'd stayed with you… It isn't just Lex's fate that's at stake here. Stay with me, and I can ensure whatever they're planning doesn't go as they hope. I'll even get you inside the King's palace. Do you trust me?"

"Do I have a choice?" Darius tried to pull the reins of his swift from Sulla's hands, but the rakkan held firm.

"You're just going, like that?" Sulla said. "You're not even going to speak with the warlords?"

"We barely have time," Aran said. "Toria's soldiers are marching towards the Arid Gorge to face your army. If we aren't quick, we won't evade them."

"Even more reason to stay!" Sulla's face flushed. "Dar, your army will need you."

"Rufus can command the army," Darius said. The Viridian Warlord was far more suited to the task anyway, and it wasn't like there were cities or towns to raze or pillage amidst a desolate gorge. Repercussions from giving him free rein would be limited this time.

"And who will stop Jason tearing through our warriors?" Sulla asked.

"He'll remain in Toria," the Chief Priest said. "Your army need not fear him, and neither do you if I'm with you. Leave Jason to me."

None of the man's barrage of information in the last few minutes struck Darius as incredibly as that assertion.

"*You* will fight Jason?" he asked.

"I didn't say 'fight.' But I can handle him."

In any event, Darius would hope for the best and assume the worst—that the Twin Blades would need to put an end to the King's Sword once and for all.

Sulla shook his head and let out a hard breath as he released Darius's reins. "You're both damned fools."

"Are you coming or not?" Darius asked.

"Of course I am!" Sulla leapt onto the back of Darius's swift. "But we should stop to let all the warlords know what's happened."

"Very well." The Chief Priest kicked his horse and set it into a sprint that saw it disappear within a few heartbeats.

Darius grabbed his own reins, but his hands began to shake so violently he worried he wouldn't control the beast.

"Easy, big man." Sulla grabbed hold of his waist. "If she's bait, she's alive."

But being dead wasn't the worst fate that could befall someone when there was a goman around.

# 53

## King's Orator – Toria

When gazing upon a face as strikingly beautiful as Alexandra's, Ophelia always had to resist the urge to maul and disfigure it to match the ugliness of her own. Women born like Alexandra had life so easy; they didn't have to earn the attention of powerful men but merely had to flit their lashes. *Sickening.*

"*Step back,*" Ipu said as if knowing Ophelia's malicious thoughts without touching her. But it wasn't like she acted upon them. Usually.

Alexandra stood behind the bars of a cell, her face and body without a scratch, a testament to Jason's skill. The King's Sword stood next to her while Ipu watched from a few yards away, bathed in rays as the afternoon sun shone through the slats of the one shuttered window into the prison block.

A lot of cities liked to encase their cells in darkness to compound a prisoner's torture by removing all concept of day and night, depriving them of sleep, normality, and humanity. But

Ophelia found such captives were often driven to madness, their minds scrambled until so incoherent that anything from their mouth was questionable at best. It was better to break a person's will rather than their sanity.

Next to Ipu stood the Numbered that they'd scoured the Empire in search of, for reasons Ophelia frustratingly still hadn't been trusted with. He was a handsome young man with a shaved head and that vacant stare common among the Numbered—or at least, that used to be common. Since Archimedes's death, many had discovered new lives for themselves and developed new personalities, even rekindling relationships they'd been stripped of. But this man… It was almost as if Ipu had recently tampered with his mind.

"It doesn't matter what you get from me." Alexandra spat at their feet through the steel bars. "Darius will attack this city soon enough and burn you all in rakkan fire. We've made no secret of our plans. We need no elaborate strategy. Toria will be overwhelmed with his might, not by any tactics you'll learn from me."

Usually, prisoners' lips had to be pried open to get them to spill so much as a word, and Alexandra's reputation was one of a woman that wouldn't even reveal the time of day if asked by an enemy. Yet, now… It was almost as if the woman wanted to speak rather than have a goman extract whatever she had hidden inside.

Ipu took a step forward and studied the algus while her eyes misted over. "*Strip her. Leave nothing in her cell.*"

Alexandra scowled but also betrayed fear.

Ipu usually respected algus enough to leave them with dignity, even traitors such as the one before them, so there must have been a reason for this command.

A couple of algus guards unlocked the cell while Alexandra slunk to the back and raised her fists as if she could best these full-grown men in such a tight space.

"*It would be better for you not to resist,*" Ipu said. "*They'll strip you anyway.*"

Lex spat again. "Liar."

"*I am goman. I cannot lie.*"

Wherever that saying had come from, Ophelia had never seen anything that made her doubt it and plenty that confirmed it.

But Alexandra tucked her chin and left her fists high.

The two algus charged in, dodged Lex's first strikes, and had her grappled before Ophelia had blinked. One held her down with his weight as she screamed in fury, while the other tore off her tunic and trousers.

"*Get the belt. Don't even leave scraps,*" Ipu said.

As an algus tossed the split belt out of the cell and at Ophelia's feet, she finally understood the reason for this.

"She'll try to kill herself?" Ophelia asked.

Ipu nodded. "*She has secrets she doesn't want me to learn. Fortunately for her, I care nothing for her mongrel daughter.*"

The words paralysed Alexandra, eyes wide and fixated on the goman now while the men continued removing anything she could use to end her life.

And Ophelia was also stunned, motionless. "Another half-breed?"

Ipu nodded. "*But don't fret. Her daughter doesn't have the abilities of an algus.*"

Alexandra suddenly thrust herself upwards, almost escaping the grips of the men, but one caught her shoulder in time and shifted his weight until pressing down with his elbow to her throat. She flared algor so fiercely that the room exploded in blue light, forcing Ophelia to shield her eyes from the sudden brightness.

"Leave…her…" Alexandra wheezed through her constricted throat.

"*Don't kill her,*" Ipu said, "*or you'll join her in death. Lock her cell once you're done.*"

The guard gave a nervous nod, then moved his weight onto her stomach.

Without waiting to ensure they followed orders, Ipu turned and began striding out of the prison, the Numbered beside her and Ophelia quickly following. Once back up the stairs and into the grand halls of the palace, Ophelia felt free to speak of other pressing matters.

"Our armies are almost in position," she said. She and her algus were always the ones trusted to relay instructions.

"*Good. Tell the swifts to be ready.*"

"They already are. Are we ready to send the Staff?"

"*Yes. Reveal it to your most trusted algus and have them ride a swift to join our main force in the gorge.*"

Ophelia knew just the man. "Consider it done." Now they just had Darius to prepare for.

Ipu gave a sigh of satisfaction, then addressed the Numbered. "*I want you to keep an eye on Alexandra; make sure she doesn't harm herself, but you're not to say* anything *to her, understood?*"

The algus nodded, but the order only puzzled Ophelia more. They hadn't searched the Empire as hard as they had just to add another guard to their ranks.

"*When I call for you,*" Ipu continued, "*you're to clothe her and bring her to the Pool of Toriamas. Hold a blade to her throat, but once I give you a signal, do not resist if she tries to overpower you. Let her do as she wishes.*"

Ophelia's frown deepened. "Any of the guards can do that. Is there not something more important he—"

"*This is why I summoned him.*"

"But...does that mean you intend for Alexandra to escape?"

Ipu shook her head. "*She won't, and she'll receive her punishment before I'm finished with her. She really will want to die, then.*"

But if she wasn't to die... "What's her punishment to be?"

Ipu halted and turned to the Numbered. "*Leave us. Refresh yourself, then return to her.*"

The algus bowed and left down the corridor, and once he was out of sight, Ipu continued walking.

"*Alexandra's punishment will fit her crimes.*"

Ophelia hurried after her again. "But why won't you execute her?"

"*Too merciful.*"

"Or will you kill her daughter?"

Ipu's voice thrummed in a laugh. "*I will eventually, but that isn't what I speak of. Come. I'll enlighten you. I think you'll be pleased.*"

And whenever Ipu had said that in the past, Ophelia had not been disappointed.

# 54

## Rufus – Arid Gorge

The smoke had barely eased over the last week, seeming to stalk them through the gorge carved through the mountains, but at least the sky had lightened with a few breakthrough moon rays making it to the ground, and the air higher up was clear enough for birds to survive, even if they could barely see the happenings below through the night-time haze.

"There's a big difference between twenty and a hundred miles," Rufus said through gritted teeth. His Subdued and commanders marched alongside him, giving yet more conflicting reports.

"The Torians are definitely less than a hundred miles ahead," one of the Subdued said.

"Clearly," Rufus said. Even an imbecile could have deduced that. "Any sign of swifts or horses?"

Every algus shook their head. If the swifts of Alogos numbered what they were rumoured to, the birds would have spotted them. That again begged the ever-lingering question in Rufus's mind: Where were they?

On each side of them, the gorge's walls towered above, weathered brown facades that looked like sand until close enough to discern the rock. The trail of a river cut through the centre of the gorge but was nothing more than a dry fossil of what it once was now, and the thin, withering plants scattering the ground confirmed the place had earned the name "Arid."

But as flat and hard as the ground was, it wasn't perfect for cavalry. Smaller cracks and dry fissures spread out like a giant web, leaving some parts uneven and many a hole that would catch a hoof and break a leg. Plenty of rocks were scattered along the ground too, giving almost limitless ammunition for Rufus's slingers in places, and the hardest ground was near the edges, where parched soil had all but blown away and left solid stone exposed, perfect for allowing any missed slinger stones to bounce and hit a foe from a lower angle. Already, the formations of Rufus's men began building in his mind, predicting the positions where they could inflict maximal damage.

"Warlord," Pollio whispered from beside him, "at this pace, twenty miles will see us face them at dawn."

That was a scenario Rufus couldn't allow. Whether their enemies were twenty or a hundred miles away, that meant a battle in the gorge, and Rufus had to use every moment he could to prepare.

"Call the legions to a halt," he said loud enough for the other warlords to hear. "We'll prepare for battle." A night or more gave them time for trenches and palisades with whatever logs they'd carried thus far, plus traps.

"I'll send my vanguard farther ahead," Warlord Varro said. "We'll need early warning of exactly how far their troops are."

Rufus wouldn't object. A few of them were riding swifts and would be able to gallop back to them in no time.

"Tell the Viridians to bring the supplies to us." Rufus paused, considering whether now was the best time to give his final order. But he had to give it because if they were facing battle, they had to use all the resources at their disposal.

He cleared his throat and casually added, "After they've brought supplies, they'll dig the trenches and palisades, then prepare for battle too."

Warlord Varro was the first to turn and stare at him but didn't utter a word of objection. After all, why wouldn't you call upon your most ferocious warriors on the eve of battle?

After some silent moments where everyone digested the order, the commands spread throughout the legions while Rufus and the warlords gathered to move on to discussing more specific battle tactics. Even the Overlord's panther joined them, apparently having found whatever she'd been searching for amongst the men for the last few days.

Rufus had just finished scratching out what little they'd mapped of the area on a flat piece of stone when Darius and the old priest came galloping up, miserable news written over their faces.

The pair gave an account of the fate of Darius's lover, but Rufus soon stopped paying attention and instead studied his map, picking up stones and cutting them into shapes relating to the types of troops at his disposal. For defence against the cavalry, a series of trenches would work best, the first to slow a charge, the second to hide his slingers as the enemy was hindered, and then a third for the slingers to retreat to once the second line was inevitably overrun. Each trench could be protected by palisades in the most vulnerable areas too.

"Rufus!" Darius's voice sliced through Rufus's trail of thought. "I asked you a question!"

"Apologies, Overlord." Rufus bowed his head a little, only now noticing the scarlet panic in his leader's eyes. "My mind was on the upcoming battle." *As it should be.*

"I asked if you're fit to lead the battle."

By now, wasn't that clear? "I am, Overlord. Like in the Silk City, it would be ideal if I could direct you to where you'll be most effectiv—"

"You didn't listen to a damned word I said, did you?" Darius shook his head and steadied his swift as the smart-mouthed rakkan behind him fidgeted. "I won't be here for the battle. I must ride to Toria and go after the King."

"Because of *her*?" Rufus let the contempt bleed from his grimace. "There are tens of thousands of people here whose fate may depend on you, and you're abandoning us?"

"One man cannot win a battle," the Chief Priest said, "but he can win a war. If we make it into Toria and get to the King, victory will be ours."

"I hardly think two people will get close to him. I think you should stay."

"I didn't ask for your opinion," Darius said, "nor do I want to hear it."

As always, it seemed Rufus was on his own. "In that case, if the other warlords are happy to follow my plans, then I'll take command."

"They will," Darius said. "Lyra will stay here and assist you. Protect her with your life. I'll know if you don't." And without waiting for a response, he kicked his swift back into a gallop and was soon nothing but a blur in the night followed by his priest.

What nerve the man had to ask the warlords to look after his pet.

However the trio would get past the army reportedly ahead of them wasn't Rufus's problem. The other three warlords and Hera huddled around his scratchings again while he began laying down the stones.

"The cliff face on the southern side is most fractured," he said. At its foot were hundreds of fallen shards of rock sticking up like giant spearheads puncturing the ground. "It provides good cover from the cavalry for some slingers and archers."

"And what if more of the cliff breaks and falls on whoever is there?" Warlord Flavius asked.

"Then they'll suffer a swift death." Rufus grabbed the rectangular stones he'd fashioned to represent his pikemen. "Toria will attack from the west, so our three trenches will be dug facing there, curving around to cover our north lest the cavalry scatter."

"And if they loop around to the east?" Warlord Varro asked.

"We'll dig more trenches there if we have time." As Rufus began to explain his reasoning in more detail, another swift charged up to the group so quickly it almost collided with Warlord Quintus as it skidded to a halt.

One of Hera's algus leapt off. "I've come from the vanguard."

Had they engaged the enemy so quickly?

"And?" Rufus said.

The man's face was grim. "We've clashed with their scouts. Their army will soon be here."

# 55

## Darius – Road to Toria

Not long after leaving his army, Darius spied shimmering torches and banners held amongst a mass of armour glinting in the night. At this distance, the Torian army wouldn't have spotted a couple of riders without so much as a candle, but Darius slowed his swift regardless to lessen the cloud of dust swirling from under its hooves.

"Dear Goddess," the Chief Priest said as he took in the plethora of tiny sparks of light. The marching column was wide and deep, not seeming to stick to a road but travelling as if ready for battle at any moment. Thick, square formations moved with purpose and deadly intent and stretched back towards the capital for miles.

But one thing gave Darius pause. "There's no cavalry," he said to Sulla behind him.

"Swifts can get into battle fast," the rakkan said. "Perhaps they're at the rear."

Darius scoffed. "You've been in enough battles to know that's a foolish place for them to be." And despite never having met the King, neither he nor his commanders were reportedly fools.

"We should head north," the Chief Priest said. "My escorts see their scouts ahead of us."

So far, the man had been correct about everything in their path. Why he hadn't revealed such knowledge until Lex's life was at stake, he wouldn't answer.

Darius gripped the reins of his horse tighter. As frustrated as the lack of answers made him, he needed to keep Aran on his side, which meant no hostility.

They did as suggested, and Darius expected by sunrise that the army would be far behind them. Yet, the plume-filled sky was bright with the afternoon sun by the time the rearguard of Toria's might disappeared from view.

"How many thousands do you think they have?" he asked Sulla.

The rakkan shrugged. "Must be over a hundred."

And still not a swift in sight. Darius steered his horse closer to the Chief Priest. "Do you know where the Alogos cavalry is?"

Aran shook his head. "My escorts have more important things to report. But I do know one thing: the swifts aren't ahead of us, and they aren't in Toria." The confidence with which the man spoke was as if he had a thousand escorts scouring the place. Who knew, perhaps he did?

By now, they were tearing across open plains so flat it was as if they'd been created to allow such rapid travel. They picked up the pace again and kicked their swifts into a gallop that they wouldn't maintain for long, but the beasts somehow managed to sustain it well, and long after the sun's rays deserted them again, Toria became visible.

At first, it was nothing but an uneven grey line that stretched out so wide Darius thought himself mistaken, thought this was a mountain range hidden beyond the horizon. But as they neared, the tall peaks formed into towers and angular structures nature could not design. The outer walls hid most of the place from view, stretching to thrice the length Laltos's had yet instead of being flat and straight there were subtle angles in them, and it wasn't until closer that he saw they weren't built facing an enemy head-on but zigzagging in and out with corners every quarter of a mile capped by tall bastions and ballistae leaning menacingly out above.

Merlons large enough for a group of men split the top of the stonework at such a height Darius certainly couldn't jump and second-guessed his ability to climb. Even his four legions would have struggled to breach these defences, and this was just the outer wall. Many had told him of the layers of defence this fortress sported.

Now without even the moon or starlight to guide him, the Chief Priest directed them from behind and seemed to set them on a course for the main gate. They weren't alone, and groups of people were crawling like insects from all across the landscape, probably fleeing some of the chaos and terror Darius had been spreading of late. At least they could hide amongst these people, and his smoking clouds had a silver lining, even if it were a thin one.

"I hope your cloak has a hood," he muttered to Sulla. His own did and was thankfully long enough to conceal the Twins hanging from his waist as well as having pockets for the pouches of powder Lex had given him to fight the King's Sword. Whether or not it would be of any use on a goman was something he wasn't sure of.

Aran slowed a fraction once they were only a few minutes away from entering.

"Leave any talking to me," he said. "There are five sets of city walls between here and the palace. The first four will be no issue, but the fifth is off-limits to anyone but the King's inner circle. Luckily, I know someone inside that can help us get through."

Darius was happy to defer to the man's wisdom, but never had he felt the lack of kuraminium armour more, felt so vulnerable. If he died today and passed to the afterlife, he'd ask the God or Goddess why they hadn't created a horse that could bear the weight of rakkan metal.

He and Sulla made themselves as inconspicuous as possible, then they headed through the main gates to the city, an imposing sight that must have taken an entire forest and quarry to construct. There were over a thousand guards standing at various levels as their swifts walked into what seemed like a kill box, lined by soldiers with crossbows in hand but thankfully not pointed at them as a few guards beckoned each group forward as they arrived for an inspection.

The one who called Aran over was a surly-looking man with armour a few sizes too small for his belly. Judging by the heavy sweat stains on his tunic and constant sighing, he'd been stood here for hours doing this, so perhaps they could take advantage of his fatigued mind.

"Dismount," the man said with a tired wave of his hand. "Let us inspect your weapons."

The Chief Priest obliged with a nervous glance back, but Darius kept his backside planted and wondered whether revealing his algor would be his best play here. Would these common soldiers dare question an algus?

"We've come from Alogos," the Chief Priest said. "My companions and I are seeking shelter from—"

"Yeah, yeah, I didn't ask for your life story. Dismount." The man locked eyes with Darius, who decided to take the chance and flared algor with a grimace.

"Out of my way, lowling," Darius said.

The man's plump jowls flushed. "Algus… I… Yes. Of course." He waved them through while the Chief Priest climbed back atop his swift and quickly followed.

"Ballsy move," Sulla said. "I like it."

"Don't think that will always work," the Chief Priest said. "The fourth and fifth sanctuaries are more heavily protected."

The man thought that was bad news, but Darius hadn't counted on it working more than once. If it could get them through three checkpoints, then he'd count his blessings.

Inside the city, the stonework used to construct the various trading halls and workshops was of softer and cheaper quality, but if the place was anything like the other cities, the palace would be a beaming sight of marble and extravagance. The rich loved nothing more than wasting their money just to prove they had money to waste. It was a wonder people gave them or the algus any respect at all.

The next two sets of gates were more heavily guarded than the first, but Darius used his apparent algus status to enter with relative ease. He reckoned as long as those demanding compliance of him weren't algus themselves, he was golden. But by the time the fourth set of gates came into view, the carved lions sitting atop the stone wall above told him they were reaching more exclusive heights, and this one wasn't left open but had a steel portcullis barring them from entry.

A woman stood outside wearing a white tunic with a black eagle emblazoned on the front, lit by the shaking light of two braziers dwindling at either side of the gate. Her mail armour was most favoured with algus, and she had tidy, braided hair along with the keen eyes of a person that didn't let much slip by them. Behind her were a few dozen other algus and soldiers mixed together that wouldn't have fazed Darius if Lex hadn't been a hostage here.

If the Chief Priest was nervous while approaching, he did nothing to show it, but he did dismount and indicated for Darius to follow his lead before they walked up to the gate with Sulla, shielding their faces from view.

"No entry tonight," the woman said, hand moving to the hilt of her sword.

The Chief Priest looked up at the dark sky. "Surely it will be dawn soon, and I have a most urgent patient for Surgeon Demetrius."

The name meant nothing to Darius, but it had the woman raising an eyebrow. "He only sees patients in the morning."

"It cannot wait." The Chief Priest turned to glance at Sulla's cloaked figure. "He has a most vile affliction that the Chief Surgeon demanded be studied at once."

"Does he." The woman took a step closer, a few soldiers behind her now craning their necks to get a better look. "Then he wouldn't mind showing me."

"Be my guest," Aran said, "but once his cloak is off, try not to breathe in. The lesions seem to infect other people through the air."

The woman suddenly halted with a wince. "I think I'll take your word for it." Then her gaze pierced Darius. "And what's your business?"

"Just here to..."—*slay your king*—"assist my brother. I'm afraid I have succumbed to the illness as well."

That was as good a lie as he could come up with, given he wasn't the best at subterfuge. When so deadly with a sword, it had never seemed pressing to develop his ability to manipulate with words.

Despite his lack of skills, the woman turned and paid him no more heed. "I'm afraid my hands are tied, regardless. No one can pass through these gates except the King's algus."

Darius flexed his fingers, readying for the hilts of the Blades and wondering how quickly he could kill two dozen algus after two nights without sleep. Before any of them screamed? Right now, his body was fuelled by nothing but fear for Lex, fatigue banished to just a pounding headache.

He spotted only a few guards stationed on the walls, too far apart for Sulla to take out with ease, but perhaps a flung dagger or two would do the trick.

The Chief Priest caught his eye with a look of warning, as if reading his intentions. Unfortunately, it was also a defeated look, and Aran's continued silence meant he hadn't another idea. It looked like the Twin Blades were their only option.

But as Darius began picking out his first targets, a crow swooped and landed on the woman's shoulder without a visible reaction from her.

Aran's face lit up. "Is that your escort?"

The woman's eyes narrowed. "It is. Why?"

"No reason." Aran clicked his tongue twice, and the bird took off at once, then flapped onto his arm as he lifted it. "It's just always nice to meet an old acquaintance."

The woman's mouth fell ajar. "It's you?" She had the same perplexed look Darius must have had when first seeing the man so well disguised. No wonder he seemed to travel the Empire so freely.

"I must apologise for forgetting your face," the Chief Priest said while giving the crow's breast a stroke, "but I don't forget animals so easily, nor they me."

Darius wondered whether the man made a habit of tampering with everyone's escorts, as he had with Lyra before.

Finally breaking her stupor, the woman came forward and hushed her voice. "Isn't it dangerous for you to be so close? If the King were to capture you, he—"

"Unfortunately," Aran interjected, "my friends' medical need is most dire. We must see the Chief Surgeon."

The woman's brow furrowed, but Darius knew a convinced person when he saw it. Aran had done enough.

"It's not so simple," the woman whispered. "Defences are in place."

Whatever that meant, Aran smiled as if it were nothing. "I know the safe path."

"If you're sure… All right," the woman said, then turned to give a signal to her men. "Let them in!"

Although seeming bewildered, the soldiers obeyed and allowed them through the fourth city gate, into a street as decadent as its entrance had suggested. This must have been where the top algus of the Empire lived, each doorway carved into a work of art, each building guarded by hundreds of statues of gods and monsters so far unweathered by the elements. Even the road had been composed of perfectly square slabs, white without so much as a speck of dirt on them.

Yet there were no people, not even guards or slaves.

Darius hooked a foot to climb back atop his swift, but the Chief Priest held him down.

"Wait," he said. "Here we walk. These streets are not safe."

A quick scan of the area ahead revealed nothing amiss, no blood, no bodies, just an eerie quiet filled only by the distant clamour of the outer city. But then he realised every shutter was locked across every window, doors closed, and not even birds or insects disturbed the unnatural stillness. Such a major city wouldn't be so desolate even at night-time.

"The defences she spoke of?" Darius asked.

The Chief Priest nodded. "Traps overlaid with traps and snares. The King took precautions when you began sending spies and assassins."

This must have been why Hera's algus had never made it into the palace, but the sheer scale made Darius's head hurt. This part of the city must have been a square mile, the palace only a distant figure making its presence known but not yet felt, and there must have been hundreds of grand houses in that mile that surely weren't just for show. People lived here once.

"I know what you're thinking," the Chief Priest said. "Only those the King deems loyal own these buildings, and they, along with their slaves, are now housed in the King's Palace—including the Chief Surgeon. They can rarely leave because of the defences now in place."

Darius grunted. "I thought the Chief Surgeon tale was a lie."

"The best lies are cloaked in facts."

"I'll take your word for that." Though the man's apparent aptitude at deceit was an unnerving revelation.

"Leave the swifts. Follow in my footsteps and do not touch anything I do not."

Sulla looked up to the rooftops. "How about we travel a little higher up? They can't have trapped the roofs."

But the tiles were at least five storeys high, not jumpable for a rakkan and a difficult climb for an old man like Aran, despite how young he now appeared.

"If you both wish to," the Chief Priest said. "But I could use a little light."

Sulla adjusted his belt as if ready to leap up, but Darius shoved him forward. "We aren't leaving him. Get moving."

Darius conjured some ferven in his hand discreetly enough it could have been taken for a lamp, then Aran led the way, each foot placed carefully but with confidence, and only ever on the centre of a paving stone.

"Are there false slabs?" Darius asked.

The Chief Priest nodded. "You'll step through onto spikes at best."

As tempting as it was to try to crack a few and see what surprises were in store, Darius resisted and focused on treading carefully. Something about the quietness made his hands yearn for his swords, but he left them for now.

The three carried on through the street for a while, every building they passed as dark and quiet inside as outside, but the shutters gave him brief glimpses of a few rooms.

"Wait," Aran whispered.

But Darius wasn't looking and bumped into Sulla's back as the rakkan came to a sudden stop.

Sulla stumbled forward. He knocked into Aran, who fell and was forced to lunge and break his fall by planting a foot firmly on another paving stone.

Darius heard the twang before he saw anything, a metallic flick of wire that saw a door to their side fling open and a dozen more twangs fill the desolate street.

Reaching out, even Darius's algus speed wasn't enough to grab Aran before bolts flew across his vision, covering the air from foot to head height.

Even an algus would have struggled to dodge. But Aran rolled with the agility of a young fighter and evaded the bolts. They grazed his back as he tumbled out of their path and came to a stop on all fours with his weight finely balanced across four adjacent paving stones.

Then the bolts slammed into a door on the opposite side of the street, and the man froze until the place quietened once again.

"Bloody quick for an old man," Sulla said with a snort. "You've been holding back on us."

Darius moved past Sulla, had a quick check around the still open door to verify it was safe, then grabbed the frozen priest and hauled him up off the stones and back onto a safe place.

"Gratitude," the man said, more with a grunt of frustration than fear at almost being skewered. "Can we please look where we're going now?"

"Sorry," Darius said. "What was that? I've never seen anything like it."

Sulla knelt and picked up a metal wire from the ground. "Must have tripped on it."

"I did not *trip*." Aran pulled back his shoulders. "I was well aware of it, which is why I said 'wait.'"

Darius had to strain to see the thing in Sulla's hand. How had the old man spotted that in the night?

"You should have been a scout," Darius said. "With that attention to detail and those reflexes, you'd have made a name for yourself." Was it these and perhaps some other hidden abilities that gave Aran the confidence to pronounce he could "handle Jason"? Because neither Darius nor Sulla had been convinced after discussing it further.

"My path is what I chose it to be," Aran said, tone still sharp. "I do not regret it and would not have changed it."

Something about the way the man spoke had Darius grasping the hilt of a sword for comfort. "You talk like you're at the end of your path."

"Perhaps I am. Perhaps all of our paths will end tonight."

As long as Lex's didn't, that's all Darius could hope for now. Lyra was in Rufus's hands, and there was no better rakkan he'd have chosen for her to be alongside in a battle. All Darius could do was pray for her and the others.

"Let's hurry," he said.

The Chief Priest returned to his careful path, avoiding more wires and spotting even more traps that no ordinary man would have noticed. Darius expected some of the man's escorts to appear and assist, perhaps a few mice or a sparrow, but there wasn't even a hint of life beyond the three of them. Even the King's palace stood tall and lifeless, like a thousand shards of grey ice pointing to the heavens around a dome rising in the centre. The only hint of warmth inside was the orange light peeking from some of the upper windows.

Darius and Sulla followed on the thankfully uneventful trek to the next set of walls, and these weren't like any others before them. They melded into the palace that, now up close, dominated the centre of the city, with its walls in a similar jagged pattern to that of the outer defences. He'd been told this place had stood for centuries, yet every stone was flawless and unchipped as if straight from the mason's table, laid out in perfect symmetry and with no hint of ever having seen hardship.

Was there some deep magic that guarded this place? No one had suggested so, but the sight had Darius wondering that perhaps the God and Goddess really weren't on his side.

The three slowed to a crawl on approach, still without a whisper of another soul in view either on the street, at the gates or even in a window or loophole.

"How do we get inside?" Darius asked.

"The door," the Chief Priest said without a trace of sarcasm.

As sceptical as Darius was at simply walking in, the man had got them this far.

The fifth gate was built into the stonework of the palace, a set of solid wooden doors hosting an iron knocker made of an eagle's shrieking head. The metal beak was so large and sharp it required Darius's strength to lift and strike, taking a chip of wood off the door in the process.

"Is it usually this quiet?" he whispered.

"The Chief Surgeon lives inside," Aran replied. "I've done him many favours over the years, and he's prepared the way for us. He should be at the door waiting."

But could a medicine man rid an entrance of all its guards? Surely only the King or his counsel could.

They waited a while with no reply, so Darius dared another knock, this time with his fist. The wood tested under his knuckles was firm but wouldn't last long under the heat of ferven, should their entry require that.

"Something's wrong," he whispered. "If your man got rid of the guards, he should answer quickly."

The Chief Priest shook his head but gave a quivering frown that betrayed he shared Darius's puzzlement.

"Let me try knocking," Sulla said. "My right foot always gets doors open."

But Aran held out a hand to stop him. "If Demetrius isn't here, he must want us to enter via a different way. We could try the western entrance." His shaking voice didn't instil confidence, though.

"I vote for Sulla's foot," Darius said.

"Wait." For the first time, the Chief Priest's eyes were fearful. "We cannot let anyone other than Demetrius know we're here. Give me a few minutes. I know another way to slip in, but you're both too large to fit. I can go and unlock the door from the inside."

It wasn't like Darius had a better idea.

"We'll give you a few minutes," Darius said. Then, Sulla's boot would be put to good use.

"No," the Chief Priest said, as stern as when he spoke of eternal damnation. "You must give me as long as it takes. Under no circumstances must you enter without me, understood?"

"Aren't I the one that's supposed to give orders?"

"I'm not ordering, I'm *imploring* you. You cannot match Jason without me, and I fear we must get past him if we're ever to free Lex."

For her sake, then, Darius nodded his agreement. "Hurry."

The Chief Priest rushed off around the side of the palace while Darius and Sulla waited with impatient huffs.

"Does any of this make sense to you?" Sulla asked.

"No," Darius said. "There should be guards, and we just walked into a place that Hera's algus failed for over a year to access. I'll wager the King is all too happy to let us inside. I just hope he doesn't know we're already here." Whether that improved or worsened his odds of rescuing Lex was unclear, but betting against a goman didn't strike him as wise.

"If the King wants us inside, he could have left the door open for us," Sulla said.

The two grumbled for another few minutes while dawn broke, the sun striving to light the city through the haze from the east and reminding Darius just how long it was since he'd had rest. How many days without sleep before he couldn't fight? Would he even make the trip back to his army should he succeed?

Before his tired mind could ponder the answers, the latches snapped open from behind the doors.

"Finally…" Darius muttered.

One door cracked open, and a face emerged from the darkness, cloaked in shadow but definitely not the Chief Priest.

"Demetrius?" Darius asked.

Then, it opened wider and gave Darius a clear view of the face. Its eyes were hollow and vacant, mouth hung open and tongue lolling out. Before Darius could utter another word, the figure fell forwards, face landing on the street outside with a crack, but he paid it no heed, because appearing behind the man was another familiar face, wrinkles stretching out at his eyes and a grey hood covering his drab hair, a man Darius had last seen in Chiva—the King's Sword.

# 56

## Rufus – Arid Gorge

Harassing an enemy wasn't new to Rufus, especially in unconquered lands, but when so defensively minded, it was difficult to commit the troops needed to break his enemy's morale.

For a day and night, the Torians had amassed almost a mile away, numbers swelling by the hour into incalculable swarms still without many horses in sight. His slingers and algus had ventured beyond his trenches to do what they could but hadn't achieved much beyond giving the diggers the time and space they needed.

And now the sun dared show its brilliance. It could only mean one thing.

"The attack will come soon," he said to the other warlords, none of whom looked surprised. "Rakkans will stay in formation and shelter themselves however they can." At least the smog within the gorge lessened the strength of that bright pest in the daytime sky.

"My elite warriors are in place," the Black Warlord said. "If there's nothing else, I'll go join them."

"Good," Rufus said. "The rest of you should join your legions too; there's little left to say." The plan had been debated ad nauseam. If they didn't know what was required by now, they never would.

A rakkan horn blared in the distance, confirming the enemy was approaching. Well, if they didn't bring their cavalry, this would be a short battle. Even if the King had a thousand algus—Hera's high-end estimate, which Rufus had no reason to doubt—the legions would stand firm and unbroken. Let them come.

Rufus set off, followed closely by Lyra, and climbed a nearby rock he'd picked to give him the best overview of the battlefield.

With him were a few warriors with horns of all colours and tones that would relay his commands, and behind him was the largest cliff face in the gorge, a towering facade of brittle rock so pockmarked it was as if a rakkan legion had unleashed their slings onto it. It would defend the south side of his army and ensure his trenches were the only way to the heart of his army while still giving them a route to retreat east. In front of him, facing their enemy in the west, the largest rakkan army the Empire had ever seen simmered and waited. Defeat was surely impossible, unthinkable. But if that were true, a goman wouldn't approve an attack.

The Arid Gorge had once been a desolate waste but now crawled with armoured life, a rippling, metallic katakto board of shifting pieces shrouded in the breath of the burning sea all those miles away.

Far in the east, Alogos was an invisible ghost city, but his gut told him to keep an eye there.

Announcing the opening of battle, the field burst with fire as the slingers began their barrage. Torians charged towards the first trench, a few algus leading them, while the first volley struck with a satisfying ring of metal that took a few heartbeats to reach Rufus's ears.

Behind the first trench were his weakest warriors and human soldiers, the freshest recruits that were no great loss to an army but had more than enough training to put up a valiant defence.

Again, he glanced to the east, the smoke thickening, and something arrested his gaze, like a shadow moving within the haze but with a will of its own, moving against the wind, directly west.

A horn blared from his army, signalling that enemies had made it over the first trench and engaged his warriors, but he couldn't pay heed now. It wasn't long until the sight from the east crystallised into the shapes of swifts setting a blistering pace towards them. They'd be here in only a few minutes, with only a single trench between them and Rufus's rearguard.

"Sound for the Black Legion to retreat," he bellowed.

The Margalvian hornmaster just gaped as if he'd asked the man to take a sword to his own gut, so Rufus grabbed the instrument from him and blew it himself.

The Black Legion turned at the noise, currently standing behind the third trench and closest to the rear. But none moved, only the Black Warlord, who hurried back and up the rock to join Rufus.

"Did my ears deceive me?" Varro asked.

"No," Rufus snapped. "Get your damned men to the rear. The swifts of Alogos are coming."

The Black Warlord's helmet dipped as soon as he focused east. "Where did they come from? We've been watching all the roads from Toria."

Did that matter? Rufus blared the horn again, thankfully answered by the legion this time as they began marching back with their pikes in hand.

What they needed to join them was more ranged defence. The Black, Branz, and Azure Legions all had slingers, but they weren't as drilled as the Viridians and hadn't as many recent years of battle experience against the Empire.

"Get me Pollio," he barked to one of his Subdued. The woman raced away without question while Rufus faced east, spotting a patch of flat ground behind the trench they could make their stand on.

It wasn't long until Pollio arrived with some of his centurions and opened his mouth to ask something. But he was stricken mute when he spotted the swifts tearing up the gorge.

"Indeed," Rufus said. "Bring all the Viridian slingers to the rear. Quickly."

"Aye, Warlord." Pollio gave a signal to one of his centurions without his gaze breaking away from the new threat. "You think the Black Legion can stop them?"

Below, Warlord Varro stomped up and down before his men, no doubt roaring words of inspiration as his helmet's front and horns glowed amber with ferven. Part of a leader's job was to inspire, to instil the courage that thousands of charging swifts would easily steal.

"Margalvia's line will hold," Rufus said. "And I'll join our men myself."

Pollio gave a nod in reply. "Our men will stand firm. Viridians do not cower."

Some did, but commanders beat that out of them young.

Rufus took his horned helmet and slipped it on, not enjoying the restricted view it gave him, but it wasn't like he wore it for practical reasons.

He glanced at his feet and caught the eye of Lyra. "Stay here, where it's safe." The last thing he needed was to give Darius an excuse to end him.

Her eyes narrowed at the suggestion, but she didn't move when the two brothers began making their way down the rock and onto the flat ground behind the Margalvian shield wall. Now lower, Rufus lost sight of the trench and the enemy but prayed their defences were enough as he came to a halt behind the Black Legion.

The rumble of running men grew behind him, and soon thousands of slingers lined up, most of them taller and thicker boned than Rufus, but he let ferven glow in his eyes and saw the fierce looks they gave him, such a stark contrast to the derisive sneers he'd received just a few months ago. Now, they saw him for what he really was—a conqueror.

Conjuring ferven in his throat, he yelled above the growing thunder of hooves. "Do you hear that?" He paused for a moment and breathed in as if savouring their enemies' approach. "They think they can surprise us at our weakest point, they think they can make fools of us! But they don't know Viridian hearts are fearless; they don't know we'd face even gods and demons without a tremor in our hand." He slid his sword free, held it out, and let them gain confidence from its calm stillness and the so-called divine tattoos on his arm. For all of Rufus's faults, at least he was cold and emotionless even in the face of a horde of beasts that should have had any veteran sweating. Even his father had been jealous of the fact, but Rufus's secret was nothing more than indifference to death. Many feared it, but did they fear falling asleep? Death was nothing but a dreamless slumber.

Pollio gave the hand signal, and every slinger fired a stone, loaded it into the pouch of their weapons, and began spinning.

"These horses have harried you for weeks," Pollio yelled, joining his brother's side, arms tense and carved with muscle. "Today is your chance for vengeance."

"They spilt the blood of your brothers," Rufus yelled as the swifts' thunder almost deafened him. "Send them to hell!"

The slingers released blind over the backs of the Margalvians, thousands of molten balls disappearing into the haze that blighted the battlefield.

Given the size of their enemy's force, it would be impossible to miss, and sure enough, after a few seconds of nothing, a crash sounded amidst the thunder.

Slingers now loosed at will while the Margalvian shield wall gave no indication they'd engaged the enemy. All Rufus had to judge events were sounds, the shrieks of horses and men, the clank of stone on metal, but then a sudden loud crash came followed by a roar of triumph from the Black Legion.

The cavalry had reached the trench, tried to run across the flimsy camouflage they'd placed on top, and met their ends on the spiked depths below.

But it wouldn't be enough. They'd dug the western trenches wide enough so a swift would need a good run up to vault them, but here in the east, Rufus doubted the scale was enough to render them impassable. This wasn't meant to be the point of attack.

"Give them no reprieve!" Rufus shouted, then grabbed one of the centurions. "Get behind. Jump and keep me updated on our range."

The rakkan took off and soon was leaping and signalling whether their stones were hitting the cavalry's front or not.

"Heads!" a Black Commander yelled from the front.

Rufus felt the air before he saw what the warning was about, hundreds of javelins arcing into and over the pikeman. He dodged to the side and let one clatter on the ground beside him while slingers rolled and weaved, some colliding with each other and others too slow to avoid a spear skewering them.

His fears had been correct; some had made it over the trench.

Many of the slingers that had dived to the ground were slow to get up, some even curling in balls and shielding their heads.

"Get up!" Rufus stomped tall and proud into the ranks, kicking every man that refused to move. "Viridians die like men; we don't live like cowards!"

His show of fearlessness seemed to work, and within a few moments, all were on their feet and spinning their weapons again.

By now, the sound of crunching metal told of the Black Legion's pikes meeting at least some of the cavalry and preventing them tearing apart Rufus's army from the rear. A couple of horns were coming from their main defensive lines in the west too, but such a chaos of screams, pounding, and crashes filled Rufus's ears that he couldn't discern their meaning.

It wasn't until a commander came bolting up to him that he knew they told of ill happenings.

"Warlord," the Viridian Commander said, taking deep breaths. "They've made it over the first trench, and most of the shield wall there has crumbled."

Rufus took a moment to believe the man's words. "*Crumbled?*" So quickly?

The rakkan nodded. "Our defences have already retreated to the second trench, where the Branzians and Azurians are re-forming ranks, but they need to retreat further. The King's—"

Rufus silenced him with a raised hand, knowing very well that without the Black Legion and slingers covering a retreat to the final trench, whatever stood now was effectively their last line of defence.

"Have the Azurians retreat alone," he said. "Dig in behind the third trench."

"But, Warlord," the man said in a panicked tone, "they can't—"

"And Hera's algus need to do their part," Rufus added.

"But they have the Staff of Arria!" the rakkan blurted out.

Rufus stared at the rakkan for any clue this was a guess or perhaps a terrible jest. But only deathly seriousness stared back at him.

For the first time that day, his heart began racing.

# 57

## Darius – Toria

Darius ripped the Twin Blades from his waist, the runes flaring in anger, while Sulla followed his lead.

But the King's Sword stood before them in the doorway motionless, weapon in hand but held in an unthreatening stance.

"The King will see you," Jason uttered in a voice so hoarse it was as if he hadn't spoken in months.

The Twin Blades spat their derision.

"What is this?" Darius asked, ready to pounce at the first flinch from the man.

"Parley." The King's Sword shrugged, opened the door further, and simply waited.

If all the other happenstances up to now weren't enough to convince Darius of a trap, this certainly was. Yet he considered going with the algus. *He* must have been what the King wanted, so did that mean he might be able to bargain for Lex's life?

"You should stay here," he said to Sulla. "I'll go and meet the King."

"I don't care if I have to break your kneecaps," Sulla said, "I'm not letting you go in there with him."

"If Lex is in there, then we should—" Darius's voice broke as Sulla rushed from beside him, gladius flaring and heading straight towards the King's Sword.

Jason stepped aside and let the blade pass his body before bringing up his sword and batting the weapon aside.

Off balance, Sulla reached out a desperate grab for one of the man's legs, but Jason had moved again, this time slicing his sword down at Sulla's wrist.

Darius lunged. He parried the strike and sent a haze of sparks across Sulla as the rakkan rolled away.

Once at a safe distance, Darius stepped back and allowed his blade to part from Jason's, the two coming to a silent staredown again.

"Finished?" Jason said in a bored tone.

Sulla moved towards the algus again, but Darius held him back.

"Aran warned us," Darius said, "we can't take him on."

Sulla growled and gave no further argument, but Darius knew he had every intention of following his lead.

"Why does the King suddenly want to parley?" Darius asked the King's Sword.

He shrugged. "Ask the King."

Either this algus was even more of a mindless slave than rumoured, or he was a liar. His sister had certainly had a devious tongue.

"Fine," Darius said. "I'll meet him." He kept his hold on Sulla, feeling the muscles of the rakkan's back tense at his words. He had to force him to stay. "I'm sorry, Sulla."

Before the rakkan could question his meaning, he moved and shoved Sulla through the doorway to send him tumbling back outside.

Curses flew from Sulla's mouth as his backside hit the ground, and Darius slammed the door shut. He snapped deadbolts across to keep the rakkan out. It wouldn't keep him out forever, but long enough.

"Lead the way," Darius said.

The King's Sword took off into the palace with Darius following closely behind, their algus speed soon leaving the door out of sight. They flew past some guards in the corridors, whose only motion was their eyes tracking the pair, but there were far fewer than Darius would have expected. Most must have marched to face his army, and at the thought, he prayed Rufus fared well.

Lyra's senses were never far from his awareness, but he couldn't focus on them now, having nothing but Lex's fate occupying his thoughts.

They carried on deeper into the palace, seeming to descend but without any stairs to mark the fact, and eventually reached a pair of metal doors gilded with strange symbols he'd only ever spotted in parts of Laltos before. They stood open and unguarded, and inside was a room that looked more like a cavern propped up by stone walls and with a dirt floor. Only clay lamps granted the windowless room light, hung on the walls all around the perimeter.

In the centre, the ground sank into a pool, shallow at the edges but darkening to depths unknown at its heart. The crystal water lay without a ripple disturbing the glassy surface, and stood next to it, a masked figure watched the motionless depths.

As they walked onto the dry, hard earth, Darius spied no other presence in the room, not so much as an insect disturbing the air, and gripped the Twin Blades ready.

The doors slammed behind him without warning, and the hush of the place revealed an ensuing quiet stampede of footsteps outside that must have been algus and guards rushing to close him in. He'd known they hadn't intended for him to leave here, and perhaps he should have been concerned, but all his focus was now on Lex and the man before him.

For years, this ruler had destroyed his life, sent foes to steal everything Darius was, and then kill those he cared for. Being so close now, all he remembered was feeling the sword now in his hand puncturing Selene, how she'd screamed in agony, pain twisting her face. Her mind had been warped into something unrecognisable, but a part of her had still been in there, a part that Darius had sent from this life to the next.

Now, the rage of that day had ferven spilling between his bared teeth. It took all his restraint to not rush at the man and end this war here and now, one way or the other.

And if the man hadn't had Lex somewhere, that's what he'd have done.

The King's Sword stopped once a few yards in front of the pool and knelt to his King on the far side, but Darius simply came to a halt and studied the wicked man before him. He'd expected someone taller, although it was hard to judge height when Medus wore such a high, jewelled crown, but the man was also more slender than he'd been told, and the black mask was more pathetic than menacing.

"Where is she?" Darius barked. Why waste time getting to the point?

No reply came, but the King turned and began walking until his toes met the water, and his long tunic and robes swept the floor behind him but betrayed no hidden weapons underneath. Whatever he was up to, it seemed like only the King's Sword was required.

"You wished to speak with me," Darius said, "so free your tongue before I cut it from your throat."

The King cocked his head a little. "*I'd cower if I actually had a tongue.*"

The sonorous voice filled Darius's mind with thunder and dread.

"So, you *are* an imposter," Darius said.

"*Did you think my husband would serve a human master?*"

This was all a little too much to process, but once he studied the King's chest, he noticed the slight bulge of breasts.

"Archimedes was your husband?" Darius asked.

The King nodded—or was that Queen? Whatever it was, it was a tyrant.

It took all of Darius's will to not rub salt in her wounds by detailing how he'd gouged out the goman's eyes and sealed his fate.

"So is all this about revenge?" he asked instead through gritted teeth.

The goman laughed, a loud thrum running through Darius's mind that gave him shivers.

"*Gomans do not succumb to such barbarian motives. Why do you think your race had been driven back to the mountains, soon to be wiped out by a people of more supreme intellect and self-control?*"

Whatever she was speaking of, Darius wasn't sure he could shoulder another tragedy.

"Where is she?" he demanded. "And what do you want? Why go to this trouble when you just wanted to call a parley?"

"*I only wanted two of you to come, not an envoy.*" The goman slowly slid the mask from her face, revealing her dark skin and the smooth patch where a human's mouth would have been. If not for the fact he despised the woman, her eyes would have struck him as beautiful. But all he felt now was hate and disgust.

She turned her attention from Darius to Jason. "*Is the priest dead?*"

The King's Sword lowered his head. "No, but the other guards should have him. He won't disturb us."

Her body betrayed her tension at the answer, her long exhalation the sign of a person calming themself. Darius wasn't sure why she'd be concerned with Aran, although the man had been insistent about "handling" Jason.

It was then Darius realised all those he'd heard rushing outside the room might not have been there just to keep him in. They'd keep others out.

But before he could figure out all the answers, the goman boomed, "*Bring her in.*"

The doors cracked open a fraction, followed by the grunts of a woman Darius recognised at once. Lex stepped into the room, jaw tense and held up by a blade stinging her throat. Behind, a man controlled her every movement and held the deadly instrument with a determined stare that told Darius he'd never reach the man before that knife emptied Lex's blood. It must have been an algus, but he wore the clothes of an ordinary citizen, without so much as mail under his cloak.

Although the King's Sword was also bereft of armour, something told Darius this wasn't due to insurmountable skill in the second man's case.

"I'll let you live if you release her," Darius said, more to test the man's reaction than to threaten, and when not so much as a flinch came back, he knew only death would stop the algus.

The man brought Lex around the pool to the side of the room, where he watched the two rulers.

Lex's eyes were wide but through anger rather than fear, and given the goman had held her captive for a while now, Darius worried she'd already been warped like Selene had been.

"*There's no use trying to bribe or threaten him,*" the goman confirmed. "*Her only hope is for us to reach an agreement.*"

Based on the pleasure lighting up the goman's face, Darius wasn't going to like the terms.

"Has she touched you?" he asked Lex.

"No," she rasped. But she could have been lying.

He looked back to the goman. "Did you?"

"*No, because we could never come to an agreement if I had.*"

"Let me guess," Darius said, "you want me to exchange myself for her, to warp me into another of your fighting puppets." He glanced at the King's Sword, who seemed to frown at the remark in confusion.

The goman shook her head. "*My terms are far more modest.*"

Darius waited for her to continue, but she instead fixated on the pool again and paused.

"So what are your terms?" he asked, anger growing unwittingly in his tone.

"*Many people think this city was built because of the River Toras and its fertile banks, but I discovered otherwise when delving into its history. Toria was built around this spring, and the River Toras named later. For centuries, this tiny pool provided enough water for hundreds of thousands, never lowering in level, never darkening with silt or impurity. Just limitless sustenance. Aeternus fired and thrown into it can be seen falling forever, never reaching the bottom—if in fact there is one.*"

"And this history lesson is relevant how?" Darius asked.

The goman's gaze snapped up to him. "*Cast your weapons into the pool and rid this world of them forever. Then your woman will be allowed to leave this city freely.*"

The Twin Blades hissed with a scarlet fury of their own volition, unwilling to be lost into a watery death. And then he realised they were the only reason for this parley.

"Because you can't throw them in yourself," Darius said, finally understanding, remembering the sphere of flames that arose when anyone so much as approached them when they had no master present. "You know that even an algus would die if they touched them." He spied the recognition in the goman's stare that told him he was correct and recalled the algus in Chiva that had tried to touch them and been consumed. He'd wondered a few times whether he'd only been able to wield them because of his algor, but it seemed that alone wasn't the reason. Perhaps he was worthy of them after all.

"Don't," Lex said.

She needn't have spoken. He knew she'd rather die than see their cause fail, but at least her urging confirmed her mind hadn't been tampered with.

"And if I do that," Darius said, "then what will happen to me?"

The goman swept her gaze up and down him as if measuring up a farm animal for purchase. "*I know you do not wish to serve me, so I'll be merciful. You'll die painlessly.*"

As troublesome as cogi powers were, at least gomans couldn't lie. Not that it made this decision any more straightforward.

"It was me that killed Archimedes," Lex spat at the goman. "I betrayed that wretch more times than I can remember."

"Lex, stop!" Darius shouted. He wouldn't let her bait the goman into killing her.

"I told the Margalvians of his plan," Lex yelled while her captor just allowed it, "and how his powers worked. It was me that came up with the plan to ambush him, that shot the arrow that blinded him."

Darius rushed forward, held the Twin Blades over the still water, and shouted at her, "Stop, or I'll do as the goman says!"

Lex froze mid-word, slurring what she'd been saying into a scream of fury.

"She lies," Darius continued. "It was the Waif Magician that shot the arrow, it was Brutus that came up with the plan for the ambush, and it was Nikolaos that slit Archimedes's throat."

The last pronouncement had the goman's eyebrows forking. "*Nikolaos killed him?*"

Darius nodded at the half-truth; it was more shameful for Archimedes to have died by that coward than to have taken his own life, as it had actually happened.

"*Then Nikolaos deserved a more painful end than he received. Now, make your choice before I make it for you.*"

The Twin Blades were now a comfortable weight in his hands, and ridding the world of them would also deprive those rakkans that would follow him. These weapons might save their kind from extinction.

And they might also avenge those that had fallen because of this monster before him, especially Selene. Just the thought of this goman with his hands on her brought bile to his throat, and now she had the woman he loved most of all.

"And what if I don't discard these weapons?" Darius asked.

"*Then Jason will finish what began in Chiva.*"

That day had given Darius only a taste of the man's rumoured prowess, one strong enough to sour him from wanting to see if the algus's reputation was earned in full.

What was Darius fighting for anyway, if not Lex's life? Revenge? Was he ready to sacrifice her for that as he'd unwittingly done with Selene?

"Do you swear she'll be allowed to leave the city unharmed," he asked, "without you or anyone else touching her?"

The goman answered, "*I swear it. I cannot lie.*"

Lex writhed, but her captor's arms squeezed and forced her to still. She'd never forgive him for sacrificing himself for her, for leaving her like all the other men she'd ever loved. But she'd have her daughter, and if Rufus won the battle, Toria would fall soon enough, even without him and the Blades.

There was only one other he had to consider—Lyra. He finally allowed himself to share her senses for a moment, and he immediately felt the heat and smoke of battle, heard the confused hollering of orders. Things didn't sound to be going favourably, but she was still in fighting shape, still well enough to share her concern over him.

*If I don't make it, stick with Lex or Gorgias. They'll make sure you're all right.* But he knew she wouldn't. She'd go back to the mountains where she'd been born and live a life free of the troubles and woes of humans, rakkans, and gomans. Perhaps that's where she should have been all along.

Feeling more at peace with his choice, he stepped towards the pool, raised the Twin Blades, and eyed the centre of the spring where the water morphed from crystal blue to unending darkness. The runes spat as if cursing him, and the air behind him moved as the King's Sword walked closer to Lex and her captor, perhaps to get a better view, or perhaps to ensure she didn't interfere.

"Don't you—" Lex's captor clasped a hand over her mouth, but she bit his finger until he yelled and yanked it away. "Don't do it, Darius!"

She twisted and wrenched her body free, slicing her throat against the knife in the process as Darius froze in shock. Her blood spilt down her front, but she carried on regardless, grabbed the wrist of the man's knife-wielding arm while he too gaped, then thrust it back into him, twisting it until the blade ripped a hole in his throat and shred his veins to pieces.

Darius moved to rush over, but Jason was faster and whipped his sword until almost pricking her eye as she stopped and let her first captor fall to the ground, blood gushing.

"*Don't move, Darius,*" the goman commanded.

All Darius cared about was Lex's new wound, but it wasn't deep, and the blood fell from her neck in a trickle in contrast to the man on the ground. He'd already stilled, red spurting and dyeing the once tranquil pool.

At one time, the sight would have had Darius retching, but he'd spilt so much blood in the last few months that the redness only numbed him, reminding him that Lex's could soon spill even heavier.

"*So predictable,*" the goman said with a shake of her head directed at Lex. "*I hardly needed to sculpt this situation to have you react so foolishly. In the hundreds of possible ways this conversation could have gone, you killed that man in almost all of them.*"

Although the words were as monotone as ever, there was something like glee in the goman's words, a fact that had Darius dreading whatever she'd reveal next.

Lex frowned but didn't take her gaze from Jason, whose sword point still threatened her eyeball.

"*It took me a long time to find that man because he was so unremarkable, so pathetic, so weak that he'd never made a name for himself and never would. Such weakness must run in family lines because you're no less pitiful now.*"

Lex's head turned towards the goman, no longer concerned with Jason's weapon as the algus moved and placed himself between her and his ruler.

But Darius's focus went to the pallid, dead man, those blue eyes staring lifelessly at the ceiling as a cold tinge took over his lips. The goman couldn't be saying what he thought she was.

"*My husband had no idea who your son was when he took him, just like he had no idea of your treachery. Long have I waited to punish you, and what more terrible curse to put on a mother than for her to kill her own son.*"

Darius knew those blue eyes looked familiar.

"Liar!" Lex shrieked.

"*I am goman. I cannot lie.*"

Lex screamed at the woman, a sound so shrill it stole Darius's breath as he saw the words register with her, realisation dawn, and her howl become like those of all the other grieving mothers Darius had been unfortunate enough to hear over the last few years. All those years of mourning, of not knowing. The pain that had made her pray for death. It was all back, an old wound open again as if it had never healed.

Her scream was unending, painful to the ears and echoing from the walls like a chorus of sorrow.

Ignoring Jason hovering over her with his sword, she turned and crawled quickly towards the man she'd just stricken, took his lifeless head in her hands as her wails continued and filled the room more until it sounded like a hundred mourning women.

Darius rushed over, keeping the Twin Blades ready should Jason move. But he didn't. Darius reached Lex and the dead man as she pulled the body into a tight hug, smearing herself with blood but with enough tears falling to rinse her face clean.

What could he do? He froze there, wanting to comfort her, wanting to ease the pain but not knowing how.

Perhaps there was no "how."

Lex clenched her jaw so hard her face shook as her scream stole her voice to leave nothing but groans and growls. Algor lit her eyes and froze the tears, but there was more than just pain there, more than just guilt, more than despair. There was fury.

"*I did nothing to provoke that,*" the goman bragged, "*and if you don't do as I asked, there will be worse to come.*"

Clearly, that meant worse for Darius, because Lex looked ready to leap into hell if it spared her this pain. Tears stung his own eyes, and suddenly he cared nothing for the choices before him or the consequences of how he reacted now; emotion overcame him, and natural urges became immune to reason, control or logic.

He moved to stand up, but Lex touched his arm weakly, caught him with the most pleading eyes she'd ever borne.

"If you love me," she began, "you'll—"

"*Do as I say!*" the goman's voice thundered over Lex's, and again when she tried to repeat the words.

He held a hand up, knowing what Lex wanted to say without needing to hear it. Standing, he gripped the Twin Blades tighter, felt their power, felt the veins of his arms bulge as if fire now ran through them.

"What you did to Selene," Darius growled at the goman, a red haze beginning to taint his vision, "I can never forgive. What you and your husband did to me, I can never forgive. And what you've done to the woman I love…" He glanced down at Lex, the rose in his vision brightening into flames. "We will never forgive."

The goman took a step back, eyes narrowed.

"You left only Jason here to face me," Darius continued, "which must mean I'd kill any others that faced me with him. And before, when I asked what would happen if I didn't toss the Twin Blades into this pool, you didn't say 'Jason will kill you,' did you?"

The goman slowly slid her sleeves up, revealing bare hands and arms that could steal his mind at a touch. "*Your presumptions are mistaken.*"

"Then tell me I'll die," Darius said. "Tell me Jason will run his sword through me. If it's true, you can say it."

But the goman only turned away from him. "*Your odds against Jason are almost nil.*"

"Almost," Darius repeated. He began walking at the edge of the bloodstained pool, away from Lex and Jason, readying his weapons as the runes lit and prepared for what could be their final furore.

"Then I refuse," he said. "Jason, let's settle this. Let's see if fate favours—"

The King's Sword leapt before he'd finished the sentence, weapon flaring blue and screaming in.

# 58

## Rufus – Arid Gorge

"Higher!" Rufus roared as he clambered onto a ledge of the cliff face where Lyra sat nervously waiting. If only all men were as good a climber as her… Hours of battle and scaling the cliff now caught up with him and his ill-trained muscles, and his men must have fared no better, especially those on the front line. Below, the trenches had been lost under a sea of Torian bodies, and the brave Laltosians held their spears and pikes in a tight formation behind the final trench while the overwhelming swifts darted in and out, tossing javelins into the mass.

The Black Legion still somehow held the east side, but the assault they faced there was weakest. Now, most rakkans had been forced from the front line by the Staff of Arria, slaughtered as they stumbled to the ground under the weight of their own armour or were trampled under the hooves of swifts. Only the Branz Legion remained, following Rufus's instructions to mix with the humans and spread out to somewhat negate the Staff's effectiveness. Meanwhile, what was left of the Viridian and Azure Legions were clambering up the cliff face, finding whatever perch they could, and beginning to force some space to spin their slings.

"How long do you think the Branzians will last?" Pollio asked, clinging on beside him.

"I'm surprised they haven't already been routed." Even Warlord Flavius had remained on the front line for hours, the horns of his helmet visible when he flared ferven in an aggressive display.

The smoke still swirled up high and itched Rufus's throat, but it wasn't too thick to spot the difference between friend and foe below. A small opening had appeared again between the Torians and Rufus's human troops, the perfect time for another daring rush.

"Sound the human horn," Rufus called to one of his men on a ledge below.

The man obliged, and soon a small mounted unit with a couple of his Subdued answered the call and began racing into the enemy's ranks. Because the mounted unit was wearing the colours of Alogos—looted from the city they just occupied—the enemy paid them little heed until one of the Subdued suddenly burst with a bright blue light, his whole body and horse overcome with the flare of algor.

"There's the target," Rufus shouted.

"Loose!" Pollio roared in a cry so loud it would have carried to Toria.

Even those far away unleashed the fiery barrage towards their target, the blue that marked where the Torians had the Staff of Arria. Thousands of molten stones rained down on the area, too far away to hear the clang of rock on metal when they hit, but the figures dropped one after another in a huge circle of destruction, including their own men. But such sacrifices were necessary in war.

Too soon, though, the flaring blue man faded into the smoke, dead but victorious. If the slingers had managed to hit the one holding the Staff, it would give Rufus a few precious minutes of reprieve.

But the hail of stones weakened.

"Keep it up!" Rufus said. "Don't take your eyes from the area. Make them pay to reclaim that fiendish weapon."

The Viridians around roared in fury, remembering the devastation and starvation that blackened staff had caused them and their families, the living off meagre scraps, the cannibalism. Today was the day for revenge.

The molten hail resumed, and with the height they had, some even reached deep into the enemy ranks, forcing the swifts of Alogos to ever farther distances to regroup and prepare for another attack.

Somehow, Rufus had salvaged some semblance of a chance for his army. Now spread out and with the high ground, the Staff's effectiveness was muted. If they could hold on long enough…

But the cliff was so sheer not many had a ledge to sit on and instead clung with their hands or feet dug into the stone. How long would they last? Once the troops below had been whittled away, the enemy would retreat and wait until the rakkans' strength waned and they fell or descended. Either way, Rufus's men would be so weak it would be like tossing lame fawns into a pool of sharks.

He glanced up to the top of the cliff, still quite a climb away but their only chance of retreat should it come to that. But then what? The swifts of Alogos would close in eventually.

Where was Darius? They needed the Twin Blades to take on the Staff and perhaps destroy it once and for all.

Rufus turned to Lyra, stared her in the eye. "Darius, we need you!" But the panther's dip of her head told him that the Overlord wasn't paying her heed, and if Darius had made it to Toria, it wasn't like he could get back in time anyway.

A flash of blue below stole Rufus's attention as another Subdued marked the Staff's new position, but this time it wasn't deep within the enemy's ranks—it was within a small group hundreds of yards behind, too far away to protect the Torian army.

"Now's our chance." Rufus watched the flaring man get even farther away as the Torians pulled back the Staff for safety. "Send the Branz Legion forward."

One of his men blared the Branzian horn, and at the first sound, the legionnaires behind the trench burst forward.

The slingers above sent a wave of support deep into the Torian army while the Branz Legionnaires leapt and crashed into Toria's front ranks. Red washed across the battlefield as Rufus watched the rakkans gain yard after yard and cut through the humans.

But then the blue flare halted, died, and once more, the Staff was shrouded in darkness.

"Call them back," Rufus said. Waves of attack were all they could afford at the moment.

The horn sounded. Many obeyed the command to retreat, but there was one who didn't—the Branz Warlord himself. With their swords and shields coated in ferven, he and the closest men continued to push; they drove away the humans around them and left an empty crater.

If they didn't fall back soon, Rufus knew the cavalry would enter and tear them apart.

But before any swifts moved, the ferven lighting the area suddenly extinguished, the men's press forward halted, and once again the haze showed Rufus only shadows of a slaughter within.

Warlord Flavius was as good as dead, but most of his men had followed instructions and returned to mix with the humans again, behind the safety of their last trench.

"Aim where the Branz Warlord was last seen!" Rufus roared.

His slingers obeyed, but with a few moments' delay that meant the Staff could have been carried to anywhere by now.

He opened his mouth to order another foray of a Subdued, but something above stopped him. Air shifted rapidly down towards his head, but it was too thin and piercing to be another rakkan that had lost their footing.

As he looked up, something small flew past his vision and cracked a man below on the top of his helmet. When it bounced, Rufus spied it was a stone larger than his head, and ordinarily, a rakkan could have withstood the blow on his armour, but the legionnaire jerked forward, lost his handhold and plummeted to the hard ground below.

Such accidents had happened when those above disturbed the rock face, but the first stone was soon followed by more than could be sensibly blamed on misfortune.

Rufus leaned out and strained to see anything above, then narrowly missed a stone soaring past his face. Above, the lip of the cliff blocked anything atop from view, but more and more stones continued to hurtle down as if materialising from the haze.

"They're above us." Rufus pulled himself close to the cliff face. If the King had a goman, it wasn't a stretch to have foreseen how this battle would play out. Did that mean the goman was down there in the army?

"The swifts." Pollio pointed towards the Black Legion. In the gorge, the swifts of Alogos had once again swept around to their eastern flank and began riding by the shield wall, hurling javelins and bolting away before much retaliation could be dealt out. But it was a smaller group that caught Rufus's eye, slower-moving and with a diamond formation, building up speed and heading straight for the Black Legion's front line.

"The Staff…" Rufus muttered, mind whirring over a possible counter to what he suspected the humans were planning. But no options came to mind.

Sure enough, when the group neared, the legionnaires closest suddenly shifted as if falling prone, and the group of swifts galloped, leapt over the east trench, and then crashed into the rakkans.

"Focus on that group!" Rufus yelled to his slingers. With any luck, they'd leave the Staff stranded amongst the Black Legion and be able to cut it off from the Torians. The fired stones began raining and would kill many of the Black Legionnaires close by too, but they were as good as dead already if he did nothing.

Meanwhile, stones from above continued to plague those on the mountainside and needed addressing.

"Gather the fastest climbers you have," he said to Pollio. "Move east, then summit." He could only hope they'd have the numbers to defeat whoever was above.

# 59

## Darius – Toria

Darius crossed the Twin Blades and took the full force of Jason's first strike, wincing as sparks from the blow prickled his face. He thrust forward, using his rakkan strength to knock the algus off-balance, but Jason had already moved back a pace, his body safely an inch from the points of Darius's swords as he reached the end of his lunge.

Darius quickly pulled back and got his weight more securely over his feet while the King's Sword waited in silence.

"*I told you to be swift,*" the goman boomed.

But Jason ignored her.

Whatever Darius tried, he knew the algus would be ready to counter. It seemed like the man wanted him to be the attacker or perhaps *needed* him to be, to counter and remain safe from his rakkan strength.

"The more we clash," Darius said, "the better my odds become. I only need you to make one mistake." He only had to land a glancing blow once, then he could get close. As soon as Darius got a grip of the man, it would be over.

The algus gave no reaction to the words, standing still with coiled energy and without so much as a tremor.

"I have no issue with you," Darius said. "Leave and let me kill your master."

He had no hopes the proposition would sway the algus, yet the frustration in the goman's eyes made him think it was worth a try.

But he wouldn't rely on convincing a mindless algus. The only way to defeat this man was Lex's powder, but with two swords in his hands, how could he take it from his pocket without being too obvious?

"*Attack him!*"

Before he could decide, the King's Sword became a blur, and the air shifted. Darius lifted a blade to parry where he felt the strike coming, but Jason moved his weapon at the last moment, lifting it up over Darius's guard and towards his face.

Darius dropped to one knee, let the sword cut through his lagging hair while reaching out for the algus's leg. It was right there, only inches from his fingers. Victory. Revenge.

But Jason leapt with a second to spare, leaving Darius grasping empty air and now fretting over his exposed back. So, he rolled forward, splashing into the pool with the ferven on his weapons exploding with a hiss and burst of steam. Water bubbled as he continued the roll through the shallow edge of the pool and regained his footing beside Lex.

Bubbles popped on the surface for a few moments before it stilled, leaving a thin film in the air that soon faded.

Again, Jason had stopped and watched. The goman had also moved during the flurry, now standing safely behind her servant.

"Coward," Darius spat at the woman. "Face me without your puppet."

She cocked her head in mockery. *"Do you really think taunts will cause someone of my intellect to do something foolish?"*

He couldn't help but be pleased the woman admitted he'd outmatch her. Hell, if Lex hadn't been in the room, he'd have summoned the full ire of Trogus, called upon the Blades' mountains of flames to flood and consume the entire room—including all flesh, bone, and metal within. But her algor wouldn't protect her, and the guards he'd heard outside would stop her from leaving.

Well, if she couldn't leave, then perhaps she could help him.

He turned his body until facing his enemies side on, the pocket containing the pouch of flash powder now blind to them.

"Your husband fell for taunts," Darius said, unsure where to go with the lie but needing nothing more than a distraction. He gave Lex a gentle nudge with his toe. "When I faced him, I didn't have the powers I do now, but I still managed to press my thumbs into his eyes."

The goman's glare spat venom as Darius brought the serrated edge of his sword to rest against his pocket, catching Lex looking at him out of the corner of his eye. He dampened the fire on the sword until it was just cold kuraminium again.

"*It won't be you that I punish for that,*" the goman said, "*but those you love.*"

She'd already done that and more.

"Eyes are horrible, slimy things." Darius grimaced. "It took weeks before the sensation of his blood left my hands. The filth ruined a nice pair of boots too."

The goman clenched her fists, looking ready to charge at him with the same foolishness she'd just ridiculed.

And as she glowered, Darius subtly ran his sword across his pocket, cutting the fabric and feeling the pouch brush his trouser as it fell behind his leg out of sight.

Lex made no movement until he spun to face his enemies again and sent tongues of ferven whirling down the Twin Blades, getting an idea from when he'd rolled before.

He stepped forward, one foot sinking into the pool, and flared ferven into it. The water roiled and bubbled within moments, sending plumes of steam up and around him that soon had his face dripping, but the haze hindered his enemies' sight, and that might give him an edge.

Still, Jason waited, sword bright and ready. He likely wanted Darius away from the water.

"*Stop hesitating.*" There was fear as well as anger now on the goman's face, constantly flitting to the door.

But Jason didn't acknowledge her, his mind no doubt running through the millions of possible futures in which Darius would overcome him if Jason were not patient.

Whatever the goman's reason for wishing to rush her servant, Darius could guess it was in his interests to drag this fight out and make the man work for a kill. If he foresaw all of Darius's attacks, he'd have a counter ready, but if *he* was the one to attack, he'd have to contend with Darius's reflexes, use feints, and avoid the power in those muscles.

While he hesitated, he felt Lex move behind him followed by something heading through the air towards the back of his weapon.

She'd thrown the pouch towards the ferven whirling about him.

Jason moved.

But Darius closed his eyes, grabbed the top of his hood, and yanked it down just as a flash of white pierced his eyelids. He squeezed them shut tighter for a heartbeat while the light grew to ever-increasing intensity; then as it dimmed, he opened them to take in the fresh white haze now blighting his vision.

He saw enough to see the hood of the King's Sword was down too. So Darius rushed forward, water and steam hissing and spitting as he leapt from the pool and thrust both swords towards his foe.

Jason flicked up his hood just in time, ducked, and rolled to avoid two strikes that would have broken his arms if he'd tried to parry. On the ground, his sword swung out and scored a cut on Darius's ankle, scratching bone and forcing Darius back a couple of steps with more blood spraying into the pool.

Perhaps the injury should have hurt, but it didn't. Rage still coloured his vision red, and all that mattered was killing these two. Just because the powder hadn't worked didn't mean he'd give up.

Although Darius hadn't paid much heed to the goman, she'd clearly shielded her eyes too and was now glaring at her servant as if Darius weren't there. "*Hurry and end him!*"

Darius moved first, ignoring the weakness when planting weight on his injured ankle, and unleashed a flurry of strikes that would have killed half a dozen ordinary algus.

But Jason danced much like his sister once had and avoided each slice of the Blades by the narrowest margins.

Darius kicked to his front in anger, but again the man skipped back and avoided it. He spat a curse, his cut ankle now definitely paining him. Perhaps he needed a new tactic. Perhaps going for the goman would be better.

He backed up, took a steel dagger from his waist, and tossed it to Lex. "Can you take the goman?"

No answer came, and he didn't dare take his gaze from the King's Sword to see her reaction. Whatever she did was up to her.

But as Darius watched the goman, the King's Sword began moving between them, away from his mistress and up to the pool's edge. Then a blue film surfaced on his feet as he stepped onto the water, freezing it in an instant and supporting his weight until he stood in the middle of an ice sheet.

Darius frowned. Clearly, the algus had no fear of him going after the goman; perhaps he was even baiting him into doing it. But why stand on ice? Darius could break or melt it with ease, as could Jason. Was that the point? Did he think if forced to swim, Darius could be made to discard at least one of the Blades into the watery depths?

With a grunt of annoyance, Darius turned back to the goman. "I wish you had a mouth, just so I could hear you scream when these swords impale you."

The goman's only reaction was a slight flex of her bare fingers, still not touching a weapon. He'd only seen goman magic a couple of times but knew those fingers were more deadly than a scorpion's sting or any sword in the Empire. One touch and he'd be warped, made to kill Lex, and then who knew what. It would be a better fate for rakkankind if the Twin Blades were lost here.

But his hatred burned until the fire of the swords spread to his arms, coated his barrel chest and shoulders and lit his enemy's eyes with reflected fire.

He rushed forward with an algus speed the goman wouldn't be able to track or match and tossed one sword to her right, spearing it into the ground to cut off her escape path while he swung the other from her left, straight at the midsection where she'd find it hardest to dodge.

A clash of metal rang from behind, distracting him for a fraction as the goman leapt backwards and out of the fiery path of his sword.

She hit the wall, one leg behind her, then sprang back forward as Darius's angry swing rocked him off balance and left his body exposed. Hands outstretched, fingers tense and eager to meet skin, she soared towards his face as he ducked, tucked his chin, and flared ferven across his whole body more out of reflex than a coherent plan. It was enough to have her rip her arm back, twist her body, and only catch a glancing touch of his shoulder that set her clothes ablaze.

Whatever happened next, he didn't see because his back was turned to her until he finally steadied himself, regathered the blade he'd tossed, then looked back again.

Lex was collapsed against the far wall, clutching a bleeding arm and without the dagger anymore, while the goman rose from the pool, drenched and very much not on fire.

What a pity. He should have just charged her like a bull on fire in the first instance.

But now, Jason stood in front of her as if aware of the shift in Darius's thoughts. Gomans were such a pain.

The reek of ash filled his nostrils as his charred tunic fell away and left the soft remains of mail still clinging to his torso.

"*Quickly!*" the goman said.

Jason moved before she'd finished the word and darted in. Darius could only block the path of the man's first swing at his head, but Jason retracted his weapon and spun low and under Darius's counter. He scored another cut across Darius's shins.

Without time to step back, Jason continued spinning and brought his long sword around and into a stab aimed at Darius's heart.

Darius shifted back as quickly as he could, took the strength from the blow, and flared algor across his chest. That gave the metal just enough strength as the point of Jason's sword struck and dug into the rings of his mail. The weapon breached the metal, pierced his skin and muscle, but his armour did enough to save his heart until he brought one of the Twin Blades up and smashed the sword away.

As the point ripped free, it took rings, flesh and blood with it, and forced Darius back a step. Rage may have dampened the pain of his legs and chest, but it did nothing for the dread building inside. This man was as fearsome as his reputation suggested.

Before Darius could recover, Jason rushed forward with another flurry he struggled to parry, deflecting the last swipe only far enough to cut his shoulder and force him back yet more steps.

His injured ankle shook as he shifted weight onto, then quickly off it, and the shoulder wound stung as the weight of the blade in his hand tugged against it.

"Don't give in." Lex struggled back to her feet, wincing in pain while glowering at their enemies. "You can beat them."

But she didn't convince him, only showed her willingness to sacrifice anything for revenge.

The goman had said Darius had poor odds, and now they must have been even worse. But he'd never give in. There were thousands of corpses that deserved justice.

Biting down against the pain of his injuries, he rushed forward again.

Jason dodged every swing of the Twin Blades and slashed low again, cutting Darius's other ankle and making it painful just to stand. But Darius kept pressing forward, trying to back the man and goman into a corner of the room where they couldn't dodge, where his rakkan strength would see their bones shatter under the force of his blows.

But the King's Sword ducked and rolled under one of his swings at the same moment the goman darted the other way. Darius started after the goman, flaring ferven across his arms, chest, bared teeth, and rushed to give the fiend a fiery death.

She had no answer for his pace as she raced to the far side of the room, trapped, no escape.

But as his weapon's point reached the goman's skin, a sharp edge hacked into the back of his legs. Despite every urge to continue after the fleeing goman, his sprint faltered, and he crashed face-first into the ground.

"Stop!" someone called, but Darius was too stunned to listen, warmth spilling down the back of his thighs and soaking into his clothes. It couldn't end like this, could it?

His heart pounded in his throat as he used his arms to crawl, to flee the one he knew hovered over his back and readied the killing blow.

The goman sprinted away to the side and left only stone in Darius's view, darkened by the shadow of the one soon to be his slayer. After him, they'd finish Lex, and any hope of justice would die with them. The thought enraged him so much his pain barely registered.

But he couldn't abandon justice. If this was to be his end, he should take them all with him.

Without time to question the urge, he lay and squeezed the Twin Blades' hilts and called upon the ire of Trogus to consume this room, this palace, and the one that had brought such death to the Empire. Perhaps it was fitting they would all die here. They all had blood on their hands. They were all guilty.

"Stop!" the voice repeated, but Darius continued his urge, vision now red as an inferno grew around him like a swelling ball. He braced for the inevitable sword through his back or through his neck, but still, it didn't come.

"Darius, stop!" This time the voice was Lex's. Was she that afraid of death?

No. Fear was unlike her.

No sword bit his back, and the flames around him dampened as he relaxed his grip, calmed his fury enough to bring the room back into focus. He pushed himself off the ground, legs too wounded and weak to be of use, but managed to turn and see the King's Sword standing over him with that long sword glinting with the remnants of his ferven.

But the man wasn't facing him; instead, he fixated on the doors where the Chief Priest now stood, robes soaked in blood, one arm held in the air with the sleeve pulled back to reveal the scars on his arm.

Lex gaped at the man as if he'd sprouted wings, and the goman looked furious, like the man was making obscene gestures towards her.

But the Chief Priest was only focused on the King's Sword, apparently freezing the algus in place.

Was this Darius's chance? To run a sword through the algus's back?

"Don't harm him." Aran walked towards them and gave Darius a telling look that meant the words were directed at him.

"*Kill him!*" The goman stooped to pick up Darius's dagger as her voice boomed, then she tossed it at the Chief Priest.

Without looking, Aran shifted his head to the side and dodged the knife like a rakkan would have. Who was this man?

Then Darius spotted something, a scar on his arm unlike the other scratches and claw marks from escorts. One was a flat, smooth shape that formed half a skull, a mark Darius had only ever seen on one person before—the Waif Magician.

# 60

## Rufus – Arid Gorge

Rakkans and stones continued plummeting from atop the cliff Rufus clung to the side of, sheltered beneath one of the few overhanging shards of rock this high up.

"It's hopeless," Pollio said, clambering back down. "There are too many algus at the top; our men are just climbing to be slaughtered even faster."

That's what Rufus had suspected when the rakkan bodies began falling, but he'd needed someone he trusted to verify it.

"Call off the attack," Rufus said. "If the Torians want to fight, they can climb down. Otherwise, we'll use whatever shields we have and weather the barrage, then send our reply with twice the malice."

Many rakkans had tossed their scutum before climbing because such a large, unwieldy weight only slowed them down when fleeing the Staff of Arria. Now, those few that had struggled up with them might be saved from a rock snapping their neck.

Pollio and the centurions sent the orders out, and soon every rakkan there was either slinging or lobbing stones far towards the enemy while Rufus sat with Lyra and simply surveyed the field.

Below, there had been a lull for a few minutes while the swifts of Alogos re-formed out of range, and the seemingly endless Torian army stood in formation, ready for something.

Rufus's front line had thinned until no deeper than the trench at their front, now filled with blood and bodies of humans, rakkans, and horses. The Black Legion had retreated until their flank was pressed into the cliff with their backs not far from the Branzians still supporting the eastern front.

Many Subdued had sacrificed their lives to give Rufus's slingers a target for the Staff, but now, there were too few to spare.

Try as he might, Rufus struggled to see a path to victory. If they tried to retreat to Alogos, the swifts with the Staff would tear them apart in the open. If the rakkans launched an attack of their own, there would be no trenches to slow the cavalry and no slinger support. That damned Staff was a variable Rufus hadn't even thought to account for before the battle. And it would be his undoing.

"We've failed," he said quietly so only Pollio would hear.

"Viridians don't admit defeat," his brother spat.

"Perhaps that's why we never won a war. Getting your men slaughtered in a losing battle just hinders your future battles too."

Pollio glared at him but had no answer. He was smart enough to see what was unfolding beneath them.

"The King has outdone us," Rufus said, "or perhaps his goman has. If Darius and the Blades had been here, we might have had a chance."

"So what?" Pollio said. "Are you going to pass me your horned helmet and dive off this cliff to end it? Defeat yourself before Toria does?"

Rufus felt disgust twist his face. "I may be realistic, but I'm still Viridian. We cannot retreat, so I'll die taking as many of these bastards with me as I can." A coward could have sneaked away, slid along the cliff face alone, and escaped Toria's wrath. But cowards were not worth the air they breathed.

Pollio gave an impressed grin, but it soon died when the Torian masses in the gorge began moving again.

The swifts were first. They wheeled and galloped straight towards the front line in a wedge formation.

"This is it," Rufus said. The Torians had weakened the shield wall enough, destroyed the morale of those defending with no means of escape. "They're going to break through." He needn't even add the words "try to" because the Torians' odds were so short.

Without needing direction, the slingers above saw the threat and began a fiercer barrage that felled many horses in the charge but didn't do enough to halt the dark mass thundering through the gorge.

The pikes of the humans and rakkans in the shield wall shot out as the swifts leapt into the trench, but they dodged the bodies and scaled the other side with enviable agility, and when the charge hit Rufus's front line, the pikes and spears of his warriors didn't slow the enemy.

The Torians at the front had their swifts leap over the rakkans, many landing within those ranks atop a dying horse, but these were algus, soon striking every human and rakkan they could before succumbing to the numbers surrounding them.

The first were quick to fall, but more followed, backed by javelins of the swift riders behind too far to join the melee. With

Torians and rakkans mingled and brawling, the slingers focused on the rear of the charge, which had slowed and begun fanning out to make space for the soldiers behind, the real might of the army.

"Tell the Black Legion to retreat farther," Rufus said to one of his hornmasters, "to get behind the Branzians." Toria hadn't devoted many to attack from the east for a while, and it wouldn't take more than a century to guard it with the palisade to use for cover.

Meanwhile, the swifts had punched a hole through the western front deeper than Rufus had feared. Now soldiers poured in and began getting to the rear of Rufus's troops with far less resistance than he would have expected, even of downtrodden warriors.

"The Staff…" His eyes narrowed as he searched the centre of the gap. "It must be in there."

Pollio stood and roared, "Focus all fire on the breach."

The hail from the cliff face sharpened and sent a thousand balls of fire to the area in only a few heartbeats, tossing up dirt and stone and blood of not just Torians but many of Rufus's warriors too.

It was no use. Even if the Black Legion could have held their line against such numbers, with the Staff there, there was no hope. At this rate, his troops would be surrounded and slaughtered within minutes.

As difficult as it was to admit, the battle was lost, and survival was all Rufus could hope for.

"Order a full retreat," Rufus said with shame.

The Viridian horn of retreat blared thrice, a shrill, foul sound that marred any warlord that commanded its use as a failure, a disgrace.

Warriors began falling back, and even the Black Legion obeyed and began climbing the cliff face, tossing gladii and scuta to hasten their retreat.

The sight must have been a wonder to the Torians, thousands of rakkans clambering up the gorge with nowhere to go and no weapons to protect them. The rocky cliff gave the slingers effectively unlimited ammunition, but what was the use? Once all his troops on the ground were dead, the Torians could wait them out at a distance. It would only be a day or two before their water ran out and the deaths began. Even if his rakkans had carried their picks and shovels up on the climb—which most hadn't—they wouldn't be able to tunnel to anywhere safe.

The Torians continued their push as every human and rakkan under Rufus's command broke. It was like watching a sheet of glass shatter—formations split, men and women routed and fighting for a path to the cliff. And now the swifts would come.

Sure enough, the cavalry sprang into a gallop through the dispersed warriors, spearing backs and hacking heads from their bodies without so much as a shout of resistance.

By the time the horses reached the cliff, only a few of Rufus's men on the ground remained alive, soon chopped down. Only half had managed to climb to a safe height. And there at the bottom, within a group of mounted algus staring up at the wriggling bodies on the sheer rock, the Staff of Arria was held mockingly up.

Many slingers leaned out and tried to slay the algus brandishing it, but the angle was too tight. Most just hit the heads of their comrades and sent them to their deaths.

Rufus was tempted to tell them to cease, but what use was it? His warriors would die anyway.

Every stone that did come within reach of the Staff extinguished before it hit, snuffed out by the weapon's power. Then, the algus wielding it shifted it to his back and dismounted, approached the face of the cliff, and disappeared underneath the lip on which Rufus stood.

He cursed. "Tell the legions to shed their armour."

Pollio's face fell as he realised Rufus's trail of thought, then he passed on the command.

All that Torian algus would need to do was get near a rakkan with the Staff, and their strength would fail, their weight sending them to their deaths. Only Hera's algus and his remaining Subdued could save them now. And they'd need the help of Aran's gods.

# 61

## Darius – Toria

Darius slid until he could prop his back against the side of the room, then he grabbed the back of his legs to stem the bleeding. The lacerations were deep and damned painful, but they weren't enough to end him.

Meanwhile, the Chief Priest stopped in front of the King's Sword, just out of touching distance. Behind him, Sulla limped into the room, gladius unsheathed and bloody, then headed straight towards Darius while watching the goman.

Jason's head twitched, his eyes opening and shutting as if a headache had just overcome him.

Could it be a mind block?

But Darius could barely focus on that man when Aran displayed that scar. What did it mean? He was good at disguises but not good enough to have been the Waif Magician. Plus, Darius had seen her die.

Only one thing made sense: a thought that sent a cold shiver through him. Aran was one of the three half-goman siblings: a sister and two reportedly dead brothers.

*That* was how Aran was always so wise, prophesied of disaster to come, and directed Darius to wherever he needed to be. And those reflexes when they'd come to the palace… Even Darius would have struggled to dodge those sudden traps, but the man's movements had been like those of the King's Sword, having seen what he needed to do beforehand.

One thing the Chief Priest had said now came back to mind too, that he'd had a brother and sister, that his brother had killed his sister, and that she too had possessed the same powers as Aran.

It had been a long time since Darius had met the woman, but he recalled her owl companion. He never had got an answer on how she had an escort, but now it made sense. She'd bonded it herself, probably had many more like Aran, and that's how she, like him, had evaded the King all her life.

How could Darius have been so blind, so trusting? This man had been around him for months and could have done anything to his mind. Darius couldn't recall a time when the man had touched him, but perhaps that memory had been stolen from him. Could he even trust his own thoughts now?

"Jason…" the Chief Priest whispered, bare arm shaking. "The King has been keeping the truth from you."

The algus glanced down at his own arm and touched the sleeve covering it.

"We bear the same mark," Aran continued, "because we are kin."

Jason's head snapped back at the words, pain screwing up his features.

"I'm sorry it's taken me so long," Aran said. "Had I known you were here sooner, I would have come. I saved you from death once before—after Shirin escaped and the executioners had us—and I'm here to save you again, brother." Then Aran moved forward, grabbed the man's arm, and pressed Jason's hand to his cheek. "See for yourself."

Jason's eyes snapped open, and the tension in his expression eased in an instant.

Taking advantage of the distraction, Darius tried to stand, but his legs trembled violently under even the slightest force, and he slumped back down as Sulla reached him with a grim frown at the pool of blood underneath him.

"The door," Darius whispered with a shake of his head. Sulla had to make sure the goman didn't escape, and he was the only one there that could touch her without fear of her cogi.

Behind the Chief Priest, the woman glared and moved forward so subtly it was as if she glided. Darius pulled back one of the Blades to toss it, but Aran spun before the goman reached him, keeping Jason's hand in contact with his head while he ripped a sword from within his robes and held it out.

The goman halted, eyes narrowed below a new sheen of sweat dripping from her brow.

"You've enslaved him for too long," Aran said, his voice deep and angry. "You made him kill Shirin."

"*Don't act so righteous, you fraud.*" The goman stepped forward until Aran's sword almost pricked her nose. "*If I'd known about you sooner, Jason would have ended you too.*"

Sulla moved as instructed, planting his body between the doorway and the goman before speaking. "Should I make it quick or painful?"

Darius knew the rakkan well enough to know the question was merely a taunt. *Quick* wasn't an option.

"Blind her," Darius spat.

Sulla's mouth curled into a grin before he pounced.

The goman moved quickly but could only dodge deeper into the room as Sulla stretched out his arms and charged.

"*Jason! Save me!*" the goman boomed as she backed up. Without the algus speed of someone like Jason, Sulla would sense her every movement enough to cut her off.

The King's Sword didn't even give her a glance, fixated on the Chief Priest with a hollowness to his eyes.

The goman reached the corner of the room. She slammed her back into the wall, head arching back and fearful as Sulla closed in and got a fistful of her dark hair.

The screech that ran through Darius's mind felt as if it were splitting his head open, but he didn't even blink to miss Sulla digging his thumbs into her eyes with a roar of triumph. Her pain was nothing compared to what she'd inflicted on those he loved. This was for Lex and Selene.

Snarling, Sulla released her and let the pathetic woman fall to the ground, her screech now softening into a haunting whimper.

Without the Staff of Arria, gomans were nothing, just pitiful creatures without the strength or speed to match a rakkan in combat. No wonder they hated the people of the night.

At the other side of the pool, Jason gasped and pulled his hand away from the Chief Priest. "Aran?" There was something different about the man's face now, a warmth as if no longer carved from stone.

"Brother." Aran smiled. "Do you see it now?"

The King's Sword nodded, then held out his hands and stared at them. "Shirin…"

Darius remembered when his mind blocks had been broken by Brutus, when he'd learned the rakkans were his allies along with his true identity. It was almost enough to pity the man that had slaughtered so many rakkans and humans in his time, Aran's brother.

*Brother…* What a liar the Chief Priest was.

Darius dropped one of the Blades, flared ferven on his fingertips, and dug them into the wall, then hauled himself to his feet and just about stood while holding still.

"What the hell is this?" he growled.

The two men turned to him, Jason's stare becoming murderous.

"He's not our enemy," Aran said to Jason.

The words seemed to hold the algus still for the moment.

"All this time," Darius said, "you've been lying to me. You said your brother was dead." He would have threatened the man hadn't he been so injured and known the brothers probably outmatched him.

"I'm sorry." The Chief Priest lowered his head. "My brother and I were separated when still young, and I long feared he *was* dead…but I've known the truth for a while."

"And what?" Darius said. "You thought I'd turn you away because you're a hybrid?"

"Of course not. It's not about you. I went to great lengths to hide the fact of our survival, and I intended to go to my grave keeping this secret. I may have hidden who I was, but I've never lied about what I can do or what I believe in. Like you, I was never accepted in this world when people knew what I was, hated and condemned with no option but to hide away like a deformed creature. But after they came for us and destroyed my life, the Goddess appeared to me and said I didn't deserve such a life, that I didn't have to become as twisted and bitter as my sister. So, I hid in the open and used the powers the Goddess has gifted me to try to help the people of this world."

The goman scoffed and lifted her head, bloody tears spilling from her mauled sockets. "*Goddess? Do not denigrate the One Mind by reducing it to such feeble terms. The One Mind is far beyond any god or algus.*"

Darius frowned. The One Mind? It sounded like some kind of deity to this broken woman and reminded him of Dianoia, Goddess of Mind.

Suddenly the source of Aran's teachings became plain, teachings symbolised by the figures hanging from Darius's neck, ones he'd struggled with but done his best to embrace.

A red tinge came to his vision as he realised and focused on the Chief Priest. "Your religion…is goman?"

Aran nodded, and there was regret in it.

As there should have been. All those ideas, all those questions, the solace Darius had tried to take in these beings… They were goman? The fact repulsed him, like the belief of his worst enemies was now his.

He looked at Lex, who was kneeling over her son once again with a horrified look at the Chief Priest that told Darius she was thinking the same things he was.

"The One Mind revealed her husband to me," the Chief Priest insisted, "and in worshipping both, the Order is not goman. I believe in everything I have taught, not that it matters now. Once word spreads about my identity, the Diagathic Order will crumble. All that work is wasted."

The sadness in the man's voice made Darius feel wrong for wanting to punch him.

"Why didn't you just tell me?" Darius asked. "Did you really think I'd reveal your secret or treat you—"

"You wouldn't put a sword in my hand?" Aran shot back. "You wouldn't have me leading your armies into bloody slaughters?"

Darius couldn't deny that would have been his initial inclination.

"I've always known the Diagathic Order would end if I revealed myself," Aran said. "Even humans would never trust a half-goman to lay his hands on them, to bond them to creatures, or even believe the words from my mouth once they knew who my sister was."

"So, you deceived us." Lex's voice was bitter and uneven.

"I did, and I will accept the punishment you mete."

"What punishment?" Darius asked. He hadn't even contemplated it.

"There are a few possibilities in my future, some more bearable than others." The man swallowed.

But Darius couldn't think of punishing him at the moment. Jason stood lost in thoughts that seemed to be rending his mind in two, and the goman still breathed, waiting for her end while her army battled Rufus.

After blocking out Lyra's senses for too long, Darius finally opened his mind to her, suddenly feeling the great height she was perched at. Below her, a sea of bodies waited, and the lack of battling made it clear they were all Torians. The mood of all those around Lyra was so dire it was almost contagious, the panther sharing in the despair. Rufus was on the cusp of defeat, a loss that would see every rakkan legion slaughtered.

And Darius became even more numb.

Using the wall for support, he limped towards the goman, grateful Jason had slashed one leg shallower than the other and left it strong enough to prop up his weight.

"Tell your armies to retreat," Darius said, "and I'll end you quickly."

A thrum of laughter filled Darius's mind in reply.

"*Never.*"

Darius spat a string of curses at the creature. If gomans couldn't lie, that meant there was nothing he could do or say to change her mind. All those rakkans would die if he didn't find some way of ending the battle.

"What about you?" He turned to Jason. "Can you tell Toria's army to retreat?"

The King's Sword eyed him for a moment. "I don't answer to you."

"I don't care whose orders you obey; I'm *asking* you."

But the algus's stubborn answer was plain on his face.

"Can you convince him?" Darius focused on the Chief Priest, desperation leaking into his voice. "Or will you let my people be slaughtered?"

But Aran shook his head. "Jason cannot give those commands, but there is another—whoever has been appearing as the King when in public. It must be a human, and if the people believe he's King, he has the authority."

"Dead," Jason uttered with no trace of care for the implications of his statement.

A thrum of goman laughter filled Darius's mind once again. "*I had that oaf killed long before you arrived.*"

The confirmation felt as if it stole the air from the room, but the Chief Priest didn't look fazed.

"Then we must use the King's Orator," the man said.

Jason's eyes grew fierce at the name. "Did she know?"

The Chief Priest didn't answer right away, as if debating whether to speak at all.

"Answer me," Jason said in as threatening a tone as Darius had ever heard from a man.

Finally, Aran nodded weakly.

"Where is she?" Darius asked. Something told him he needed to get to her before the King's Sword.

"*Don't do it, Jason.*" The goman knelt and held out her arms. "*All we've ever done is to protect our kind. If it wasn't for me, Hadrian would rule the Empire and Goma would be facing insurmountable odds. Now that the sea has calmed, he'd have been building ships and planning the invasion of our homeland. But he's dead.* This *is what we've achieved. I've taken much from you, so take your revenge on me. Don't make the Empire suffer for my deeds.*"

Darius had tired of that voice invading his mind, and it was time to silence it for good. Although it would have been nice to drag her from this palace and parade her in front of his army before killing her, she was too dangerous to be left alive. His only regret was he didn't have the strength to deliver justice himself.

He caught Sulla's eye and said, "Shut her up."

The glint the words triggered in the rakkan's eye was vicious.

"*Don't ally with them, Jason.*" Every word became hurried. "*You mustn't—*"

Sulla's fist hit the goman's temple with a crack, knuckle sinking into her shattered skull as her head jerked to the side and then fell with her body. It smacked into the ground. Finally, the thrum of her voice left Darius's mind in peace, but like with the deaths of all his enemies, it brought no solace or relief from the torment they'd inflicted.

Lex glared at the body with disgust before pressing her eyes shut and cradling her dead son again as if he were all that mattered.

Now that Darius couldn't have children, he realised he'd never feel the pain she was in, never feel that kind of devotion to a child. Perhaps that was a great loss to him, but at this moment, he was glad of the fact.

"Jason," Aran whispered, "there are thousands of lives at stake if we let the battle in the gorge continue. If you can lead us to someone that can end the bloodshed, please do."

The King's Sword remained silent for a few moments, studying everyone in the room with suspicion.

And who could blame him? Although the goman had warped his mind and betrayed him, Darius was still an enemy.

"Read my thoughts again," the Chief Priest said. "See the future I have seen, where the war begun by the tyrants that have used you is finally over and we'll be free of their control at last."

The King's Sword glanced at Darius, clearly suspecting *he* was just another tyrant. And after the recent conquest and horrors, perhaps the title was fitting. But Jason did as the Chief Priest suggested and reached out to touch Aran's head again, eyes clouding over and lost inside himself.

While the two shared thoughts, Sulla returned to Darius, wrapped an arm around him, and gave enough support that he needn't lean on the wall any longer.

"Thanks," Darius said, still watching the brothers. "What do we do if this doesn't work?"

Sulla shrugged. "Search the palace ourselves, I guess."

But Darius knew from Lyra's senses that they hadn't the time.

After the brothers stood tied to each other for so long that Darius became restless, Jason broke away and murmured under his breath. "Ophelia can give the order." There was something different about his tone now, no less anger than before but this time, it didn't feel directed at Darius.

Aran bowed his head in acknowledgement. "Lead the way."

"No. She must see this." Jason tipped his head to the dead goman. "I'll bring her." Without waiting for a response, the algus took off and was through the doorway before Darius could decide whether to trust him going on his own.

"What about the guards?" Darius asked.

"I took care of them," the Chief Priest said with another look of shame.

That explained the blood on his robes. To think he'd been hiding such power until now… Perhaps the man was right and Darius would have put a sword in his hand.

"And do you trust Jason?" Darius asked. "What did you show him?"

"A possible future," the Chief Priest replied. "But much now is uncertain."

"How so? Isn't Jason going to help us? Won't the battle be halted?" Not only were thousands of people facing death, but Lyra was among them, and Darius was in no fighting shape to help now and nowhere near close enough even if he had been.

"This isn't about the battle," Aran said. "Even if your army is saved, what you choose to do next will decide the fate of the Empire."

Darius couldn't figure out what the man was speaking of or why he should listen. Everything he thought he knew about Aran wasn't true, was a veil that had shrouded the real man and the source of his ways.

"How can I trust you now," Darius asked, "when you told me tall tales of gods and goddesses backing me in this war?"

The Chief Priest's face darkened into a glower. "I told you no such thing. I voiced my doubt over that many times. We cannot know for certain the intentions of the God of Justice nor the Goddess of Mi—"

"Don't you mean the 'One Mind'?"

"Call her what you will. Whatever divine patronage you believed supported your carnage is nothing more than a bastardisation of my teachings. Don't you dare lay the blame for that on me."

This was the first time Darius had seen the man so incensed; it was hard to doubt a man's truthfulness when speaking from a place of such raw emotion. But how dare he try to pass the blame.

"You bastardised your own teachings," Darius said, "when you passed off your gifts as if from a goddess. But it's just cogi, isn't it? That's how Archimedes was able to tamper with my bond to Lyra… Tell me it isn't your goman magic that lets you bond humans with animals. Tell me you were truthful about it, and I'll bow down now and call you the new King of Toria."

The Chief Priest's lips pressed into a thin line. "Perhaps it is cogi, but my goman father could never do it, only Shirin. I've never lied about my powers, never claimed anything that they were not. What else are they but a gift from the Goddess? Who are you to deny the one I pray to and that answers me?"

"And why did you not use these powers when it mattered? Why didn't you warn me about the slaves in the Silk City, about Psinara, about Chiva and the great fire?" So much of the destruction could have been avoided.

The Chief Priest's gaze darkened. "*You* started the fire that blighted these lands?" He shook his head. "Of course, that makes sense now. Perhaps I shouldn't have left you, but what choice did I have after Psinara? Mark my words, had I foreseen what I witnessed there before it was too late to prevent, I would have taken up arms to stop it. But alas, my cogi is too weak and does not see far enough, and by the time I saw my future amongst the desecration in Psinara, the Viridian Legion had already committed the act. As for the Silk City…I accept the blame for that. Long before the executions, I knew they were a possibility, but I ignored it, prayed in earnest to Agathos that one of the many other possibilities became reality. But I was clinging to a foolish hope."

Darius cursed and turned away from the man. This conversation was achieving nothing other than making him angrier than he already was when it should have been a moment of triumph; the King was dead, the war could soon be over, and he and Lex could finally be together.

But to look at her now, to look at that same broken face he'd seen after she'd killed Omid, only this time worse… How could he feel anything but rage? Justice hadn't been done, not by a long way.

The figurines hanging from his neck weighed him down now, made him want to discard them and lose all hope in any goodness in this world. But he didn't; some part of him believed in what the Chief Priest said. If this goman hadn't gone to meet the God of Justice, what could he do other than despair that she and many others had died without the punishment they deserved?

The goman had shown no remorse, even taunted him before her death, and something about what she'd said came back to mind, something that had suggested she hadn't seen this as the end of the war.

"What did the goman mean," Darius said, "when she said 'the sea has calmed'?"

Before the Chief Priest could answer, the door opened and in walked the King's Orator with Jason right behind her.

Her peeling face dropped with horror as her eyes latched onto everyone in the room. She tried to turn for the door, but Jason blocked her way and grabbed her arm for good measure.

"What is this?" she shrieked.

Forgetting the Chief Priest for now, Darius turned and faced the woman. "The end of the war."

# 62

## Darius – Toria

Darius took a few steps towards the King's Orator with the help of Sulla and said, "I suggest you cooperate."

Her eyes searched the room and widened even further when she spotted the dead goman.

"That's right," Darius said. "Your mistress is dead, and I'm the one in charge here now. The war between rakkans and humans has cost the lives of too many. Let's end it now."

"You only say that because your army is on the cusp of annihilation," the King's Orator said, voice stiff with the force of a woman battling to control her fear.

"So you're in close contact with them," Darius said. She must have had algus with escorts there or vice versa. Communication lines would be fast between the two.

He conjured a little ferven in his throat to fire his next words. "Call off the attack."

She shook her head. "Only the King can. You shouldn't have—"

"Liar," Jason muttered behind her.

Her head twisted, face contorted as if the man had just whipped her back. "Why?"

"He knows the truth." The Chief Priest looked down his nose at her. "He knows how the King poisoned him and how you've covered up the fact all along."

A wet shine came to her eyes as she turned pleadingly to the King's Sword. "I had no choice, Jason. You must understa—"

"Save your apologies for later," Darius said. "Tell your army to surrender, or we'll force you to. But have no doubt, you *will* give the order in the end."

"I'll die before I do," Ophelia said, and the courage in her voice told Darius she wasn't lying.

She squared up to him as if that would give her any hope of defying his commands. But when he didn't break his unblinking glare, she turned to Jason, and that stubbornness just alight within her cracked.

"Do it," Jason said.

She shook her head, mouthing words that didn't come out until the last few whispers. "…you too?"

Jason slid his sword from its sheath. "Or you'll feel my blade."

Just by the horror that came upon her face, Darius could tell that was a fate more intolerable to her than any other, so he didn't break the silence in the room and let the algus make threats on his behalf.

"But the King…" Ophelia said.

"Was no king," Jason said. "Only a liar."

At that moment, her head fell, revealing the scabby patches on her scalp as broken as her will just was.

"I'd need a stamped decree," she said.

"I took one." Jason pulled a roll of parchment from his pocket along with a reed pen.

She seemed a little shocked that the algus had thought to collect one along with her, but she took it without argument and began scribbling something above a wax stamp already dry at the bottom.

"My man has an escort with our army's commanding algus," she said as she wrote. "If you take this to Phineas, he'll relay the command." After a few more silent moments writing, she scratched a large, eloquent signature next to the wax seal.

"Is it enough?" Darius asked the King's Sword.

Jason studied the message for a moment.

"Please, Jason." Ophelia turned, grabbed the man's sleeves, and fell to her knees. "I had no choice. I tried to tell you at first, but the mind blocks… And the King knew everything. I'd never have survived if—"

Her voice broke away when a thin blue light surfaced on Jason's sleeve as she clutched it, and soon it swept down to her hand. She gasped as the bright film carried on over her fingernails, knuckles and wrist before gathering pace and consuming her entire arm with what must have been an excruciating freeze. But the look on her face as she watched the deadly algor wasn't one of pain or fear but sorrow and guilt. When it enveloped her shoulder, her gaze lifted back to Jason, pleading with the killer—not to stop, not to spare her, but to forgive.

But all he gave her in return was his notorious iciness.

She gasped as the algor seized her neck, breached her lips and nose before it solidified with a crack and morphed her into an agonised ice sculpture, the last part to freeze and die being her grey eyes.

Jason took another glance at the parchment before answering Darius's earlier question. "This is enough."

Then, as if he hadn't just slain a woman he'd known for decades, as if his mind had been wiped clean again of all that made someone human, he turned and walked calmly out of the room, leaving his frozen friend grasping at the air.

Although unsure whether to trust the message would get to where it was supposed to go, Darius was glad to be rid of both the fearsome man and woman. He'd never met her before, but according to what Lex and others had told him, she had more blood on her hands than anyone in the Empire. It would have been her that gave the command to slaughter the slaves in Xavala, to destroy the Great Bridge, and to leave the Viridian Legion to raze Laltos.

And how pathetic had the woman been at the end, to grovel not to Darius, but to a man she'd known and betrayed. Her death wasn't punishment enough.

He stepped forward and punched high, put all his rakkan strength behind it, and connected with his fist to Ophelia's frozen head. Her body shattered into a thousand shards of red-and-purple ice, leaving not even an outline of the woman that had done the goman's wicked bidding.

So ended the legacy of the King's Orator. Now all they needed to do was nullify the goman's last commands.

"Tell me good news," Darius directed at the Chief Priest. "Tell me Jason will do as he said."

"He will," Aran said, but there were nerves in his voice. "What remains of your army will be spared."

Darius prayed what remained was enough for whatever was to follow.

"I sense I'll need every man and woman I can get," he said. "What troubles you?"

The Chief Priest took a few moments to pick his words, staring at the now bloody pool at the centre of the room. "The Aretean Sea has calmed."

Lex and Sulla exchanged a worried glance, but Darius struggled to understand what that meant.

"The sea to the north?" he asked.

Aran nodded. "Its waves once stopped the gomans and us from crossing to one another, apart from a few brave and fortunate souls. But the shifting of the world has stilled it, and now we'll meet more than a couple of them soon enough."

"That bitch spoke like *we're* the threat," Sulla said with a scoff at the dead goman, "as if we're the ones sending people over to warmonger."

"I don't doubt what she said," Aran muttered. "If it weren't for her, Hadrian might rule Rakka and the Empire; he'd already be building the ships to invade."

"The wretches would deserve it." Darius gritted his teeth, wanting to stomp angrily about the room but without the legs to do so. There was much to think over now. Whatever the gomans did next, Darius had to be ready.

"The Torians are good shipbuilders." Lex's voice was weak and hollow, but she finally stood and left her son's side. "The fishermen often brave the Toras Delta, where the river meets the Aretean Sea. Their ships could survive even a storm as long as the sea has calmed enough."

The Chief Priest paled. "That's your first instinct? Did my years of—"

"How long would it take to build enough ships for my whole army?" Darius interjected.

Lex shrugged. "I'm sure someone in this palace knows. We should act quickly; if we delay, there may be others that try to claim Toria's throne. Once you're king, the shipbuilders will obey you."

If Sulla hadn't been holding him, Darius would have fallen over at her words. "'Once I'm king'?"

The look she gave him was fierce, not the look of a woman ready to sheath her sword and retire as they'd planned but one ready for many battles to come.

And Darius could only gape at her, confused. *Him*, king? The thought hadn't even crossed his mind since their discussion about their future, these Twin Blades being enough of a burden for one man. All this time, he'd only dreamed of destroying the Empire, not becoming its new ruler.

So why was Lex expecting this of him now? Had she forgotten their promises to one another, that she was the one who hadn't wanted him to wear a crown, or was she ready to discard their promise so readily?

One look at her dead son reminded him her emotions would be unimaginable now, similar to his had been when Archimedes had taken hold of Omid, followed by watching the boy die in Laltos. Neither of them was in the best state of mind to make such a decision now, but did fate always wait for the right moment to demand answers from them?

With every passing heartbeat, Darius considered what Lex said more, imagining himself sitting on Toria's throne. What power would that give him? Would children like Omid and Lex's daughter be spared living in fear? Would the algus lose their power, no longer needed to defend the people from rakkans? They could all live in peace and under a ruler who cared about justice for once.

"Think about what you've just done," Lex said. "You killed a goman impersonating King Medus, and I know the king was once real because I saw his mouth myself. You aren't a conqueror; you're a liberator! The humans will welcome you, and Toria's armies will be added to our might."

"Darius," the Chief Priest said, holding his bare hands out submissively but not close enough to touch anyone. "You must think carefully before you act. What you do next will determine the fate of more than just our lives, but hundreds of thousands. I do not pretend to know what it was like to live your life, and your anger and thirst for vengeance is understandable, but I beg you to see reason."

"What reason? Yours?" Darius glared at the man. "Why should I not take Toria's crown? Haven't I earned it? Will I not treat the people better than those before me?"

"I do not speak of Toria's crown." Aran clasped his hands together. "Take it if you wish. But do not start a war with the gomans. Just look what only two of them have done to us."

"Yes…just look. Look at the death they've brought to this land, look at the tyrants they've had squeezing Rakka's neck for over a decade. You dare ask me not to start a war when they've already started it! Should I not judge them by what I've seen? Can I not infer their intent from those they have sent to hound us?"

"You cannot judge a people by only two of their kind!"

"They've taken everything from us," Lex said, "not just from the rakkans, but humans too. Children taken from their mother's arms, warped into unfeeling killers with no conscience, no humanity. Do the gomans not deserve the war they fear? There can only be one reason they came here." Her eyes grew murderous. "They fear the rakkans; they know their cities will burn in ferven before the end."

Aran shook his head. "No… You can't—"

"Are we not owed goman blood?" Darius asked. "Doesn't Agathos demand it?"

"Agathos?" Aran snorted an appalled laugh. "He sees through you, knows you better than you know yourself. He curses those who sacrifice justice on the altar of revenge!" The Chief Priest's last words howled through the room and echoed as Darius took them in.

Over the last few months, Darius still hadn't figured out the difference between justice and revenge, only the emotion behind them. Justice was blind, unfeeling, and fair. Revenge was meted while looking your enemy in the eye, relishing in your hate for them, and enjoying their agony. But wasn't the result the same?

"What's the difference?" he asked the priest.

"Remember the fountain in Laltos." Aran held up his arms, mimicking Dianoia's statue that had stood at the centre of the water, crying out to her husband. "The Goddess doesn't cry for the executioner's axe; she cries for mercy." The man paused as if that answered the question.

But Darius just frowned.

"Mercy," the Chief Priest continued, "is compatible with justice, but not revenge."

"You want me to be..." Darius struggled to get the words out without shuddering, "merciful to the gomans?"

"I promise you, peace is possible. I have seen it achieved sooner than you'll believe."

*Peace?* The man had a lot of nerve to expect Darius to trust him, but there was something about his pleading expression that tempted Darius to believe what he said.

"They don't deserve it." Lex spat at the dead goman as she came right up to him, still trembling. "We'll build the ships. We'll finish the war they started."

"And what more will it cost you?" The Chief Priest screamed the words as he pointed at the dead boy behind her.

Her son lay staring at the ceiling in a state Darius couldn't look away from, lips blue, another dead boy sacrificed on her quest. How many of those she loved would have been alive now if she'd given up on revenge? Omid? Selene? Brutus? She never betrayed an ounce of regret, but perhaps that wasn't a strength but a fault.

She'd already lost everything, and a war with the gomans would curse countless more to make the same sacrifice.

Lex's glare shifted, fixated on Darius. "You're actually considering peace, aren't you?" Her pitch was laced with disgust.

But as much as Darius was tempted to blindly follow her wishes and hope it might in some way ease her pain, he couldn't deny he was torn. From all he'd seen over the years, he knew the price for revenge, the debt of blood it left.

Was he ready to see cities massacred again? Thousands of men crucified in a show of brutal dominance to assert power? The land rent beneath his feet? Hundreds of miles choked by fires that could rage for years? Wasn't all that enough for one lifetime?

Sulla shifted under his arm, giving him a little more support to stand while remaining quiet for once. Although never a rakkan to shy away from war or battle, Sulla's silence told Darius that the rakkan didn't agree with Lex yet didn't want to openly back a man that had lied to them for so long.

And it was then that Darius saw the difference between the choices before him. Deep down, the Chief Priest's words had resonated. He knew that peace was the course he *should* take.

On the other hand, Lex shared his fury, his malice, all the darkest urges that may have originated in his conscience but ended in a path with no regard for fairness. Her reaction marked a way he *wanted* to take.

"I'll take my crown," Darius said, dealing with the simplest decisions first.

Lex began to nod, but her agreement would be short-lived.

Darius continued, "And I'll use it to shatter this empire. What do I know of ruling Alogos or Psinara or Laltos that their regents do not?"

Lex frowned. "You'll have—"

"Nothing. I know nothing. Let regents rule their cities, and the only crown will be their own." That made the most sense.

And that decision helped him clarify the broader issue and remember what he wanted most in life.

"As for you, Aran," Darius said, "perhaps one day I could trust you again, perhaps I could look at you without feeling the sting of betrayal… But we'll never know. You're banished from this land, and I don't expect to see you again in this life."

The Chief Priest lowered his head with what seemed more relief than disgrace. It was no surprise that he seemed to know what Darius intended.

"If this war has taught me anything," Darius said, "it is not to repeat it. You're right; I won't judge the gomans by the only two I've met. We'll find a ship, then you and Jason will travel to their homeland. Make the peace you are so confident of with only this condition: no goman, human, or rakkan will ever cross the Aretean Sea again."

The Chief Priest fell to his knees. "I swear, this is the right decision. I foresee they will be open to your terms, and we can reach their shores within only a couple of weeks."

But Lex's expression twisted in disgust, as if she couldn't bear any of the words Darius had just uttered, as appalled as if *he'd* been the one to just kill her son.

"Don't they deserve war," she hissed, "after what they've done to us?"

"Perhaps," Darius said, "but do we? Don't we deserve peace? Don't the people of Rakka and the Empire deserve peace for once?"

She turned away from him with a snarl, and he knew her well enough to know it would be a mistake to try to convince her to agree with his decision right now. She needed time, and Darius hoped that's what they'd have from now on.

"Before we do anything," Sulla said, finally breaking his silence, "we need to get you bandaged up." He helped Darius down to the ground and began wrapping his thighs while the Chief Priest muttered some prayers to himself and Lex returned to her dead son.

Not long after, Aran opened his eyes as if struck by something. "If I may be so bold as to ask a question, if the Empire is to be broken, what do you intend for the slaves?"

Darius hadn't gone so far as to think about the details, but the destruction of the Empire could involve far more than letting cities govern themselves. So far, the slaves had been the most open to aiding him and had paid in blood for it. Darius owed them something, or at least, owed those still alive something.

"You wish for me to free them?" Darius asked.

The Chief Priest nodded.

"And is it possible without anarchy ensuing?"

To that question, the Chief Priest's nod was more hesitant. "The algus fear you, and if Jason leaves with me, no one will be your match."

Darius turned his attention to the King's Sword, aware the man hadn't said whether he'd accept his banishment or fight against it.

"Will you go with your brother?" Darius asked.

Jason looked at Aran for the longest time, uncomfortably long for any normal human, but the Chief Priest showed no signs of unease, only a warm smile so inviting any man or woman would have been hard-pressed not to want to follow him.

Finally, after mulling the question, Jason nodded.

"I am glad," Aran said. "We'll be much happier with our own kind, and I promise they aren't all as manipulative as *that*." Aran turned up his nose at the dead King.

"When will you leave?" Darius asked. "Does your cogi show you when is the most opportune time for the voyage?"

"I'm not sure. My range barely extends far enough to see my arrival in Goma, but they are receptive to me. I should probably go at once."

Despite all the questions Darius had for the brothers, what good would it do to go over the past now? What was done was done, and perhaps it was best not to dwell too much on what-ifs.

"Then go," Darius said. "Let it be over."

The Chief Priest stood and bowed. "One of my escorts will contact you when I've arrived and let you know what the gomans have said."

"There, done." Sulla tightened the knot on the last bandage on Darius's leg. "What next? Shall we return to the army?"

"And risk someone seizing power here in Toria while we're absent?" Darius said. "No. The armies will come here, and my enemies will listen to me as I sit upon their throne."

# 63

## Darius – Toria

Toria's throne was uncomfortable, built from cold steel that even cushions couldn't soften. As impressive as it looked, Darius had been tempted to melt it while under the watch of the most powerful men and women in Toria, just to prove he could, to mark the end of the Empire.

But he'd resisted the urge over the last couple of weeks. The orders sent from the King's Orator had worked and spared his army, and tonight, they'd finally arrived in the city and were making their way to the palace with Lyra at their head.

Waiting inside, all the algus of Toria and Alogos had gathered to witness this. They hovered around the dais he sat upon, most only daring to steal a brief glance until he met their eyes, then hurriedly looking away as if his gaze could kill. Perhaps they saw the conflict within him, the anger that victory hadn't quenched.

Since the goman's death, he'd done his best to ignore his violent urges, to forget these were the same people that had sought to slay him and his people not long ago. Peace was harder to stomach than blood, it seemed, but any unease Darius had to suffer for the sake of it would be worth it in the long run.

The Chief Priest and Jason had set sail on the first day, and then Lex had also left without another word. All Darius could do was give her time and hope she understood his decision. Meanwhile, he'd asserted his authority in the palace with the help of only Sulla, and once he'd revealed their king was a goman imposter, he'd found the Torians surprisingly receptive to his demands—or rather, distinct lack of them. He didn't demand fealty or riches or even honour. Only an end to the conflict that had blighted his life.

Perhaps they were as tired of blood and death as he was, or perhaps brandishing the head of a dead goman had scared them into submission, but they'd been open about their plans to invade across the River Toras and allowed Darius to put an end to them, as well as sent the soldiers back to their families. Surprisingly, he'd been able to avoid any more fights altogether and let his legs heal. All that remained was to free the slaves as he'd promised Aran, and for that, he wanted the might of his army behind him.

As for the Chief Priest and the Diagathic Order, Darius hadn't uttered a word about his identity, yet it had spread through the Empire like a contagion. The religion had crumbled as Aran had predicted, some algus in Toria even going so far as to slay their escorts in gruesome public displays, no longer trusting them.

That was only one of the new issues wrestling for Darius's attention, but so far he'd been able to devote little time to it because one other thing had come to light once he'd stopped blocking out Lyra's senses.

The Staff of Arria not only wasn't lost but was with the Torian army. They too had arrived back tonight, and all Darius could contemplate was what to do with the thing. The deep spring inside the palace was a tempting place to toss it, as the King had urged him to do with the Twin Blades.

But what if that wasn't enough? He'd thought it had been lost into the depths of the world once before, and now he couldn't shake the worry that it would plague the world again.

Not only did that thought haunt him, but the Blades at his waist did too. They gave him such power over the rakkans and had almost been taken by Hadrian. Even if Darius kept them for the rest of his long, natural life, what would happen to them after he died? Another would then wield enough power to dominate the land, and who knew what they'd do with it.

As he scratched his chin, thinking of no answers, the doors to the room swung open to reveal hundreds of figures clad in black kuraminium outside.

"Finally," Sulla said beside him. "I was beginning to feel lonely being the only rakkan here."

The heavy thudding of their boots made many of the Torians flinch at every step, but it was welcome music to Darius, the sound of allies and friends.

Lyra and the warlords of each legion except the Branzians marched up to the dais on which Darius sat, and when they reached the edge, they stopped and bowed. Only Lyra carried on, leaped up the steps of the dais, and gave Darius a long-overdue greeting while letting him run his fingers through the fur on her head.

"Missed you too," he muttered to her. But there was something else she was telling him besides her relief at their reunion. She was accompanied by a presence that hadn't been with her for a long time, one Darius had been waiting for—Aran's pteron.

One of the warlords below cleared their throat and reminded him of their arrival and Darius's lack of manners. The pteron could wait.

"I'm glad you all made it," Darius said. "I bet a month ago, you never thought reaching the heart of Toria would be such an uneventful journey."

Warlord Rufus sighed. "We suffered more than enough 'events' in the gorge, Overlord."

Although Darius hadn't paid attention to what Lyra had seen at the time, he'd witnessed the aftermath through her eyes and nose. Such a stench of death wouldn't leave his memory quickly.

"You did well to bring any men back at all when against the Staff," Darius said.

The Viridian Warlord grimaced. "Speaking of which… What do you intend to do with it?"

"Toss it into the sea?" Sulla said. "Or how about we finish the job of burning it?"

Judging by the horrified looks that came upon the Torian algus in the room at the mention of that, they weren't thrilled by the idea, and who could blame them when they'd fought with the rakkans for most of their lives, the older ones remembering a time before the Staff, when the Viridian Legion ravaged swathes of the Empire?

Even if Darius had wanted to throw the Staff into a furnace, he doubted the weapon would be touched by fire when even ferven extinguished before it. According to legend, only the Twin Blades had been able to burn it into its blackened state.

"They already tried losing the Staff once," Rufus said. "My great-grandfather told me of the day they captured it and buried it deep in the dungeons of the world, where they thought no one would find it. Those brave rakkans that took it under were sealed inside, its location dying with them."

"Apparently not," Darius said. Who knew whether that tale was true—old rakkans had a habit of misremembering things—but the warning still resonated with him regardless.

"What do you think, Varro?" Darius asked. The Black Warlord was always a cautious man, and something told Darius this task required someone to assume and plan for the worst-case scenario.

Varro took a step forward. "If I may approach, Overlord."

Darius nodded, and the Black Warlord leapt up to the high platform with as much ease as a human taking a step. He came close and dropped his voice so that only the two of them could hear.

"You must destroy it." Although Varro worded it as a command, Darius took it as advice, and he assumed that was a shared opinion amongst all the rakkans. But what about the humans? He needed another perspective he could trust.

"I don't suppose you've seen Lex," he asked Varro.

The rakkan frowned. "She isn't with you?"

"Never mind," Darius said. He instead cast his gaze across the humans among his army and spotted a welcome face near the Viridians. "Gorgias. Come here."

The tired-looking algus looked to Rufus for permission.

But Darius interrupted. "No. You're no longer under his power. The arrangement is over, as it is for your mother, Rufus." Who Hera had last assured him was well.

Gorgias bowed nervously and climbed up the steep stairs onto the dais. "What do you need, master?"

Darius lowered his voice. "What do you think the humans' reaction would be if I destroyed the Staff?"

The horror that came over the man's face gave his answer before his lips could, and it gave Darius pause; the last thing he needed was to do something that would cause a fight to break out in the throne room.

"I don't think it would shock them," Gorgias whispered after collecting himself, "but you can understand how afraid they'll be."

"And how might I assuage their fears?"

Gorgias's gaze fell to the Twin Blades for a moment before flitting away. "… I'm not sure."

Darius ran a thumb across one of the hilts, feeling its ferven stir as he realised what thought must have occurred to Gorgias that he dared not utter.

"I see…" Darius said. Just the thought of abandoning the swords felt uneasy, like leaving behind two allies on the battlefield after they'd just won you a war.

"Where's the Staff now?" he asked.

"It's waiting outside the room with Regent Berenice of Alogos," Gorgias replied. "My mother chose to travel with them. She used to be on good terms with her, so they didn't object."

After never fully trusting the woman, Darius was surprised she'd done that. As tempted as he was to deal with the Staff at once, there was one last thing he needed to wait for, something Lyra had assured him was on the way.

He spoke with Varro and Gorgias a little longer, letting them fill him in on the battle, but not long after getting into the gory details, Lyra nudged his leg and turned expectantly to the entrance to the hall.

Flapping through the doorway, a pteron soared inside with only the rakkans noticing something stirring above, and it paid them no heed and headed straight to Darius and landed at his feet. Most escorts looked no different to wild animals, but Lyra knew this was Aran's.

There was no note attached to the bird's leg, and it did nothing to convey any message using its wings or head. But a feeling soon came over Darius, a message in more than words or actions—one in emotion. It was warmth, joy, relief, and more convicting than any written message could have been. Lyra felt what the escort did, which no doubt stemmed from the Chief Priest. Peace with the gomans had finally been achieved.

But while Darius was relieved, he was far from sharing the priest's joy. The costs of the war had been great, and although they wouldn't be added to, joy felt like something he might never experience again. Relief would have to do.

"I have news!" he yelled to bring the already quiet room to utter silence. "My envoy to the gomans has reported back. We have peace. There will be no invasion. There will be no more bloodshed between our races."

Not everyone there looked happy at the news, and Darius shared their concern. Bitterness and grudges didn't fade within a few days or weeks. It might only be their children that let the enmity die, but it would be best for them if they did. After all, according to myth, the grudge between rakkans, gomans, and humans had been running ever since the Creator bestowed two tribes with powers via their leaders, Arria and Trogus. That grudge had given birth to the most fearsome weapons, and perhaps it was only fitting that the end of the war also marked their destruction. Because Varro was right; these weapons were too dangerous to be hidden away.

Darius raised his voice again. "Bring it in!"

No human or rakkan in the room needed clarification on what "it" he spoke of. The rakkans began shedding their armour and moved to the sides of the room while Darius took hold of the Twin Blades tightly, readying them to resist the weakness the Staff brought.

It took a few minutes for the Torians carrying the Staff to enter, and before anyone had seen the weapon, rakkans started dropping to one knee or holding each other for support. Walking through an emptied space leading from the door to the throne, a group of algus surrounded a red-headed woman carrying it on her back, the black shaft poking above her neck as the Twin Blades began to hiss.

The noise filled the now silent hall, and a thin wisp of fire rose from the runes of the Blades and streaked towards the Staff as it neared, like an orange thread connecting them. Weakness battled to take hold of Darius's muscles, but the metal in his hands gave their cold strength to him and allowed him to stand and begin stepping off the dais towards the rakkans' most loathed nemesis.

The algus parted and allowed Darius to approach the woman at the centre, whose hard features bore a pride Darius saw was that of a regent. He'd seen such pride before, in algus after slaying countless in battle without remorse.

"Regent Berenice," Darius said.

The woman gave a cold nod that drew his gaze to a weighty diamond hanging around her neck. She must have been the most wealthy and powerful algus left in the Empire now.

"Lay it down," Darius said. "Then step away."

The Regent's eyes narrowed as if tempted to resist, and Darius considered slaying her for hesitating, to let there be no doubt in the minds of anyone there the consequences of defying the newfound peace.

But was that a "peaceful" act? The Chief Priest sure wouldn't have approved, and the more Darius considered it, the more it seemed counterproductive to humiliate the Empire's algus further.

He spun one of the Blades, made it hiss louder. "I do not repeat myself with words."

The Regent looked to some of the other algus in the throne room, but none seemed willing to look her in the eye, and after a few more heartbeats of hesitation, she finally unslung the weapon from her back and laid it down as ordered.

But she didn't back away.

Darius sighed and shook his head. "So much death from so small a thing." He watched the swirls of light as they were sucked from his swords into the cracks in the ashy wood. "So much power to be wielded, and by whom?" Now he lifted his gaze to the woman again. "Who is now worthy of possessing it?"

The Regent gave only a twitch of her nose in response.

"No answer?" Darius said. "Then I agree with you. No one should."

Before the Regent could frown at the words, Darius rushed forward, knocked her aside and towered over the Staff while bringing the Twin Blades high above his head. Ferven spilt from the runes and erupted around him, but it was restrained, thin, and piercing like a tornado of flames boring from the high ceiling and into the Staff.

Whatever power resided in these swords, Darius prayed it was enough, because the time had come to test the legend of the Staff's charred state.

He tried to thrust the swords down, but they hardly moved, as if a force resisted and made it like pushing them through stone. Both weapons now screamed fury while everyone—human and rakkan alike—fell back and shielded their eyes from the radiance filling the centre of the hall.

Darius pushed down harder.

Fire stung his hands and cheeks, and although he conjured algor to save himself from the heat, it still burned, just like when he'd first taken the Blades and proved his worth.

The Staff trembled on the ground as the points of the Blades neared inch by inch, deathly sharp kuraminium that was the only part of the swords still dark and stained. Without his full rakkan strength, Darius gritted his teeth and pushed with everything he had. He felt his weapons near, but it was as if the swords too resisted, unwilling to approach their rival, afraid.

But Darius didn't care. With one last push, it was as if their resistance crumbled. The swords thrust down and pierced the wood with a snap as loud as the quaking world. Torrents of blue flames escaped the Staff's wounds and consumed the red fires until they sent a cold bite to replace the searing pain against Darius's skin.

But only a heartbeat after the algor had extinguished the fire, it died along with it, leaving only a bright, ghostly flicker in the throne room.

He let the swords fall to the ground with a clang, sending a breath of air that saw the Staff crumble to ash.

Now, the only sound in the hall was his fevered panting. He glanced around quickly, checking whether the sudden torrents had harmed anyone. But apart from a few blackened faces, everyone seemed unharmed.

"I probably should have done that outside," he said, wiping the sweat from his brow. He stepped onto the pile of ash and crushed it under his feet, just to check the wood was indeed gone.

And something odd struck him as he did. The Twin Blades lay there without a whisper, no longer giving off that glint of ferven like they craved his touch.

Feeling a newfound emptiness like a void inside himself, he knelt and touched the runes to find only deep grooves in cold kuraminium, and even when he grasped the hilts and willed their power to come forth, nothing but his own magic stirred. The Staff had killed them, and even though he hadn't intended it, he could only be relieved at the fact.

"And so it's done." He stood with the weapons in his hands once again, only then realising that, not only was everyone in the room staring at him, but they were still backing away, as if they faced a true Slayer of Gods.

Is that what he really was? The hell he'd brought to the land testified to that.

He'd never seen such fear in the humans and realised this was probably the first time they'd witnessed the true ire of the Twin Blades.

And he could use that to his advantage.

He walked towards Rufus and offered the hilt of one of the Blades to the only rakkan there that hadn't backed all the way to the wall. "Take it."

Rufus eyed the sword with sensible trepidation, then extended a finger first and brushed the metal. When nothing flared to life, he slowly took the hilt in his hand with a disgruntled murmur under his breath. He knew what these weapons symbolised, the power they gave the rakkans that had now been lost.

"What have you done?" Regent Berenice was the only one brave enough to disturb the quiet, grimacing as the ash scattered with the hall's draughts.

"Ended this feud." Darius turned and squared up to the woman. "You've lost your greatest weapon, and we've lost ours."

"And you call this peace?" The Regent shouted the words towards the high ceiling, trying to rile up the Torians. "We will not stand for this affron—"

"Hold your tongue!" Darius flared ferven across his sword, sending bright orange light to fill the once red runes. "Or I'll cut it out! Don't think because a crown is not atop my head that I'm not the one in charge here. You think what you just witnessed was because of these weapons? Do you think that power was not my own?" He snorted a cruel laugh. "I could destroy this city as easily as I just destroyed the Staff. Be grateful I do not."

The Regent leaned away, seeming to believe every word of what he'd just said. And the looks on the faces of the rest of the algus said they'd bought it too, that standing before them was not only an enemy but one with true godlike powers.

Little did they know how powerless he really was, how he'd repeatedly failed to turn the face of fate from those he loved. And they called the algus gods? A real god could reverse the water flowing from a clock or bring back the dead when taken before their rightful time. What power he had was of this world and would die within it, and as much as others seemed to hunger only for that, Darius still felt it wasn't enough, like there was more to life than savouring the fear of the people now surrounding him.

Still...he'd use the power he did have to finally bring up his most contentious decree before leaving this all behind.

"I choose not to take Toria's crown," he roared, "but do not think I cannot snatch it whenever I want to. I am gifting you the freedom you have denied the rakkans for too long, and in return, that freedom will be extended to everyone, not just you algus." He waited to see the reaction as the brightest there inferred what he was about to say, and when none dared so much as utter a murmur of discontent, he gave the command. "I was born of a slave, and to slaves I owe much. I will repay them with their freedom across the whole Empire."

He waited for the jeers, the spits, the scoffs...anything. But all he received were hollow looks of terrified humans. Despite their claims of being gods, these people were nothing but vulnerable mortals, just like he was.

As he scanned the mass of people there, he was surprised to catch sight of Lex watching from amongst the crowd, and the sheen of sweat on her face told him she'd watched the chaos he'd just unleashed. He suppressed a smile and was now all the more eager to finish this spectacle.

"It is over," he roared to the room. "Go home to see your wives, husbands, children, dogs…whoever, and raise a cup to the end of the war. We'll leave your city, so sort out amongst yourselves who will govern here as regent."

A few of the algus exchanged greedy looks that had Darius second-guessing his decision.

"Don't make me return here," he warned. "I'll know everything that happens throughout the Empire. Govern wisely, or you'll lose your heads in the night."

Many algus at the back of the room rushed straight out as if they'd been waiting for an excuse, but the initial rush turned to a more tame exit led by Regent Berenice. Many walked past the remnants of the Staff as if struggling to believe what they'd witnessed.

Ignoring the algus, Darius headed straight towards Lex while trying to judge her mood from the cold blue of her eyes. But he couldn't, even when only inches away from her. Regardless, he wanted to take her in an embrace, to kiss her, but he kept a slight distance for now.

"Lex… Where have you been?"

"Walking…thinking…laying my son to rest." Still, her expression gave nothing away, much to Darius's concern given what she'd said.

"You buried him near here?" he asked. She wouldn't have had time to travel to Laltos with the Great Bridge destroyed.

"No. I couldn't decide where, so I burnt him and scattered him to rest near..." Her last word was nothing but a breath.

Wanting to ease her sorrow, he embraced her and felt the tension pour from her body as she squeezed him.

"I would have been there with you," he said. Why had she gone through that alone?

"Later." She leaned back, ran a hand down his cheek, then gently pushed him away and made him aware of all the rakkans still staring at him and awaiting instructions. There was so much more he wanted to say to her, but it would have to wait.

"I'm almost done," he said. "Stay close? I have somewhere to go, then we'll retire for the night."

She nodded and reached out to touch him again, giving his chest a light stroke, at which point Rufus approached him with the Twin Blade still in his grasp.

"Overlord," he said. "What next?"

Darius held out his hand and waited. Although without their power, the Twin Blades were his, a relic of the war that would hopefully never be repeated, and when Rufus handed it back, he vowed no rakkan would ever wield them after him.

"Warlords!" he called, and they all lifted their heads. "See that your men are well-fed and drunk, then load up the wagons. You have three days, then I don't want there to be a rakkan left in Toria."

# 64

## Darius – Toria

Before finding somewhere to stay that night, Darius led Lex out of the throne room once the others began to drink, eat, and sing in what would hopefully be a time when the former enemies could toast their fallen brothers and sisters and bury ill feelings—or at least avoid devolving into fisticuffs with each other.

But if he didn't wish for any rakkan to wield the Twin Blades again and spoil this costly peace, regardless of whether the swords had power or were nothing but a status symbol, then he had to rid the world of them forever. Lex didn't ask where he was taking her. Neither of them conjured algor to light the passageways as they descended and the surroundings grew darker. Regardless of how much he had to say to Lex, he first had to end this conflict before they began what was hopefully a life together.

He headed straight back to the room with the Pool of Toriamas, and she continued in silence as he walked right up until the still waters touched his boots. He finally conjured ferven for a little light, then held the powerless Twin Blades over the pool, pausing and half expecting her to object to what he was doing. But instead, she watched with what looked like relief. And that gave him all the confidence he needed in this decision.

As soon as he relaxed his grip, the heavy swords slipped through his fingers and stabbed into the water, sending hardly a ripple across the surface as they plunged in and sank into the black depths of the world they had once ruled. For the last time, he saw a flicker from the runes on the Blades, but it was nothing but a reflection of his own light before they sank to their end.

Perhaps people would record these acts in the tablets of history, and perhaps people in the future would curse him for destroying weapons that might be needed one day. But he suspected he'd never regret what he'd done. The war of today had cost too much blood.

"It's finished." He could hardly believe the words but soon realised they were true.

Lex didn't reply, and they both stood and digested the fact for so long that Darius's muscles began to plead for respite.

But he took Lex's hand and gave her some more time. There was something comfortable about the silence, though. They both knew what this meant, and just the little squeezes of each other's hands conveyed more than words would have. Sooner or later they'd need to discuss things, but for now, Darius enjoyed the silence for what it was.

Once she was ready, they left and headed towards the tallest tower of the palace, where Darius had been told the King's chambers were.

He'd sleep there tonight because why the hell not? When they entered, he found that the servants in the palace had lit lamps all around and dressed the King's bed in clean, royal-blue linen that looked similar to the banners in Laltos. But Lex didn't seem to notice as she sat and rubbed her shoulder under her mail with a sigh.

Now in better light, he could tell she hadn't slept much in the couple of weeks since he'd last seen her, and he could no longer hold his tongue.

"I was worried for you." He settled down beside her, glad to finally have time to talk.

"Why? The war is over; I wasn't in danger." There was no anger in her voice like there had been when he'd first opted to cease fighting.

"You weren't too happy about that fact the last time I saw you," he said.

"No… But it's all that I've had on my mind of late. Perhaps it's for the best. They say revenge only keeps your own wounds green, and mine…"

Such torment was apparent in the worry lines on her brow, but they took nothing from her beauty, only deepened his admiration for her because he knew the pain that had caused them would have broken many others.

"I hope your wounds can heal," he said. Although so far, his own still felt raw at times. All those loved ones lost, yet incomparable to her losses.

"I hope so too," she said.

"Does that mean you've forgiven me?" he asked.

She sighed again and leaned her head onto his shoulder. "What's there to forgive? You're my king now. I acquiesce to your wishes."

At least she didn't seem too angry. She never jested when annoyed.

"Am I really a king?" he asked. "I refused the crown."

"A crown needn't be worn to be seen."

"Fair enough." He wrapped an arm around her waist. "But in any case, I'm more than your king. I'm your man."

She lifted her head and turned to him, stared into his eyes in a way she usually avoided. "Yes… We did promise that, and I'm a woman of my word, my king."

Trust her to make this feel like bartering.

"You know, you're making me feel like the Silk Regent," he said, "pressuring a woman with my power."

She smiled at him in that teasing way that made him want to kiss her. "Don't you enjoy feeling your dominance, my king?"

Darius growled, "Will you stop calling me 'my king'? I'm no king, not even an overlord anymore." Since the Twin Blades were gone, it felt like a relief. Who knew how the warlords viewed him now, but he had no intention of continuing in the position he'd been in.

"Don't think because you've rejected your seat," she said, "that you're not still the one with power here, my king. Did you not command the Torians to free their slaves without even a whisper of opposition?"

As much as he wanted to deny it, she was right, even if she spoke light-heartedly.

And something else struck him; every time she called him king, she glanced at his lips with a hunger she'd rarely showed before, as if she enjoyed being in the presence of his power.

"Then, as your king," he said, "I won't allow you to call me by that title again."

She raised an eyebrow. "And how will you stop—"

He pulled her closer and pressed his lips to hers, feeling her kiss him back without hesitation. Soon after, she shifted out of his arms, swung her leg over, and mounted him while their lips stayed locked together, grabbing a fistful of his hair for good measure.

His body heated, needing conscious control of his ferven to stop it from leaking out and melting her armour as their bodies pressed together.

But after a few moments, she broke away with a gasp, gave him a fretful look as if something awful had just occurred to her.

"Wait…" she said.

That's all he'd ever done for her. "What's wrong?"

"Cynthia."

"She's fine. My grandfather sent a message not long ago."

"No, I mean, what will we…" She moved to climb off his lap, but he held her, gently pulled away the hair that had fallen across her eyes and slipped it behind her ear, sending a visible shiver down her neck.

"Tell me," he said.

"I can't just think of myself. If I'm not fighting the war anymore, I need to be with her."

"And what's the problem? You want to leave right now?"

She shook her head. "I just don't know what your plans are now, and before we start anything…"

Finally, Darius understood what was troubling her. "When I said I was yours, I had kind of assumed you both came as a pair. Unless you don't want me around her."

She breathed a laugh and relaxed into his lap, taking his head in her hands as she eyed his lips again. "I want you with us."

"Good. As long as we get *some* time alone." But that did remind him of one thing he'd never brought up with her despite wanting to a while ago. It had been lost among the streak of devastation in the last few months.

"Speaking of Cynthia," he said, "you should speak with Varro. Isn't it time he knew the truth?"

She frowned, pulled back a little. "What is there to discuss? He already knows about Cynthia."

"What?" Darius had known as much, but Varro had acted like she was oblivious. "You mean you told him?"

"No, but I saw him watching me and her when we fled Laltos. He's not a fool, and if he wanted anything to do with her, he would have approached me."

It seemed the pair of them were as bad as each other at communication.

"He's waiting for you to approach him," Darius said. "He told me as much. He's probably afraid of pissing you off and losing any chance of seeing her."

"Afraid? Varro? Please."

But even Darius knew the Black Warlord's fear, despite being unfazed even in the face of death.

"He's not facing an opponent with a sword," Darius said. "You could hurt him deeply, probably already have."

Lex considered his words while she ran her hands harshly through his hair as if to relieve stress.

"Fine," she said at last. "But not tonight. Can we just relax? After everything, I just need to forget."

"Sure." He pulled her a little closer again. "What did you have in mind? I saw a katakto board in the other room. We could have a game, winner gets to—"

She cut off his words with another kiss so intense it had him forgetting games or the worries of life. She pushed her weight into him in a way that let him know she wanted him lying on the bed. His rakkan strength must have made him hard to move around, but he let her shove him, fell back as she began unfastening the belt around his tunic.

It took her longer than he feared his patience could last, and as soon as she slid it free, he took hold of the bottom of her tunic and mail, ripped it open as easily as tearing cloth, and sent iron rings scattering across his exposed chest.

She gasped, then took hold of his flexed arms and squeezed with a lustful grin. But his eyes slipped from her lips onto what he'd just uncovered.

"That armour was expensive, you know," she said.

"A king doesn't have to worry about expenses. He can buy anything, do as he pleases."

"That's true." She bit her bottom lip. "And what would please my king right now?"

He gripped the top of her trousers and began to tear. "His queen."

# Epilogue

## Darius – South of Margalvia

Waves crashed into the shore and wet Darius's toes while the coastal winds tussled his hair and he waited for the dawn sun to rise further and share its heat. For the last couple of months, he'd spent all his mornings enjoying the breeze from the southern sea, and it still wasn't tiring.

The war was over, and every city was working out their fate without blood spilling in the streets. The fires in the east had burnt out to leave the land unblighted once again, and the slaves were free as ordered. Darius finally had no figurative weight of a crown on his head or swords at his waist, only the light sea air.

Lyra curled into a ball beside him, not as much a fan of the chills but grateful to have been beside him now for far longer than usual. And so it would be for the long years of his life, with any luck.

"Must you come here every morning?" Lex's voice came from behind him, a more pleasing sound to his ears than even the calming lap of water.

"It's the best time of day," he said with a sigh. "Rakkans across the land tuck themselves into bed while the humans rouse for a new workday. And me… I have another day of doing as I please." Which usually involved fishing with his grandfather.

When he'd first arrived back here, he'd avoided Eugenius for fear of running into his mother, but he'd soon been relieved to find she'd left some time ago. Now the two retired leaders met often to enjoy life's natural treasures.

Lex sat on the other side of him to Lyra and huddled close. "I'm cold."

Making use of himself, he flared ferven across his forearms and held them out for the pair to enjoy the warmth.

"I don't like waking to an empty bed," Lex said.

That was a first. In the beginning, she'd been so unused to sleeping next to someone that she'd often elbowed and kicked him in the night. That's how he'd got into the habit of waking so early.

"Is the little madam awake?" he asked.

"Thankfully not," she said, then began playing with the necklace resting on his chest. "You're still wearing these?"

His Agathos and Dianoia figurines still hung with his aeternus, now probably rarely seen in the Empire. He'd considered discarding them but found himself reluctant to. It wasn't just because of their sentimental value, which was reason enough to make them precious, but he had a hard time letting go of many of the Chief Priest's words and teachings. For all the man's secrets, Darius had come to trust he'd at least genuinely believed what he taught, and there had been a ring of truth to it.

When the Chief Priest's ship had returned with a message and full report of what had happened, it had confirmed the gomans' intentions and that Aran had verified their truthfulness himself. The sailors had said he'd been in good spirits to be with one half of his lineage for the first time, and Darius hoped it lasted.

But the Chief Priest had also left Darius a full confession of sorts, revealing nothing new but his reasons for his actions. It could have been more lies, but Darius saw little reason for the man to keep up the pretence now. He seemed to genuinely seek Darius's forgiveness but never asked for a word of reply. Perhaps he believed he'd discover whether he had it in the afterlife.

"You're handsome when you're pondering." Lex touched his stubble. "Do the God and Goddess occupy that much of your mind?"

"Don't start," Darius said. "You'll begin sounding like my grandfather, always trying to drag me into some highbrow debate about them when we're out on the raft."

She kissed his cheek. "Don't worry. I'd never think of having a highbrow debate with you."

It took Darius a few moments to determine whether or not that was an insult. Given it was from Lex, he concluded it was.

But before he could respond, he sensed someone approaching, trying to hide their movements within the chaotic winds but not well enough to fool a trained warrior such as him.

"You need to do better," he shouted, extinguishing the ferven on his arms. "Even a deer would feel you coming, madam."

The air suddenly shifted even faster, and a small figure sprang from behind him and landed on his stomach, knocking the wind from him.

He groaned and grabbed the girl, quickly getting her into a hold tight enough she couldn't do any more damage.

"Who dares disturb the Slayer of Gods?" he growled with a godlike depth to his voice.

"I got closer that time!" Cynthia said triumphantly, although her muffled voice stole some of the achievement.

Darius released her and slid the girl to go bother her mother instead. It was still a shock to him how much energy children had at the break of dawn. Why couldn't they be like a pet panther and be quiet and half-asleep for the first couple of hours of the day?

"I suppose you're hungry," Lex said.

Cynthia nodded, her blonde curls flailing and almost raking across Darius's eyes. So much for a relaxing morning.

"Go and wake Eugenius, then," Lex said. "He likes preparing your food."

Cynthia grinned, then scurried back into the hole in the ground as instructed. At times, Darius envied the girl. She'd been so filled with joy that Lex had returned it had almost been infectious. There was a simplicity in children that thankfully hadn't been stolen from Cynthia. For all Lex's faults, it seemed she had made the right choice to keep Cynthia away from the Empire and spared her the welcome to life Darius recalled as a child. Although he remembered nothing of his youth after the day the algus had called at his mother's house, he knew his childhood innocence had likely died with his baby brother.

And showing her own scars, Lex's face fell as soon as Cynthia disappeared, and she stared out at the sea in a way Darius had quickly learned to decipher.

"You're thinking of him again," he said.

Lex nodded, nestled closer to him. Who knew how long it took to get over the loss of a son, never mind being the one to cut a knife through his neck. But in their long talks about it, she didn't regret killing him; her son had died many years ago, as it had been with Selene.

They both knew each other's pain and were rehearsed enough in grief to know that time made things a little easier to bear. Meanwhile, they let the weeks and months pass and leant on each other for support when at their lowest.

"How about another trip to Margalvia?" he said. He hadn't seen Sulla in too long, and now that Lex and Varro had cleared the air about Cynthia, they'd promised to bring her regularly.

Lex sighed. "Tomorrow. Today, I just want to lie here and listen to the gulls and the ocean with you next to me."

That sounded like the perfect day to him. One thing he'd learnt in the last few weeks was that nothing healed old wounds like the warmth of the one you love.

Other books in the series:

# A Mark Of Gods

*Prequel to the Rakkan Conquest series*

**Available for FREE at AndyBlinston.com**

**The Slayer of Gods is coming**

Javad dreams of the eastern sands, of a life where he and his family are free from slavery to the Empire's gods. But those dreams are fading.

When a panther is attacked outside his town, the blame is wrongfully laid on his brother. He tries to convince the people of the truth, but they aren't interested; they only want someone to take the wrath of the panther's master…

The Slayer of Gods is bent on revenge.

Javad's brother will be offered in appeasement, but Javad won't stand by and watch them condemn an innocent boy.

Even if it kills him, Javad will save his brother from meeting the merciless Slayer.

Printed in Great Britain
by Amazon

13398856R00349